PRAISE FOR

THE BARTENDER'S TALE

National Bestseller

A *Washington Post* and *Seattle Times* Best Fiction Book of 2012

Library Journal's Best Book for Teens 2012

Booklist Editors' Choice for 2012

"Doig cranks into motion a dense valentine of a novel about a father and a small town at the start of the 1960s. . . . Doig writes the tenderness between Rusty and his father vividly, and his facility with natural, vernacular dialogue is often hypnotizing. . . . *The Bartender's Tale* is thoroughly engaging, and the book's soft focus of nostalgia is in itself a kind of pleasure." —NPR

"The rewards of *The Bartender's Tale*—a subtle and engaging narrative, characters who behave the way real people behave, the joys of careful and loving observation—remain very great and extremely rare." —*The Washington Post*

"Looking for a good story? A well-written and engrossing tale that leaves you feeling satisfied? Give Ivan Doig's latest novel a chance. . . . The perfect book for your bedside table. Pick it up, lose yourself in the past, and remember what it was like to be twelve years old, when your world and all the people who entered into it felt as fresh as the Montana mountain air." —The Associated Press

"Doig is a master of Americana details, and he layers this old-fashioned family saga with considerable nostalgic charm." —*Portland Book Review* (five stars)

"Doig is at his best with coming-of-age stories. And he is masterful at exploring the emotional complexities of family and community through the eyes of a precocious youth. . . . [He] has fashioned a moving tale of tolerance, self-discovery, and forgiveness in which a child comes to terms with his own origins and in the process opens a new door to his future." —*The Seattle Times*

"With this expert novel, [Doig] sets himself a larger canvas and fills it with a diverse cast. . . . Fact and fiction are skillfully fused to document a boy's last days of youth and a history his father can't leave behind. . . . Rusty's youthful adventures are enchanting, but Doig does something more—he punctuates them with the colorful local idiom." —*The Daily Beast/Newsweek*

"Doig is one of those gifted writers whose unique voice leaves indelible images of time and place through characters so vividly drawn that they linger long after you close the book. . . . Chronicling the western way of life has become his trademark . . . It is no coincidence that a pivotal character in *The Bartender's Tale* is a young man with a tape recorder whose quest is to capture the expressions and times that are rapidly being lost to a homogeneous blend of sounds and lifestyles. We hear in those voices the echoes of the mid-America in which many of us grew up." —*Bookreporter*

"This is such a satisfying novel from one of America's premier living writers." —*Harbor Light*

"Doig expertly spins out [the] various narrative threads with his usual gift for bringing history alive in the odysseys of marvelously thorny characters. . . . Possibly the best novel yet by one of America's premier storytellers." —*Kirkus Reviews* (starred review)

"Essential reading for anyone who cares about western literature."
—*Booklist* (starred review)

"Highly textured and evocative . . . Doig gives us a poignant saga of a boy becoming a man alongside a town and a bygone way of life inching into the modern era." —*Publishers Weekly* (starred review)

"[An] enjoyable, old-fashioned, warmhearted story about fathers and sons, growing up, and big life changes." —*Library Journal*

PRAISE FOR

WORK SONG

"As enjoyable and subtly thought-provoking a piece of fiction as you're likely to pick up this summer. . . . A pleasure to read."
—*Los Angeles Times*

"Not one stitch unravels in this intricately threaded narrative . . . infectious." —*The New York Times Book Review*

"If you were looking for a novel that best expresses the American spirit, you'd have to ride past a lot of fence posts before finding anything as worthy as *Work Song*." —*Chicago Tribune*

"Doig has delivered another compelling tale about America, epic as an Old West saga but as fresh and contemporary as the news."
—*The Seattle Times*

"Richly imagined and beautifully paced."   —The Associated Press

"A classic tale from the heyday of American capitalism by the king of the Western novel."   —*The Daily Beast* (Hot Reads)

THE WHISTLING SEASON

"Along with his much praised, incantatory gifts for evoking quintessentially American prairie life and history, the National Book Award finalist brings . . . a bushel and peck of irresistible characters, each so full of spunk, wit, ambition, or sheer orneriness that not one of them will lie down on the page and sleep for a moment. . . . Both elegiac and life-affirming, *The Whistling Season* takes the chill out of today's literary winds."   —*Los Angeles Times Book Review*

"*Whistling Season* does what Doig does best: evoke the past and create a landscape and characters worth caring about. . . . It's lovely storytelling, whether you're in Montana or New York."   —*USA Today*

"A deeply meditated and achieved art."
     —*The New York Times Book Review*

"You feel as if you're in the hands of an absolute expert at storymaking, a hard-hewn frontier version of Walter Scott or early Dickens. The landscape and characters are vivid, the prose flawless, and like the earlier masters, Doig imbues each scene and his spacious story with deep emotional understanding and a sense of possibility and personal adventure. *The Whistling Season* is a book that strives for more than beauty, which it achieves: It reaches for joy."
     —*O, The Oprah Magazine*

THE BARTENDER'S TALE

IVAN DOIG

RIVERHEAD BOOKS

New York

RIVERHEAD BOOKS
Published by the Penguin Group
Penguin Group (USA) Inc.
375 Hudson Street, New York, New York 10014, USA

USA I Canada I UK I Ireland I Australia I New Zealand I India I South Africa I China

Penguin Books Ltd., Registered Offices: 80 Strand, London WC2R 0RL, England
For more information about the Penguin Group, visit penguin.com.

The Library of Congress has catalogued the Riverhead hardcover edition as follows:

Doig, Ivan.
The bartender's tale / Ivan Doig.
p.   cm.
ISBN 978-1-59448-735-4
1. Fathers and sons—Fiction.   2. Bars (Drinking establishments)—Fiction.
3. Life change events—Fiction.   4. Montana—Fiction.   I. Title.
PS3554.O415B37   2012   2012017498
813'.54—dc23

First Riverhead hardcover edition: August 2012
First Riverhead trade paperback edition: August 2013
Riverhead trade paperback ISBN: 978-1-59463-148-1

PRINTED IN THE UNITED STATES OF AMERICA

10   9   8   7   6   5   4   3

Cover design by Wednesday Design
Cover photograph © William Albert Allard / Getty Images
Book design by Nicole LaRoche

To Mark and Lou Damborg,

friends over many a magical meal and beyond

THE
BARTENDER'S
TALE

✳ 1 ✳

MY FATHER WAS the best bartender who ever lived. No one really questioned that in a town like Gros Ventre, glad of any honor, or out in the lonely sheep camps and bunkhouses and other parched locations of the Two Medicine country, where the Medicine Lodge saloon was viewed as a nearly holy oasis. What else was as reliable in life as sauntering into the oldest enterprise for a hundred miles around and being met with just the right drink whisking along the polished wood of the prodigious bar, along with a greeting as dependable as the time of day? Not even heaven promised such service. Growing up in back of the joint, as my father always called it, I could practically hear in my sleep the toasts that celebrated the Medicine Lodge as an unbeatable place and Tom Harry as perfection of a certain kind behind the bar.

Which was not to say, even the adherents comfortably straddling their bar stools might have admitted, that he added up to the best human being there ever was. Or the absolute best father of all time, in ways I could list. Yet, as peculiar a pair as we made, the bachelor saloonkeeper with a streak of frost in his black pompadour and the inquisitive boy who had been an accident between the sheets, in the end I would not have traded my involuntary parent for a more standard model. It is said it takes a good storyteller to turn ears into eyes, but luckily life itself sometimes performs that trick on us. In what became our story together, when life took me by the ears, what a fortunate gamble it was that my father included me in his calling. Otherwise, I'd have missed out on the best seat in the house—the joint, rather—when history came hunting for him.

I turned twelve that year of everything, 1960. But as my father would have said, it took some real getting there first.

MY MOTHER, who was my father's housekeeper when domestic matters underwent a surprising turn and I was the result, long since had washed her hands of the two of us and vanished from our part of Montana, and for all I could find out, from the face of the earth. "She up and left," was his total explanation. "Pulled out on us when you were a couple of months old, kiddo." Accordingly, he handed me off to his sister, Marge, and her family in Arizona, and I spent my early years in one of those sunbaked Phoenix neighborhoods where saguaro cactuses had not yet been crowded out entirely.

It was not an easy existence. My cousins, Danny and Ronny, were four and six years older than I was, and infinitely more ornery. Aunt Marge was loyal to me—or at least to the checks my father sent for my support—but she took in laundry and ironing as well as running the household, and so her supervision of her unruly sons was sporadic at best. None of us saw much of the husband and father, Arvin, a fireman who usually was trying to catch some sleep in the back bedroom or on shift at the firehouse. My enduring memory of that period of my life is of the big Zenith console radio saving my skin the same time every afternoon, when the bigger boys took a break from tormenting me and we all slumped down on the living room floor to tune in to serial adventures far beyond what Phoenix had to offer. So I survived, as children somehow do, and occasionally I was even reprieved from Danny and Ronny. A time or two a year, my father would show up and take me off on what he declared was a vacation. We saw the Grand Canyon more than once.

As time went on, my situation started to slip drastically. Ronny was about to become a teenager, and turning meaner along with it. Among other stunts, he liked to grind his knuckles on the back of my head when Aunt Marge wasn't watching. All the while, copycat Danny was just waiting for his turn at me. The saying is that what does not kill you strengthens you, but sometimes you wonder which will happen first.

By the summer I turned six, I was desperately looking forward to the first grade, when I would be out of Ronny's reach at least that much of the day. It all culminated one hot afternoon when we were sprawled on the rug in the living room, listening as usual to *The Lone Ranger*. Ronny was alternately mocking Tonto—"Why it never your turn to sweep the tepee, Kemo Sabe?"—and spitting sunflower seed husks at me, Danny was giggling at such good fun, and I was wincing at how cruddy a life it was when a person had to put up with relatives like the pair of them. Then, more dramatic than anything on the radio, there was a thundering knock on the front door, which brought Aunt Marge rushing to see what it was about.

She opened the door to my father, head and shoulders above her even though she was a large woman. "Hey, Marge. How's tricks?" I was too surprised to jump up and run to him as usual. Seeing him materialize in that doorway—he looked like he always did, his hair slicked back and his lively eyebrows cocked, although his usual blinding white shirt was unbuttoned at the neck in concession to the Arizona heat—challenged my imagination more mightily than the masked man and his faithful Indian companion ever could. What was wrong? Why was he here, suddenly and unannounced?

The perfectly bland answer confounded me as much as the question. "I came to get the kid."

Aunt Marge laughed in his face. "Tom, you can't drag Rusty off on some dumb vacation right now. He starts school pretty soon."

That did not seem to perturb him the least bit. "Last time I looked, Montana has schoolhouses."

She was speechless, although not for long. "You don't mean you're going to try to raise him! That's crazy!"

"Yeah, well, that's one description of it." My father's wallet now entered the conversation, a riffle of bills as he counted out more money than I would have ever dreamed I was worth. Thrusting the wad of cash into her nearest hand and adding "Much obliged, Marge," he peered past her to our three gaping faces amid the unheard palaver of the radio.

In that moment, my life stopped being cruddy. Maybe I was imagining, but I thought I heard a scared gulp out of Ronny as my father sized up him and the sunflower seed shrapnel. Then he was looking at me as if we were the only two in the room. "Let's grab your things and hit the road, kiddo."

WE SWEPT OUT of Phoenix in one of those tubby Hudsons made after World War II, which maybe accounted for its family resemblance to a tank. I could barely see over the dashboard of the thing, in contrast to my father, who just fit under the car roof, tall even sitting down. By then I was catching up with the full implications of what had happened and was thrilled through and through with my escape from those stinker cousins. But was he? Every time I stole a look at him, he was squinting at the highway ahead as though something more than driving was on his mind. Surely he wouldn't turn the car around and deliver me back to Aunt Marge's madhouse, would he? Would he? Squirming in the passenger seat as the desert whipped past—he drove the way Montana people did in those days, as though the speed limit was merely a suggestion—I badly wanted to look however far ahead to when our trip would be safely over. "Daddy, how long—"

"Cripes, let's get rid of that word right now," he muttered, fishing out a cigarette and punching the lighter on the dash. "Makes both of us sound like we're still dealing with diapers."

Cautiously I tried again. "Father?"

"I'm no priest, am I," he said gruffly.

"Wh-what should I say?"

He lit his cigarette and waved the lighter as if extinguishing a match. "Don't sweat it. We'll think of something."

There matters stood until we pulled into a gas station in the first little town. As luck would have it, past the pumps I spotted a cheery enameled sign for Orange Crush soda, my favorite, and blurted: "Uh, Pop, can I please have some pop?"

He shot a look at me across the space of the front seat. His eyebrows went up in what seemed to be fresh consideration of his passenger. "Didn't I tell you we'd think of something?"

WE HAD TRAVELED together a little on those "vacations," but this trip was beyond anything even a daydreaming type of child like me ever imagined. Half of a state might go by in an afternoon, with Pop giving the Hudson's gas pedal no mercy. Interstate freeways hadn't yet bisected the West, and the highway went through towns, so that you felt you were visiting each one. Pop would slow whenever the road became a main street and ask, "Need to take a leak?" I almost always did, and he would aim for a sign that said Mint or Stockman or some other saloon name in plain tubular neon—this was 1954, take into account, before everything began flashing like Las Vegas—and in we would go. "My kid's got a quick call of nature," he'd tell the bartender, and be sure to buy a couple packs of cigarettes or some gum or candy bars for me to give the bar a bit of business, while I went to the toilet. On our way out he would always say, "Nice joint you have here," even if the place was gloomy as a funeral parlor. I suppose I learned something about professional courtesy from those stops.

To pass the driving time, Pop was trying to follow the fortunes of the Great Falls baseball team. They played in a Class D league—about one step up from picnic softball—and we took turns twiddling the car radio dial to pull in their games. I practically squinted an ear at first, trying to figure out what I was hearing. "Why are they called the Slick Tricks?"

He told me that wasn't the case, fishing in his shirt pocket to toss me a matchbook. "Here's where the name comes from, see?" Back there at six I already could read, and had not too much trouble with the fancy red script lettering that blazoned GREAT FALLS SELECT—MONTANA'S BEST BEER!

"I sell oceans of it," he spelled out further for me. "Seems only fair to root for the team." It sounded like they needed it, against the Pocatello Cowpokes. The broadcast signal faded in and out, as the Selectrics—as they proved to be—also seemed to do. *There's a grounder through the infield, one runner is in to score, here comes another. Seven to two, 'Pokes. The ball has eluded the Great Falls center fielder . . .*

"Damn," said Pop with a frown as the Selectrics wavered off the dial to their fate. "It's real too bad they don't live up to the beer."

Nights were a time neither of us was quite prepared for. Auto courts still existed then, and after parking the Hudson in the garage stall as if putting the horse in the barn, the two of us had a cabinlike room and all evening ahead. With that in mind, before pulling in for the first night, Pop had let me buy my fill of comic books at a drugstore. His own reading preference turned out to be paperback mystery novels, usually with a cover showing a beautiful blond woman in a bad situation. But we both read restlessly in the unaccustomed company of each other. My head was too full of what-ifs: What if I didn't like Montana, which I had not seen since I was an infant? What if they didn't have a desk for me, surprise newcomer that I was, when I started school? What if I didn't like living with Pop, or he with me? What if he didn't know how to cook? What if he didn't even have a house, just the saloon? What if he had met some woman and I was going to have a new mother; there must be some reason, mustn't there, why he had whisked me from Aunt Marge's after all this time?

Worst of all, what if he changed his mind at some point and delivered me back into the clutches of Ronny and Danny?

It was a boggling amount for a six-year-old to think about, all because the human mystery across the room, who happened to be my father, had appeared like a white-shirted genie in that Phoenix doorway. Somewhere in any of us is the memory of how it was at that age, elbow-high to the almost incomprehensible world of parents. In my case, one newly materialized parent, almost more incomprehensible yet.

After a long enough spell of trying to stick with his book, Pop got up and prowled the room. Television had not yet invaded everywhere, and the radio on the bedstand when he tried it seemed to carry only the 50,000-watt station in Del Rio, Texas, broadcasting lovelorn country songs and constant commercials for quack cures. He clicked that off in no time and went over to his suitcase to see what it had to offer. It appeared he must have packed in a hurry, or maybe not unpacked from some other trip; what I glimpsed were primarily mussed white shirts. However, he rummaged a bit and came up with more detective stories, and under those, a deck of cards. Eyebrows lifting, he looked over to where I was flipping the pages of a Plastic Man comic book and eating a candy bar.

"You know how to play cards?"

"Sure!"

"Gin rummy?"

"What's that?"

"How about pinochle?"

"Huh-uh."

"Okay, cardsharp, you tell me."

"Old Maid."

"I don't have a deck like that."

"I do! You sent it for my birthday. Along with *My Friend Flicka*, remember?"

"Oh, yeah, sure. Aren't we in luck." He sighed. "I suppose it beats solitaire. Okay, one game." He thought it over as I scrabbled in my suitcase for the cards. "Hey, if anybody ever hears about this, we played cutthroat poker, got that?"

"Sure! I won't forget! Cut-rate poker. Here's my deck, Pop."

He did the shuffling and dealing, since he was countless years better at it than I was. And here was another strange thing, engraved in memory: time suspended itself as we studied our cards, drew from each other's hand, took turns discarding, over and over. I see us yet in the dresser mirror of that boxy room, civilly playing cards on the kind of nubbly bedspread used before artificial fabrics came along. My father was a figure to behold, by any standard. The long, big-shouldered body, as if the whole world was meant to look up to him the way I did. The skunk streak in his black hair; expressive, thick eyebrows, just as dark with a little silvering in them to match. A widow's peak starting above the temples, pushed by the forehead's set of lively wrinkles. Deep-set eyes, of a surprising light blue. Eyes the color of sky and active eyebrows can do you a lot of good in dealing with people, and his fit him as if made to order. But it was the lines in his face that told the most about him. History sees to it that certain countenances become visages of an era. Lincoln and Grant and Lee of their time. Mark Twain and Teddy Roosevelt of theirs. The man on that unlikely magic carpet of bedspread with me that night was etched with the Thirties, with that deeply creased survivor's look so many times photographed as the image of the Depression generation. Hollywood further put that kind of face into our national memory by casting its most believably gaunt leading man, Henry Fonda, as Tom Joad in *The Grapes of Wrath*. My time-scarred father was no movie star, nor was he a Dust Bowl Okie, but his face was a badge of the decade as surely as if printed on a coin.

And the smaller figure in that mirror reflection? My mop-headed self, the early draft of some decade yet unwritten? Other than the shock of hair as shoe-polish black as his, I was not any miniature of my father. Complexion-wise, Pop's was merely the washed-out sort that comes from years spent under fluorescent lights, while I had the hopelessly pearly pale skin that generally is found on someone blond, the kind that always sunburns, never tans. Beyond that, my features were more regulation boy-ish, more—for lack of another word—cozy than his rugged ones; Lassie would have licked my face by the hour. Where resemblance was concerned, then, time had its work cut out for it on the boy and the man paired in that mirror.

"That's my last card, Pop! I win!"

"Cripes, just my luck you're such a cardslick." Stuck with the Old Maid, he tossed in his hand, frowned for a moment, then scooped the cards together for a shuffle. "Let's play another one."

Another led to another, and while I did not manage to skunk him entirely, he ended up the Old Maid several times more than I did. At last he let his wristwatch come to the rescue. "Hey, look at the time, we'd better turn in. Tomorrow's another real stretch of road."

He let me choose which side of the bed I wanted, and we undressed. Pajamas were in my suitcase, but Pop got under the covers in his shorts and undershirt, so I bravely did, too.

I was too excited to go to sleep, my mind going every which way, the what-ifs still buzzing in me like bees. My father was no example of repose, either. I could tell he was lying there awake with his hands under his head. Before very long he sat up in bed and I heard the scratch of a match, and the draw of breath as he lit a cigarette.

I turned on my side, toward him. "Uncle Arvin says people who smoke in bed are sticking their necks out."

"He's a fireman; it affects his judgment."

I stayed the way I was, watching the red end of his cigarette as he took slow drags and expelled the smoke into the dark. "Pop? Can I ask you something?"

"Ask me no questions and I'll tell you no lies." My heart stopped a little at that. The springs creaked as he leaned to tap an ash into the bedside ashtray. "Only kidding. Ask away."

"Is it gonna be just us? At"—I didn't know what other word to use—"home?"

He did not say anything until he had finished his cigarette and ground it out in the ashtray. "We're enough, kiddo. Catch some shut-eye."

GOOD-BYE, SAGUAROS, hello, sagebrush. After the days of our long drive north, the Two Medicine country and its anchoring town were all at once the world around me, and I had some real adjusting to do. Phoenix had mountains of a kind around it, but nothing like the great high snowy peaks of the Rockies that now stretched farther than I could see, to wherever Canada was. Hay fields green with alfalfa, also new to me, were tucked along a wooded creek that wound all the way from the mountains, and white igloo-like things that Pop identified as sheepherders' wagons stood on distant ridgelines. And from the sign at the city limits as he slowed the Hudson to a more reasonable speed, I realized that the town I had always heard him speak of as Grow Von was spelled Gros Ventre. I asked why and drew the reply: "It's French, so it doesn't need to make any sense."

I craned my neck at the strange storefronts—a store that called itself a mercantile, with rolls of barbwire stacked on a loading dock; another place of business that identified itself as the Top Spot, and left it to the curious to figure out it was a cafe; next to that, Shorty's, the smallest barbershop I'd ever seen; what looked like a clothing store, called the Toggery; and finally something I could recognize, a movie theater marquee, with ODEON spelled out in bright red letters—as Pop drove along the shady main street, in no hurry now. Halfway through town, he slowed down even more and pulled over. "Welcoming party for you," he said, cracking a grin. I peered over the hood of the car at sheep, sheep, and more sheep, filling the entire street and coming right at us like a woolly stampede.

"Wh-what do we do?"

"Sit tight and think of lamb chops." He explained that the flock of animals stamping their hooves at us was being trailed to the ranch from summer range and the town was used to this sort of thing. In back, whooping the sheep along with the help of a busy dog, were a stumpy herder who looked like he needed a bath and a longer-limbed man in clean clothes and a good Stetson hat. Under their push, what must have been a thousand fleecy eye-rolling ewes, the lambs beside them nearly as large and agitated as they were, rapidly surrounded Pop and me where we sat; their stupendous blatting sounded as if the sight of us was making them lose their minds. I wasn't really scared, but not very far from it either. As the sea of sheep parted around the car, Pop rolled down my window to call to the long-limbed man. "Hey, Dode! Got the kid, come meet him."

"Keep the sonofabitching old biddies moving, Dan, I'll catch up," the rangy figure yelled to the herder, then came and poked the brow of his hat in the car window. "Huh-uh," he declared after a close look at me. "Been a mistake. Better take him back."

Much alarmed, I shrank far down in the car seat. The frozen expression on Pop didn't help.

Our visitor broke out in a generous smile that had a tooth missing. "How can this one be yours, Tom? He's way better looking than you."

Relieved, Pop instructed me to shake hands with Dode Withrow, sheep rancher and prize customer. "Pleased to make your acquaintance." The ranchman went through with the ceremony as if we were equals. "Randall, do I remember your front name is?"

"Russell," I piped back. "Most everybody calls me Rusty."

"Then I guess I better, too. So, Rusty, are you all set for the derby?"

"He's gonna be," Pop answered stoutly for me while I blinked at this revelation. Thanks to the Wheaties box that Aunt Marge plunked down beside my cereal bowl practically every breakfast of my life, I knew there was such a thing as a soapbox derby, in which Wheaties-filled boys surely no braver than me were depicted scrambling into homemade miniature race cars and letting gravity guide them to glory on a downhill track. How lucky I was! Never mind the what-ifs! I had a father who fetched me all the way from Phoenix to put me in the cockpit, if that's what it was, of my very own soapbox flyer. I couldn't wait to see the wheeled wonder.

"This old man of yours generally has something up his sleeve," Dode Withrow confided to me with a wink, turning to go. "See you on the big day."

"Why didn't you tell me about the derby, Pop?" I asked, bouncing with excitement.

"How the hell could I, when it's supposed to be a surprise?" he stated with irrefutable logic, putting the car in gear and nosing it through several last panicky sheep, up the street to the Medicine Lodge saloon and all that came with it.

THE BUILDING WE pulled up to was a lot like Pop—taller than ordinary, showing its years somewhat but not giving in to them, and impressively two-toned at the very top, where the biggest black letters I had ever seen were painted onto the whitewashed square front to spell out MEDICINE LODGE. Beneath that in lesser lettering but still about a foot high was BEER—SOFT DRINKS—FULL BAR AND THEN SOME. I was to learn that the triumphant previous owner added that line once Prohibition ended, and when Pop bought the place not many years later, he saw no reason to change the wording.

Wisely, the brass-trimmed doorway below the signs was inset against the weather, while on either side of it, department store–size plate-glass windows provided anyone sitting at the bar with a full view of the activity on Gros Ventre's main street, such as a passing parade of sheep. This saloon was already more personable than the Mints and Stockmans of all our toilet stops since Phoenix, and I could hardly wait to go inside. But Pop made no move to get out of the car.

"Kiddo"—his brows drew down as he looked over at me—
"there's something we need to get straight. Did Aunt Marge
ever say anything about me and"—he inclined his head toward
the saloon—"this?"

I thought. "One time I heard her tell Uncle Arvin that a bartender wasn't the absolute worst thing you could be."

"That's high praise from Marge." He continued to look at me
intently. "What about those cousins of yours?"

"They said stuff all the time. I didn't listen, honest."

"Smart use of your ears." His creased face showed relief for a
moment, then he turned serious again. "Okay, here's the straight
scoop. I'm in business here"—he nodded to the Medicine Lodge,
and I wouldn't have been too surprised if it had nodded
back—"just like somebody who sells candy bars or jelly beans.
Only what I sell has alcohol in it. You know what that is, do
you?"

"Sure. It makes people drunk."

"Too much of it can, just like you can get a bellyache from eating too much candy." I could tell he was putting every effort into
making me understand. "People are gonna drink and have a
good time, that's just the way it is. Even the Bible says so, Jesus
doing that stunt with the water and the wine at the wedding,
right? But customers who are feeling thirsty don't need to get out
of hand, and I see to it that they don't. If they want to drink
themselves blind, they can go down the street to the Pastime. If
they want to have a few snorts in a decent joint, they can come in
here." He turned his eyes to the waiting saloon. "Cripes," he said,
more or less to himself, "churches are for sinners, too. What's the
big difference?" His gaze shifted to me and he cleared his throat.
"Follow what I'm saying?"

"I guess so."

"That's that, then. Let's head on inside."

———

THE JOINT, as I right away learned to call it, was not yet open for the day, but behind the bar, a scrawny man in an apron that fit him like a tent was setting up for business.

"Hey," Pop called out as we entered, which seemed to serve as *Hello* and much else in his vocabulary. "Didn't manage to give the place away to some bigger fool than me, I guess?"

"That would take too much looking," came the croaky reply. The sparely built part-time bartender gave me, or at least my existence, a bare nod of acknowledgment, then cocked an eye at my father. "Can I trade in this apron for my rocking chair, now that the prodigal has returned?"

This was Howie, bald and cranky and indispensable to Pop for filling in as needed. You can't run a saloon like a country club, and Howie was an old hand at handling customers of all stripes, having owned a roadhouse and row of cabins during the war, when the Great Falls air base was going full blast. "Howie knows the tricks of the trade," Pop would say in a certain kind of voice. In the fullness of time I eventually figured out what trade was plied in that row of cabins.

"Not so damn fast," Pop told him now, "I haven't even had a chance to change my shirt yet. Let's take a look at how the cash register did in my absence." Remembering me as he rounded the bar, he reached into the pop cooler. "Here"—he handed me an Orange Crush—"entertain yourself while I count the take, okay?"

So, wide-eyed at the new surroundings, I was temporarily left on my own in my father's prized place of business. "Your old man makes his money off of a bunch of drunk sheepherders," knucklehead Ronny had told me plenty of times. Whatever the quantity of truth in that, at the moment there were none of those on the premises, and the venerable barroom was mine to explore. I still see the Medicine Lodge of that day as clearly as if it were a stage set.

The highly polished surface of the classic bar, as dark as wood can get.

In back of the bar the colossal oak breakfront, as ornate as it was high and long, displaying all known brands of liquor. According to what Pop had heard from the oldest of old-timers, it had taken a freight wagon usually used for huge mining machinery, with ropes up, down, and sideways, to haul the tall, teetery thing; coming across the prairie, it must have looked like a galleon sailing the sea of grass.

A lofty pressed-tin ceiling the color of risen cream. Walls of restful deep green. Original plank-wide floorboards as substantial as a ship's decking.

Fake-leather maroon booths along the far wall where only strangers and loners ever sat, and a baize poker table looking a little lost at the absolute rear of the room.

Crowning it all, literally, my father's notion of decor, or as he pronounced it, *dee-cor*: his menagerie of stuffed animal heads protruding from the walls. The buck deer, mostly antlers. The mountain goat and the antelope facing one another, glassily. Cougar, bobcat, even coyote, lopped and mounted. The one-eyed buffalo over the front door was particularly dramatic, dark and mangy, a ghostly relic of the great vanished herd of the plains. This wildlife motif achieved a last flourish in the gilt-framed painting dominating the wall across from the bar, a reproduction of a hunting scene by Charlie Russell, the cowboy artist who painted Montana in dreamy sunset colors no matter what time of day. Called *Meat's Not Meat Till It's in the Pan*, it showed a hunter in the high country scratching his head in bafflement as he gazed down at the mountain sheep he had shot on a ledge impossible to reach. A good many of the Medicine Lodge patrons had hunted since they were big enough to hold a rifle, and they heaped scorn on the unfortunate in the picture who had pulled the trigger inadvisably, always referring to him as the Buck Fever Case. As far as I know, Pop never turned a hair when crude remarks were directed at his chosen masterpiece, evidently convinced the artwork was doing its job, giving the audience something to think about.

Such was the saloon of near-mythic status, which stayed substantially the same in the span of time when I went from a half dozen years of age to a full dozen. I would like to say I felt its inimitable atmosphere from that first moment. Actually, all I could think about was a derby-winning soapbox race car waiting somewhere for me.

"Ready?" Pop called to me after he had counted out the take at the cash register. "Done all the damage we can here. Let's head to the house."

WE WERE PRACTICALLY THERE by the time I settled onto the car seat and resumed gawking over the dashboard. The house stood across an alley from the back of the saloon; Pop could walk to work in about half a minute. I had to get used to the fact that although we were in the middle of town, there were more trees than anything else. Nearby English Creek and its good, steady water table accounted for that, cottonwoods growing to such tremendous size that Gros Ventre was practically roofed over with leafy limbs. An old giant of the species loomed beside the lofty two-story structure we pulled up to now, the yard white where its seed fluff had drifted down. Pop stopped the car in the dappled shade of the big overhanging limbs. When we got out, he laughed comfortably at the fluff falling on us like confetti, and said: "Say hello to Igdrasil."

I looked all around the yard for a dog or a cat. Nothing barked and nothing meowed.

Then the horrible thought hit me. Maybe Pop had another kid, another version of me, waiting there in the house, that he had spared telling me about until now. Which meant I would have a brother or a sister to compete with for his affection, to call it that. How was that in any way fair?

I asked fearfully: "Who's . . . who's Ig-somebody?"

"The tree, savvy?" I watched in relief but still some confusion as he stepped over and patted the enormous wrinkled trunk. "Had a customer in the old days," he shook his head, remembering, "Darius Duff, how's that for a name? He was kind of a political crackpot, but he knew things. He'd start feeling his oats after enough drinks, and one time he got going on Igdrasil, the tree of existence. It's an old Norskie legend, according to him. I can't do his Scotch brogue, but the words stuck with me. 'Igdrasil,'" he recited, squinting to get the words exactly right, "'the tree of existence. Its roots watered by the fates of past, present, and future. Its top reaching to heaven and stirring the colors of the rainbow. Its bower spreading over the whole universe.'" Gazing up at the mighty expanse of green leaves and gray bark, he shook his head again. "When I bought the joint and the house, the biggest tree in town came along with. That's Igdrasil for you." He met my blinking gaze. "I know it's a headful, but you'll catch up with it someday. Come on, let's see if the house is still standing."

My new home looked as aged as Igdrasil, gray and knotty in its own way. The outside hadn't tasted paint for a good many years, while the interior was well kept but as old-fashioned as the time it was built, with a dreary parlor and a milkmaid room off the kitchen and those high ceilings of the Victorian era that defied rationale and heating system alike. Perched as it was on a stone foundation of enough height to allow for a dirt cold-cellar where people used to store the canning and potatoes, the house had a cool, earthy smell, even on a summer day like this.

"So, kiddo, this is it," Pop said as he dumped our belongings by the stairway at the end of the hall and lit up a cigarette. He blew out a wreath of smoke and his brows went up an inch. "Got something for you. Let's go out back."

At last! My reward for waiting through a welcoming party of sheep, an excursion through the saloon, and meeting the king of all trees. Nearly skipping with excitement, I followed him through the dining room and the kitchen and into the backyard. At the end of the driveway sat an old car, long and black as a hearse, but no soapbox racer was parked anywhere that I could see. Well, of course, something that precious would be kept in the garage, wouldn't it? I looked around for the garage. There wasn't one.

"Here you go." Pop reached back inside the porch doorway and pulled out a junior-size fishing pole. "All yours. Now, all you have to do is give the fish hell, day after tomorrow."

An awful truth descended on me as I unsurely held the awkward gift. "Is it going to be a, uh, fishing derby?"

He gave me a look. "What did you think it'd be, a Sunday-school picnic?"

There is that memorably rueful line in Shakespeare, *The soldier's pole is fall'n*. Despite my effort to be stoic, my newfound one definitely drooped.

Somewhat belatedly, I remembered manners. "Gee, Pop. Thanks. Can I try it out?" English Creek chattered past only a strong cast away, if a person knew how to cast.

"Not here," he shook his head decisively, "the creek's too roily. I'll take you to the real place tomorrow. Come on back inside, we need to get you squared away."

I followed him in and upstairs, to a warren of bedrooms; the house went with the saloon, I learned, so the original Medicine Lodge owner must have sired a batch of children. Pop thought for a moment and assigned me a room at the back, farthest from his own at the head of the stairs, on the theory that I wouldn't be disturbed when he came in at all hours from bartending. A bedroom of my own eased disappointment about the lack of a soapbox racer somewhat; at least for now I was under the same roof with my singular father, rather than the world's worst cousins.

But I could see his mood change markedly while we were putting away my things. He had a habit of squinting while thinking, his eyebrows drawing together until they nearly met. The deeper the squint, the deeper the thought. Whatever was on his mind now appeared bottomless. After kicking my suitcase under the bed—not far enough under to suit me—he stood there facing me, running a hand through the gray streak in the middle of his hair.

"Listen, Rusty," he said, as if I hadn't been all ears since the instant he showed up in the Phoenix doorway. "The joint takes damn near every hour I have, day and night, so I can't be playing nursemaid to you all the time, right? You can stand your own company, can't you?"

"Sure, I guess."

"You don't miss Danny and Ronny?"

"Huh-uh. I hate their guts."

"That's pretty much what I figured." He muttered, "Too bad they didn't run down Arvin's leg."

"Too bad they didn't what, Pop?"

"Never mind. You're here now, that's what counts." He started to say something more, then gruffly broke off to: "Dress warm tomorrow for fishing."

TOMORROW CAME all too soon. Pop must have believed fish got up before dawn. Cats were just then scooting home from their nightly prowls, eyes glittering at us in the Hudson's headlights, as he drove out of town and onto a gravel road that seemed to go on and on. I was more asleep than awake when eventually he stopped the car. "Here it is. Set your mouth for catching fish."

Groggily I climbed out after him, and Montana opened my eyes for good.

The Rocky Mountains practically came down from the roof of the continent to meet us. The highest parts lived up to their name in solid rock, bluish-gray cliffs like the mightiest castle walls imaginable, with timber thick and dark beneath and the morning sky boundless beyond. Canyons, mysterious by nature, led off between the awesome rims of stone. I know now that the clear air and time of day made it all seem so wonderfully near and distinct; in the first morning of the world the light must have been like that.

Such was my introduction to the Two Medicine country, larger than some eastern states and fully as complicated. The Two, taking its name from the Two Medicine River in ancestral Blackfeet land some thirty miles north of town, was an extravagant piece of geography in all directions. The sizable canyon of the river cutting through the eastward plains was joined by a succession of fast-running creeks, with generous valleys nicely spaced along the base of the mountains. Benchlands flat as anvils and dramatically tan as buckskin separated these green creek valleys, while to the west, the peaks and crags of the Rockies went up like the farthest rough edge of everything. The Two Medicine National Forest began in the foothills and stretched

up and over the Continental Divide, and that forest grazing land
and the wild hay in the creek bottomlands had made the Two
Medicine country a historical stronghold of sheep ranching,
with one huge cattle ranch, the Double W, thrown in for contrast. That restless landscape working its way up to the summit
of the continent seemed to me then a dramatic part of the earth,
and still does.

Taking in the view between assembling our fishing poles, having a cigarette, and drinking coffee from a thermos, my father
summed up the surroundings in his own way: "Nature. Damn
hard to beat."

What he was viewing most appreciatively, I suspected, was
the body of blue water in the foreground, so big that it stretched
around the nearest mountain and out of sight. RAINBOW
RESERVOIR, according to the sign at the edge of the lake. I
was to learn that the dirt dam of the reservoir—rezavoy, Pop
pronounced it—impounded the South Fork of English Creek,
there at the canyon that rounded the towering rimrock called
Roman Reef. At the time, it was simply an oversize fishing hole
I had been dragged to.

Rocks large enough to stand on lined the inner curve of the
dam, and Pop scrambled down to the water's edge, with me following uncertainly. Perching us on a boulder that seemed to suit him,
he blew into his hands to warm them and began fiddling with our
fishing poles and a bait can. "This is just our secret, got that?" He
glanced around, even though there wasn't a sign of anyone for
miles, then carefully shook out a few of the grayish slimy contents
onto the rock and started cutting small strips with his jackknife.
"Fish knock each other's brains out trying to get to these."

"What are they?" In what I hoped was the spirit of fisher-
manliness, I picked one up to examine it, drippy and sort of
oozing though it was.

"Chicken guts."

I determinedly did not puke. Close, though. Pop busied himself showing me how to hold the fishhook steady by its shank and work the hunk of icky bait past the barb so that it covered the shine of the hook.

Trying it, I was nervous and stuck myself. I yelped, and tears started.

"Cripes, don't bawl," he soothed, getting me to wash the spot of blood off my finger in the frigid lake. "Stick it in your mouth and it'll stop bleeding. Here, I'll bait up for you, this once."

I sucked on the finger and sniffled myself dry, watching as he took up his pole, fussed with the line and reel, drew back, and sent the hook and sinker sailing to where the fish were dreaming of chicken guts. "Now you try."

Awkwardly I whipped my pole and the line plooped into the water about six feet from the bank. "That's a start," he commended my effort to the extent he could. "You want to go a little more easy when you cast, okay? It's not like you're chopping wood."

Another swish, another ploop, maybe seven feet out from the bank this time. And, again, no interested response from any fish. I was beginning to get the feeling that progress came slowly in fishing. Not only that, but my hands and feet were cold, and the rest of me in between was not much better. Beautiful as the crisp scenic morning was, it would have been even more attractive from inside the car with the heater on.

"Don't sweat it"—Pop at least was undiscouraged—"you'll get the hang of it."

Not, as it proved out, before losing my bait every few casts and having to deal with the hook and chicken guts a number of times more.

Something else troubled me. I could accept that the sign was

right about this being a reservoir, but the other part I had my
doubts about. Any rainbow I had ever seen—Arizona at least
had those—needed its distance, an expanse of sky to stretch its
band of colors from end to end. Here, though, the way the lake
was pressed against the mountains, you would sprain your neck
looking overhead for any sign of one. I asked Pop about it, and
he just laughed. "It's on the fish. Rainbow trout. The rezavoy is
stocked with them."

"Really?" I was more interested now, if chicken guts were going
to lead to amphibians with red, yellow, green, blue, and purple
stripes. Time passed, however, and cast after cast, with me growing more and more numb and no tug at my line—or, for that matter, at Pop's—from any trout, rainbow-colored or otherwise.

Ultimately I was saved by the wind, which kicked up a strong
riffle on the water and made his casts hard to control and mine
hopeless. "Well, hell, they aren't biting anyway," he conceded at
last, securing his hook into the cork handle of his pole and doing
mine for me. "It just leaves that many more for you to catch in
the derby." I shivered from more than the cold as we climbed
back to the car.

BACK IN TOWN, it began to dawn on both of us that my father
did not quite know what to do with me once the fishing poles
were put away. So there I was again, tagging after him as he
went to tend to business at the saloon. Howie, smoking a cigarette as if he couldn't breathe without it, was doing the same
things behind the bar he'd been doing twenty-four hours before,
but with a fresh gripe.

"Tom, you're gonna have to do something about Earl Zane.
Teach him to read, if nothing else." He jerked his head toward
the sign prominent above the cash register: MOSES FORGOT

THE ONE ABOUT CREDIT: THOU SHALT NOT ASK. "The no-good son of a bitch wanted to keep on drinking after his money ran out, but I told the prick to—"

"Hey, not in front of the kid," Pop cut him off, just when I was getting interested. At least in my vicinity, my father brought his own rules to the etiquette of bad language. *Damn* and *hell* salted and peppered his remarks to me as well as to everyone else, but he made an effort to swear off, so to speak, the worse words when I was around. *Cripes* stood in for what Bill Reinking, the newspaper editor and the town's acknowledged wise man on matters of language, would have called invoking the Nazarene. And *ess of a bee* I soon figured out was his abbreviated version of *son of a bitch* rather than anything to do with collecting honey. *Bee ess*, on the other hand, baffled me until some overheard conversation enlightened me with the key word *bull*.

Now Howie tucked his tongue in his cheek to keep from saying anything, which nevertheless made all the statement needed about protecting my tender ears, and resumed his bar chores. Pop meanwhile was scooping unpaid bills from a drawer by the cash register. "Come on in the back while I'm busy being busy with these damn things," he told me as if he saw no other choice. "You can help me count the booze."

I HAD NEVER been in a museum, but the colossal back room of the Medicine Lodge immediately fixed that. The two-story space was like some enormous attic that had settled to the ground floor under the weight of its treasures. Ranch things were everywhere, most with the dust of time on them. Saddles, bridles, pairs of chaps, sets of harness—one entire wall was leather items of that sort, as if the horses had just left. Automobile jacks and tires neighbored with the equine gear. Elsewhere, axes and shovels and even a sledgehammer shared space with softer goods such as bedrolls and bright yellow rain slickers and hats of the Stetson sort. A guitar leaned against a pile of well-traveled suitcases. I couldn't help but notice a clutch of fishing poles poking up in one corner, in with some long-handled crook-headed things that proved to be sheep hooks. As though one floor wasn't enough for it all, the room had a loft—doubtless the haymow in the early days, when this extensive space had been the stable behind the saloon—and lighter items such as lariats and hay hooks, like the kind stevedores used, hung from the rafters there.

"Wow," I let out, openmouthed, "where did you get all this?"

"All what?" Pop asked absently, shedding his suit coat but not his bow tie as he prepared to deal with the month's bills. He followed my gaze around the menagerie of items. "The loot?" He half laughed. "It accumulates. See, customers don't always have the ready cash when they want a couple of drinks. Or maybe need bus fare to somewhere, or are in the mood for a better pair of boots or a new hat. So," he shrugged and lit up a cigarette, "I'll take whatever they bring in, if it's of any use. Maybe they get it out of hock eventually and maybe they don't. After long enough, I sell it off, a bunch at a time." He contemplated the motley collection again. "Some of the stuff goes way back, long before me. An old Scotchman owned the joint for a lot of years, in the early days. They say he knew every nickel about life, and he's the one who started taking things in when cash was short. Kind of comes in handy eventually, doing it that way." Tobacco smoke wisped over him as he stood there thinking out loud. "Gonna have to lay down the law to Earl Zane, though. He's dumber than a frozen lizard. You got to watch out for people like that, kiddo," he philosophized to me. "Hell, if the ess of a bee is short of money, he's got those belt buckles he won riding at rodeos when he was a bronc punk. Hold up his pants with one hand and drink with the other—it'd be good for him." Laughing the way he ordinarily did, quick and sharp like exclamations, he climbed the stairs to his check-writing chore.

I followed him, eager for the next sideshow attraction of the back room. The stairs to the loft were interrupted halfway up by a long, wide landing, and there Pop had his desk and a table and other office requirements, as if staying above the tide of stuff below. I thought it was a sensational perch, and I didn't yet know the best thing about it as I gawked around from up there: a sizable air vent was cut through the wall at one end of the desk, and all of a sudden, the sound of Howie smashing ice behind the bar came through clear as anything. It took me hardly any time to figure out that when the vent's louvered slats were open like that, a person could hear everything—and see everything, by peeking—that was happening out front in the barroom. No wonder my father had the reputation of being the lord of all he surveyed, if he could do it secretly whenever he wanted.

He dropped the stack of bills to pay and his checkbook on the desk and turned around to me. "The deal is, you're gonna count up the booze for me, right?" His forehead furrowed. "You do know how to count, don't you?"

Anything above ten was a challenge, but I didn't want to appear as shaky at arithmetic as I was at fishing. "Sure! I do it all the time."

"Okay, then, see those cases down there?" They were hard to miss, stacked halfway to the ceiling along the sidewall. "Count each kind and call it out to me. Start with the beer."

That was the next scene for a while, me scrambling around the boxes of alcoholic beverages and out of his way while he sat there at his lofty desk tackling the financial chores. That image of him with his clattery adding machine and fountain pen and checkbook I suppose sounds as quaintly manual now as a monk with an abacus and quill and scroll, but calculators then were still the human sort cranking out sums up there on the landing and, to a lesser degree, the six-year-old one laboriously enumerating the pyramid of booze down below. Starting with the beer—the vast majority of it Great Falls Select; the beverage of the Selectrics!— I would count the cases twice to make sure I had the number right, call out the total to Pop, he would say "Got it," and write it down somewhere and go back to his calculating, and I would move on to the next brand of intoxicant. It was educational. *Booze* was a new word to me, and toward the back of the pile, I was thrilled to find included with the bourbon and scotch and all the rest a case of Orange Crush, proof of my father's discriminating taste. The thrill diminished somewhat when I counted the Coca-Cola, six cases, but I still ended up happy to have been entrusted with the inventory.

"All done, Pop."

"Okay, swell job," he responded without looking up. "Keep yourself amused awhile, I'm not done writing these damn checks yet."

"Can I have some booze?"

"What? Hell no!" He scowled down from the landing, until he saw me disconsolately tracing a finger along the carton of orange pop. "Oh. Sure, help yourself to a crushed orangutang." He tossed me an opener.

Bottle of sweet, sticky soda in hand, I circulated through the maze of things, eager for discoveries. One that puzzled me was tucked behind a stack of spare tires and covered with a tarpaulin, several toolboxes identically new and shiny. Still in my counting mode, I asked: "How come there's so many of this?"

Fanning a check in the air to dry the ink, Pop glanced over at what I'd found. "Never mind. Pull that tarp over those like it was."

"But there's"—I had to think hard to remember what the number is when you have ten and two more—"twelve?"

"The customer must have been a dozen times thirstier than usual," he said as if that was that, and went back to what he was doing.

I kept on prowling the wonders of the back room. Propped against the wall where the rain slickers were hanging was a sizable wooden sign standing on end. Pushing aside the curtain of coats and turning my head sideways, I managed to read the big lettering: BLUE EAGLE. Between the words, in fading paint, a fierce-looking sky-colored bird swooped as though it meant business.

"Pop, how come the eagle is blue instead of eagle color?"

"Hmmh?" The adding machine was coughing out a long result, which he waited for before answering me. "That's the name of the joint, is all."

"I thought it was the, uh, Medical Lounge."

"Not this one," he replied crossly, setting me straight about the Medicine Lodge and that the other joint was somewhere he'd been way back when, long before I entered the world. "That's another story," he said, which told me he didn't want to be pestered further about it. Getting up from his desk, he straightened his bow tie and shrugged into his suit coat. "Come on, let's mail these damn bills and grab some lunch."

DERBY DAY WAS a repeat of the circumstances Pop had introduced me to at Rainbow Reservoir twenty-four hours before: brilliant weather, matchless scenery, and chicken guts.

What was decidedly different, though, was his method of getting us there. This time, when he gathered fishing poles and bait can and thermos and so on, he headed not toward the

Hudson but to the old car parked at the far end of the driveway. Trying to get my bearings on a day that was strange enough already, I asked: "Does it run okay?"

"Hell yes." His reply sounded a little hurt as he tumbled our gear into the back seat. "It's in top-notch shape."

That may not have been too far from the truth, I saw when I drew closer to the lengthy black vehicle. I learned it was a 1932 Packard, its characteristic hood nearly as long as the four-door passenger compartment, which looked like it could hold a baseball team. Up close, there was a certain old-fashioned elegance to the car, from its gleaming grille and white-sidewall tires to its outsize headlights mounted on fenders that swooped all the way back to the running board at the door frame. "How come you"— I corrected that as I circled the automotive behemoth—"we have two cars?"

"The Packard still has its uses"—he was busy unfurling something—"you'll see. You don't get rid of a good thing just because it's got a little age on it, right? I've had it since Blue Eagle days, up at Fort Peck." I took in this news with some confusion. My father had been at a fort? But didn't he tell me the Blue Eagle was a joint, like the Medicine Lodge? That did not seem to go with being a soldier, nor did possessing the biggest, fanciest car I'd ever seen. He was not about to explain anything further, though, cheerfully going at the task at hand. "Here, help me with this banner."

Accordingly, I held one end of a large oilcloth banner while he tied it across the car's extensive trunk. Twice a year, it developed, the Packard attained this kind of starring role, this time with the banner reading: THE MEDICINE LODGE SUPPORTS THE GROS VENTRE FISHING DERBY. CATCH 'EM TO THE LIMIT! The other occasion was rodeo time, when it was prominently parked in front of the saloon,

bannering the message: THE MEDICINE LODGE SUP-
PORTS THE GROS VENTRE RODEO. RIDE 'EM TO
THE WHISTLE!

"There," he said in satisfaction, standing back with his hands
on his hips. "Ready to go. People get a kick out of seeing the old
heap. Besides, it never hurts to advertise."

So we went to the rezavoy in what Pop regarded as style, and
joined what appeared to be the entire populace of the Two Medicine country at the water's edge. Setting off where he assured
me was the best spot on the lake, he was right at home in the
festive throng, meeting and greeting people in wholesale numbers, looking like a million dollars in his dress hat, a pearl-gray
stockman Stetson, while I felt out of place in my dumb cloth sun
hat from Phoenix. Headgear was really the least of what was on
my mind, though, in this looming situation of me versus what
appeared to be every kid in Montana ready to compete for mysterious rainbow-hued fish.

Churning with apprehension as he assembled my pole for me,
I listened distractedly to his recital of the fishing contest rules. He
could bait my hook for me in preparation for the initial cast, but
after that, "It's up to you, kiddo." He reminded me to bury the
hook in the bait so it would look good to the fish. And then,
when I caught a trout—a prospect I wasn't at all sure I looked
forward to—I would need to land it myself, but he could help
me take the hook out of its mouth, because sometimes it got
snagged so hard it had to be torn out with pliers. Fishing was
more gory than I'd thought. At least there were prizes, in each
age category, for catching the biggest fish and the most fish.
"Two shots at packing home the money, you can't beat that,"
Pop topped off his pep talk. "Ready? Let's go give the fish hell."

First we had to sign up, atop the approach to the dam, where
a truck was parked with a loudspeaker crowning its cab. White

water was picturesquely gushing through the floodgate out in the middle of the causeway, and the sky could not have been more blue. As Pop and I approached the registration table, the announcer on the flatbed of the truck boomed out, "WELCOME TO THE ROD AND REEL EXTRAVAGANZA YOU'VE BEEN WAITING FOR, THE SECOND ANNUAL RAINBOW FISHING DERBY!" as if just for us. The woman who took the entry money and pinned a number on my back seemed considerably less hospitable for some reason, eyeing me and then Pop, as if to make sure we matched. He didn't seem to pay that any mind, kidding with the announcer and the Chamber of Commerce organizers of the festivity who were standing around, looking important. The civic side of my father was complicated, as it can be in a town where everyone knows everyone else's business. For example, he would not have anything to do with the Rotary Club. "Not until the esses of bees quit stealing money out of my pocket with that beer booth of theirs." The Kiwanis and Toastmasters, younger strivers hoping for a station in life higher than a saloon, were not sure they wanted anything to do with him. Leave it to Pop, he sorted it all out without blinking: he had no argument with commerce, nor it with him, so the local Chamber received his wholehearted backing.

As now, when he steered me past the army of adults attacking trout with rod and reel to the stretch of lakeshore reserved, according to the banner flapping in the breeze, for JUNIOR ANGLERS. Boys my age or a year or so younger, and a sprinkling of girls, were being stationed far enough apart that we wouldn't spear one another with our fishpoles during energetic casts. Pop got me settled in my spot, slipped me the bait can of chicken guts cut into gooey strips, told me again to give the fish hell, and retreated up the bank a safe distance, where other parents were clustered. My head was spinning. *Second* annual extravaganza; why wasn't I plucked from Phoenix for this a year ago? Another nettlesome thought: If it wasn't for the fishing derby, would I still be . . .

I did not have time to dwell on that, because the announcer's voice was booming again. "AND NOW WE COME TO THE SPECIAL FEATURE OF THE DERBY, THE CONTEST WHERE THE KIDDIES SHOW US HOW IT'S DONE. READY, JUNIOR ANGLERS? GET SET . . . START FISHING!"

Hooks and lines swished through the air at all different altitudes, and the tips of more than a few fishing poles dunked in the lake, mine included.

A pause ensued, as those of us who had thrashed bait into the water wondered what to do next, beyond hanging on to the fishing rod with both hands, while the grown-ups shouted conflicting advice—"Try a longer cast!" "Keep your hook in the water, not in the air!" Stealing a peek over my shoulder, I saw Pop standing with his arms folded, the picture of patience, confident that the secret bait would lure fish in my direction in a frenzy. Even though my line sagged out into the lake only a little way, I decided to let it sit there. The breeze had picked up—it would have been news when the wind wasn't blowing at Rainbow Reservoir—so I didn't want to risk another cast; the fish could jump ashore if they wanted chicken guts badly enough, as far as I was concerned.

To my surprise, suddenly there was a sharp tug on my line. I yanked my pole up and back as hard as I could, the hook and line sailing over my head in a mighty arc. But no fish. Worse than that, I realized, no bait.

"Hot damn, they're biting!" Pop yelled encouragement. "Don't horse it like that, though, just pull the next one in real easy. Bait up and go get him."

During this, the boy nearest me had actually landed a fish. "Way to go, buckshot!" His father, a chesty man with a red face broad as a fire bucket, came charging down the bank to unhook the catch and gill it onto a stringer. The trout was a good size, but I was disappointed to see it was not striped like a rainbow, merely brightly speckled on the sides. As both of us faced the challenge of baiting our hooks, I said to the chunky kid in sportsmanlike fashion, "Nice fish."

"If you like something slimy as snot." He made a face. "I hate fishing, I wish it had never been invented." Narrowing his critical view of things to me, he demanded: "Who're you, anyway?"

I told him, which drew me a beady look and the remark, "Huh, you're that one. My daddy gets a snootful in your daddy's saloon when Mom isn't looking."

"Uhm, what's your name?"

"Duane Zane." He smirked. "I don't take up much alphabet that way, my folks tell everybody." By now he had shaken little doughy pellets of some kind out of a bait can and was jabbing his hook through one.

"What're those?"

Duane smirked again. "Pink marshmallows. My daddy says they're our secret weapon." Before I could even blink, he picked up his pole and whipped the line—*whizzzz*—over my head and into the lake.

Gulping, I managed to bait my hook with a sloppy bit of chicken gut and get everything into the water again. As if I didn't have enough on my mind before, now the holy terror next to me already had another bite and was sidestepping in my direction as he tried to haul the fish to shore. It was then that the wind strengthened, and somewhere down the rank of junior anglers from Duane, a gust caught a line being weakly flung out and blew the hook back onto the boy making the cast. He screeched and threw his pole aside, unfortunately toward the kid next to him. That one panicked, too, and I gaped at fishpoles toppling like dominoes toward Duane and me, with lines and hooks flying crazily. Busy trying to land his catch, he glanced down in irritation when a hook caught in his sleeve, yelped when he saw what it was, and yanked his pole so hard, the fish flew off and his hook flew at me. I yowled as it caught my ear.

Pop was right there in the stampede of parents rushing to tend to aggrieved children. "Don't get in an uproar," he told me, cutting the fish line with his jackknife and tilting my head so he could see how the hook was embedded. I had quit yowling, but the tears of fright and pain would not stop.

During this, Duane Zane seemed mostly put out that I was in possession of his fishhook, but his father hovered in, full of advice. "Push it on through and snip the barb off, why don't you, Tom?"

Pop shook his head grimly. "It's caught too hard." Now I was so scared I couldn't even whimper, thinking of pliers tearing the hook out of my ear the way it would from a fish's mouth. At least, it turned out, Pop was not going to do it himself, saying he had to get me to town to the doctor.

The CATCH 'EM TO THE LIMIT! banner flapping madly behind us, he drove the gravel road at high speed while I hunched down against the passenger door, a picture of misery, at least to myself. Neither of us had anything to say until he asked, "Doesn't hurt, does it?"

"Yes."

"Okay, okay, we'll get you to the doc in no time." And the Packard somehow picked up even more speed.

His day off interrupted, the doctor was grumpy, as if someone else's fishhook sticking in my ear was my fault. Sighing at what people get themselves into, he sat me on the examining table, numbed my ear with something, used a needle-nosed instrument to maneuver the hook out, dabbed some mercurochrome on my wound, and told me I was as good as new. There wasn't even any blood in sight, which I have to admit disappointed me.

As we went home, Pop tried to make me feel better by telling me about worse things that had happened to people in his experience. Unloading our fishing gear in the driveway beneath the bower of Igdrasil, he paused when I still hadn't said anything.

"The ear still bothering?"

"Huh-uh."

"What's the matter, then?"

"Are you going to send me back?"

"Where? To Phoenix?"

"Uh-huh."

"What for?"

"The derby's over. And I didn't catch anything, I got caught."

We looked at each other for a long moment, pretty much a life's worth, as it turned out, before he muttered: "What kind of an ess of a bee do you think I am?" The fishing poles clattered in his grasp as he headed for the house, motioning me on in. "School starts Monday, we need to get you some pencils and tablets and junk like that." At the back door, he stopped and looked at me again, his eyebrows cocked.

"Kiddo? About today—the fishing and all. Don't sweat it. You'll show them how, next year."

S O MY SUITCASE stayed under the bed and I stayed on as half-pint participant in the world of my bartending father. He and I occupied the house behind the saloon like a pair of confirmed bachelors, rattling around in the big old place by ourselves except when the cleaning woman came and moved the dust a little. Having learned his lesson about housekeepers, Pop employed Nola Atkins for this, who was seventy-five if she was a day. Otherwise, the two of us were free to go about domestic matters in our unrestricted male way. Actually, the house was where we slept and kept our clothes. We lived at the Medicine Lodge.

"—THE GUY LOOKS over at her in bed when they hear her husband come in downstairs and says, 'Can you cache a small Czech?' Get it, Tom? The c-a-c-h-e kind of 'cash,' see, and he's—"

"Can't help but get it, Earl. You rich enough for another Shellac or do I have to cut you off?"

"How would you feel about a silver inlaid belt buckle, on account?"

"On account of you're broke again, you mean? Let's see the damn thing."

The Medicine Lodge did not have a monopoly on the drinking trade in Gros Ventre and the Two Medicine country, but close enough. The main competition, the Pastime Bar at the other end of town, was, well, past its time; run-down, erratic in its hours, gloomy, smelling a little funny. And the lounge bar across at the hotel had the hereditary failing of its kind, lack of pep. This meant that besides the jackpot of Saturday-night crowds—"Saturday night buys the rest of the week, kiddo" was one of Pop's favorite pronouncements—the singular saloon with FULL BAR AND THEN SOME added beneath its name drew a day-in, day-out traffic of steady customers. This imbibing community, to call it that, which showed up in my father's venerable place of business, was mainly wetting its collective whistle now and then as people have done since time immemorial, exchanging gossip or talking just to be talking. The back-and-forth whiled away time and its concerns, of which those last years of the Fifties held their dire share, as was usual in human history. The familiar voices would start up in the late afternoon, when Earl Zane slipped in to swap a joke barely worth telling and whatever was loose on his person for a series of beers before his wife appeared to drag him back to their gas station. To be followed, more often than not, by gray-mustached Bill Reinking on the way home to supper after putting in his day as editor, star reporter, and linotype operator of the Gros Ventre *Weekly Gleaner*.

"What you have in your hand looks like just what the doctor ordered, Tom, bless you."

"It's the best scotch in the joint, comes in a bottle and everything. The world going to hell enough to suit you?"

"It keeps me in business, alas. Any juicy news in here I can hold up to the light of day?"

And in the clockwork of human habit, no sooner would Bill Reinking be out the door after his single drink than Velma Simms would sail in for hers. By the nature of things, the Medicine Lodge was a watering hole for men, just as the beauty parlor down the street served as a social oasis for women. This particular customer did not treat that as a fact of life; quite the contrary. Her husky voice never varied as she headed for her usual booth. "It's that time of day, Tom."

"Funny how that happens about now, Velma." Pop did not quite treat this patron as if she was radioactive, but it approached that category. She'd had four or five husbands, and her history of divorce settlements scared the daylights out of every man in town. Velma was around Pop's age, so the chestnut hair surely had help from the drugstore, but in tailored slacks and a silky blouse, she still drew second looks. Her custom was to nestle into the booth, instantaneously get a cigarette going with a flash of her silver lighter, and begin riffling through her mail, in all probability on the lookout for alimony checks. Pop meanwhile mixed a G-ball, conscientiously using a decent bourbon and opening a fresh ginger ale so the drink wouldn't taste flat. After delivering it to the booth, he would retreat all the way behind the bar before initiating conversation.

"Been anywhere?"

"Hawaii. Waikiki Beach isn't what it used to be."

Those regulars and others, early birds before the saloon became fully populated for the evening with ranchers on their way back from tending sheep camp, tourists on their way north to Glacier National Park, fishermen who had tried their luck at the reservoir, seasonal hunters hoping to do better than the Buck Fever Case on the wall, state highway crews on perpetual maintenance jobs, construction workers passing through at the end of their workweek on the Minuteman missile silo sites starting to dot the northern plains of Montana, roughnecks who maintained the donkey pumps and storage tanks of the minor oil field south of town, hay hands from the big Double W cattle ranch, local couples treating themselves to a night out, sheepherders in for a spree; if the ocean ever comes back to the Rockies, archaeologists of that time can dive to the site of the Medicine Lodge and determine how a segment of mid-twentieth-century America assuaged its social thirst.

I absorbed every bit of this, because, thanks to the father I happened to have, the joint became something like my second parent.

"GOT AN IDEA, kiddo. Let's cross our fingers and toes it's a good one."

Things happened fast around Pop. After my rescue from Phoenix and induction into fishing and all else, I had been in school barely a week before he concluded that our household, such as it amounted to, needed serious adjustment. He had been smart to start me in Gros Ventre when he did; in the first grade everyone is a new kid, the ABCs see to that. Thus, school itself was no big problem, if I didn't count Duane Zane snickering at my wounded ear until he grew tired of it, but after school was another matter. That time of day and on through the evening was when the Medicine Lodge did most of its business and Pop had to be there to maintain the level of bartending that made the saloon's reputation, leaving me to the sparse company of the empty house and Igdrasil the tree. Even as inexperienced as he was at raising a kid, it evidently didn't feel quite right to him for us to see each other only at breakfast, supper, and after closing time at the joint. Which is why he reached the decision that needed fingers and toes crossed. He announced it as usual, with a puff of smoke.

He stood there outlined in the doorway of my darkened bedroom, bow tie loosened against white shirt, the next-to-last cigarette of the day—one of my worries was that he continued to smoke in bed just as if Uncle Arvin the fireman never existed—aglow between his fingers. Already it was a ritual between us that I would snap awake when I heard him come in late at night and as soon as he finished in the bathroom I would call out, "Is that you, Pop?" and he would answer something like, "No, it's the Galloping Swede." The notion of Montana's immigrant governor, Hugo Aronson, galumphing in on Scandinavian size-fourteens to use our bathroom would set me off into a fit of giggles, and Pop would lean against the door frame a minute and ask me what I'd been up to since supper, which was seldom much beyond listening to the radio and reading comic books until my eyelids drooped. After a little of that exchange, he would say, "Let's catch some shut-eye—don't let the ladybugs bite" and tread down the hall to his own bedroom. So I grew even wider awake than usual this night as he hung on there in the doorway, squinting and smoking.

"It gets kind of lonesome over here by yourself so much, I bet."

"Maybe just a little."

"Not that you aren't doing real good at getting along on your own, don't get me wrong."

"Uh-huh. I mean, huh-uh."

"If I could be two places at once, we could do some things together. Go fishing after supper and stuff like that."

"That'd be, uh, nice."

"But I can't, can I. Be two places at once. It wouldn't work even if I was Siamese twins."

"I guess maybe not."

"So here's my thinking." His forehead furrowed with it. "I don't dare let you be in the barroom when the joint is open, the state liquor board would nail my hide to the wall if they caught us at it." He spelled out his decision probably as much for his own benefit as mine. "But I see no reason why you can't be in the back room some when I'm busy out front. After school and maybe until your bedtime. How's that grab you?"

On those hasty vacation trips of ours to the Grand Canyon, he had let me do what he somehow knew a kid most wanted to do. Held in his strong arms and big hands there at the rock parapet on the rim of the canyon, I would stick my head over the edge as far as I dared and spit a mile, fully believing I was adding my contribution to the Colorado River way, way below. A similar sense of unprecedented thrill took hold of me now. My face must have lit up the dim bedroom, because he added in a hurry, "That don't mean you can run wild back there. You have to behave yourself around the hocked stuff, it's like money in the bank for us."

"I won't hurt any of it, I promise."

"There's something else. The air vent." His eyes locked onto mine. "You know what I'm talking about, right?"

"Uh-huh." Who could forget, how sound from the barroom came right in through it, clear as a whistle, when he was at the desk busy being busy with bills and checkbook.

He took a drag on his cigarette, still looking hard at me. "I know you're gonna listen in to the bar talk, there's no getting around that. You're liable to hear some rough language—"

"That's nothing, Ronny cussed all the time."

"—and that's my point, I don't want you picking up the bad habit." I shook my head vigorously against the possibility of that ever happening. He had a further thought. "If you're playing around up there at the desk and the vent's open, just don't make any racket and disturb the inmates," meaning the customers out front. "Savvy that?"

"Sure!"

Hesitating a moment, he drew a deep breath that had nothing to do with smoking. "I've got to trust you back there, Russell." It was the first time within memory that he had used my given name.

"I'll be good, Pop. Honest!"

"Okay, kiddo, we'll give it a try." He turned to go. "Don't let the ladybugs bite."

I FELL IN LOVE with the back room of the joint from the first possible moment.

I could scarcely believe my good fortune in being allowed to spend hours on end at that comfortable desk perch on the stair landing, reading comic books or building model airplanes or following the misfortunes of the Selectrics in the Great Falls *Tribune* or letting my imagination wander through the ever-growing collection of hocked treasures piled below. And of course, most of all, listening at the vent, silent as a ghost. Any kid is a master spy until that talent meets itself in the mirror during the teen years and turns hopelessly inward, but life could not have arranged my surveillance of the grown-up world more perfectly. From the barroom side, the air vent high on the rear wall wasn't even noticeable amid the stuffed animal heads, but there in the back room, that same slatted metalwork grille close by the desk was almost like a fabulous radio I could take a look into and have each scene come to life. I needed only to stretch my neck a little to peek through the vent slats when the street door swung open and a customer appeared, and see and hear everything as my father lived up to his reputation as the best bartender imaginable, his shirt and apron crisp as table linen, his black bow tie lending an air of dignity, his magical hands producing a drink almost before it was thought of, his head tilted just so to take in whatever topic was being introduced on the other side of the bar. The reliably contrary weather of the Two Medicine country? "Sure enough, it's all gonna dry up and blow away if we don't get some rain." The storms of the human heart? "She did that to you? No bee ess?" Philosophy needed after some grievance against fate? "All you can count on in life is your fingers and toes." And if a known face came in, not saying much of anything, I could count on hearing "Hey, you look like you need a Shellac," and then the whish of a Great Falls Select being drawn from the beer tap, and the sounds of Pop puttering patiently until this set of vocal cords, too, was oiled enough to reward the waiting ears, his and mine.

I know, I know; the listening bartender is a standard character, probably ever since Chaucer. But Pop filled the role so completely, those years when I was the eager but secret audience behind the vent, that the Medicine Lodge became the repository of lore in much the same way as material items piled up in the back-room collection. Sooner or later, everyone has a story to tell, and his tireless towel rubbing up a special sheen in front of a customer seemed to polish the opportunity. If it wasn't Dode Withrow in from the ranch with yet another tale about one sheepherder or another quitting for the twentieth or thirtieth time, then it was one sheepherder or another there on a bar stool, drinking up his wages and recounting, like the other half of an old married couple, Dode's shortcomings as an employer down through the years. If it wasn't absolute strangers relating things that sent Pop's eyebrows climbing, and mine, then it was the afternoon regulars contributing their share of episodes as well.

Earl Zane's sagas of himself tended to be blowhard accounts of rodeo bronc riding, during which he seemed never to have been bucked off. If the mail happened to be short of alimony checks, then Velma Simms might have a second drink and begin dreaming aloud about her latest cruise of Greek islands, through seas if not wine-dark, at least ginger-ale highball tinted in her recollection. Bill Reinking, with his newspaperman's memory, often harked back to the 1930s, the testing time of his and Pop's younger years; Pop kept an old election poster of Franklin D. Roosevelt taped to the mirror beside the cash register in tribute to the president who pulled the nation out of the Depression. And even I, underage occupant of the 1950s, could feel the close breath of history when Turk Turco, the state highway maintenance man, in his distinctive twang, would relate some hair-raising episode from his time as an infantryman in Korea at Pork Chop Hill, and his buddy and arguing partner, the Montana Power lineman Joe Quigg, would match that with the sobering memory of the mushroom cloud shrouding the Pacific sky when he served in the Navy during the hydrogen bomb tests in the Marshall Islands. The voices of the vent still seem so vivid to me, so distinct. It is a sensation I even yet find hard to describe, how those overheard stories kept me occupied, in the truest sense of that word, taking up residence within me like talkative lodgers in the various corners of my mind. As the father who was doing his bachelor best to raise me would have said, I didn't lack imagination in the first place, and I certainly had no shortage of it as the clandestine eyewitness—or earwitness—to the variety of life as it passed through the Medicine Lodge.

"POP? DID YOU HAVE to bounce anybody?"

This was the big question, as regular as Saturday night, the minute I heard him in the hallway. Weeknights, regular as clockwork, he would break off anything he was doing in the barroom, serving drinks or negotiating with a customer wanting to hock something, to step into the back room when it was my bedtime, and if I was still there, ritually shoo me home. Saturdays, though, his busiest night, I had to evacuate to the house right after supper—"Just to keep the decks clear, kiddo"—and spend those evenings wondering what I was missing at the saloon.

"Relax and get your beauty sleep," he usually answered, tired after his long night behind the bar, "nobody got out of hand." Usually.

The price of my cherished private spot in the back room was a pair of nagging thoughts that would not go away, no matter how I tried to put them out of mind. I will come to the other one soon enough, but my first concern was that Pop served not only as bartender and proprietor and all the other lofty jobs of the saloon, but as bouncer as well. This was tricky, since it almost always involved someone who'd had a drink too many. If asked, Pop would have pointed out that people have been getting intoxicated since the first ripe grape dropped on Adam and Eve. To him, Prohibition was the dumbest thing ever tried, resulting only in bad bootleg booze. But the Medicine Lodge had a reputation to maintain as a respectable joint, and he did not tolerate what he called squirrelly behavior. "Hey, this isn't the Copabanana," he would directly warn anyone growing too loud or just plain sloppy drunk. Persist, though, and the offender would be told in no uncertain terms to tone things down right then or clear out. Every once in a while this ultimatum would put the balky customer in a fighting mood, and if he could not be talked into taking it outside, Pop would have to throw him out. The first time I happened to witness this through the vent, scared to watch but too thrilled to look away, I held my breath as he came out from behind the bar, his apron still on and not a hair out of place in his silver-striped pompadour, and got hold of a drunken and combative oil field roughneck. In nothing flat, the guy was in the street; you did not argue the point with Tom Harry.

As soon as I saw him bounce that unwelcome customer, though, the what-ifs swarmed. Suppose the guy had been carrying a knife? A gun? What if he had been an ex-prizefighter, mad at the world and more than capable of beating Pop's brains out? What if things really got out of hand some Saturday night, always the drinkingest night of the week?

When I confessed that I worried about his role as bouncer, Pop seemed surprised. "I'm not selling milk to kittens, am I. Don't bother your head with it."

Mostly, I did not have to, the majority of the evenings of the week when I was across the alley there, seated at what I regarded as my rightful place, with the familiar sounds from the barroom sifting in through the vent. The click of washed glasses lining up on a shelf. The release of metal and air when a fresh beer keg was tapped. The *ching* of the cash register. Much like being backstage while the theater came to life out front. But all you can count on in life is your fingers and toes, right? The script changed mightily for both of us when the page was turned from one decade to the next and the curtain went up on 1960.

"CAN'T I GO with you this once, Pop?"

"You sure as hell can't." Bent over like a bear in a berry patch, he was rummaging through the hocked items piled along the walls of the back room, selecting things, rejecting things. "Get that idea out of your head before it leaves a puddle, okay? Cripes, you'd have to miss some school."

I knew it wouldn't do any good to argue the point. It never

did, when something would set him off this way. This was the other worry I carried through those years, these periodic trips of his to sell off some of the back-room loot, as he jokingly called it, when he would park me with Howie and his wife, Lucille, while he was "away on business" days at a time. He always went alone, so that part did not surprise me now. This abrupt journey, though, was right after New Year's, a time of year when I thought we were safely settled in for the season, maybe for many frigid months. Out the top of the frosted back window, I could see Igdrasil's spreading branches humped with snow from the unusually hard winter we were having.

"You didn't tell me you were gonna do this again."

"Yeah, well," he answered without looking up, "things come up and need something done. Rule number one is, don't wait until you hear from heaven."

Except for times like this, he and I by now knew each other's habits blindfolded. Our nearly six years together had taught me that when he said, "Maybe," it meant "No," and when he said, "We'll see," it meant "Maybe." When I asked him in those nighttime conversations in my doorway how the day's take was, if he said, "Not bad," that meant "Good," but if he said, "So-so," that meant "Bad." Pop could sound gruff—no, wrong, he could be gruff—but I had grown used to that, just as he'd had to become accustomed to my tendency to get carried away by matters. He generally coped with any of my thorny questions about life by giving some vague answer that ended with "That's the how of it," while I always wanted the five Ws and an H—who, what, when, where, why, and then the how. If I persisted, he might say something like, "Don't be a plague of locusts" or he might sigh and provide some actual Ws. It depended.

At various levels, then, there was give-and-take between us, maybe more so than in some supposedly normal households.

When it occurred to him, he taught me things for their own sake—I was probably the only kid who could tie a bow tie at the age of six—and I figured out for myself certain habits that made our life easier, such as fixing my own lunch for school, invariably jam sandwiches. I suppose with only each other to count on, reciprocity was a necessity. Whenever I had a class project I needed help with, he leapt to it as if I were an Einstein in the making, and whenever he took a notion to go fishing at Rainbow Reservoir on a summer Sunday, I fished loyally alongside him for as long as the chicken guts held out. True, we occasionally got on each other's nerves—those ironclad habits of his did not always coincide with my own—but we got off again just about as fast. In short, we probably were as used to each other as two people can get. We ate, slept, and went about life as suited us; one of Pop's middle-of-the-night hallway pronouncements was, "I don't give a flying fig what anyone says, we're not doing too bad with what we got to work with, kiddo." We weren't, except for times like this. The truth of the matter was, bad weather was not the only hazard agitating me as I watched him gather to go.

Was he seeing someone on these trips? "Someone" could only mean a woman, in my mind, and "seeing" carried all manner of implications I didn't want to have to face, ever. I hated to be suspicious of him, but what other explanation was there for these urges that seemed to come over him unpredictably? He wasn't much of a drinker—in the joint, he was notorious for saying, "I'll take mine in the till," and ringing it up whenever someone tried to buy him a round—so I was pretty sure he wasn't going off on drunken binges. No, man's other leading temptation was the only thing that made any sense to me about these trips of his. And that one frightened me almost as much as the threat of a blizzard, the danger that he would repeat the kind of ill-advised romance he'd had with my mother, and a woman, a female stranger, would invade our bachelor existence. She would barge into my life as a stepmother, and I'd had enough of being a stepped-on child in the Phoenix part of my life.

So I was spooked by the prospect of us being hit by rough weather of different kinds, but I stuck to the variety out the frosty window. "Pop, it gives me the creeps. What if the car runs off the road and you freeze to death? The radio says there's another big snowstorm coming."

"Let 'er come, I was here first," he said stoically.

"Aw, crud, though," I switched complaints trying to find one that would work, "can't you at least take the other car?" The successor to the Hudson was a Buick we called the Gunboat for its series of stylized chrome insets in the lengthy hood like portholes—he liked substantial cars—but parked in the alley, waiting to be loaded, was the old Packard.

"Naw." He wrestled down a saddle from the wall collection and added it to the growing pile of stuff. "Like I told you before, the old buggy holds more." That was inarguable. The Packard's roomy back seat and big trunk had probably the capacity of a small truck. Pausing to catch his breath, he checked on me where I was slumped at the desk on the landing to see how genuinely worried I was. Reading me like an open book, he sighed. Pop could really sigh, what I came to think of as the sigh of ages; like the expelled breath of time itself. If that isn't in Shakespeare, it ought to be. "Don't get all worked up." He followed that with, "Canada is real good about keeping the roads open." The fact that many miles of blizzardy prairie lay between Gros Ventre and the Canadian border did not enter into the matter, apparently. "I'll be back before you know it."

Fat chance of that, my long face said. Why did he always have to go to Canada for this, anyway? Why not direct his urges, whatever they were, to the city of Great Falls, a mere few hours

away? Every time I pointed this out, I was told I didn't understand back-room commerce.

"Come on, cheer up." He cocked an eyebrow at me. "Tell you
what, I'll bring you a plane kit. What was it that you wanted?"

"A Spitfire."

"Easy done. Figure out where you're gonna hang it." Suspended
by fishing line from the rafters above the stair landing and the
loft was the swarm of other plane models I had assembled, from
his other trips. With the least stirring of air in the back room,
the P-39 Airacobra fighter plane and Grumman Avenger torpedo bomber and others danced in little aerial duels with the
hanging lariats and hay hooks, an effect I liked. Pop was standing under the swaying aircraft, mentally calculating his load for
the car in a way that told me he was mostly done. Mostly.

"Okay, I'm about ready to hit the road." Looking up, he saw me
still morosely watching. He frowned the way a person does when
trying to be super-patient. "Don't you have schoolwork to do?"

"Arithmetic, is all. My book's at the house."

"Just make sure to get at it. Numbers aren't as easy as pie." I
have since wondered whether he actually meant pi; it was tricky
to know how much to read into him.

Giving me another serious look, he made a shooing motion.
"Go get yourself some supper at the Spot."

"Can't I help you load?"

"Go get yourself some supper," he repeated, as if I hadn't
heard him the first time. "Howie and his missus are ready for
you these next couple of nights." One last look of that kind and
he said, as I expected him to, "Don't put beans up your nose."

I can smile now at his usual proscription against doing anything foolish. At the time, though, I was too busy nursing my
grievance to appreciate it. By then I was very nearly twelve, as I
liked to think of it, even though my birthday was months off, an

age when notions can come into a person's head as fast as chain lightning and it's hard to tell which of them are crazy or not. This particular conviction had been growing in me since the first big snowstorm, on Thanksgiving Day. I was convinced we were in a thirty-year winter.

That was not to say that I expected the deep snowdrifts and below-zero temperatures gripping the Two Medicine country to last for the next three decades, like a meteorological version of some medieval war that hopelessly went on and on. No, when Pop and the Medicine Lodge denizens spoke of a thirty-year winter, they meant a hard one such as came once in a generation, season-long weather disasters that stood out in history. The cattlemen's winter of 1886, when the open range was dotted with cow carcasses in the tens of thousands by the time spring finally came. The sheepmen's winter of 1919, when ranchers' hay sleds had nothing to offer starving animals but measly slew grass. The snowbound winter of 1948, when airplanes dropped medical supplies to communities cut off from the world by impassable roads. Tales of those last two still were told and retold in the Medicine Lodge every time a siege of freezing weather set in. Not only did I hang on those sagas at my listening post at the vent, but there was always something like the twangy exchange between Turk Turco and Joe Quigg, over which of them had it worse in this kind of winter.

"You in here warming your insides already, Turco? It must be nice to be on a state pension."

"Try running a snowplow for twelve goddamned hours when you can't even see the goddamned side of the road, and then tell me if it's the soft life, Jojo."

"Hah. Try hanging forty feet off the ground in the goddamned wind with the goddamned snow in your face."

Every such morsel fed my imagination, my conviction that this was a time that still would be exclaimed about—"Back there in '60, it'd freeze parts right off you!"—when I was old and gray. True, there was the point that it had been only a dozen years since the last thirty-year winter. But that might mean this one was so ferocious it overrode the usual weather arithmetic, mightn't it?

Besides, if any further proof was needed of the nature of this season, Velma Simms had pulled out for Mexico, saying she wasn't coming back to this icebox of a town until June.

In short, a killer winter, and Pop somewhere out there in it in an old crate of a car. I tried my best not to think about him swallowed up in the polar wastes of Canada, although I could not get it off my mind for very long. If this was a fair sample of being fatherless, it gave new meaning to *cruddy*.

My spirits did begin to lift—the only direction for them to go—the day he was due to come home. All I had to do was to get through the hours of school, I kept telling myself, and there he'd be behind the bar, the same as ever, fresh white shirt putting the snow to shame, when I burst into the joint through the back door, and that would be that, no more of his trips until this weather monster was in the record books. You can talk yourself around to almost anything when you really try.

Accordingly, by noon hour the main thing on my mind was the game of horse the usual fifth-grade bunch of us gathered for in the gymnasium. The junior high boys were hogging the basketball court as always, but in the alcove leading to the locker room there was a hoop mounted on the wall for practicing free throws, and that served for us.

"Who's first?"

"Jimmy's turn. He was horse's wazoo last time."

"Ruhss-ull keeps track." Duane Zane perpetually thought it was funny to mock my name in caveman syllables. "Ruhss-ull *always* keeps track."

"Somebody has to or it'd be your turn all the time, brain pain."

Jimmy Hahn and Hal Busby, my closest friends, laughed plenty at that, and even Duane's buddies, Sid Musgreave and Ted Austin, had to snicker.

Trying again, Duane sneered, "DDT, simp," short for "drop dead twice."

"And look like you? Huh-uh, nothing doing."

Giving me a last dirty look, he flipped the basketball to Jimmy.

"Jump shot," Jimmy decided. He gave a little hop and with a grunt catapulted the ball toward the basket, hitting the rim. We were just at the age where the basketball no longer seemed as big as a pumpkin to us, but it didn't yield easily to our shot-making efforts.

Catching the rebound, Sid crooned, "Nice try, guy," the latest word fad—*guy* this and *guy* that—we had picked up from somewhere. "Watch this." With a grunt, he shot and hit the backboard, but not the basket.

"Rusty's up," Hal said, bouncing the ball to me. "C'mon, guy, show them how."

To my surprise, if nobody else's, I did, although my jump shot clattered around the rim for what seemed an interminable time before dropping through.

"Unreal! How'd you make that?"

"How'd you miss it? H," I announced, because one of our countless and probably unique rules was that you had to call out each letter of H-O-R-S-E as you earned it with a basket; if you forgot to do it before the next player shot, you lost that letter.

"How about that"—Duane still was on my case—"the guy thinks he can spell."

"'Duane' starts with 'Duh,' that's easy enough," I came right back at him. I had long since learned the one great lesson of

early education: To fit in, stand your ground. Duane, my neme-
sis since that first fishing derby and always the loudest mouth at
school, at first had been in the habit of making cracks like,
"C'mon, Harry, show us your hairy part!" I noticed, however, he
did not join in when someone smarted off with, "Hey, Rusty,
had any of your old man's medicine lately?" A few playground
fistfights settled the worst of that, and by now I wasn't picked on
any more than anyone else. To keep it that way, I made sure to
join in on things at the proper volume, loudly playing work-up
softball and touch football and horse with the other boys and
whispering answers in class to selected girls; you would have had
to look hard to single me out from my couple of dozen classmates.
It was each day after school that I turned into the loner an only
child tends to be. My close buddies, Jimmy and Hal, rode the
school bus to where their families ranched, and neither of them—
nor anyone else from school—ever laid eyes on the back room of
the Medicine Lodge. That was my special spot in life, mine
alone, and I intended to keep it that way.

"You guys know the difference between beans and peas?"
Duane halted our game, smirking his face off. "You might spill
the beans, but you can always take a pea."

"Funny as a crutch, Zane. C'mon, you gonna shoot the ball or
hatch it?"

"It's not his turn anyway, it's mine."

"You're crazy, it's mine."

"He's right, it's his."

"Then let's see him do something."

"Here goes, losers."

"You shoot like a girl, guy."

"I do not, sparrowhead. That's a two-handed set shot. Try it
and die."

Overflowing with energy and slander, the half dozen of us

took turn after turn at trying to make the basketball go in the basket. In our rules of the game, as fixed as the laws of nature, every player not only had to attempt a shot from the same spot as the first shooter, it had to be the identical kind of shot. That first one, though, could be as creative as any eleven-year-old athlete could come up with. Sometimes we were totally silly in shooting it, sometimes we were cutthroat serious.

With Duane Zane, you couldn't always tell which was which. "Free throw," he declared when it came his turn to start the round. His version, however, proved to be an exaggerated underhand heave from down around his ankles.

Wouldn't you know, the damn ball went in. Just then a blast of wind rattled the high windows at the end of the gym. Most of us let out *brr*s and yearnings for spring, but not Duane.

"I hope it storms for a month, so my dad keeps on making money pulling people out of ditches with his wrecker," he proclaimed, his voice strutting with the rest of him after that basket.

Oh, how I wanted to bounce the ball off his fat head. Instead I managed to take revenge by swishing my shot through the net to match his dumb free throw. "Way to go, guy!" cried my adherents, while Duane made a gagging sound.

Noon hour was nearly over after that round, but we always believed if we hurried, we could squeeze in one more before the bell rang. I especially wanted to. With the lucky day I'd been having, all I needed for horse was *E*. Even better, it was my turn to start, and my choice of shot was as unpopular as I'd hoped.

"Aw, not that!"

"Be a guy, give us a break!"

"You and your pukey hook shot."

Even Jimmy and Hal moaned with the others. A hook shot may not have seemed a likely accomplishment for me—I wasn't a bad athlete, though I definitely was not a really good one—but at the start of the school year, Pop had put up a basketball hoop for me in a back-room corner that must have been a horse stall originally, and I endlessly practiced over-the-head shots there, pretending I was Wilt Chamberlain or some other hook shooter two or three times my height. Those solo hours paid off now as I catapulted the ball one-handed over the top of my head and it ricocheted off the backboard hard enough to rattle the rim, then toppled through the hoop, to everyone else's groans and my cry of joy.

The basketball hadn't hit the floor yet when it was intercepted by the school principal, Mr. Naylor.

"Whoa, boys. We're sending bus students home early"—he singled out Hal and Jimmy—"on account of the roads. Grab your coats and books and be ready to go."

"Lucky guys," Duane mouthed off, while they went to be bussed home through treacherous weather.

I forged my own way from school at the regular time, the slow afternoon hours like enormous shadows dragging behind me. What was the saying, something about the driven snow? This snow was doing its unerring best to drive down my neck, the wind flinging the fat flakes right at me no matter how I turned my head. If this wasn't the recipe for a thirty-year winter, I didn't know what was. Beneath the bare cottonwood trees, English Creek was frozen over, an icy pond that went on for miles. The entire town of Gros Ventre looked like something that had been left in the freezer too long.

Anxious, I did not take time to go around to the back of the Medicine Lodge as usual but stumbled in, overshoes, mackinaw, cap, scarf, and mittens coated with snow, through the front entrance. I couldn't wait to see Pop, safe, sound, big as life, bartending incomparably as usual.

But Howie was behind the bar. The saloon's only other sign

of life was a pair of the red-eyed sheepherders who were fixtures in the Two Medicine country, Canada Dan in from the Withrow ranch on one of his frequent spells of unemployment, and Snoose Syvertsen, likewise in from any number of places he had been hired and fired from down through the years, sitting out the winter in town and hoping for some charitable soul to attend to their thirst. They especially pinned their hopes on "tursters," as they called tourists, who could be trapped into conversation and free drinks. Pop ritually grumbled about this scruffy pair leaning a hole into the bar but let them hang around because, he said, you couldn't leave the damn old fools in the lurch; the lurch always sounded like the worst kind of place to be left in.

"Hi, Eskimo." Howie's croaky greeting past the cigarette nursed in the corner of his mouth did not tell me what I wanted to know.

"Isn't . . . isn't he back yet?"

A shake of the old bald head.

Despair gripped me to the bone. This was my worst fear coming true. What might have been a sympathetic guttural sound came from Canada Dan at the far end of the bar. "It's sure too bad Tom's not on hand, ain't it?" he observed, as if to the world at large. "Depressing weather like this, he'd stand loyal customers a drink now and then to cheer things up."

Snoose Syvertsen backed that up with vigorous nods. "That's hunnerd percent gospel truth."

"You're so keen on the weather, just keep watching until it hits forty below in hell," Howie advised them acidly. "That's about when you'll get a free drink from me in this joint." He turned his attention back to me. "You better scoot on over to my place again, you're still dressed for it. Lucille is gonna be looking for you."

All I felt like doing was collapsing in a heap, but I put it differently: "I could just stay on here until Pop gets home."

"No, you aren't. That father of yours would skin me alive if I let you do that. Besides, I'm pretty quick gonna kick these two out and close the joint early. This weather's a bugger." He made a sour face, more than usual. "I'm getting too old for this."

"Why isn't he back by now?"

"He's delayed, is why," Howie said crabbily. He parted with his cigarette long enough to pluck a shred of tobacco off his tongue. "The road's closed, up there." Apology was not in Howie's vocabulary, but his tone softened a trifle as he said, "He'll show up. Now scoot."

Head down, I traipsed the length of the barroom to go out the back of the saloon. "Your old man's away for quite a while, eh?" Canada Dan remarked as I glumly went past. "He's sure missed around here."

Snoose Syvertsen wagged his head sadly. "Hunnerd percent."

LIKE NANOOK RETURNING to the ice floe, I trudged through snowdrifts to the bungalow across town, where Lucille greeted me in her nice, quiet way. She was as aged and sparrowlike as Howie, and while both of them treated me like a best guest, theirs was a house that had not known a child for many years. Prominent on the living room wall was the photograph of their Marine son who had been killed in the invasion of Tarawa in 1943.

This night was the darkest of my life in every way. I lay under strange old heavy blankets in that musty bedroom, listening to the wind, knowing it was whipping up the snow into a ground blizzard, the absolute worst thing for Pop if he was out there somewhere trying to drive home. My thoughts swirled and whirled as well. I blamed him for going by himself in this terrible weather, I blamed myself for not throwing such a fit he'd have taken me with him, for if I had gone along he would not have dared to let anything disastrous happen, right? In theory, anyway. This night I resented the existence of thirty-year winters, this night I could not get rid of the fear under the covers with me, fear that this time Pop's trip was going to lead to unimaginable disaster, except I was imagining it.

There in the bone-chilling dark, the two dangers of his trips merged treacherously in my mind. If he had a love interest that kept drawing him north, there was an insidious side to such an affair. Namely, what if he stumbled into "maddermoany," as he'd done once already, and this woman didn't want a kid around? Wouldn't he be forced to abandon me, in one unwelcome direction or the other? Then which was worse, Arizona or somewhere unknown? In my years with him, Phoenix had gradually diminished to Christmas cards and birthday cards curtly signed, "Ever, Aunt Marge." It still was very much on the map, though, down there with the sand and sidewinders and cactuses. Ending up back in Aunt Marge's maniac den with Ronny and Danny seemed to me a one-way ticket to hell. But against that known peril was the great unknown one, my vanished mother. I simply knew virtually nothing about the woman who had borne me. She existed only in my father's extremely few remarks about her, mainly this one: "We split the blanket when she pulled out on me and you, and that's that." It wasn't, as far as I was concerned.

I had learned her maiden name the hard way, by innocently asking Pop after I understood enough about marriage to be curious about that. "Joanie Jones if there ever was one," he let out in one long, exasperated breath. "Why?" My stammered answer must have amounted to, Because. He reminded me yet again she had pulled out on us when I was still in the cradle and it was best for all concerned to have her out of our life. And while that was that one more time, I came out of it finally able to fit "Joanie Jones" onto the hazy outline of the woman who gave me birth. I went to school with a Janie and a Susie, so the girlish first name did not trouble me, although if you had a choice, you'd want your mother to be named something nice like Gwendolyn, wouldn't you. "Jones" I found harder to deal with; how anything about her could be figured out from that, I hadn't arrived at. In any case, her name could not tell me why she up and left a husband and a baby, and I harbored my own version of what must have divorced her from Pop and, for that matter, me. The Medicine Lodge, what else? It made sense. If, say, she disapproved of liquor, as there were people in the world who did, would she stay married to a bartender? Plainly not. Admittedly, leaving me—by way of Pop—to the clutches of Aunt Marge's clan did not win her any high marks as a mother, but parents do whatever suits them, for good reason or not, every kid learns that.

Yet, gone from almost my entire life though my mother was, what if I was handed over to her if the worst happened to Pop? Would she even want me, reared in saloon circumstances as I was and by a man she couldn't stand? For that matter, would I want to be with her, a total stranger, a dozen years of separation the only thing we had in common?

My thoughts kept jittering back and forth: better the demon I knew—Ronny—or the phantom I didn't—her—if this diabolical trip did my father in, one way or another? Everything churned in my mind, except anything resembling a right answer. I huddled miserably under the covers, ashamed that I was near tears not only for him but for myself.

I heard Howie get up in the night. The toilet flushed, the slap-slap of slippers stopped at my bedroom doorway.

"You're awake, aren't you." I could see his bald head in the light from all the snow.

"Uh-huh."

"How about some warm milk to help you sleep?"

"No, thanks. It would just make me have to get up and take a leak."

"There's a path wore in the floor about that," Howie readily granted. He shuffled back to bed, but not before saying: "Your old man generally knows what he's doing. He'll make it back tomorrow, you'll see."

Grown-ups are full of painless predictions like that. I was in no mood to have reassurance spooned into me. My worries were altogether too big, nobody else could understand the fix I was in with Pop lost and gone, as I was more and more sure he must be, the inside of my head would give me no rest for as long as I lived, I just knew, and more to the immediate point, I wasn't going to be able to go to sleep ever again.

"HEY. KIDDO. Rise and shine."

It was either bright daylight or a dazzling dream. Pop was shaking me awake, peeling away my cocoon of blankets.

"Wh-what time is it?"

"Saturday. Come on, upsy daisy, let's get over to our place."

Groggy, so surprised to see my missing father back in existence that I couldn't put words to it, I fumbled into my clothes while he tidied my bed in the manner expected of a guest. The silence of the house said Howie and Lucille were not up yet.

The two of us floundered out to the Packard, purring like a limousine, through fresh snow up to the top buckles of our overshoes. He looked like he'd been pulled through a knothole, mussed, weary-eyed, distracted. But he drove home capably enough, taking advantage of the deep set of wheel tracks someone earlier had left, then, at the untouched snow of the alley and our driveway, he floored the gas pedal and fishtailed the old car to its natural parking spot beneath the bare-bone branches of Igdrasil. The gunboat Buick, in its spot, was under so much snow it resembled an igloo, and I wished for the same to happen to the Packard, if that's what it took to keep Tom Harry home.

"Here we are," he said, calm as cream, and I gave him a look he pretended not to notice.

The house was so chilly, we kept our coats on at first. Neither of us saying anything, I set the table and things like that while he made coffee. He crucially needed some, I saw. He still was looking nearly done in, the lines in his face deeper than ever, his pompadour flopping to the sides. Worst of all, his pouring hand shook a little in filling the coffee cup. But when the house warmed up some, he shed his coat and took over the kitchen as though he were back in the barroom, getting out the soup bowls and big spoons.

"So, kiddo. What'll it be this morning?"

"Oyster."

We never fussed any with breakfast, merely heated a can of soup, almost always tomato or chicken noodle, so my choice was enough out of the ordinary that he scrutinized me before going to the cupboard.

"Okay, let's splurge. Get out the milk and butter."

When it was ready, we each crumbled crackers into oyster stew until it was nearly solid, and commenced to eat. He still wasn't saying anything, so I did.

"Howie said the road was closed."

"Howie is not the last word on every damn thing." He started to dip his spoon, then felt my look. "It was shut overnight, is all."

"Then where did you spend the night?"

The only answer was a slurp of soup, which he chased with a swig of coffee.

"Pop? Did you hear? Where'd—"

"In the car, if you really have to know."

At least he hadn't been with some woman. Or had he? "Were . . . were you stuck?"

"Hell no. There was just a roadbock until the snowplows got things cleared."

The trickle of fear in me ever since last night pooled into terror. "But . . . don't people die from the exhaust, sitting there like that?"

Irritably he tried to spoon up an oyster, which slipped back into the bowl. "I didn't, did I . . . Will you get your mind off this? The Mounties are the highway cops up there, and they kept checking on all the cars so nobody went to sleep with the motor running. Satisfied now?"

Not by a million miles. I swallowed hard, which had nothing to do with breakfast, and spoke the plain truth. "I don't want you to go on these trips like you do."

"I wouldn't need three guesses on that."

"They scare me worse than anything."

"Hey, don't exaggerate," he gruffly instructed.

I didn't think I was. The look on my face told him as much.

With an exasperated sigh he quit trying on his soup and sat back, frowning at me. "Damn it, kiddo, you want to save being scared for something really worth it."

"I can't help it." I was determined not to blubber, but my eyes were getting moist and my voice had started to quiver. "You go away like that, and I don't even know where for sure, and then there's a blizzard, and if you're out in it froze stiff or gassed to death and I don't have you anymore—how am I supposed to not be scared?"

"Rusty, I don't like doing it," his voice was as strained as mine, "any more than you like me doing it."

"Then why do you have to?"

"There are things that just won't wait."

"What things?"

"Things," he despaired, as if those were too numerous to face over breakfast. "You see me fighting the bills like I do, sometimes it's just worse, is all." He started to say something more, but stopped and ran a hand through his hair, smoothing the black in with the silver. "Rule number one is, you got to play the hand you been dealt."

"I thought it was don't wait until you hear from—"

"Don't split hairs at this time of day, okay?" With obvious effort he steadied his voice and his gaze at me. "The back-room loot helps out with things, that's all there is to it."

"But why do you need to go all the way to Canada? Why can't you just make a trip to someplace close for a change, like Great Falls? When it's not snowing like crazy?"

"It pays off better up there," he said in frustration. "Cripes, I'd have thought you figured that out a long time ago."

I must have looked immovably skeptical.

"All right, then, Mr. Dubious." He rose and went to where his coat was hung. Reaching into a pocket I didn't even know was there, he pulled out an envelope and dropped it on the table next to my soup bowl. "Take a look."

It was bulging with money. Nothing smaller than tens and twenties, either. More money than I had ever seen, even when the bar's cash register was full after a Saturday night.

"Really? That much? For those old things?"

"Miracles happen, if you give them enough help." He sat back down heavily, retrieving the money, as if to make sure it didn't get away. "There's your answer on these trips, okay?"

"Now you don't have to do it again," I pressed on hopefully, "until winter is over, I bet."

"We'll see. Pass the crackers."

A SATURDAY, even in the heart of winter, meant getting ready for Saturday night, and so he pretty soon directed himself to the saloon, and I stuck right with him, making up for lost time if I could. Howie wisely had left the heat up overnight and the place was livable when we stepped in and started doing things. Pop took a look in the barroom, where the floor showed all the evidence of snowy feet tracking in while he was away, but he only muttered, "First mess first," and climbed the stairs to the landing to contend with the stack of bills that had come in at the end of the year. I kept busy down below at my small chores of sorting empty bottles and seeing to the supply of towels and aprons while he sat at his desk, writing checks. I noticed him looking at his watch a number of times, and when the phone rang, he already was frowning as he answered it.

"Wouldn't you know it," he groaned after hanging up. "The Finletter kid didn't make it home last night—the basketball team's snowed in up at Cut Bank. Not the first time he's stood me up that way." A high school boy always was hired—they came cheap in those days—to clean up the barroom on Saturday morning for that night, the peak of the week's business. "I'm gonna have to can him and find a new swamper, that's all there is to it."

I would like to say I had been waiting for this chance. The truth is, I spoke up before really thinking about it.

"Can't you just hire me? I can do all that stuff."

He looked at me in surprise. "You aren't even—"

"Yes I am! Almost."

"—twelve." He eyed me the way he did a customer asking to be put on the tab. "You really think you can do everything that needs doing?"

"Sure!"

"Sweep and mop and dust the whole joint?"

"Uh-huh."

"Clean the spittoons?"

I hesitated, then nodded.

"The toilets?"

I had to gulp hard on that, but managed to nod again.

He still did not look entirely convinced. "Okay, I'll give you a try. But you better be up to the mark. I'd hate to fire my own kid."

THAT WAS MY INTRODUCTION to broom and mop and toilet brush. And in one of those tricks life likes to play on us, that first Saturday forenoon and the ones to follow I came to truly know my father as a bartender.

Spending the time there in the front of the joint with him as he puttered behind the long, dark bar getting everything ready for opening time, his reflection playing hide-and-seek behind him in the breakfront's angles of mirror as he arranged glasses and bottles, was altogether different from the constrained view through the vent. The tall man with shoulders that stretched his white shirt roved from one housekeeping chore to the next in the room-long aisle in back of the bar, as if primping delicate blossoms. *Loving* may not be the most apt word for the kind of care he gave to his bartending domain, but it's close. With him, finesse equaled preparation; his just-so way of doing things gave me plenty to live up to in my new role as swamper. Seeing out of the corner of one's eye is not an entirely unusual ability, but I swear, he seemed to have such second sight all the way back to his ears, as I found if I failed to clean out the dried-up spider parts in some tucked-away corner and would immediately hear, "Missed a spot. Get with it, kiddo."

In spite of such scrutiny, I was proud and pleased to have the job and particularly the pay, not that it was much. My favorite part of swamping out the saloon was mopping behind the bar, where I got to see what a master bartender kept out of sight under the bar top. A sock filled with metal washers to bust apart ice cubes. Bottle openers of every design. Countless swizzle sticks. A hot plate with a coffeepot to keep him going through the long shifts. A plump stash of fresh towels, the secret behind his always having a clean white one in hand. The Medicine Lodge clientele preponderately took its drinks straight, but just in case someone came in wanting something more fancy, he had a storehouse of makings ready under there: maraschino cherries and a few limes and lemons and bottled olives and even cinnamon sticks—a regular little grocery shelf, it seemed to me. And down at the far end of the bar, the amen corner as he called it, was tucked away a stack of those paperback mysteries with racy covers for reading when business was dead, and a pair of bedroom slippers to give his feet some relief in the long hours behind the bar. All this was like seeing a secret side of Pop, and as Saturdays went by, I never was back there in his working domain with the winter light casting a kind of hush over everything without feeling I was someplace special to him, and therefore to me.

The one thing he did keep out in the open, prominent and practically as big as life, was that FDR campaign poster, always in place on the breakfront mirror, right next to the cash register. And before 1960 was very far along, it was joined by another. Looking over my shoulder then as I swabbed the floor was not only Franklin D. Roosevelt, eternally jaunty in his fourth successful run for president, sixteen years before, but also the current Democratic hopeful making his way through the primaries, John F. Kennedy, combed and groomed until he shone. Pop was more than ready for a new political champion, having suffered through two Republican terms of Eisenhower, whom he always called Eisenhoover. I was dutifully sweeping the floor one of these mornings, not far along in my career as swamper, when he let out a "Cripes!" that made me look up. He had noticed that the campaign posters were peeling away from the glass, a state of affairs that could not be tolerated. "Get me the Scotchman tape, why don't you."

When I fetched it from the back room, he ever so carefully Scotch-taped the corners of the campaign posters that restored Democrats to their rightful eminence, and stood back.

"This Kennedy maybe has what it takes," he said with satisfaction. "FDR, though, he topped them all. A giant among men. We maybe wouldn't be up against so much of it," he ruminated, as if to a listening customer, although I was the only one around, "the Russians acting up the way they do and this Castro in Cuba and the country going to the dogs, if Franklin Delano Roosevelt was still the man in charge." He gazed at the large face of FDR some moments more. "I heard him give a speech once, you know."

"Really? Here?"

"Not by a long shot," he dismissed Gros Ventre's eligibility for a presidential visit. "Up at the dam." I could tell he spoke the next two words simply for the sound of them. "Fort Peck."

This was new of him. I knew vaguely that he had tended bar there during the construction of the big dam, sometime before working his way up to buy the Medicine Lodge. Occasionally someone he had known in those years, such as J. L. and Nan Hill, who now ranched on upper English Creek, would drop in for a drink on their way home and they would get going on something that happened in the old dam days, as they liked to call that Depression period. From school I knew a little about the Fort Peck Dam, built by the government in the 1930s, when projects of the New Deal were being set up as fast as the alphabet could be divvied out. According to the schoolbook, the enormous dirt-fill dam on the Missouri River had given ten thousand people jobs and wages and hope. Doubtless they were ready for a drink, too, after all that shoveling or whatever other manual labor dam workers worked at, and from the sound of it when the Hills and Pop got to laughing about some saloon episode back then, tending bar there must have been a good job for someone starting out in life. I had never paid any great attention to such reminiscing as it drifted through the vent, the way we can't quite credit parents with real existences before we came along in their lives. But this time, perhaps it was the look on Pop's face as he stood there studying his political hero that made me prompt him: "You never told me about that."

"Didn't I?" He came to life. "It was a doozy of a speech, all about the Missouri River and how when the water was put to work, so were people who hadn't had a job in years." He tapped the Scotch tape in the palm of his hand in some odd rhythm of memory to envision the scene for himself as well as me. "His train came right to the dam, see, and they had loudspeakers rigged up so when the man himself came out on the rear platform, you could hear that voice of his for a mile. I tell you, kiddo, it was like hearing from heaven, him that day." Stretching to the FDR poster one more time, he pressed a thumb on a top corner, as if to make sure the tape would hold a good long time. "If Frank Roosevelt walked in here right now," he was saying pensively, "I'd stand him a drink on the house, you better bet I would." His brow knotted in brief contemplation. "Cutty Sark and soda, is my guess. He was always classy."

"Pop, wasn't he in a wheelchair?"

"Don't sweat the small stuff, okay?" His gaze still lingered on

the posters, the foxy old campaigner side by side with the youthful president-to-be. "Damn it, some people just shouldn't have
to die. They're too good to put in the ground." He shook his head.
"Life cheats on us sometimes."

Handing me the tape to put away, he noticed the way I was
looking at him. "The toilet needs another scrubbing," he said
gruffly. "Better get at it."

THE BIG ROUND NUMBER of a new decade on the calendar
always brings anticipation with it. After the Depression years of
the Thirties, the World War II years of the Forties, the Cold
War years of the Fifties, people of my father's generation were
more than ready for the world to behave itself better in the Sixties. All I knew was that 1960 was bringing surprise after surprise, some bad, some good.

"Guess what, Pop!"

The weather was still at it, new snow on top of old, old snow,
some weeks later when I hurried home from school, as determined as I was excited. I had shed my coat, cap, and overshoes in
the back room and rushed through to the quiet barroom, where
he was drying beer glasses. "We have a class assignment about
'Family History and What It Means to Us.'" I wasn't going to
pass this up. "Things like—"

"History, hey? That's a deep subject, as the well digger said."
He tossed me his towel. "Snow on your eyebrows."

I mopped that off. "Things like, how come—"

"Better have a sunshine juice while we think about this." He
uncapped an Orange Crush for me and lit a leisurely cigarette
for himself. It was not the first time personal matters of this sort
stalled with him. While this father of mine seemed to know
everything worth knowing about anyone who ever stepped into

the saloon, he never talked about himself. Not for lack of trying, I didn't know his precise age, and he wouldn't even let on to me when his birthday was. "Same as last year," he'd say, and that was that. He stayed equally vague on the subject of genealogy; to judge by him, we might be the only living people without ancestors. Perhaps this murky lineage should not have bothered me as much as it did—a Harry family tree, after all, might be full of rotten apples, if those Phoenix cousins were any example— but I had developed a burning reason for wanting to know more. As I persevered with now before he could sidle away from the topic behind a cloud of cigarette smoke.

"Things like, how come I'm named Russell?"

It bothered me every time I had to write my full name on a school assignment such as this one, or when the teacher called on me, or when some grown-up who didn't know any better would simper, "My, my, Russell, you're growing like a weed." Worst of all, of course, was when Duane Zane would drag it out so it sounded like it was in some idiot language. Thank heaven for "Rusty," which bought me survival in the schoolyard, but my given name did not seem to fit with anything I could figure out. Half the males in the Two Medicine country were called Bill or Bob or Jim or Joe or, for that matter, Tom, so why had I been tagged with something that seemed more than a bit out of place? Now I looked the question to the person responsible, deter- mined to get an answer out of him.

He barely paused in his toweling of an invisible spot on a glass. "Old family name. Didn't Marge tell you all that stuff way back?" I shook my head. "Doesn't matter"—he breezed past that—"nobody amounted to a hill of beans before us anyway. Do your report about you and me and Igdrasil and going fishing and junk like that, why not."

I wasn't satisfied, and immediately wrote to Aunt Marge,

airmail, in my careful fifth-grade fashion, asking about my namesake back there in family history. She wrote back, saying she had no idea what my father was talking about.

Confronted with this, Pop swabbed the wood of the bar this way and that, studying me out of the corner of his eye. "Okay, if it'll make you quit asking." He pointed his chin to where *Meat's Not Meat Till It's in the Pan* hung slightly askew on the far wall. "You're named after him."

I gawked at the scene of the hapless hunter. "That guy? The Buck Fever Case?"

"Hell no, use your thinking part," came the impatient answer. "The painter."

Now I gaped at the father who had plucked a name for me off the nearest Charlie Russell purplish rendering. My dismay surely showed, as he said defensively: "You had to be called something."

"I guess so, but I can't just hand in that I'm named after somebody I'm not even related to, can I. That's not family history, Pop." Suddenly something cunning came to me. Now was the time, now if ever. "Hey, I know what! I bet I'd get an A on stuff you can tell me about"—how to put it?—"the other side of my family."

He winced the way he always did when things led in this direction. "Rusty, you're better off if I don't say anything about your mother." Rubbing the side of his head as if it ached, he continued: "When you go through a gate, close it behind you, right? That's how it is with me and her." A shrug. "I've told you she was nothing but a Jones, anyway. Hard to do anything with that."

I was disappointed but not surprised; so much for anything maternal, one more time. He was determinedly steering matters back toward the namesake who had done the Buck Fever masterpiece on the wall. "If I was you, I'd stick with good old Charlie Russell and—"

When I wailed that I'd flunk the assignment if I didn't have anything better than that to turn in, he held up his hands like a traffic cop. "Don't get hydrophobia about this. Make something up."

"I can't, Pop. It's school."

"What"—his eyebrows climbed—"getting yourself out of something that has you stuck doesn't count? You've got to learn that, too." My dubious expression made him sigh hard. "Well, hell," he said to himself, "there's always the proxy method," whatever that was supposed to mean. Then to me: "All right, we'll come up with some kind of pedigree and you can put your name onto it like you're trying it out for a little while, okay? It's sort of like renting a house." It did not sound exactly okay to me, but I was past the point of arguing. He checked the clock. "Your whole class has the same assignment to dig up family stuff?"

"Huh-uh," I said, although I couldn't see why it mattered, "just us in the first half of the alphabet. The others are doing town history and what it means to them."

"You've got it made, kiddo. Grab your tablet and get up there in the back room, where you can hear."

I did so, my ears practically into the air vent. Very nearly to the minute, in came Earl Zane, practically licking his chops for the beer my father was already drawing from the tap. Large-headed and bigheaded both, he was one of those characters who had to be put up with in a town as small as Gros Ventre, where not only people but businesses needed to get along with one another. Pop normally gassed up at Earl's service station, and unfortunately Earl returned that kind of patronage, strutting in as he did now with his belly lopping over his belt buckle, a moonfaced grin breaking out on him as usual; he was the kind who winked with half his face. I could tell from the set of Pop's shoulders he was braced to be civil, even though this customer was the town's leading windbag.

What passed for conversation with Earl Zane ensued. "Ever hear the one about Pat and Mike and Mustard and the toilet brush, Tom?"

I never would understand why two Irishmen and someone named Mustard figured in half the jokes told by Earl and, for that matter, the entire male clientele of the Medicine Lodge, but they seemed indispensable. Biting my pencil to keep from groaning out loud as the joke played out, I sneaked a peek through the vent slats at Earl toasting himself with his beer. "Know where I first heard that? Around the bucking chutes, at the Calgary Stampede in the old days. Laugh, I thought I'd cry."

"Nobody remembers them like you, Earl, that's for sure." Pop manfully chatted for a couple of minutes while the beer went down in swigs. "Ready for some more holy water?"

"I meant to talk to you about that. This month's caught me a little short of—"

"Don't sweat it, catch up next time." As he slid the foam-topped glass to a surprised Earl, Pop said casually, "Hey, speaking of the old days, somebody was in here the other day saying he knew some Zanes in North Dakota, back when he was yay-high. Relatives of yours?"

"In North Dakota? I'd rather have relatives from South Hell than there." Earl got his mouth in gear. "Didn't I ever tell you we're Minnesota people, as far back as it goes?" Getting the idea, I made that Wisconsin in the Harry family version. "We'd still be there, breeding with Swedes, if it wasn't for my granddad Herman." Scribbling away, I drew a decisive breath and changed that to Russell. I suppose I should have been remorseful about pirating Duane Zane's forebears, but because he was Duane, I wasn't. "The old boy hopped on a train back there in Saint Paul in nineteen-aught-three," Earl rolled on, "he'd heard there was all this free land in Montana being thrown open to homestead—"

I wrote as fast as it spilled out of him, more than enough history for any family to rent. And it got an A.

THAT BIG WINTER of '60 kept up its weather tricks, storming as if it would never quit and then abruptly thawing everything with a chinook wind warm as an opened oven. This happened time and again, until the calendar finally said it was spring, whether or not the weather agreed. In between snow squalls, the Two Medicine country waded in mud up to its shoe tops, which gave me plenty to do in my job as swamper. One of those Saturday mornings of what was supposed to be spring, Pop considered the tracks on the barroom floor and joked, "Maybe we just ought to hose out the joint." At least I thought he was joking. But he wasn't when he contemplated the white slushy street. "So much for the opening day of fishing at the rezavoy."

Secretly I didn't mind if fishing season was delayed. As far as I was concerned, the rainbow trout could swim in peace indefinitely. I was content to be in the company of my busy father and the zoo of animal heads and the other comfortable surroundings of the barroom—even the dumb hunting painting by my namesake painter—on mornings like this, with Pop more like his old self now that we both had settled down some after that Canada trip of his. Money makes a difference in life, I had to admit, and since that trip he showed no sign that we were running out anytime soon, paying bills with only the usual muttering to himself.

Things were back on track enough that I was daydreaming a little when I started my chores with the push broom to get up the worst of the mud before mopping, still in the thrall of living through a historic time, although even for me, the winter had proved its point by now. This latest surprise storm had dumped several inches of heavy, wet snowfall not twenty-four hours before, and now the day was innocently bright and clear. The barroom was washed in light from sunshine reflecting off the snow, although *washed* may not be the most appropriate word, given the dusty places atop the booths and other surfaces showing up in the unaccustomed brightness. Pop had not pointed out my housekeeping lapses yet, but I knew I was in for an extended session with the dust cloth after I finished sweeping and mopping, and I felt put out at the weather. I wasn't the only one. "This isn't exactly great for business," Pop muttered, irritably flicking his towel at an imaginary mote on the bar.

He scarcely had the words out of his mouth when, to our surprise, Canada Dan slogged in, stomping snow onto the mat by the door and grumbling to himself while he kicked his overshoes off, even though we weren't open for business yet.

"Hey," Pop met him with, "I thought you went bunch herding for Dode." Curious myself, I perked my ears while I swept dried mud into the dustpan. Lambing time had started weeks ago, the season when sheepherders migrated back to work on ranches all across the Two.

"I did," came the sour reply. "He canned me. Ran me off the place. I caught a ride in with the county plow."

Pop and I almost had to laugh at this latest in the long-standing story of cantankerous herders and fed-up ranchers. But the look on Dan's face stopped us. We watched silently as he hoisted himself onto a bar stool with a grunt and grimaced toward Pop. "Something wrong with your pouring hand?"

"It hasn't woke up yet," Pop said mildly, taking his time about reaching for a shot glass and bottle.

"I ain't mooching, Tom, if that's what's bothering you." Canada Dan pulled out some crumpled bills and loose change in a spill onto the bar. "Gimme some bar grub while you're at it." This was another bad sign. Only someone too drunk to leave a bar stool ever ate the pickled pigs' knuckles and preserved boiled eggs swimming in big jars of bluish brine at the very back of the breakfront. Canada Dan plainly wanted to get that way as fast as humanly possible. Reaching for his drink almost before Pop finished pouring it, he said in a deadened voice, "Here's to them things called lambs. What's left of them."

Pop stood motionless and my broom and dustpan halted.

The grizzled sheepherder clutched the shot glass so tightly he seemed to be drinking out of his fist. "I lost a couple hunnerd in this storm," he said hollowly, "never had it happen before in all the years. Had them out in bunches like I was supposed to, so the ewes could eat a little new grass to help their milk. It started blizzarding so goddamn fast I only got about half the bunches into the shed. The others, they're froze under snowdrifts." Shoulders hunched miserably, he looked like he was about to cry. "It wasn't only my fault. Dode listens to them radio forecasts like they was religion. And he never did drive down to the lower shed and tell me a foot of snow was gonna hit, whatever the hell got into him." He tossed down the rest of his drink as if the whiskey was water. "Then this morning first thing, here he comes and blows up at me something fierce. Tells me to get out of his sight. What kind of a way is that to treat a man, I ask you." Choking up, Canada Dan twirled the shot glass on the bar wood. "C'mon, Tom. I know you got more where that came from."

"Hold on to yourself a minute, okay? I need to get a bottle from in back." Pop signaled me with the slightest jerk of his head and I followed him to the back room.

The instant we were there, he said low enough for only me to hear: "He's gonna drink himself blotto. Call Dode."

I dialed the ranch number, letting it ring about twenty times as you have to when a rancher is in the lambing shed. Finally the familiar voice answered, sounding testy, and I hurriedly said who I was and why I was calling: "My father thought you'd better know Canada Dan is in here."

"He's *what*? The phone line practically sizzled. "We're still in the middle of lambing! What's he doing in town?"

"Getting drunk as fast as he can."

There was a silence and then a burst of swearing that swelled to the question, "What in hell brought this on?"

"Dan says you, uhm, ran him off the place."

"Silly son of a bitch." Shocked, I nearly dropped the phone before realizing that meant Canada Dan, not me. "I only told him to get out of my sight when I found out about those lambs. I figured he'd stew in his wagon until I cooled down. Tell your dad not to let the idiot get too boozed up before I get there."

For the next while, Pop kept up a conversation with an increasingly slurred Canada Dan. The sheepherders of the Two Medicine country were a familyless tribe, single men with kinks in their lives that sent them into the hills like hermits for months on end and then deposited them in town to drink up their wages as fast as possible. Canada Dan was only one of the more habitual of the many who passed through the Medicine Lodge in the course of a year, the saloon and the Top Spot cafe and cheap rooms at the back of the hotel their way stations before the last stop of all, the cemetery on the hill overlooking Gros Ventre. "They're just waiting for the marble farm," Pop set me straight when I once said something about always having smelly old sheepherders around the joint, "and they'll get there soon enough." Canada Dan looked halfway there now as he hoisted his shot glass to his lips with a trembling hand. I slowly wiped down booths and fiddled with other chores so I could watch what would happen when Dode Withrow got hold of him.

Something of the sort must have been in the back of Canada Dan's mind, too. "Here's what I owe, ain't it." He shoved some money along the bar toward Pop and jammed the rest of it in his nearest pocket. "I'm going down to the Falls," he declared, as if Great Falls was on the next block, instead of ninety miles away. "See what's happening on First Avenue South." Even I knew that was the wino district where whores hung out.

"Are you," Pop said, as if he had heard this too many times. "How you gonna get there?"

"Thumb."

"Don't be a horse's ass." Pop's language was unusually strong. "You'll freeze to death on the side of the road before anybody comes along to give you a lift." Squinting toward the street in vain for any sign of Dode, he resorted to direct diplomacy. "Just go over there in a booth and simmer down, why don't you, and I'll bring you some more bar grub and another drink."

"Nope. I'm going, you watch and see," the herder lurched off his bar stool and unsteadily pointed himself in the direction of the door. "Had enough of old Dode and his dead lambs."

"Damn it, you're not going anywhere in this weather." Pop came around the end of the bar to head him off. Canada Dan was toddling off toward the door, his gait as rolling as a sailor's, when he hit the glare from the snowfield outside, and with a grunt flung up an arm just as Pop reached him. To my horror, his elbow clouted Pop smack in the eye, knocking him off balance and sending him to his knees with a sickening "Uhh."

"Pop!" I squealed in fright, throwing my dust rag away and tripping over myself in my rush to him. "Are you okay?"

That was the dumbest of questions, with him down on all fours and groaning in pain, but the sight of my father so vulnerable in the barroom that was his kingdom shook me to my roots. My imagination had never even come close to this. I was afraid to touch him for fear of what I'd find when that eye was revealed.

Blinking in confusion, Canada Dan swayed over him. "You hurt yourself, Tom?" he asked considerately.

"What in blazes is going on in here?"

Dode Withrow had just now come in, stopping short at the sight of tottering sheepherder and paralyzed boy, both useless as bumps on a log, hovering over the figure of Pop struggling up onto one knee. "Get out of the way." The rancher was a portrait of temper in a plaid mackinaw as he roughly pushed the two of us aside and grappled Pop onto his feet. "What did the son of a bitch do to you, Tom?"

Both hands covering his eye, Pop gasped to steady his breath. "Dan's crazy bone got in my way, is all," he managed. "These things happen." Mustering himself, he directed: "Get me some ice in a towel, Rusty." And to Canada Dan: "How about planting your stupid butt over there in a booth like I told you?"

"Hunky-dory," the herder said, as if he was the soul of cooperation, and staggered over and sat down.

With Dode and me helping to steer him, Pop made it to the amen corner and dropped onto the high-backed stool there, clasping the ice pack to his eye. "Don't take a fit," he told us, mostly me, "see, it's only a shiner." It was going to be spectacularly that, all right, a real raccoon job of a black eye. I was relieved, but still shaken, too, aghast over that image of him collapsed on the floor until Dode helped him up. As a unit, the three of us looked across the room to the booth where Canada Dan was mumbling his trials to the Buck Fever Case in the picture on the wall. "I hung on to the ess of a bee until you could get here," Pop told Dode in a resigned exhalation, "he's yours to deal with now."

Dode studied the hunched-up herder a trifle longer, then offered: "What do you say I just take him outside and beat the living daylights out of him?"

"You know better than that."

"Yeah, I'm afraid I do." The weary sheep raiser grimaced and headed over to the booth, shaking his head. "This is the damnedest year."

Canada Dan addressed him indignantly as he approached. "Couldn't wait to track me down and hand me my pay, huh? Write 'er out."

"I will like hell," Dode said back to him angrily as he slid into the opposite side of the booth. "I need a herder with those sheep. Even if it's you."

Canada Dan sniffed. "I ain't said I'll work for you ever again, have I." He sat in woozy dignity before demanding: "How come you didn't tell me it was gonna snow so goddamn much?"

"I didn't catch up with the forecast," Dode said in a dead voice. "Midge and me were in Great Falls at a woolgrowers' meeting and didn't get back until late. Never gave it a thought we'd get dumped on this time of year."

"That wasn't any too bright of you."

"Tell me something I don't know."

Long silence.

"You still sore at me for losing them lambs?"

"No more than I was."

Longer silence.

"That's sore enough, ain't it."

"Yeah, it'll do. You ready to quit tearing the town up and go back to the ranch?"

"Why didn't you say so in the first place?" Wobbling to his feet, Canada Dan called over to where we were watching: "Sorry if I inconvenienced you any, Tom."

"It could happen to a nun," Pop said past his ice pack.

The two of us watched through the plate-glass window as the unsteady herder put his arm over his eyes against the glare of the snow and let Dode lead him to the car. Then Pop winced and took a look at his mostly shut discolored eye in the breakfront mirror, and said to my distressed reflection: "Better get at the mopping, so we can open the joint on time."

THIS GOES TO SHOW you how much I knew about handling the embarrassment of a black eye. I'd have been sick with mortification until the telltale mark of a losing battle was fully gone. Not Pop. He practically turned that record shiner into a public attraction, imperturbably tending bar in the same style as ever and answering the obvious question by saying no more than, "Hey, you should have seen the other guy." And guess what, in the course of all the razzing he took about learning when to duck, customers often had a second drink or a third. "Business has picked up, kiddo," he reported in my bedroom doorway, untying his bow tie with a flourish, a week or so after the incident in the barroom. "I probably should cut Canada Dan in on the proceeds, but I'm not gonna."

Relieved as I was at that outcome, it still bothered me to see him going around with that doozy of a shiner, which turned various sickening colors on its gradual route to fading. On the other hand, he hadn't vanished on a trip since that nightmare one at the start of the year, so if I didn't have an unblemished father, I at least had one steadily on the premises. Even the weather improved now that the winter that threatened never to leave finally went away for the next thirty years or so, and spring, what little was left of it, settled in.

True, it rained notably more than usual as June approached, but that merely revived the old saying among the customers in the barroom that in Montana too much rain is just about enough, and beside our house, English Creek ran high and lively and

Igdrasil greened up in cottonwood glory. I sprouted, too. Almost before I knew it, I awoke one morning a year older than when I had gone to bed. Twelve at last, which immediately felt tremendously better than being merely eleven. In my newfound maturity, I managed to sound enthusiastic—if not totally sincere—about the new fishing pole Pop gave me for my birthday.

The better present was school letting out for the summer. A kid's dream, always, an entire untouched season of liberated days ahead. By habit and inclination I right away all but moved into the back room of the Medicine Lodge, spending as much of my time as I wanted casually listening in at the vent or practicing basketball shots or building model planes or entertaining myself any of the other ways an only child so well knows how, while Pop's performance of his bar duties went on as clocklike reliable as ever on the other side of the wall. This was how I always wanted things to be, and at last in this peculiar year, here they were, along with summertime and every new day of nature's making.

Therefore I was unprepared, soon into those first days of freedom, when Pop came back from a meal at the Top Spot, the cafe down the street that was best described as reliably mediocre, with news of a major change. We invariably ate supper at the Spot, although usually separately, because he needed to grab an early bite before his evening of tending bar.

"New couple bought the place," he reported while slitting open a whiskey case in the back of the saloon. They were Butte people, and his guess was that Pete Constantine, the husband and cook, had been in some kind of scrape—a lot of things could happen in Butte—and the wife, Melina, was determined that the cafe would keep his nose clean, as Pop put it. "I hope to hell they make a go of it. The food's not any better, but at least it's no worse."

Straightening up, he flicked his lighter and lit a cigarette, cocking a look at me in my favorite perch up there on the landing, where I was gluing a challenging twin-tail assembly onto my latest model aircraft, a P-38 Lightning fighter plane. His black eye was down to a greenish purple that I had now almost grown used to. "Guess what. They got a kid about your age."

Aw, crud, was my first thought. Every youngster knows the complication of such a situation, the burden of being expected to make friends with a new kid just because he was new. Why weren't twelve-year-olds entitled to the same system as adults, to merely grunt to any newcomer, "How you doing?" and go on about your own business?

"What's his name?" I asked with total lack of enthusiasm.

"Go get yourself some supper"—Pop blew a stream of smoke that significantly clouded the matter—"and find out."

As soon as I walked in, the Spot showed it had indeed changed, because Melina Constantine herself was behind the counter in the cleanest waitress apron the cafe had seen in ages. Mrs. Constantine was squat and built along the lines of a fireplug, but with large, warm eyes and a welcoming manner. She greeted me as if I were an old customer—actually, I was—and plucked out the meal ticket Pop had just inaugurated. Activity in the kitchen sounded hectic, and her husband, the cook, hurried past the serving window, giving me a dodgy nod. No kid my age was in sight, which was a relief.

"Now then, Russell," Mrs. Constantine said, smiling in motherly fashion as I hoisted myself onto my accustomed stool at the end of the counter, "what would you like for supper? The special is pot roast, nice and done."

Her smile dimmed a bit when I ordered my usual butterscotch milk shake and cheeseburger, but she punched the meal ticket without saying anything.

Wouldn't you know, though, muffled conversation was taking

place in the kitchen, and from where I sat, I could just see the top of a dark mop of hair as someone about my height stood waiting while Pete, cook and father rolled into one, dished up a plate of food and instructed that it all be consumed. I heard the new kid groan at the plateload.

Listening in, Mrs. Constantine beamed in my direction again and provided, "You're about to have company." I waited tensely as you do when someone from a different page enters the script of your life. Would he be hard to get along with? Would I?

The kitchen's swinging door was kicked open—it took a couple of thunderous kicks—and, meal in hand as if it weighed a tragic amount, out came a girl.

"Hi," she said faintly.

"Hi," I said identically.

Zoe was her name, and she seemed to come from that foreign end of the alphabet, a Gypsy-like wisp who slipped past me to a table in the back corner before I finished blinking. Her mother corrected that in nothing flat. "Russell, I'll bring yours over to the table, too, if you don't mind."

You bet I minded. All my years in Gros Ventre, I had been contentedly eating supper at the counter. In the manner of old customers, I felt I owned that spot at the Spot. But tugboat that she was, Mrs. Constantine had me maneuvered into changing seats before I could think of a way out of it. "Sure, I guess," I muttered, and reluctantly slid off my prized stool to go over to make friends, as grown-ups always saw it, or to meet the opposition, as kids generally saw it.

At the table, the two of us sat across from each other as trapped as strangers in a dining car. Given my first full look at Zoe, the wide mouth, the pert nose, the inquisitive gaze right back at me, I must have just stared. My education until then had not included time with a girl. Male and female relationships in school were literally a joke. "Your eyes are like pools. Cesspools. Your skin is like milk. Milk of magnesia." But the incontrovertible fact facing me was that Zoe Constantine possessed deep brown eyes that were hard to look away from, and she had an olive-skinned complexion that no doubt suntanned nice as toast, unlike mine. Her hair was not quite as richly black as my own, but at the time I thought no one in the world had hair as dark as mine and Pop's. For all of these arresting features, she was so skinny—call it thin, to be polite—that she reminded me of those famished waifs in news photos of DP refugee camps. But that was misleading, according to the indifferent way she toyed with her food while I waited edgily for mine. I was close to panic, thinking of endless suppertimes ahead with the two of us about as conversational as the salt and pepper shakers. How was this going to work?

She spoke first.

"I bet your dad was in a knock-down, drag-out fight, wasn't he. That's some black eye."

"Uh, yeah. You should have seen the other guy."

"People get in fights all the time in Butte," she said in worldly fashion. "It gives them something to do." Idly mashing potatoes that were already mashed, she caught me even more by surprise as she conspiratorially lowered her voice enough that neither her mother behind the counter nor her father in the kitchen could hear:

"How come he and you eat here? Where's your mother? Can't she cook better grub than this?"

"She's, she's not around anymore."

Her voice dropped to an eager whisper. "Did they split the blanket?"

"Uh-huh," I whispered back, although I wasn't sure why divorce was a whispering matter. "When I was real little. I wouldn't know her if I saw her."

"Wild! Are you making that up?"

"You can't make something like that up, nobody would believe it."

"Ooh, you're a half orphan, then." That jolted me. Even during my time in Phoenix, trying to dodge Ronny's knuckles, I had not thought of myself that way. That was nothing to what she said next. "You're so lucky."

I was so stunned I could hardly squeak out: "Because I don't have a mother I've ever seen?"

"No, silly, I mean because you've got only one parent to boss you around," she whispered, with either world-weary assurance or perfectly done mischief, it was impossible to tell which. "That's plenty, isn't it?" She peered critically toward the kitchen. "I'd give up my dad, I think, if it came to that."

"Wh-why?" I sneaked a look at her father in his undersized cook's hat, flipping a slice of Velveeta onto my cheeseburger as if he'd just remembered that ingredient. "What's the matter with him?"

Zoe waved that away with her fork. "Nothing much. He's just not swuft about a lot of things."

This was another stunner from her. *Swuft* did not merely mean quick at handling things, it meant swift-minded, brainy, sensible, and quite a number of other sterling qualities she evidently found lacking in her father.

"He couldn't beat up anybody in a fight, like I bet your dad can," she was saying, as if she would trade with me on the spot. "Besides, my mom could have made your burger while he's standing around looking at it." In fact, Mrs. Constantine kept revving the milk shake machine as she waited for the cheeseburger to find its way out of the kitchen; my shake was going to be thin as water.

All kinds of doubts about the Top Spot under its new management must have begun showing on me, as Zoe now amended her view of fathers for my benefit in another fervent whisper.

"I bet *your* dad is plenty swuft, you can tell that just by looking at him, can't you. Besides, I heard the old owners tell my folks"—her whisper became even more whispery; what a talent she had—"this cafe gets a lot of its business because the Medicine Lodge brings customers to town from everywhere. I guess it's real famous around here?"

I nodded nonchalantly. Fame was right up there with swuftness in her estimation, I could tell.

"Do you get to be in your dad's saloon"—she wrinkled her nose at the less than impressive confines of the cafe—"ever?"

It was my turn to astonish. "Sure! All the time."

She gave me the kind of look you give a bare-faced liar.

I began convincing her by recounting my job as swamper every Saturday morning. Disdainfully she let me know this did not win me any bragging rights, *her* parentally ordained job was to fill the sugar dispensers, salt and pepper shakers, ketchup bottles, and napkin holders and things like that every single day, from her tone a life sentence of cafe chores.

No way was I going to be trumped about the joint, though. "Yeah, well," I responded, elaborately casual, "I just about live in the saloon, I'm there so much. In the back room, I mean."

Her ears perked up. I expounded about the privileged position provided by the stair landing, and went on at some length about the trove of hocked items housed from floor to ceiling.

Zoe listened as if she had never heard of such a thing, as I suppose she hadn't.

"All kinds of stuff?" she whispered eagerly. "Years' and years' worth? And people are still doing that?"

"You bet. Sometimes the same people, over and over."

"How do you know that?"

"I hear them at it, don't I, out front with my dad. Everything that goes on."

"Whoa, are you serious? Is there some rule," she scoffed, mischief in her gaze, "they have to talk at the top of their voice to get a drink in this town?"

"Don't be silly," I got back at her for that word, "it's not that. All it takes is—"

Carried away with myself, I told her about the vent.

"Really?" Her voice dropped again to the lowest whisper humanly possible. "You can see and hear them but they can't see you? They're down there drinking and carrying on and everything, and you're up there, invisible?"

"Uhm, yeah."

Her eyes shone. "That sounds neat! Can I come listen to them, too?"

Before I had to commit to that, my milk shake and cheeseburger were delivered, along with Mrs. Constantine's smiling wish for me to have a good appetite and her instructive frown at Zoe's barely touched victuals. "Eat, missy, or you'll blow away," she recited, and left us to it. I attacked my meal. Zoe sighed and speared a single string bean off her plate. It dawned on me I had better make sure just how much we were destined to be around each other, apart from what looked like disconcerting suppertimes ahead. Between milk shake slurps, I inquired, "What grade will you be in?"

"Sixth. Same as you."

"How'd you know?"

A quick, devilish look. "Your father bragged you up."

"Uh-huh." I swirled my milk shake in man-of-the-world fashion. "We'll have old lady Spencer for a teacher."

"Is she hard?"

"Terrible. She catches you whispering, you have to stay an hour after."

The mischievous look again. "In Butte, they cut your tongue out."

By the time I was done snorting milk shake out of my nose, I was in love with Zoe. I have been ever since.

"POP, IS THAT YOU?"

"No, it's Nikita Khrushchev."

I had not yet gone to sleep by the time I heard the nightly sounds in the bathroom and then the hallway, my mind turning over and over all that was to be digested from my first meal with Zoe. It should have been exhausting, but it was the opposite.

Pop came and leaned against the doorjamb, smoothing the cloth of his undone bow tie between his hands as he peered at me in the dim bedroom. "How'd you do with your supper partner?"

"She's"—I cast around for the right way to put it—"different."

That immediately turned him into the listening bartender.

"Not *bad* different," I spelled out. "She's real smart, for a girl."

"They can be like that," he said drily. "Try to get along with her, okay? It puts us in a bind if we can't grab a meal at the Spot. We'd have to live on pig knuckles and embalmed eggs." That was meant to be a joke, I understood, but it was not that far from the dietary probability if we had to fend for ourselves every suppertime.

"Sure thing, Pop," I said, as if there really was such a thing.

PEOPLE COME AND go in our lives; that's as old a story as there is. But some of them the heart cries out to keep forever, and that

is a fresh saga every time. So it was with me and the unlooked-for
supper partner who quickly became so much more than that. Zoe
proved to be something like a pint-size force of nature, thin as a
toothpick and as sharp. Her face was always a show, her generous
mouth sometimes sly, sometimes pursed, the tip of her tongue
indicating when she was really thinking, her eyes going big
beyond belief when something pleased her, and when something
didn't, she could curl her lip practically to the tip of her nose. To
say that she was not the kind of company I could ever have
expected in that summer of my life is a drastic understatement.

Whether or not we were made for each other, the two of us
were definitely made for the back room of the Medicine Lodge.
From the very start of our exploring of its wonders together, she
couldn't get enough of the assortment of stray and odd items
that had been traded in down through time, and I couldn't get
enough of her prodigious imagination. Prowling in some clut-
tered quarter, she would stumble onto a stray article such as a
suitcase made of that old pebbled phony black leather and away
she would go. "Ooh, I bet this has been lots of places. Let's look
in it." We would. Empty, every time. No matter, the lack of content only spurred her speculation. "Just think, all he has is the
clothes on his back. I bet there was a fire. In the bunkhouse. He
was all played out from punching cows all day and was laying
there smoking in bed and went to sleep and the old army blanket caught fire"—for a twelve-year-old, Zoe had a remarkably
graphic view of life—"and everything burned up, and he had to
run for his life, and the only thing he had time to grab was his
suitcase. Everything else, *ka-whoosh!*"

You always hate to disrupt an artist, so I did not tell her the
inspirational piece of luggage actually was owned by some snoose-
chewing herder whose belongings were securely in his sheep
wagon out in the foothills while he hocked the suitcase when his

money ran out before finishing off a big drunk. Besides, Pop's habit of that last cigarette at bedtime made *ka-whoosh!* something I didn't like thinking about.

I had to ask, though. "Does your dad smoke in bed?"

"All the time," she said, rolling her eyes to fullest effect. "I bet your dad knows better."

"Oh, sure."

That was cast into doubt, however, by her next find. The shoe box half full of metal cigarette lighters. Zoe's eyes went big in amazement. "Who smokes this much?"

"No one guy," I responded like the back-room veteran I was. "See? They're engraved. Soldiers trade them in." And had been doing so for a long time. Rummaging, we found a tarnished lighter with the engraving MONTANEER JUNGLE FIGHTERS, which dated back to the Montana National Guardsmen who served in the tropical hell of New Guinea in World War II. Another one read INCHON SEPT. 1950 THE MARINES HAVE LANDED from the Korean War. Newest and shiniest were some engraved with MINUTEMAN MISSILEMEN—AMERICA'S ACE IN THE HOLE, from Air Force troops, flyboys, as we somewhat inaccurately called them, stationed in missile silos out there under the prairie. "Pop takes one out and uses it until the flint wears out," I explained the plenitude of lighters. "He says he got tired of running out of matchbooks all the time."

"Smart," Zoe commended, but by now her attention had been caught by a collection of shoes ranged along the bottom of one wall: cowboy boots and work shoes but also well-shined oxfords. "That's wild!" she gasped. "People even trade in their dress shoes?"

"You bet. Like Pop says, they can't drink with their feet."

She giggled and went over to the footwear assortment, drawn by one particularly extravagant-looking pair of items. They resembled cowboy boots, but were higher topped and the leather was of an odd texture and funny greenish shade. "What are these fancy things?" she wondered, fingering one.

"Snake boots."

"Rusty, you're making that up." Nonetheless she jerked her hand away.

"Huh-uh, cross my heart up, down, and sideways. It's snake-skin of some kind, they're made in Texas," I held forth knowledge-ably because I had asked Pop the identical question a few days before, when Earl Zane traded them in to drink on. I started to fill her in on the Zane family propensities, but she was so canny she had already caught on to those, including Duane's. "That kid at the gas station?" She curled her lip dismissively. "What a weenie."

Snooping past the boots and shoes, she next found the hiding place of the Blue Eagle sign under the rain slickers, just as I had when the back room was a new world to me. Watching a dark-eyed imp of a girl repeat my discovery so exactly was remarkable and somewhat spooky. I've said this was starting off as not a usual summer.

Unlike me, however, Zoe saw nothing odd about the eagle being blue. "I bet it's the only paint they had that day," she resolved the question, and moved on.

As inevitably as B follows A, she next stumbled onto the lat-est quantity of items tucked away even farther with the tarp over them. "What are all these tools for?"

My guess was that they were implements used in oil field work, but I only repeated what Pop told me whenever I hap-pened to ask about the stuff that every so often multiplied under the tarpaulin, as if it was a magician's cloth. "It's just surplus somebody didn't know what else to do with."

"This place is really something, Rusty," she marveled.

And that was before I even introduced her to the vent.

"It's that time of day, Tom," the alimony purr in that voice drifted up to us when we hunched in at the desk on the landing and I grandly levered the vent slats open.

"You're living proof of that, Velma." Pop's reply was punctuated with the sounds of a ginger-ale highball being mixed. "I can quit winding my watch now that you're back."

Zoe pressed so close to the metal grille, her ear practically kissed the slats. "Ooh." She turned to me, instinctively whispering, "It's just like you said, we can hear every word! This is wild!"

Veteran eavesdropper that I was, I welcomed her to the club with a smug smile.

"How was Mexico?" Pop's voice kept its distance from Velma's.

"Same as ever. Fiestas and tortillas."

Craning her neck, Zoe took a good look at Velma's tailored outfit and eternally chestnut hair. "She looks pretty swuft," she murmured over her shoulder to me. "How come your dad doesn't fall for her?"

"She's too"—I almost said *old* before remembering Velma Simms most likely was close to my father's age, whatever that was—"divorced." I noiselessly closed the vent so I didn't have to whisper my way through the long history of the town's record holder for broken marriages.

"That's a lot of split blankets," Zoe said sagely when I was done. "I bet that's why your dad is such a bachelor. He doesn't want something like that happening to him again, don't you think?"

"Yeah, sure."

Zoe looked at me keenly. "You don't ever hear from your mom at all?"

"Not really," I blurted, surprised into dumb honesty. I was not yet used to the fact that the mind of Zoe was like a pinball machine; the flips and bounces came so suddenly you were left blinking, trying to know the score.

"Christmas or anytime?" she pressed the point.

"It doesn't matter."

"Not even," she wondered in a hushed voice, "on your birthday?"

I might have answered, *Especially on my birthday*, since my arrival in the world seemed to have so colossally done in the marriage of my mother and my father. "She, ah, doesn't believe in that sort of thing. I don't blame her." I tried to sound worldly. "When you go through a gate, close it behind you."

Zoe blinked in thinking that over, and the vent came to my rescue. "Oh, hey, listen," I whispered, opening it again to the clocklike happenings of the barroom.

"Ring me up one, Tom." Bill Reinking had walked in on schedule. "Something to get my mind off the state of the world again this week."

"Shot of scotch, water on the side," I stated without looking.

Peeking to check on that, Zoe bobbed her head in fascination. She listened avidly to the trials and tribulations of the *Gleaner* editor as told to Pop, then when Bill Reinking left, dropped back into her chair with a gleam in her eye. "Know what?" Her whisper turned even more confidential. "Priests do this all the time."

Pop and I weren't remotely Catholic or anything else, but I was pretty sure the confessional booth had something more to it than a vent in a saloon wall did.

"How's it any different?" Zoe insisted. "People come and tell their troubles, and they get to feel better because somebody is listening to them."

"Yeah, but it's my dad they know is listening, not us up—"

"Same thing, him or us," she breezed past that. "People just want somebody to spill to." Her eyes sparkling, she provided final proof of her expertise. "In Butte, they have a confessional on every corner, like a phone booth."

I gave my new best friend a look and a knowing laugh. "I bet they need to."

THAT WAS THE start. Zoe quickly became as regular in the back room as some of Pop's customers out front. In no time, we were thicker than thieves, as that accurate enough saying goes. When we were together, almost anything tickled our funny bones, particularly overheard snatches from the barroom that arrived to us through the vent. In no time we adopted old sheepherders' "Hunnerd percent" and "Wouldn't that fry your gizzard" equally with young flyboys' "Listen up, troop" and "Outstanding!" and any number of other gleeful bits we made our own, lingo overlapping in us as though we were time travelers. Inevitably added to that was every particle of radio serial and comic strip and movie dialogue we'd ever encountered that was silly enough to remember, piled up and waiting in two active twelve-year-old brains like ingredients filling a flour sifter. All it took for that powder of imagination to sieve through in good measure was for one or the other of us to turn the crank.

"Ace, what do you think this doohickey is?" Zoe might take on a persuasive growl—she could be a deadly mimic, and I wasn't bad myself—as we prowled the holdings of the back room.

"Get a brain in your head, Muscles." Gangsters who talked sideways out of their mouths were one of our favorites. "Any dumb cluck can plainly see it's a whatchamacallit, a bootjack."

"Now that you give me the skinny, boss, I can see you hit the nail on the noggin."

Zoe had yet another surprising side to her. With boyish trepidation—she was first and foremost a girl, after all—I had given her a hasty tour of my aspiring air force of Hellcats and

Spitfires and Airacobras and the like hovering on their fish lines
from the rafters, figuring she would have about as much interest
in model-plane building as I would in learning to sew. How wrong
I was, luckily. Whether it was the pugnacious aircraft names or
what, she took to my balsa wood kits as though they were magic
sets. "Neat! Show me how it all fits together." I did more than that,
finding the courage from somewhere to show her my most precious possession, the X-Acto knife Pop had given me for Christmas. "Ooh," she breathed, just that, exactly the right response to
the beautiful little instrument that was a cross between a pen and
a scalpel.

"You suppose"—for once she was almost shy in asking—"I
could try it out sometime?"

I didn't have to think twice. "Right now, if you want," I said,
with my heart thumping as I pulled out the model kit I had been
saving for after the Fourth of July rodeo, when summer started
to stretch on. "I'm going to build my biggest one yet. A Flying
Fortress."

There were more *ooh*s from her as I laid out the balsa wood
sheets of the framework of the B-17 bomber. With the care of a
surgeon I cut out the first wing to show her how it was done,
and then handed her the X-Acto knife to do the other one herself. She handled it like a treasure, I was gratified to see, tracing
the wing outline with the sharp point as slowly and precisely as
I could do it myself.

That settled it. From then on, so many of those afternoons
and early evenings, Zoe and I were to be found together at the
desk on the stair landing, alternately tuning in on the barroom
doings and giggling at each other's tomfoolery and holding our
breath as surgical cuts on balsa wood were made. Somewhere in
the back of our minds lurked the disturbing knowledge that
when school started in the fall, I would have to turn into a boy

among other boys again and she would have to find a best friend among girls. But that fact of life lay whole months away yet, and in the meantime, all we had to live up to was for each of us to do half the laughing.

Early in all this, Pop came in from the bar side to wrestle a keg of beer out to the taps and glanced up at us, innocent as angels there on the stair landing. He paused for a long moment, his eyebrows working on the matter. "Your folks know you're in here as much as you are, princess?"

Zoe swore, cross her heart and hope to go to heaven in a flash of fire, that they did.

He went back to grappling the keg, but not before reciting the warning about beans and nose with an oddly pensive look at the so youthful pair of us.

IT WAS RAINING cats and dogs again, another weather parade the Two Medicine country wasn't used to, the day not much farther into summer, when she came in the back door shaking her wet hair and caroling up to me on the landing, "What's the story, morning glory?"

"Hi."

She gave me a little look, but then bounded up the stairs as usual and started to settle in next to where I'd been dithering over our half-built Flying Fortress. I had the louver slats of the vent open to try to improve my mood, and right away we heard the bar phone being answered. Nothing got past Zoe in the sieving of voices from the barroom—at times like this, I wished it would—and at the first guttural word, she went alert as a sentry.

"That's not your dad," she whispered.

Trying to sound offhand—it's hard when you're whispering— I told her it was only Howie, filling in.

"Is he sick?"

"Who, Howie? He always talks that way."

"No, silly, your dad."

I was badly out of sorts, even with her. "No, nosy, he's not sick."

"Then why isn't he tending bar like always?"

"He's . . . away on a trip."

"He is? For how long?"

"Couple of days."

"Oh, good, that's not much." She read my face. "Although it's kind of a lot, too. Why didn't he take you along?"

"I didn't want to go," I said, hoping the opposite of the truth would end this. "All he's doing is selling some of this old stuff."

"Really? Ooh, I see what you mean, the snake boots are gone. Too bad." Those and a whole lot else I crossly had watched Pop pile up for loading in the Packard early that morning, before he shooed me to the house and told me not to put any you-know-what up my nose while he was away. By now Zoe knew the holdings of the back room as well as I did, and she could tell from the crumpled look of the tarpaulin back by the Blue Eagle sign that the tool collection had vanished, along with a lot else. Her curiosity wasn't quenched about the comings and goings of the hocked merchandise. "Where does your dad go to sell all these kinds of things?"

When I told her, her eyes reflected dark mystery. "Canada! Why there?"

"Uhm, he makes more money."

"Just by going across the border? How does that work?"

"They're short of American stuff up there, I guess."

Zoe gazed around at the motley accumulation that was left. "They won't be, if he makes enough trips."

———————

SAME PICKLED BEDROOM. Same slap of Howie's slippers on the way to the toilet. Same sleepless mood, that first night, fretting myself to a frazzle about my father. I couldn't get over it. One minute we were in our usual comfortable routines in the house and the joint, and the next thing I knew, he was gone in another puff of smoke. True, this time he had not driven off into the jaws of a thirty-year winter, but it had been the rainiest spring and start of summer anyone could remember, and there was flooding up north on the Milk River. I had a really bad feeling about this sudden trip of his, even more so than that New Year's excursion into the blizzard, maybe because Zoe had taken my mind off the matter and I was caught utterly unprepared when he told me he was about to load up and go. I wasn't even sure why, weather aside, this time scared me so. What was it about life that kept tiptoeing back and forth so unpredictably across the back of my mind this odd year? Or was it just the age I was at, still a kid with a kid's nightmares (Phoenix!) but growing older if not wiser at what seemed an accelerating rate? In any case, here the situation was again, him gone and me stewing in the dark.

Yet when I look back, this is possibly what it took to encourage me into what I did that next day. Desperation can serve as a kind of encouragement, after all.

Zoe and I were back at the B-17, the X-Acto knife doing most of the talking as we traded back and forth at cutting out delicate small parts and gluing them into the complicated bomber fuselage. Worried sick and not able in the least to keep it from showing, I knew she deserved better company than I was managing to be. She was all sympathy, I could tell, but she had that carefully pursed expression a person has around someone something is

wrong with. Mustering myself, I cast around for some way to
make up for my mood. Fortunately I was not without resources,
Pop having given me a couple of dollars of conscience money
before he left.

"Hey, want to go to the show?" Our evenings were pretty
much second helpings of afternoons, inasmuch as television literally wasn't in the picture before relay stations began beaming
the signal to small western towns like ours; it is strange to think
how much distraction the curvature of the earth spared us back
then. The new movie at the Odeon once a week was exactly
what it sounded like, the only show in town.

"You bet," said she, ready for anything. Until she thought it
over for a second or two. "You think we both should? Together,
I mean." She picked at her elbow uneasily. "That's kind of . . .
you know."

Yes, it was awfully public. Gros Ventre was a small town
where people knew one another's business almost before it happened. We could be teased to death if the wrong party—Duane
Zane came to mind—spotted us sitting together in the movie
theater. That was a chance we would have to take, and I had an
inkling of how.

"Leave it to me, Bucky"—I did my best radio-serial voice—"we'll
foil those devils yet."

With enough pleading to her parents and my dogged negotiation with Howie, we managed to get permission to go to the
late show rather than the early one on the unique premise that it
was a shame to waste a nice summer evening inside. Even so, it
still was only dusk when we slipped out the back door of the
Medicine Lodge and down the alley until we were across the
street from the Odeon. The first show had just let out, and as
the crowd dispersed to cars and pickups, we waited until the

traffic died down and then hurried across to where the marquee read:

THE ALAMO
STARRING JOHN WAYNE
DIRECTED BY JOHN WAYNE

Charlie Hooper, the Odeon's owner, was at the ticket window, counting his take, and was surprised to see customers already for the next showing. He was even more surprised when I pushed our price of admission through the little wicket and requested urgently: "Can we please be in the crying room? She has a real bad cough."

I swear, Zoe immediately took on the look of a consumptive who would cough her head off throughout the show. As Charlie Hooper peered at her through the ticket window glass, she ducked her head and gave a piteous hacking sound. Figuring I was the emissary from her folks or my father, Charlie surmised: "Bashful, is she?"

"Scared of her own shadow."

"Well, all right, but you'll have to clear out if there's a squaller."

We would cross that high water when we came to it. Meanwhile the crying room, a small soundproof cubicle next to the projector booth where a parent or two could sit with a squalling baby, was all ours. Unseen by the audience below, we could watch the show in royal privacy and make cracks about it out loud to our hearts' content. Zoe was already nearly giddy with our fortunate spot and I was glad to have my mind somewhat off my absent father.

"Outstanding, Rusty! Hunnerd percent!"

"Almost." I ran back down to where Charlie Hooper doubled

as clerk at the candy counter and bought us each a roll of Necco wafers. This was pure kid instinct. The thin candy discs of a variety of flavors, all of them faint, were kind of like sucking on nickels, but I had a hunch Zoe would be as crazy for them as I was.

"Boy oh boy, Ace"—Zoe grinned a mile as she crackled open her Necco roll—"this hideout is the best idea ever."

One thing about a movie called *The Alamo*, there was no doubt about how it was going to come out, so instead of following the plot very closely, we could sit back sucking Neccos and evaluate the actors and the funny way they were dressed. Laurence Harvey played Colonel Travis, in charge of the mission fortress threatened by the Mexican forces of Santa Ana, and whatever anyone in Texas was actually wearing in 1836, this version of the colonel raced around in tight white pants and a really big hat. It was headgear so wide-brimmed it wouldn't have lasted a minute in Montana wind, and we couldn't help snorting laughs whenever a camera angle caused it to dwarf the head under it. It seemed like in every scene, Colonel Travis tromped around in the same bad mood. For the whole first part of the movie, he and Jim Bowie, played by Richard Widmark, with the trademark knife—about the size of a dozen X-Actos—strapped to his hip, were so mad at each other that the Mexican foe somewhere out there seemed an afterthought.

As history dragged along at the Alamo, Zoe said impatiently, "Isn't John Wayne even in this?"

"He must be waiting for something to happen before he shows up." I rolled what was left of a mint Necco around in my mouth. "Guess what, that's not even his real name."

"You're making that up."

"Not either," I said, confident of what I'd read somewhere. "Bet you anything it's really Marion Morrison."

We both snickered at the sissy sound of that, or as it would have been in the schoolyard, the thithy thound.

"You suppose back then," Zoe giggled her way into a lisp, "when someone asked what his name was, he didn't like to have to thay 'Morrithon'?"

"'Marion' ithn't tho hot, either, ith it."

Finally the supposed star of the show showed up on-screen. However he came to be John Wayne, he sure was a-talkin' slow when he came on the scene as Davy Crockett, coonskin cap and all in the blazing Texas sun. A ragtag bunch with him were his Tennesseeans, and promptly enough they were in a big drunken fight scene in a cantina, the most action yet in the movie. Then appeared a busty señorita, whose main role seemed to be to stand sideways so John Wayne could get a good look.

"Wooh, how about the front porch on her," said Zoe, which freed me to grin appreciatively.

The movie slowed down drastically after that—after all, it *was* a siege—and we spent more of our time peeking down at the audience to see what was going on. Attendance at the late show ran heavily to couples on dates, so there was sometimes interesting behavior in the dark. It must have been some of the more evident necking that brought the question to mind in Zoe.

"Rusty? What if"—it was eerie to hear her say my most haunting two words there in the dark—"what if your dad met somebody he liked on one of these trips? A Canadian lady, maybe? Would you want a new mother?"

Zoe had an incredible knack for zeroing in when a person least expected it. Blinking in the dark, I answered thinly: "Are you kidding? You said it yourself, remember? One parent is plenty."

"I know."

"Then why'd you bring it up?"

She rattled out a Necco before answering. "That was real dumb of me, wasn't it," she said in a small voice. "Excuse me all over the place." She did her best to erase all doubt. "Besides, your dad is too swuft to do that to you."

He'd better be, I thought but didn't say. Instead, I resorted to: "Boy, if this movie doesn't end sometime, we'll be eating Neccos for breakfast." Relieved to change the subject, Zoe piped up: "Maybe they lost track of the ending, you think, Ace?"

In the course of time, with a lot of preachy dialogue along the way, things actually were building to a climax at the Alamo, and the arrival of Mexican soldiers on-screen by the apparent thousands for the attack was really something, we had to admit.

"This is kind of like Custer, isn't it," Zoe observed, both of us back in movie-critic mode.

"Reckon so, ma'am," I responded, John Wayne–like. "It don't look good for the Texicans."

The Alamo battle scenes were serious blood and guts; heaven help the human race if war ever ceases to be sobering, even at its most make-believe. And yet, right there amid the explosions and bodies falling everywhere, the scriptwriter and the director included a scene where two mortally wounded Tennesseeans are pinned against a wall and one of them asks, "Does this mean what I think it do?" The other one answers, "It do," and they both expire.

And we had something new for our vocabulary of the summer.

THE NEXT NIGHT was another story. I went to bed at Howie and Lucille's in hopes of a call of "Hey, kiddo" rousing me. It didn't happen. The third day came, and Pop didn't show up and didn't show up. Zoe did her best to cheer me up—"Maybe he has to look real hard to find anybody to buy the snake boots, is all"—but by nightfall, I knew I was in for another spell in that tomb of a bedroom.

Breakfast the next morning with Howie and Lucille had me downcast about as far as I could go. As they ate their stewed prunes and took their pills, I fed on toast and jam and watched the clock. Theoretically, I was free to come and go now that it was broad daylight, but I didn't want to miss Pop when he came for me, if that ever managed to happen. From the concern on Lucille's kindly face and Howie's crabby expression—awfully early in the day for that—I was not the only one wondering why he hadn't shown up long since. I had some more toast and jam and stayed sitting there, waiting.

At last came what we had all been straining to hear, the Packard's heavy crush of gravel in the driveway.

I was outside before Pop had time to climb out of the car. "Hey, where's the fire?" He sounded like always, but didn't look it. His shiner had finally gone away, but there were dark pouches under his eyes, and the deepened lines in his face told how tired he was. He had been driving with the window rolled down, I saw, something a person does to stay awake at the wheel.

I babbled a greeting of some kind, cut off by the slam of the screen door behind me. Unexpectedly, Howie had followed me out.

"You're stretching it some, Tom. The boy was getting awful worried."

"I'd just as soon that didn't happen," Pop said levelly, looking from one of us to the other. "Anyhow, here I am, right? Climb in, kiddo."

He drove home as if the huge old car knew the way by itself, his mind elsewhere, and for the first few blocks I didn't say anything. The streets that had been whited out with snow the last time were now a tunnel of leafy trees, the dappled green that happens when a breeze stirs a column of cottonwoods. Every house lazing in the shade possessed a carpet of lawn or at least grass outdoing itself to be green, from the moist spring and summer. Lilacs were blooming like big purple bouquets left at porches. If there ever was a market for momentary Americana, a day like this was the time to sell off the town of Gros Ventre, complete and entire. My mood didn't match the pleasant scene, however, emotions going every which way in me. I was dizzily relieved Pop was home in one piece, and at the same time I was so mad at him, I could taste it. Something needed saying, even if I wasn't sure what.

"Did you get a lot of money from the loot?" I asked sullenly.

He looked at me from the corner of his eye and then back to the road. "I made enough. Don't sweat it."

"What, did you have trouble selling the things this time?"

"I got it done."

"Did you have to drive through the flood?"

"It wasn't where I was."

The next logical question was whether he'd been too busy with some floozy to come home on time, but I managed not to ask it, quite. "Then how come it takes longer every time?"

"I hadn't noticed."

"It's longer. Every time."

"If you say so."

"Even Howie thinks so."

He let out a sigh of ages. "This is one of those days. Right away Howie takes an ornery fit, and you don't seem to be in the absolute best frame of mind, either." One hand on the steering wheel, he knuckled the bags under his eyes with the other. "How about letting me catch a couple of hours of sleep, and then we'll tackle the joint, would that suit you?"

I looked at him blankly.

"It's Saturday, remember?

That had skipped my mind entirely—this summer every day was Zoe day, I wasn't keeping track of much else—but I stiffly maintained: "Howie and I were going to do the setting up and the swamping by ourselves if you didn't get back."

"Saint Peter will put you both in the book," he said wearily, and aimed the car into our driveway, where Igdrasil waited with its top reaching to heaven and its roots watered by seasons of fate.

"IMAGINE THAT," Pop stepped into the saloon, still yawning after the few hours of sleep he'd snatched but with his bow tie in place and his apron on, "the place didn't fall down without me." While that was true enough, the barroom definitely had missed his presence, glasses mouth down in the breakfront slightly out of line from usual, stools not quite squared up to the bar, ashtrays emptied but not washed clean, and so on—Howie had his own way of doing or not doing things. Somehow the long old room welcomed its proprietor back, as an empty theater changes when a leading actor strolls onstage. Even the familiar gallery of taxidermied heads up on the walls appeared more hospitable with my father and his black-and-white mane on the premises. And he looked miraculously recuperated, now that he was back where he belonged. Why couldn't he just stay here forever and tend to the business of bartending instead of vanishing off when I least expected and maybe getting himself in some love situation I didn't even want to think about?

Still burning inside, I'd trailed him into the barroom with broom and mop and bucket, ready to get at my swamping job, but he circled the floor a couple of times, looking around at things, lost in thought, having a leisurely cigarette.

"You're getting as bad as Howie," I complained for the sake of complaint, "I wish you didn't smoke so much."

"That's funny, I wish that sometimes, too," he said, taking a deep drag. "Usually between cigarettes." Taking philosophy further, he mused, "If you're in the habit, you might as well stay there. Saves confusion."

He glanced my way. "Hey, didn't I tell you to go down to Shorty's and get your ears lowered while I was away? You look like a beatnik." We wouldn't have known a beatnik if one thumped his bongo drum at us, but it was what he customarily said when I needed a haircut.

"I forgot."

"That's what I do about quitting smoking." He squinted at me critically. "Cripes, Rusty, don't tell me you just sat around being down in the mouth to your eyeteeth all the time I was gone."

"No-o-o." I dragged it out to the fullest extent of indignation. "Zoe and I went to the show."

"Yeah? Good for you, I guess. Get all the training you can in dealing with females." Next came one of those grown-up pronouncements as hazy as the blue nicotine cloud following him around this morning. "You'll need it."

Now that we had thoroughly gotten on each other's nerves, he turned back to contemplating the barroom. I couldn't sweep with him there stargazing like that, so I hinted heavily: "Aren't you going in the back and pay bills?"

"Right away," he said, showing no sign of going. Finishing his cigarette, he tossed it in a spittoon, then cocked a look at me different from any yet. "Tell you what. We need to do something else first. I'll help you at it. Get out the stepladder."

"What for?"

"It's time to shine the eyes."

Time to what? I goggled at him, then around at the ever-staring eyeballs of the stuffed heads. "Theirs?"

"Hell yes. We don't want the deecor going dim, do we?" He gazed up at the one-eyed buffalo over the front door as if it might nod in agreement. "Better get at it. I'll hold the ladder for you."

Feeling vaguely foolish, I fetched the stepladder. "Start with him." Pop still was in communion with the cyclopean bison. "Break you in easy."

"I've never, uh, shined eyes before that I know of. What do I use?"

"Tickle your brain a little," he advised. "Didn't some fancy writer say eyes are the windows of the soul?"

I went and got the Windex bottle and a rag.

While I climbed up and positioned myself beside the huge bearded head, Pop steadied the ladder and watched the procedure critically. The buffalo's single eye, like a sizable black marble, could use some help, I had to admit. However lifelike it may have looked when the taxidermist inserted it, over the years it had gone dull and cloudy from cigarette smoke and other tolls of midair life in a very active saloon. Rather tenderly I spritzed the bulge of glass and wiped with the tip of my finger wrapped in the rag until a gleam came up. It was uncanny, the feeling that grew in me as that dark eye brightened almost to life. In such a situation you know perfectly well the shaggy old beast has been dead for an eon, not to mention decapitated, yet there is the odd illusion that its gaze matches yours. The buffalo in fact had the advantage with that staring eye, and the other socket squinted closed in a shrewd, piratical way.

Curious about that, I wondered out loud: "What happened to the other eyeball?"

"It's somewhere in the back room."

"Really? It fell out, you mean?"

"Hell no," Pop answered offhandedly, "I had it taken out, long time ago. You'd be surprised how hard it is to find a taxidermist who'll do that. Professional ethics or something. I had to pack that head all over Great Falls before I found one who would agree to it."

I felt a little dizzy, not just from the altitude of the ladder. Wild! Wait until Zoe heard this!

"Okay, Pop, I'll bite. Why'd you have poor old bruiser here operated on like that?"

"Think about it," he said, as if telling me I had missed a speck of dust. "Isn't a customer gonna be more interested in a one-eyed buffalo than one with twenty-twenty vision? Maybe he'll get to speculating about where that eye went, like you just were, and order another drink while he's at it." He shrugged. "If the guy doesn't care how many eyes a buffalo has, we don't want the ess of a bee for a customer anyway."

I couldn't argue with any of that. Pop and I moved on from the twinkling buffalo to the elk, with the coyote and deer and bobcat and the others beadily waiting their turn, every eye in the joint starting to shine, mine included. Every little while I looked down at the lord and master of the Medicine Lodge, this father of mine with his bag of secrets, like chicken guts and one-eyed animal heads and who knew what else. Damn, he was difficult to ever stay mad at.

✢ 3 ✢

Was it that spirit of imagination, which seemed to cling to the Medicine Lodge like the smell of fresh bread to a bakery, that accounted for the next turn of events? Whatever was in the air, Zoe and I found our calling in life that heady summer of 1960, no small achievement for twelve-year-olds.

She's always claimed she was the one who spied the story in the *Weekly Gleaner* unfolded on Pop's desk, and I've always maintained I spotted it first. There is no argument whatsoever that we both reacted less than surely to that headline lying in invitation on the desk: SHAKESPEARE TO VISIT GROS VENTRE.

"You want to go?"

"I dunno. Do you?"

"I guess. If you do."

We went. Even if all the world's a stage, it still was something of a surprise that our own scanty public park in an elbow of English Creek qualified. Or at least a patch of grass there large enough to hold a dozen or so actors and actresses in full raiment. Drama students from the university in Missoula, they were spending the summer traveling around the state in a repainted school bus with THE BARD ON WHEELS on its side. The play, cleverly, was *As You Like It*, which let the troupe get away with any kind of outdoor setting; the creek-side cottonwood grove where the park sat served just fine as an eventual forest of exile. Zoe and I settled in a shady spot to spectate. The audience wasn't numerous, and pretty much predictable: high school teachers, library staff, some women's clubs, key members of the Chamber of Commerce that had put up sponsorship money, Bill Reinking from the newspaper, and even his wife, Cloyce, who generally held herself above civic doings.

The performance commenced with a herald stepping from behind the bus and announcing, "We begin our revels in the garden of Sir Oliver." A pair of actors strutted out, speaking in round tones, and the world changed for two twelve-year-olds.

Miracles sometimes come in disguise, and certainly this one came in costume, wearing pumpkin-style pants and puffy dresses long enough to step on and speaking a language such as we had never heard. *As You Like It* is wordy Shakespeare, if that's not redundant. Much of the ornamented dialogue was over our heads, although lines about copulation of cattle and laughing like a hyena were not. Yet we could catch the strangely wonderful melody of it, issuing out of the characters like spoken music. And things didn't drag along at an Alamo pace, everybody was always coming, going, thinking out loud to one another.

Zoe sat entranced, as did I, soaking up every gesture and straining to take in every curlicue of language as the student actors exclaimed "How now!" and snapped their fingers grandly to summon or dismiss one another. Under the phony beards, drawn-on mustaches, and lopsided wigs, the cast was miles too young for the parts they were playing, but in some strange way the obvious makeup made them all the more convincing. I am going to say it hit both of us at the same time, like forked lightning. The realization that living, breathing figures, with a sprinkling of greasepaint and a few ruffs of wardrobe, could not only imitate people of centuries before but could mimic life. Life with anything imagination could add onto it, even.

The disguised identities and all the costumes the Bard always had up his sleeve clinched it for us. Zoe's eyes shone as she watched Rosalind strut around bossily in men's clothes. I wanted to be Orlando, the suitor dressed to the hilt like a gentleman. Or possibly the chamois-shirted shepherd Silvius—I certainly knew a lot about sheepherders—driven hilariously cross-eyed by love for Phebe. Better yet, maybe, the fast-talking clown Touchstone in crazy, floppy rags.

"We will begin these rites," the rosy-cheeked actor with a scruff of beard that made him a duke proclaimed, forming up the dance after all the lovers finally got their identities sorted out, "as we do trust they'll end, in true delights."

Truer words were never orated. The play ended, but not our state of excitement as we left the park.

"So let's get this straight, he was proposing to her even though he didn't know it was her—"

"Sure, silly, because she was pretending to be a man—"

"—who he thought all the time was just rehearsing him—"

"—for when he proposed to her for real. Wild, huh?"

"Weren't they great at talking that stuff?"

"Wow, their tongues must be tired."

Hearing us at this, the Reinkings slowed down in front of us until we caught up with them. "Vox populi, I believe I hear," Bill addressed us gravely but with a glint behind his eyeglasses, "just what an overworked editor needs to fill space. So tell me, as patrons of the thespian art"—despite the jokey way of putting it, he appeared to be professionally curious—"what did you think of the play?"

"Swuft!" we cried simultaneously.

His mustache twitched. "I'll have to try to work that plaudit into my column."

"I've never heard of anything you couldn't, Bill," his wife twitted him puckishly, if that was the word, as Zoe and I fell in step with them. Cloyce Reinking was generally known around town for being as frosty as her silvery hair—the story was that she came from a family that made movies in the early days, and Gros Ventre was a longer way from Hollywood than a map could measure—but even she seemed to have liked *As You Like It*, although that didn't stop her from assuming the role of drama critic. She went over the finer points of the performance to her patiently listening husband while we drank it all in, until she came to Silvius, the cross-eyed shepherd, when she had to outright laugh in tribute. "The business with the eyes, wasn't he good at it, Bill? That goes back to Ben Turpin, before talkies. Remember? It's been years and years since I've seen anyone do that bit."

Those last three words went off with a bang in twelve-year-old minds. Instantly Zoe was looking at me, mouthing a silent *Ooh*, and I must have done the same. What a revelation, that when we did gangster talk or mimicked sheepherders, it wasn't just kid stuff of trying to be funny—we were doing bits! Performing little tricks of stage magic as old as Shakespeare, and we hadn't known it! Then and there, the two of us entered into the company of Groucho Marx wiggling his eyebrows like caterpillars and Bette Davis dropping the words "What a dump" like a stink bomb and the rest of history's glorious virtuosos of lasting gags. How those careers got started, we had no idea, but for us, we had just been given a license—learner's permits, of course—to dream up the performing mischief that went under the honorable old theatrical name of "shtick."

After the Reinkings turned at their street to go home, Zoe and I jabbered about the play and the performers' bits, as we now collegially knew them, all the way back downtown. Still in the spell, one of us finally dared to say it.

"We could be like them, I bet. Be actors, I mean. When we're a little older."

"Yeah. Wouldn't that be neat?"

"Traveling around that way—"

"Dressing up like that—"

"—getting paid for it and everything."

Out front of the Top Spot, Zoe sighed a gale at having to part with Shakespeare and me. "See you at supper."

Never let it be said of me that, at such an opportunity, I did not do my bit. Goofily I crossed my eyes, more or less, and gabbled, "How now?"

She stifled a giggle and snapped her fingers bossily. "Be gone!"

My mind going like an eggbeater, I cut through the alley to the rear of the Medicine Lodge. The back room seemed newly magical to me, the biggest costume trunk imaginable. I seemed to float up to the desk on the stair landing. Eagerly checking through the vent, I was in luck. The saloon was empty except for Pop, who was on the phone. "No, that's okay, I appreciate it, really. . . . Yeah, g'bye." As soon as he hung up, I raced down the stairs.

"Pop!"

Looking spooked, he whirled from where the phone silently sat.

"Guess what, I'm gonna be an actor!"

His brow cleared slightly, then clouded again. I knew I was not supposed to be in the barroom when the saloon was open and wouldn't have been, except for my uncontainable excitement, but he simply looked at a loss about how to deal with me. "Rusty, listen, kiddo—" He stopped, whatever he was about to say eclipsed by the gleeful shine on my face.

"Actor, hey?" he switched to, flicking his lighter a couple of times to start a cigarette. "Better drink an orange and tell me about it." Digging the bottle of pop out of the cooler and handing it to me, he studied me with a deep squint. "Like the shoot-'em-up guys in the movies?"

"No, in plays! Shakespeare and stuff!" As I rattled on about the performance in the park, he smoked and listened.

"That's really something," he provided when I finally ran down. He gazed at me a moment more, then started busying himself at the sink under the bar. "An actor has to memorize a lot, you know." I nodded nonchalantly; he himself said I had a memory that wouldn't quit. "And learn how to walk around without knocking over the scenery." That hadn't occurred to me in the acreage of the park. Still making conversation with his head down, he went on: "Slick work if you can get it, I suppose. Spend a couple of hours pretending to be somebody else and get paid for it. Not bad. Beats running a joint, I bet." He cleared his throat and looked up from the sink work. "Speaking of that, it's business hours and you better scoot into the back before some ess of a bee reports us." He made enough of a face to soften that, and I grinned my way out of the barroom, each of us drifting back to our clouds of thought.

I SPENT DAYS after that in that same stagestruck haze, sneaking off to a mirror every so often to practice crossing my eyes and other actorly expressions. I know Zoe was doing the same when we weren't prancing around the back room dressed up in rain slickers and cowboy hats and other costumes Shakespeare surely would have approved of if he'd had the chance.

Suppertimes at the Spot, we had to behave ourselves like civilized people, but that didn't stop us from whispering up a storm about what life as actors would be like, all the while secretly watching the cafe customers for bits to do later. The tourist couple from somewhere unimaginably South, for instance, who had to ask Zoe's mother three times whether there was a grudge in town where they could get their tar fixed before she figured out to direct them to a garage that fixed tires. Or the Double W hay hand, a little worse for wear from a prior stop at the Medicine Lodge, blearily holding the menu so close it appeared he was about to kiss it. Pickings were good and the two of us were gliding along in our amateur mischief until the mealtime when Bill Reinking came in, which was unusual in itself, and went straight to the counter to lean over and say something to Zoe's mom and they both headed into the kitchen to talk to Pete.

Watching, Zoe groaned in concern. "I hope my dad didn't stiff him on this week's ad." Aw, crud, was my own reaction to the kitchen conference; now my milk shake was going to be lumpy and my cheeseburger burned crisp as a shingle.

Directly, the gray-mustached editor emerged from the kitchen and startled us by coming in our direction, even though there were plenty of empty places to sit. "May I join you?"

"Help yourself," we blurted in chorus, both trying to think what we had possibly done to attract the attention of the Gros Ventre *Weekly Gleaner*. The saying was that a newspaper was the first draft of history, and the *Gleaner* week by week told the story of Two Medicine country to a remarkable degree. Far and wide, people read it to catch up on the doings of their neighbors across the distances of benchlands and prairie and mountain slopes, and for perspective on the world beyond. A life could be changed by those words in ink, because an article in the *Gleaner* meant that some set of ambiguous circumstances had been distilled by Bill Reinking or one of his rural correspondents into recorded fact, replete with those basic ingredients of truth, five *W*s and an *H*. Zoe and I then had only a beginning grasp of this, but we understood that a very important grown-up was pulling up a chair to our table for some reason.

"You're no doubt wondering why I called this meeting," our visitor joked seriously to start with. Taking off his glasses, he breathed on each lens and polished them with a paper napkin as he deliberated to us. "I've checked with the powers that be"—we understood that to mean Zoe's folks and evidently Pop—"to see if it's all right to offer the two of you a job."

Zoe with her Butte smarts asked first: "What kind of a job, and what would we get?"

"It's one well suited to junior thespians," Bill Reinking was saying gravely as he fitted the specs on one ear at a time. Zoe and I traded glances. Did that mean what we think it do?

Evidently so, as the *Gleaner* editor, who was said to be smart as a dictionary, now invoked Shakespeare. "The play's the thing, and all that. Cloyce"—catching himself, he cleared his throat significantly—"Mrs. Reinking, as you may or may not know, sometimes performs with the Prairie Players in Valier when the proper role comes up. There's one such now, and she needs someone to help her with her lines before rehearsals start. This has created a crisis."

Glancing around the cafe as if the three of us were conspirators, he lowered his head and looked at us over the tops of his glasses, confiding: "The crisis is, if you don't do it, I'll have to."

Naturally we were wild to, and the dab of pay he named for each session of thespianism or whatever it was didn't hurt.

"You've spared me." He smiled with relief and told us the curtain would go up, so to speak, at ten the next morning at their house. "If you want to stay on the good side of Mrs. Reinking"—he cleared his throat again—"be on time."

"HOW ARE WE doing?" Zoe asked anxiously.

I was carrying the pocket watch, complete with a Benevolent and Protective Order of the Moose tooth fob, that someone must have dug out of a father's or grandfather's trunk to hock and Pop had let me borrow from the back room for the occasion. It was raining torrents again and I had to wipe the watch crystal to read the time.

"Three minutes till. Slow up, there it is at the end of the block."

The Reinkings lived on the west side of town. Houses were nicer here, the ground a little higher, the view to the mountains more grand. Coming up the front walk to their big, generously windowed house at a robotic pace dictated by my sneaked looks at the watch, we arrived at the door at ten, straight up.

At our knock, it swung open to Cloyce Reinking, regal and bone-dry and eyeing the dripping pair of us as though wondering whether to mop us down before she let us in. I was wearing the rain slicker Lucille had cut down for me, although it was still voluminous, and Zoe looked aswim in more ways than one in the long gabardine coat her mother had foraged from somewhere.

"This weather," the rather forbidding woman in the doorway said, as if we had brought it with us. "Well, let's hang your wet things over the cat box, that's what I do with Bill's when he's been traipsing around, getting soaked in the name of higher journalism. Sheba can't complain too much." Maybe not, but the fluffy black Siamese or whatever it was meowed and scampered off when it saw the ominous cloud of clothing over its bathroom spot.

"That's done, come on in." Mrs. Reinking briskly led us to the living room, the kind with a rug that almost tickles your ankles and chairs too nice to sit in comfortably and pictures certainly not painted by Charlie Russell. I tried to take it all in without staring impolitely, while Zoe couldn't help making a little O with her mouth.

"Now, then," we were being addressed with a mild frown, "I suppose the Svengali I'm married to told you why you're required?"

We nodded in mute unison. Cloyce Reinking did not appear to lack requirements of any other sort in life. Tall and straight, with prominent features that on a man might have been horse-faced but looked distinguished on her, and natural frost in her perfectly kept hair, she seemed to us the living picture of a rich lady, although Pop had said that wasn't entirely so. "A little more money than most of us, maybe. She just wears it different."

"This may be foolish of us, of Bill and myself, I mean," she surprised us with. "All I said was something about not knowing what to do with myself in this awful weather, and he said he knew just what it took to change the climate, and rang up the director in Valier. And here we are. But I don't know." All of a sudden she was looking like she wished she had shooed us back out into the rain. "Today may be a waste of all our time. It's been so long since I was on a stage."

Zoe and I traded looks of dismay. This did not show signs of being long-term employment. I stammered, "We thought you acted with the Prairie Players all the time."

"Years and years ago, yes," she waved the past off. "*Arsenic and Old Lace. The Man Who Came to Dinner.* All the old warhorses that audiences find impossibly funny. Speaking of which," she said doubtfully, "we may as well give this a try."

Busying herself setting three straight-back chairs around a

coffee table as we stood there awkwardly, being no help, she asked over her shoulder: "Bill didn't say—have you both been in school plays and such?"

"Sure," I vouched for myself, "every Christmas. I'm always a shepherd because I have my own sheep hook."

"The innkeeper's wife every time," Zoe similarly reported her theatrical experience. "In Butte, the Catholic girls were always Mary."

"I see. Well, sadly enough, there are no Nativity scenes in this."

Sitting us down and then herself, she handed us each a play-book with a cover of that bubblegum color that boys at least called panty pink. Zoe clutched hers in both hands and studied the author's name.

"Oscar Wil-dee?"

"'Wild,' my dear."

I was trying to figure out the title, *The Importance of Being Earnest*. "Is that how that name is spelled?"

"You're getting ahead of the play," she cautioned me with a slight lift of her eyebrow. "Now, then, how to begin." She gave us a gaze that seemed to estimate our capacity for inspired non-sense, although little did she know. "I'll just read a straight run-through," she decided, putting on glasses, the newer horn-rim kind rather than her husband's type of wire frames, "until we reach the pertinent part. It'll give you some idea of the play."

It did, all right, although that was not the same as under-standing it. Some of the first act, such as the butler who didn't think it was polite to listen as his master fooled around on the piano, was funny enough, and some of it went right over us, cucumber sandwiches and high-toned exchanges about going to the country and so on. Regardless, while we followed along in the script Mrs. Reinking read all the parts, Algernon and Jack and the butler, in distinct voices, and Zoe and I shifted more and more uneasily in our chairs. If this woman could perform Oscar Wilde's witticisms all by herself, what did she need us for?

Then she reached the section with the lines "Ah! That must be Aunt Augusta. Only relatives, or creditors, ever ring in that Wagnerian manner" and our role, or roles, in this began to come clear.

"Now we get down to business," she said, fanning the script book in front of her a few times, as if clearing the air. With a tight-lipped smile she turned to me. "You are no longer Rusty, but Algernon, and occasionally Jack, also known as Ernest."

Zoe giggled.

"And you, child, are Gwendolen now and Cecily later." That sobered Zoe right up.

"And I," said our star performer, "am Lady Bracknell."

The part seemed to fit. Cloyce Reinking was famous for her New Year's Eve parties, where everyone who was anybody in the Two Medicine country showed up. We were never invited, Pop being busy with one of his most profitable nights of the year. Not that we would have been anyway, I suspected, mentally comparing the housekeeping here with our approximate sort. I figured Zoe's folks probably shouldn't hold their breath, either. Telling myself that was neither here nor there or in between, with a feeling of mild panic I scanned the swaths of fancy-pants talk Algernon and Jack/Ernest were responsible for, trying to figure out how to say it anywhere near right. Zoe's lips were moving uncertainly too as she encountered Gwendolen going on for half a page at a time.

Mrs. Reinking was paging ahead, marking her pieces of dialogue with a red pencil. "This ought to come back to me more than it is," she said with quite a sigh, in character or not, I couldn't tell. "I've played Lady Bracknell before, during the war."

Zoe began to ask "Which—?" before I shot her a warning glance.

"Nineteen forty-three doesn't seem that long ago"—the silver-haired woman probably no older than my father knitted her brow over some paragraph that took a lot of marking—"but I'm not as young as I was."

Why grown-ups always said that was beyond me. Zoe stated what seemed to us logical: "That's okay, neither are we."

"What?" Putting the pink playbook facedown on the coffee table, the lady of this house took off her glasses and twirled them in one hand while rubbing the bridge of her nose with the other. "I didn't have to wear these things then. They say the eyes are the first to go." She shut her eyes tiredly. "The gray cells aren't what they used to be, either."

It began to dawn on Zoe and me more fully why Bill Reinking had enlisted us, if his wife was going to approach this play as if it was the clap of doom.

"Well, that's why we're here," I sang out, Zoe bobbing her head like a bouncing ball to back up my bit of phony cheer.

"So you are." Straightening herself up, Mrs. Reinking turned back to the page where she had stopped reading aloud. "Let's take it from the start of this scene."

Shortly I was alternating back and forth between Algernon and Jack, telling Gwendolen she was smart and quite perfect, and Zoe was trilling back she hoped she was not that, it would leave no room for developments and she intended to develop in many directions. Then Lady Bracknell's part began in full gale force, with her recounting the call on a friend whose husband had recently died: "'I never saw a woman so altered; she looks quite twenty years younger.'"

The grand manner Mrs. Reinking put into this made the two

of us snort little laughs. Her lips twitched a bit. "Don't get carried away. I gave that line too much. Farce has to be played straight."

We sobered up, and went on feeding her lines that produced Lady Bracknell's wacky pronouncements. Most were reasonably funny, although by the time Jack told her he had lost both his parents and she responded that to lose one parent may be regarded as a misfortune, but to lose both looked like carelessness, Zoe and I were cutting glances at each other. If we were in over our heads, though, Cloyce Reinking showed no sign. At the end of act 1, she whipped off her glasses again. "That's enough stretching of the brain for one day," she said with a wintry smile apparently intended for herself. Zoe and I waited anxiously. She hesitated, seeing the look on our faces. "Well, we'll take it from the top again tomorrow and see whether my memory held up overnight."

"WHAT'S THIS play about, again?"

Pop lounged against the doorjamb, trying to fathom Oscar Wilde, which I had to admit was not easy. I sat up higher in bed and patiently explained that one character was using the phony name Ernest when in town and his real name of Jack in the country, and there was all other kinds of sleight-of-hand as to who was a guardian to whom and who was left as a baby in a handbag, but it all worked out in the end with Jack, now Ernest for good, free to ask for the hand of Gwendolen and Algernon entitled to woo Cecily, with Lady Bracknell presiding as loftily as imaginable.

"That's pretty deep for me," Pop said, then asked what he really wanted to know. "How'd you get along with Cloyce Reinking?"

"Good enough, I think." He caught my slight hesitation. "I mean, she's kind of hard on herself about gearing up to be Lady

Bracknell. She doesn't sound like she's sure she can do it any-more. And that seems to really bug her."

He considered that in silence, then shifted his weight on the doorjamb. "Let me tell you a little something about her so you don't get yourself in hot water, okay?" He ran his hand through his hair. "Don't repeat it, this is just some skinny between us."

That flustered me. "But Zoe's there with her just like me, too, and if there's gonna be any trouble—"

"All right, you can tell your partner in crime," he granted. He drew the kind of breath needed to begin the story. "Cloyce Reinking started off with all the advantages in life, see, down there in Hollywood. As I heard it, her folks made a pile of money in the movie business in the early days. But these things happen," he shrugged fatalistically, "she lost out on all that somehow and she ended up here, with Bill. You couldn't ask for a better human being than him, but she's, how would you say, never taken to the town the whole way. Some people are like that, they like a bigger pond to swim in. Get what I mean?"

"I think so."

"She's not my all-time favorite person"—he stuck his nose in the air indicatively—"and I doubt that she thinks any too highly of a run-down bartender. None of that matters. My guess is, getting up in front of an audience and being Lady What's-her-name means a lot to her. You don't want to mess that up for her, you wouldn't want that on your conscience, would you." I shook my head that I certainly wouldn't. He made himself clearer than clear. "So even if she has to gripe her way into it every inch of the way, just lay back in these rehearsals and give her some rope, right?"

"I will, honest. Zoe, too."

"Okay, that's that." He shoved off from the doorjamb and headed for his bedroom. "Don't let the ladybugs bite."

"Pop?" I called after him.

"Yeah, what now?"

"What's a Svengali?"

"It's a Swede who says 'Golly' a lot." His voice grew muffled as he went on down the hall. "Although you might check that against a dictionary."

"LET'S TAKE IT from the top again. There has to be a better approach to this."

We were in the third or fourth straight day of Cloyce Reinking despairing at doing Lady Bracknell theatrical justice. Practically ramming her glasses into the bridge of her nose, she faced down into the script and tried in a fluting voice:

"'I have always been of the opinion that a man who desires to get married should know everything or nothing. Which do you know?'"

The script said Jack should hesitate before answering, so I did. "'I know nothing, Lady Bracknell.'"

"'I am pleased to hear it. I do not approve of anything that tampers with natural ignorance.'"

Zoe patted her hands together in silent applause, but Mrs. Reinking wasn't having any. With a groan, she pulled off her glasses. "It would help," she was back to her own throaty tone, "if Oscar Wilde were less clever and more substantial." She eyed the script as if feeling sorry for it. "This is such a flimsy piece of work in the long run, isn't it," she reflected. "There's an old saying that there are only two stories that last and last. A mysterious stranger rides into town, and somebody goes on a big journey. There you have it, from *Shane* to *The Odyssey*."

Truthfully, that did seem to match up with the experience of two twelve-year-old drama critics, recalling John Wayne cantering into the Alamo and the entire cast of *As You Like It* transported in the turn of a phrase to the Forest of Arden. For that matter, Zoe's magical arrival was the story of my summer so far, and her parents' consequential migration from Butte to the Top Spot was hers.

"But it's funny." I felt I had to stick up for *The Importance of Being Earnest.* "Isn't it?"

"Very well, Rusty," Mrs. Reinking granted with a twitch of her lips, "it has its moments. I wish I had mine anymore." She snapped her fingers like a shot. "The time was when I could absorb a script like that and know by instinct how to play it. Now?" She shook her head in that way that made us afraid she was about to call it quits. Instead she just murmured, "Well, let's take a break."

Perhaps to make up for the play's lack of reward, this day she had fixed a pitcher of Kool-Aid of some strange flavor— persimmon, maybe—and set out a plate of tired macaroons. I went right at a couple of the cookies while Zoe took one for politeness and, after licking off a shred of coconut, put it aside.

With an eyebrow arched, Mrs. Reinking watched this. "Child, do you ever touch food?"

"Y-e-esss," Zoe said back. True as far as it went; I had seen her move it around on her plate like a card-trick artist. Mrs. Reinking was getting to know us, but she still had a lot to find out, such as how fast Zoe could change the subject. "Did you really live in Hollywood?"

"Of course," came the surprised answer. "Why?"

"What was it like?" Zoe said eagerly, and I followed up with, "Who was there?"

Cloyce Reinking shifted restlessly. "You really want to know, do you. All right, my parents were among the pioneers, you might say, in the film business. Movies were silents then, so at parties, there might be Charlie Chaplin and Mary Pickford and

Douglas Fairbanks, people of that sort." She twirled her glasses while thinking back to that time. "Everyone had mansions, including us—I sound like Lady Bracknell, don't I," she laughed slightly in spite of herself. "But it was true. I suppose"—she looked uneasily at us and our circumstances—"it made me a little spoiled. For instance, my parents let me use their roadster whenever I wanted when I was only a few years older than you." Zoe and I goggled at that. "Of course I couldn't drive in public quite yet," she went on, as if even the rich faced certain drawbacks, "but up and down our orange groves, I probably was a holy terror."

Plainly, living in Gros Ventre was small potatoes after that. But that's where we all were, and Zoe now brought matters back to earth.

"Boy oh boy, they sound like the best parents ever. Are they still around?"

The woman in the chair opposite us went rigid, as if she might not answer. But then: "They were killed in a car wreck. Right after Bill and I were married. We were young, still teenagers really, and the movie company fell into other hands." She made a gesture as if brushing all that away. "These things happen in real life."

"Wow," one of us said softly, it may have been me.

"Well," Mrs. Reinking stirred uncomfortably and picked up her script but didn't open it. "Back to *The Importance of Being Earnest*." The dubious expression had returned to her. "Or not." Abruptly she threw her glasses down on the coffee table. "Bill must be out of his mind, pushing me into this," she said angrily. Zoe and I traded apprehensive looks. "I'm sorry, children, but I really think we're not getting anywhere and had better give this up as a bad—"

We had talked this over and agreed it would be best coming from Zoe. "Mrs. Reinking?" she interrupted. "Before we start again," just as if we were going to. "Can you do that bit for us? The Ben somebody one you told us about after Shakespeare that day?"

She frowned, taking a minute to remember. "The crossed eyes? No, why should I fool around with that?"

I leapt in. "Don't you think it might be kind of funny if somebody as, uh, stuck-up as Lady Bracknell did that? Not all the time, but every once in a while?"

Drawing farther into her chair as if backing away from the suggestion, she looked askance at our eager faces. "Children, I don't think that's in my repertoire."

"Just try?" we pleaded.

With considerable reluctance she did, slowly directing her eyes as if trying to see the end of her nose. Her attempt was more wall-eyed than cross-eyed, but it altered her looks fantastically, pulling her strong features into a comical prune face.

Zoe and I grinned, giggled, outright laughed. "You should see yourself."

"You two." She shook her head, but looked around for a mirror. Getting up swiftly, she led us into the hall, interrupting the cat at its business in the box. "Scat, Sheba, that will have to wait." Posting herself at the mirror beside the hat rack, she drew herself up, took a breath to compose herself in the reflection, and said: "Give me a line, please."

Zoe recited in her Cecily voice: "'Mr. Moncrieff and I are engaged to be married, Lady Bracknell.'"

"'I do not know whether there is anything peculiarly exciting in the air of this part of Hertfordshire,'" even the dowager voice sounded better, "'but the number of engagements that go on seems to me considerably above the proper average that statistics have laid down for our guidance.'"

The three of us gazed into the mirror as she held the expression leading up to the finish of that. Her try at crossing her eyes at the climax of this did not actually yield dueling eyeballs, but it did produce a classic caricature of a snooty lady looking down her nose.

Letting her face relax, Mrs. Reinking nodded slowly to her reflection and the pair of us. "It has possibilities."

GIDDY WITH THE assured prospect of further rehearsals—"Ten sharp, remember," we had been reminded with a smile that was at once tart and sweet—Zoe and I practically sailed back downtown, talking a mile a minute. As we rounded the corner to the Medicine Lodge, however, I caught sight of something that made me tighten inside. Howie's bald head instead of Pop's dark one showing through the plate-glass window. Zoe was so busy chattering she didn't notice, and I managed not to say anything beyond our usual "Later, gator" as she sashayed off to her chores at the Spot.

Hurrying around to the back of the saloon, I checked across the alley. The Packard was parked where it always was, so at least Pop wasn't loading up for another trip. Yet.

I charged into the back room and there he was, idly rambling around the room to no clear purpose that I could tell, hands in his hip pockets, gandering at this and that like a museumgoer. "Hey, how'd it go today?" he greeted me, still looking around. "Did Cloyce Reinking need much help being theatrical?"

"What . . . what are you doing? Why's Howie here?"

"Just kind of looking things over," he said, gruff at having been caught at it. "Howie's handling a shift while I take a little inventory up here." He tapped his temple, circling the room some more. "Cripes, there's stuff tucked away here I'd forgot about."

I watched him, not knowing what to think. He looked the way

he had lately, as if there was a lot on his mind. Maybe the weather was getting to him. There hadn't been a chance to go fishing yet this crazy year. That was the least of it, though. Summoning my courage, I sneaked a look at the tarp. To my surprise, it didn't appear to have any surplus under it. Still, I asked suspiciously, "You're not gonna make a trip again already, are you?"

By now he was over at the shoe box of cigarette lighters, burying a played-out one to the bottom and trying out a shiny Ace in the Hole type. When it flamed on first try, he grunted and closed the lid, tapping the lighter in the palm of his hand contemplatively as he looked at me. "Naw, not right away, anyhow, you don't have to worry your hair off about that." He held his gaze on me. "Guess what. If and when I do, it'll be a short one, maybe a day." He made this sound casual, although it was anything but. "Down to the Falls, most likely."

Did I hear him right? Those trips that plagued me like nothing else, over and done with, in just that many words? My voice thick with hope, I made sure: "Not Canada anymore? Ever?"

"That's about the size of it," he said, resuming his inventory stroll again. "Tell me about the rehearsal."

IT WAS AMID this run of luck that I stepped out of the house one morning to the strangest sight: All over town, the cottonwoods were suddenly snowing, the fluffy seed filaments they were named for drifting down like the most tardy flakes of the thirty-year winter, and there, through the heart of this soft storm out of old wrinkled Igdrasil and fellow trees, a rainbow was glowing. I stopped, amazed, as if the mighty seasons of this year were colliding in front of my eyes. Glimmers of rainbows had not been uncommon after all the rains, but this was a true one, a hypnotic arch stretching from somewhere beyond the

Medicine Lodge and the other downtown buildings to the far hay fields of the creek valley. I watched, riveted, its full band of colors from red through yellow to violet phenomenally mixed with the snow-white fluff, until it gradually faded, and I think of that signal morning whenever I look back to that time now half a century ago, as if to the pigments of that many-hued year.

Still under the spell of that spectacle, I went on my way across the alley to the Medicine Lodge to await Zoe as usual, for our next session of being Ernest and Algernon and Cecily and so on. The beer truck with GREAT FALLS SELECT blazoned on its side in big red letters—and below, that immortal slogan *When you Select, it's a pleasure!*—was backed up to the rear door, as it was every week. The beer man Joe greeted me like an old comrade as he rattled a last case of empty bottles into the truck, while Pop was occupied in reading something that must have come with the usual invoice. I noticed that the more he read, the more his eyebrows climbed. Finally he could not contain himself: "No bee ess? This on the level, Joe? They chose this joint?"

The beer man laughed and thumped him on the back. "Says so right there in the letter, don't it? You've been an A-one customer all these years, Tom, it's only fair. Have a helluva good time in the Falls." Climbing into the truck, he gave us a beep of salute and pulled out, leaving Pop standing there reading over the piece of paper, looking as pleased as I'd ever seen him. I almost didn't want to interrupt the moment.

"Who's it from, Pop?"

"Some bigwig at the brewery, no less. Guess what, kiddo. The Medicine Lodge is the Select"—he drew it out into *Seee-lect*—"Pleasure Establishment of the Year. It beat out every other joint in the entire state. How about that, hey?"

"Wow! Is there a big prize?"

"Let me see here." He ran his thumb down the letter. "A

twenty-five-percent discount on next week's beer order—that's better than a kick in the pants, anyway—plus a tour of the brewery, an award luncheon, and guest seats in the company box at the Selectrics game this Sunday."

"Outstanding, Pop! Can I—"

"Don't sweat it, you're along. It says right here 'honoree and family.'"

"Can Zoe come with us?"

"What am I, an adoption agency?" That did not sound promising, but if I played my cards right, it might not be the last word, I sensed. Seeing my face fall and stay that way, he reconsidered. "Just the two of us"—he rubbed his jaw as if taking count—"I guess we are a little short on family. If her folks say it's okay, I don't see any overpowering reason why she can't come."

THE DAY DAWNED bright and clear, like stage lights turned high. Dressed to the teeth as Pop and I also were, Zoe sat in the middle in the car, because that's what females did in those days of front seats that held three people. The drive to Great Falls felt like a storybook journey, the polar crags of the Rockies beyond, the nearer fields so unbelievably green the color needed a new name, the creeks and rivers running high, wide, and handsome in a countryside usually starting to gasp for moisture this time of year. Pop declared he could not remember a summer quite like this, and Zoe and I could readily believe it. He was in an expansive mood as our route stepped us down from the altitude of the Two Medicine country, pointing out for my benefit a landmark square butte that Charlie Russell had painted any number of times, and for Zoe's, the sky-high smelter smokestack, visible from thirty miles away, where copper mined in Butte ended up. Never mind the Pyramids, the Alps, the topless towers of cities of legend, we had sufficient marvels to behold as the Buick gunboat sailed us along.

As the name implies, Great Falls has a river at its heart, the renowned Missouri, and the broad, powerful current was brimming almost into the bank-side brewery, as though the water could hardly wait to become beer, when we pulled up to the front of the big brick building. The brewery looked disappointingly like a factory, one from long ago at that. There could not have been anything more up to date, however, than the gigantic electrical sign up on the roof spelling out GREAT FALLS SELECT, with that vital last word blinking bright red every few seconds.

"This seems to be the place," Pop said with a straight face as we got out. While he bent down to adjust his bow tie in the reflection of the car window, Zoe and I gawked around. Both of us had trouble keeping our eyes off the hypnotic sign. Suddenly the thought hit Zoe: "Mr. Harry, is this the beer they call Shellac?"

"The exact same one, princess," he replied, straightening up to his full height, "although none of us are going to say that word again today from this minute on." He looked at her forcefully, then the same at me. "Got that?"

We bobbed our heads like monks in a vow of silence, but you know how difficult it is when you deliberately try to put something out of your mind. *Shellac, Shellac, Shellac,* the huge sign seemed to register in its every blink.

Checking his watch, Pop hustled us into the brewery. Waiting for us was a well-dressed man of large girth, who introduced himself as the vice president in charge of brewing operations. "I see to it the barley comes in and the beer goes out." He gave an encompassing sweep of his hand as if that explained everything.

Talking every step of the way, he led us off on the tour of the brewery. There was a bewildering variety of vats and boilers and other equipment strung throughout the building, with an army of workers reading gauges and adjusting dials and opening and closing valves and so on. The manufacture of beer, it turned out, was full of words that Zoe and I thought we knew but took on evidently far different meanings when spoken by the vice president, such as *malt* and *mash* and *hops*. It might not be everyone's idea of a prize outing, but trooping through the Select production maze behind our indefatigable tour guide was decidedly educational, I suspect even for Pop, although he kept nodding wisely and murmuring *mm hmm*, as if he knew all about how beer was made.

Naturally the brewery had an intoxicating aroma, a heady odor that seemed to go farther up the nostrils than other smells. While the vice president gabbed to Pop, with us trailing behind, Zoe could not resist crossing her eyes as if she was drunk, and I had to make myself not dissolve in giggles. I got back at her by whispering, "Don't look so shellacked." She puckered up at the forbidden word, and now we couldn't help it, both of us laughed through our noses as if sneezing.

Pausing in his discourse to Pop, the vice president turned and smiled indulgently at the sunny pair of us. "Cute children you have, Mr. Harry. What are they, twins but not the identical kind?"

Pop shook his head and gave the kind of wink that passes between men of sophistication. "Different mothers, if you know what I mean."

"Oho," said the vice president, not entirely as if he knew what that meant.

When at last we had been shown everything there was about beer making, our host leaned toward Pop as if confiding a business secret.

"Of course, we can brew our product until it runs out our ears, but we can't sell one drop without superb skill such as yours behind the bar. That's why we here at Select were so pleased to"—he chuckled—"select your establishment for this year's award."

Pop took this as imperturbably as a captain of industry. Nodding gravely to the activity in every precinct of the brewery, he responded: "I'm glad to see I've got your crew working Sundays to keep up."

"That's saying a mouthful!" the vice president acclaimed that. He thumped Pop on the back as Joe the beer man had done with the delivery of the award letter; I mentally tucked away the bit of behavior as the Great Falls Shellac—whoops, Select—salute. "Well, onward to the luncheon," our host exclaimed. "I'll meet you at the Buster." He smiled tolerantly at Zoe and me again. "I hope you brought your appetites with you."

LIKE THE BREWERY, the Sodbuster Hotel—so named in tribute to the grain-growing region that Great Falls was at the heart of—was a place Pop and I, and for that matter Zoe, might never have encountered in the ordinary course of our lives. Classy enough to invert itself into the Hotel Sodbuster in the terracotta name on its facade, it also made sure to boast GREAT FALLS' FINEST! in a banner over the front entrance. The marble lobby and overstuffed furnishings and potted greenery showed that it was not merely claiming that honor by default, and in those surroundings I'm afraid our threesome looked like just what we were, Sunday visitors who were in over our heads in a fancy hostelry. Not a thing in the brewery excursion had seemed to faze Pop, but he looked nervous about this.

A desk clerk a lot better dressed than we were coolly directed us to the banquet room. Pop halted outside the big oaken doors, though, and jerked his head for Zoe and me to follow him down

the hallway. "Anybody who has to take a leak, now's the time."
Zoe did not yet have the skill of blushing on cue, but she otherwise acted ladylike enough as she minced into the properly labeled
restroom while we went to the one marked GENTLEMEN.

The Hotel Sodbuster had restrooms deluxe. More of that
marble on the floor, and sinks that nearly snowblinded a person.
Even the places to pee gleamed, and, thinking of my dreaded
latrine duty at the Medicine Lodge, I wished out loud its facili-
ties were as nice as these.

"Sure," Pop muttered as we lined up side by side to do our
business, "just what the joint needs, a Taj Mahal toilet."

"Pop? Are you worried about something?"

"What do you think? It's an award ceremony, isn't it, so
they're going to expect me to get up and say something, aren't
they. And I'm no public speaker, am I."

"Can't you just say, 'Gee, thanks,' and sit right back down?"

"What kind of an ess of a bee wouldn't have any more manners than that?" He zipped up, and checked me over to make
sure I had done the same. "Okay, let's collect Zoe and go get this
over with."

Stepping into the gathering in the banquet room of the
Buster was like entering a forest of business suits, with a few of
the dignitaries' wives sprinkled in to coo down at Zoe and me.
The vice president from the brewery greeted Pop and ourselves
like old friends and led the trio of us around to be introduced.
The roomful was quite an assortment—the slickly dressed
mayor of Great Falls and sunburnt farmers from the barley
growers' association and up-and-comers of the local Chamber
of Commerce and burly beer distributors from all over the state;
names flew by us in bunches as Pop shook hands endlessly. With
his height and the silver streak in his hair, he stood out in the
crowd like a cockatoo, and I could tell he was uncomfortable

with the marathon of one-sided conversations people were making with him. This was one of those occasions where much was spoken, but very little was actually being said. Zoe and I were asked over and over how old we were. It was a relief when the vice president clattered a spoon against his beer glass and announced it was time to take our seats.

Thanks to Pop's eminence, ours were at the head table, and with a roomful of people in front of us to be spied on just by looking, Zoe and I now were in our glory. We sat watching, keen as magpies, as the grown-ups socialized variously. I was storing away the tongue-tied expression on the barley farmer who had ended up next to the mayor's wife when I heard a finger snap under the table, a signal either from the ghost of Shakespeare or Zoe.

Leaning toward her in response, I whispered, "How now?"

She giggled, but whispered back with concern: "Your dad looks awful serious. Isn't he having a good time?"

"He has to get up and make a speech of some kind."

"So? He doesn't have stage fright, does he?"

"He doesn't have a speech."

"Ooh, that's not good." She thought for a moment. "Maybe he can tell them it fell out of his pocket back at the brewery and went into one of those big vats, and so the next time they have a beer, they'll have a taste of what he meant to say."

"I don't think he'd go for that."

As if by radar, Pop turned from valiantly keeping up a conversation with the vice president and said under his breath, "Don't get carried away, you two." We obediently straightened up, mute as puppets.

Waiters in white jackets flocked into the room, and the food came. I studied my plate to learn what a banquet consisted of. Mashed potatoes, no surprise there. String beans, harmless enough. Roast beef, pink in the middle. Very pink. In Gros

Ventre, someone would have been sure to joke that they had seen critters worse off than this get well.

I had never met anything yet I couldn't eat, so I went right at my meat. Zoe, though, only tweaked hers with her fork.

Observing this, Pop told her out the side of his mouth, "Dig in, princess."

"It's not cooked," she whispered to him.

"It's rare, is all. Give it a try."

"I can't. The color turns my stomach."

"Better chew with your eyes closed, then. Come on, people are watching. Saw some off the edge and eat it."

"Do I have to?"

"Hell yes," he said, giving her a look. "It's good manners."

I knew that look, and braced for trouble. The last thing we needed in a roomful of important people was a contest of wills between my father and Zoe over a chunk of meat. But miracles do happen. Swallowing hard before the really hard swallowing, she cut a bite and ate it. Then another. I was amazed; in our suppers together in the cafe, I had seen her throw a fit over an undercooked pea.

Thus the banquet proceeded without warfare, and after sufficient beer had been served to the grown-ups, the vice president rapped his glass with a spoon again to draw everyone's attention.

He introduced the mayor, who said a few pleasantries and doubtless won some votes by promptly sitting down. The vice president got to his feet again and talked on for a while about the long and warm relationship between the brewery and establishments such as Pop's; I noticed the word *saloon* never crossed his lips, let alone *joint*. In conclusion, he said it gave him the greatest pleasure to present this year's award to "an owner and bartender known as one of a kind, Tom Harry, for an establishment which also has no equal, legendarily the first place of business in the town of Gros Ventre and still its leading one, the Medicine Lodge!"

At that, Pop had to stand up and receive a copper plaque that surprised him with its size and heft. As he wrestled it into security in his arms, Zoe and I craned for a look at the thing. Besides the fancy inscription, it was a representation of that scenery around Great Falls we'd seen on the drive in—the river valley, the Charlie Russell square butte, the mountain background—but where the smelter stack would have been, a gigantic Select beer bottle loomed over everything.

Pop studied the engraved scene for a few moments, then said as if thinking out loud: "I have a customer this bottle is about the right size for." That drew a laugh—Earl Zane would never know he had been his own best joke—and I felt relieved for Pop.

However, he looked not too sure about what he was going to say after that as he ever so gingerly deposited the award onto the table and faced the waiting audience. He ran a hand through his hair, as if trying to comb his thoughts into place. "Something like this comes as quite a surprise, although I guess it's a long time in the happening. Down through the years, I've sold oceans of Shel—"

"*Ooh!*" Zoe squealed in the nick of time, as if I had goosed her.

"Kids these days." Pop recovered hastily, giving her what amounted to a grateful frown. He cleared his throat and started again. "Like I was saying, I have sold oceans of *See*lect"—he all but buttered the word and handed it on a plate to the brewery vice president beside him—"down through the years. Years of beers, hey?" he said, as if just noticing the rhyme. Now he squinted as he followed one thought to the next. "My, ah, establishment, the Medicine Lodge, does go way back. I'm kind of getting like that myself." He shook his head as if thinking about the passage of time. "According to this nice piece of metal"—he tapped the plaque, making it ring—"all the days and nights behind the bar maybe do add up to something."

There, that did it up perfectly fine, I silently congratulated him. Proudly I waited for him to say "Thanks" and sit down.

Instead he said, "It reminds me of a story."

What? Since when? My father who would not tell the least tale about anything? The man who made an art of listening, not shooting the breeze? I wanted to disappear under the tablecloth. I just knew the banquet room would become a tomb as people grew bored. Zoe caught my stricken look.

I will say, he did the familiar man-walks-into-a-bar cadence as if it was second nature when he began: "A bartender whose time is up goes to heaven.

"Saint Peter is sitting there on a cloud with his gold-leaf book." Pop pantomimed the celestial gatekeeper. "'Hmm, hmm, remind me . . . what did you do in life that brings you to heaven?' The visitor scratches his head over that, he's a little embarrassed." Deliberately or not, Pop acted this out sufficiently. "'I'm a bartender,' the visitor finally comes right out with it, 'and I have to tell you, I'm surprised to be here.' 'You're right about that,' says Saint Peter, 'we haven't had one of your kind in quite some time.'"

That hit the funny bone of the brewery vice president, who started chuckling unstoppably. Encouraged, Pop squared himself up and continued, "'Come in, come in,' says Saint Pete. The bartender follows him through the golden gate, and there are all the angels, sitting up to a beautiful bar that's so long it goes out of sight off into the clouds. The spittoons are made of gold, and the bar grub in jars on the back shelf"—Pop sketched this with his hands rather longingly—"is caviar and hearts of beef. Everybody is having drinks, but this being heaven, no one gets out of hand."

A more general murmur of laughter around the room at that,

with Pop wagging his head about the comparative behavior of drinkers. He resumed: "'Come along and meet the Proprietor,' Saint Peter says now, and leads the bartender over to where the saints are sitting in the booths. One booth is bigger and grander than all the others, and he realizes it's the throne, and there's God Himself sitting there, bigger than life.

"'This is the bartender I was telling you about, Lord,' Saint Pete says by way of introduction.

"God's voice is the size of a thunderclap, of course. 'Welcome,'" Pop imitated to the best of his lung capacity. He did it again. "'Welcome. We've been waiting for you.'" I still rated it a miracle, but a lifetime across the bar from storytellers now paid off in his delivery of the ending: "God turns to the person sitting there in the booth at his right hand. 'Jesus, have this fellow show you a thing or two about wine.'"

As laughter swelled, led by that of the vice president, Pop modestly said, "Thanks," and sat down.

"THIS IS SO MUCH FUN. I could spend forever with you and Rusty."

"Don't get too carried away, princess." Pop himself was looking pleased with life, though, regally puffing on a cigarette as he navigated the Buick across the Missouri River bridge to the ballpark, the final installment of our honorific day. The vice president had given him a congratulatory smack on the back after his speech, if that's what it was, at the hotel, and said he would leave word at the ticket office for us to go right on in to the company's box and he'd meet us there. As Zoe chattered, I stayed mum, dreamily looking forward to seeing the Selectrics, those phantoms of the radio, play baseball, even the hazardous way they'd historically played it.

The instant we set foot into the grandstand I fell under the dazzling spell of the emerald-green outfield and the inset diamond of infield; I was an American male, after all. An usher materialized to escort us as if we were the most important people in the park, Zoe prancing in our lead. Watching her bound down the steps ahead of us, Pop shook his head, saying aside to me: "Isn't she a heller. How you holding up, kiddo?"

"Hunnerd percent."

He looked at me oddly. "Since when did you start talking like a sheepherder?"

There at the roped-off box, the vice president met us with a glad cry and we took our seats, almost in the third base coach's back pocket, only to hop right back up as the tinny public-address system played the national anthem. Then the Selectrics bounded onto the field, and the leadoff hitter for the other team, the Fargo Fargonauts, scuffed his way into the batter's box and it was unmistakably baseball, slower even than fishing.

Like me, Zoe had never been to a game before, and I could tell she was fiendishly finding bits to store away, such as the coach's signs to the batters, which had him touching himself in surprising places and tugging at his earlobes and nose as if keeping track of his sensory parts. I concentrated on what was happening on the field, which was instructive in a way, some of the Great Falls fielders proving to be about as athletic as the recess bunch of us playing horse.

Chatting away next to Zoe and me, Pop and the vice president shook their heads every so often at the local version of the national pastime. Surprisingly, however, Fargo did not manage to score, inning after inning, despite all the chances the Selectrics handed them.

Then, in the bottom of the fourth, the first Great Falls batter let a pitch hit him in the butt, the sharpest play of the day by the home team. ("Ouch!" Zoe let out a little mouse cry that drew her a look from Pop.) There followed what passed for a rally on a team of anemic hitters, the lineup scratching together a pair of runs out of the hit batsman and some walks and bloop singles. GREAT FALLS 2 VISITORS 0, the score flopped into place in the slots of the center field scoreboard, and hope sprang eternal that the Shellactrics, such losers on the radio, might actually reverse that in person.

Not for long. In the top of the fifth, errors produced base runners, a couple of Fargonauts hit three-run homers, and that was obviously that—another shellacking, to put it disloyally— although there were still four innings to go.

Zoe was starting to shift in her seat on a regular basis, and I confess I was losing interest in every ball and strike. The vice president noticed we were turning into wiggle worms.

"Say, how would you like to see a little of the game from the press box?" He checked with Pop. "If it's all right with you, I'll get the traveling secretary, he can show the kids a good time for a couple of innings." He chuckled meaningfully. "We can have some of our product to keep us company."

Pop eyed the pair of us squirming hopefully, and with only the slightest fatherly hesitation okayed the proposition, and the vice president shepherded us through the grandstand all the way up to the press box, then went off to find the traveling secretary.

This was more like it, Zoe and I agreed without having to say so, luxuriating in our lofty new seats. The press box was like a long, low shed hanging from the grandstand roof. At the far end was the glassed-in radio booth, where the sportscaster could be seen gamely trying to milk excitement from the proceedings on the field. Also at that end of the booth from us, a few sportswriters were occasionally pecking at typewriters, but mostly talking among themselves in bored tones. Which left the two of us in splendid isolation to take in everything now below us, the pool-table green of the ball field, the players in harmless miniature, the beer vendors going through the stands shouting, "Seee-*lect*," the Sunday crowd a universe of details we could peer right down onto, even the bald spots on men and women's hair roots under bleach jobs. We grinned at each other, smug as spies atop the Empire State Building.

"Rusty, what if"—how something like this is possible I still can't explain, but I swear I knew Zoe's mind was about to go in some direction not on any compass—"a person couldn't see any of this?"

My heart beat faster. "You mean do a blind bit?"

"I bet all I'd have to do is—"

"Hi there, I'm Irv," fate announced itself to us in a cheery voice. "Glad to have you as guests of the Great Falls Selectrics."

The traveling secretary was a chubby young man with the hearty attitude that so often substitutes for genuine ability; if I didn't miss my guess, he was the son or nephew of someone in the team's management. Smiling broadly, he asked what our names were, how old we were, where we were from, right down the list. We answered by rote, Zoe giving him an unblinking gaze throughout this, until he confidently wanted to know if we were having a good time.

This caused her to stare, still as blank as a fish, toward the ball field and sigh heavily. "I suppose so."

Irv's heartiness diminished somewhat. "What's wrong?" he asked me.

"Nothing. She's blind, is all."

"Oops. I wasn't told that."

The crack of a bat and the groan of the crowd interrupted things. Zoe did a good job of gaping vacantly at the sky. "What was that? Lightning?"

"Don't be afraid, sis," I provided in my best phony-faithful manner, "it was only Fargo hitting another home run."

"Ooh, I wish I could see one of those just once."

By now Irv was glancing around nervously at the circumstances of the press box, where a person could fall out and a foul ball could fly in. "Your folks don't mind if you're up here by yourselves?"

"It's just our dad with us, and he's busy with the brewery man." I took the opportunity for a fantasy of my own. "Mom"—Zoe perked up her ears at that unexpected word from me—"is home, tending bar."

"She is? I mean, well, your family is really dedicated to selling beer, isn't it."

"The Select Pleasure Establishment of the Year," Zoe recited. "When our dad read those words to me, I cried, I was so happy." She sniffled a little at the memory of it.

"Well, ah . . ." Irv cast around for anything to head off tears. "Would you like a hot dog?"

A swift intake of breath by Zoe. "I've heard of those! I'd love to taste one just once."

"You haven't ever—?" Irv looked at me. I meekly shook my head.

"We'll fix that, right now. Sit tight, don't move." He bounded out of the press box to hunt up a vendor.

Zoe blinked about twenty times and rubbed her eyes. "Whew. All that staring is hard."

"But it's working! Anybody would think you're blind as a bat."

"If my eyeballs fall out of my head from this, I will be."

"*Shh.* Here he comes."

Irv came hustling back bearing hot dogs. Mine he handed me without trouble, but Zoe's he couldn't decide what to do with as she sat there staring into space. "Let me," I said tenderly, lifting her hand into midair like a marionette's and then depositing the hot dog into it.

"Mmm. *Mmm.*" Actually munching away at the roll and wiener, she was really giving this her all. Talking with her mouth full, she wondered, "You're the traveling secretary. Do you go all around the world?"

Irv laughed, although not much. "Only to Canada, actually. Saskatoon and Medicine Hat." I knew those were the towns, not far over the border, of the Saskwatches and the Toppers, two more teams that habitually trounced the Selectrics.

"I bet it's nice," Zoe said dreamily, "flying everywhere, stewardesses bringing you pillows and stuff to eat."

"Actually, we go everyplace on the team bus," came the uncomfortable admission.

"Mister Irv?" She dabbed at some mustard on her chin and deliberately missed, which I thought was overdoing it somewhat. "I was too embarrassed to ask around the brewery man— but what are they doing out there? I mean the baseball players. It sounds like one side throws the ball for a while, trying to hit the other side, then the other side gets to throw the ball at them. Doesn't it hurt, all that getting hit with the ball?" She gave me an apologetic stare. "My brother tried to explain the game to me, but he has trouble figuring it out, too."

More perplexed than ever, Irv asked me: "You haven't even heard baseball on the radio?"

"There's a lot of static where we live."

He turned back to Zoe and her big blank eyes. "Well, see . . . oops, I mean, if you can visualize," he pursed up with the effort of this, "the field is made up of the infield and the outfield, and there are nine players on the field—"

"Lined up, but not very straight, I bet," Zoe put in knowledgeably. "I heard somebody say the Selectrics don't have a very good lineup."

"That's . . ." Irv stopped to regroup. "That's actually not what a lineup means. The players are more like . . . scattered around," he summarized as if just noticing this. He was spared further attempt at description by another crack of the bat and one more muted groan from the crowd.

"What was that?" Zoe asked excitedly. "Another home run for the Fargoes?"

I deferred to Irv to see what would happen. "A ground ball to the shortstop," he reported for her benefit.

"Isn't it mean to call him that?" she scolded. "How short is he?"

"What? No, he's only called that because the position he plays is between second base and third, it's, ah, a shorter space than the other infielders cover."

"That doesn't sound fair to the other players. Do they get to take turns at being shortspot?"

"Short*stop*, as in he *stops* the ball from getting through the infield—"

"Aren't they all supposed to? Rusty." She pouted as if betrayed. "You told me the players run all over the place after the ball, but now it sounds like there's only one in charge of stopping it."

"It's a funny game," I said.

Searching around for help, Irv had a sudden inspiration. "You know what," he confided to me, man to man, as though Zoe were deaf as well as sightless, "this is a terrific human-interest story, your sister at her first ball game. I'll get the *Trib* writer over here and—"

"NO!"

My outcry set him back on his heels. "No, please don't," I rattled out desperately while Zoe sat frozen, "our dad feels too awful about her being blind. It would ruin his day." Ruin a pair of smart-aleck twelve-year-olds along with it, for sure. I could already hear, drumming in my head, Pop's everlasting admonition: *Don't put beans up your nose.* And from her paralyzed look, Zoe knew as well as I did we had gotten ourselves into a noseful of trouble. What were we thinking—what was *I* thinking—in pulling a stunt like this, today of all days?

"Well, gee," Irv stood on one foot and then the other, "I sure don't want to upset anyone. It's a shame to pass up such good publicity, though. Why don't I go and try to talk your dad into—"

Just then a Selectrics batter was called out on strikes, ending the inning. A leather-lunged fan below the press box hollered: "That was ball four if there ever was one! You're blind, ump!"

"Ooh!" Zoe came to life and clapped her hands. "They hire blind people in baseball? That's so kind of them."

While she furnished that distraction, I wildly tried to think of how to get Irv to evaporate. It would take a miracle and I couldn't think how to produce one.

"Could you get me a job here"—Zoe was improvising like a trouper but she couldn't keep it up forever—"when I grow up? As a—what is it, umper?"

"Ah, chances aren't good," Irv equivocated. "See, I mean, you can imagine that to be an umpire you have to be able to—"

All of a sudden, as if the entire stadium of people had decided to give up on the Selectrics and go home, people in the grandstand below us and out in the bleachers were getting to their feet, but only standing and rubbing their tired behinds and working various kinks out, and I realized we were saved.

"Sis, remember? It's the seventh-inning stretch—"

"All right." Staying in her seat, Zoe stretched her neck like a languid swan, although telepathy told me she was as ready to bolt as I was.

"—and we're supposed to go back down to where the brewery man and Dad are, aren't we. Let's hurry."

"I'd better go with you," Irv prepared to spring into action. "Miss, if you could manage to take my arm and we'll—"

"That's okay, I'll lead her, I do it all the time at home," I babbled, and beat him to Zoe's side by a whisker.

"My seeing eye," she said fondly. I made a big show of helping her out of her seat and she made one of clinging to me to be guided. "Oh, Mr. Irv? Thanks for the hot dog," she called over her shoulder to him as he peered after us in concern, while I steered her urgently out of the press box and down the stairs.

"Is he still watching us?" Zoe moaned as we reached the grandstand aisle. "My eyes are getting really tired."

"Hang in there, we've almost got it made," I said out of the side of my mouth. With everyone still standing around and stretching, we were able to slip into the crowd in the aisle and become our normal selves, more or less, as we neared the guest box.

"Was that great or what?"

"You were fantastic!"

"No, you were!"

"Actors get paid for that! Can you believe it?"

We were welcomed like the long-lost by the vice president and Pop as we clambered into seats on the far side of them, away from prying eyes in the press box. Feeling the effects of the bottles of Select, Pop sat back like king for the day, turned to Zoe and me, and grandly asked: "How was it up there? Could you see good?"

"The whole bit," we chorused.

THE JOURNEY HOME, in my memory, capped the day perfectly, Pop driving and smoking in contentment, Zoe smiling as she dozed between us, while a sunset that would have made Charlie Russell grab for his paints drew down over the mountains and prairie. When the car cruised into Gros Ventre with the darkened trees over the town like a canopy of night and the lights softly on in the houses beneath, Pop roused Zoe with a gentle "Hey, princess" as we pulled up to the cafe. Sleepily she got out and thanked him for the day and yawned us a good-night. But before I could close the car door, she whirled like a dancer and whispered as if giving me full credit, "Your dad is wild!"

THE PLAQUE PROUDLY went into place in the barroom below the buffalo head, where no customer entering the Medicine Lodge could possibly miss it, and on the other side of the wall Zoe and I eagerly resumed our routines after the triumphant Great Falls trip. Rehearsing Cloyce Reinking into cross-eyed high-toned perfection in her role, doing ballpark bits to each other like old vaudevillians reciting beloved punch lines, rooting around in the treasures of the back room, listening hungrily at the vent for fresh lingo from the loosened tongues of Pop's clientele, life at the moment was just right for the two of us, the midsummer air fairly bubbling with laughing gas, every minute together promising fresh intoxication of our imaginations. Could I have told even then that, like the thirty-year winter, this was a summer all others would have to be measured against? Everything in me says so.

A week spilled past, and in practically a blink, here was Sunday again and I was up so early and so full of life that I trotted across to fetch the Great Falls *Tribune* from the front doorway of the Medicine Lodge to read the comics and sports sections while waiting for Pop to get up and fix breakfast. Walking back, I idly thumbed the brown wrapper off the hefty Sunday paper.

FARGONAUTS FLEECE SELECTRICS 11–3, not a surprise. But the photo near the top of the front page surely was.

"Pop!" I tore into the house and up the stairs to his bedroom. "You're in the paper!"

"Hmpf?" He struggled upright in bed, rubbing sleep from his eyes as I waved the newspaper at him. "Let me see that."

The newspaper picture did him justice, the merciless way a camera does, highlighting the lines in his face, the furrows of his forehead, the stripe in his hair that looked even more startling in black-and-white. He looked more than ever like the etched visage of the Depression generation, the survivor with those past hard times written in his face. The photographer at the Sodbuster Hotel award luncheon had caught him cradling the plaque the awkward way a new father holds a baby. Squinting at his likeness as if it hurt his eyes, Pop tried to yawn himself more fully awake. "It took the Shellackers a week to get a mug shot like that in, hey?"

"No, there's more!" I flipped the newspaper for him to the story beneath the front-page fold.

Still bleary and hunched in his undershirt, he spread the *Tribune* on the bedcovers, with me reading along with him over his shoulder.

THE MAN BEHIND THE BAR

Beneath that headline was Bill Reinking's account of the Medicine Lodge and its one-of-a-kind bartender.

> If you bottled Tom Harry, bartender of possibly the oldest continuous pleasure dispensary in Montana and surely the most engaging, you would have the hundred-proof pure stuff of legend.

His Medicine Lodge saloon, the comfortable old gathering place on the main street of Gros Ventre, has been in operation since territorial days, and Tom Harry has been in business long enough to qualify as a historic landmark himself. Recently the brewers of Great Falls Select beer honored his beloved joint as the Select Pleasure Establishment of the Year, and all that needs to be said further about that is, what took so long?

His barroom has the look and feel of that vacation lodge you have always dreamed of finding, one small surviving corner of an earlier time but absolutely professionally up-to-the-minute in service. The man behind the bar looks almost too much like a bartender—bow tie, pompadour, lived-in face—to be real, but then he seemingly only glances in your direction and here's that drink you had in mind. You'd like to talk? He'll listen hard enough to turn you inside out, if you want. You prefer to sip in silence? Not another word is heard.

Tom Harry makes it all look easy—and does so while finding time to be father to a bright twelve-year-old son, Russell—but presiding over the clientele that unerringly finds its way into this western outpost of civility in a parched land is no small task. Behind the bar on a busy Saturday night, he is Clyde Beatty in the lion cage. Mandrake the Magician doing the pouring. Lamont Cranston using his wizardry judiciously.

"Who the hell is Lamont Cranston?"
"He's the Shadow, on the radio," I was an authority on that, all

those Phoenix afternoons of cringing on the carpet to listen to serials finally paying off. "He has the power to cloud men's minds."

There was more, much more, in the newspaper piece, but I had to force myself to concentrate, my head swelling fast. Bright! I'd been called that right there in the newspaper. Pop was wide awake now. He broke off reading long enough to snatch his cigarette pack off the nightstand and light up with a big puff. "Bill poured it on thick," he muttered, "whatever got into him."

"Yeah, wow, Pop, you're really famous!"

"Don't go overboard. Famous around here isn't so famous."

"No, see what it says?" Beneath Bill Reinking's byline, in smaller print, was the wording NORTH AMERICAN PRESS FEATURE SYNDICATE. "North America is a lot to be famous in, right?"

"Cripes." I couldn't tell from Pop's exhalation whether he was pleased or not to be continentally famous.

We read to the bottom of the newspaper piece.

Tom Harry's decades as the ideal bartender have carried forward the historical standing of the Medicine Lodge as an institution in its special corner of the world. The cavalcade of customers has gone from homesteaders and cowboys and sheepherders to tourists and businessmen and missile warriors, but the presence behind the bar has stayed steady as the mountains of the Two Medicine country.

On a recent Saturday night, with the joint full and rollicking, this bartender of the ages found time to listen to some fisherman's lie he had heard so many times before, his towel restless on the polished bar but the rest of him keen and still, until the punch line came and all that was left was for him to cock an eyebrow and chip in his own:

"Sure gonna miss you when I'm gone."

Customers of the Medicine Lodge hope that will not happen for a long, long time.

"Cripes" again, from pop as we read that ending. I was open-mouthed.

"Did you really say that to somebody?"

"I must have. Bill Reinking is an honest ess of a bee in what he writes."

"What did you mean about being gone?" The phrase brought a chill around my heart.

"Hey, don't get constipated about it." He mashed out his cigarette in the ashtray next to the bed, trying to think. "It's a what do you call it," he mumbled, "figure of speech. Somebody I used to know said it all the time. She was always saying something." He caught himself. "I don't know why it popped into my head."

She?

Pop returned to the newspaper photo, wishing he'd gotten a haircut before the awards luncheon so he didn't look like a beatnik. I scarcely heard, my mind so taken up with "miss you when I'm gone" and the phantom who said it all the time. Who else could she be but my mother? A dozen years ago when they were splitting the blanket—and me into half orphanhood—how had she spoken it then to him? With the snap of drama, fit for Shakespeare's ear if the Bard were still around? Or did it come out plain and bitter, good riddance to him and his booze business and everything that came with it, including an accidental kid? And *gone*, the question that hung off that. Did it admit a longing that she knew she could not entirely escape by pulling out on us, as Pop put it? Or did it mean the opposite, we'd never be missed as long as she lived? And if she saw the newspaper story, wherever she was, what would she think now? A Jones among the world full of names, how must she have felt at seeing our distinctive ones reappear like ghosts from another life?

During my daze, Pop had absently lit another cigarette while he frowned down at the newsprint, the bartender for the ages smoking in bed. Still shaking his head, he sighed acceptance.

"What the hell, maybe it'll be good for business. How about we celebrate being famous by going fishing?"

IN NO TIME, the article was not just good for business, it was wildly so. There was such a flood of tourists stopping in to experience the historic saloon and its fabled bartender, besides the Two Medicine country proudly paying its respects by ordering up round after round, that Howie had to be summoned to help Pop behind the bar for hours on end. One particular brand of beer sold at a fantastic rate, as customer after customer—"even the Schlitz yayhoos," Pop had marveled to me in one of our bedtime conversations—ordered up a Shellac in tribute to the towering bottle on the plaque. Earl Zane got so carried away, he hocked his Calgary Stampede belt buckle for a week's worth of beer credit.

During all this, Zoe could not get enough of the vent's events, nor could I, once I somewhat got over the mystery of that utterance of Pop's that now existed in every newspaper under the sun. It was as intoxicating a time for the pair of us as for anyone bellied up to the bar, what with mornings of Cloyce Reinking steadily perfecting Lady Bracknell bit by bit and then the dialogues of the Medicine Lodge awaiting us the minute we climbed to the familiar comforts of the landing. Grinning widely at each other, we silently cheered Bill Reinking to the skies the first time he came in after the momentous newspaper story, although

Pop folded his arms instead of producing a shot of scotch, water on the side.

"How come you couldn't have warned me I was gonna be plastered on front pages everydamnwhere?"

Old friend looked at old friend across the expanse of that question.

"Alas, Tom, I didn't find out in time the story for the *Trib* was being picked up by the syndicate. I haven't had that happen for a while. You make good copy, as we knights of the press say."

"Yeah, well, maybe. But did you have to make that last line sound like something at a funeral?"

"A story can have more than one ending, you hear enough of them in here to know that," the newspaperman said mildly. "It's a question of what fits best with the rest of the tale, isn't it."

Through the vent slats, Zoe and I memorized their expressions, the hopeful smile lifting the gray mustache of the old customer and the deep frown creasing the face behind the bar, like the two masks of drama. We could hear the tick of the clock behind Pop. Then a shot glass and water on the side appeared like magic. "It's on the house today."

"Swuft," Zoe breathed, and my heart danced in agreement.

That set of days passed like a parade, and before Pop's fame showed any sign of wearing off, Saturday dawned and it was time for me to swamp out the barroom as usual.

This particular morning, I didn't mind even the snottiest of chores quite as much. After proudly dusting the plaque on the wall, first thing, I emptied spittoons and swept and mopped and all else, while Pop seemed wrapped up in his own thoughts, doing little things behind the bar. A couple of times I noticed him checking the cash register, as though making sure the money piling up in the till wasn't a mirage.

Busy dreaming up the next bit to do with Zoe, I wasn't paying any special attention when he picked up a towel and began polishing the bar as always, but this time in a single long, slow lick from one end to the other. When he reached the end nearest to where I was doing swift justice to the floor with my mop, he called over to me.

"Got something to tell you."

He took a longer look than usual around the saloon, from corner to corner, and I expected to be told I'd missed a spot in my mopping. Instead, he said, "I've made up my mind I might as well sell the joint."

The barroom floor seemed to give way under me. I stared at him as if he had declared he might as well drown himself in the creek.

Like wrong pieces of a puzzle, the words refused to fit together sensibly in my mind. Sell? The joint? *You can't!* Out loud, the best I could do amounted to, "But, but . . . why?"

"All kinds of reasons." He had that shrugging look, and I was afraid he was going to be as impenetrable on this as about those trips of his. I was wrong.

He started to say something, then didn't. The lines in his face deepened as he searched for where to start.

"Seeing you in here like this set me to thinking," he began in a strained voice.

Me? Now I was horrified as well as shocked. By taking on the job of swamper, I caused us to lose the Medicine Lodge? I was the pebble that started this avalanche?

He was fumbling out something about how damn hard a decision like this was, which barely registered through my daze. Finally he simply shook his head. "Rusty, I don't want you to end up running the joint."

"I'm gonna be an actor, remember?"

"Kiddo, listen." His blue eyes softened as he looked into mine. "Things don't always work out the way they're supposed to."

He saw that didn't help at all, and tried again.

"I mean, sure, let's say you're gonna be an actor and set the world on fire. But first you've got to grow up, right? And that's years down the line from now, isn't it. I . . . I don't want it on my conscience that you might have to shoulder more than you already do around here." He employed the towel on an already spotless corner of the bar so as not to look at me. "You know as well as I do what it takes to operate the joint. You have to be a working fool, your time is never your own, it adds up on a person after a while."

Now he did shrug, as if what he was going to say next was merely the tag end of that, although it was anything but. "I'm getting middle aged, you know. In the middle of getting too damn aged." Seeing my doubting expression, he sighed. "Hey, maybe you don't notice it, but I do. The body doesn't lie." He patted his stomach regretfully. "My belly's coming over my belt more all the time. When you can't see down to your business end, you know you're starting to hit trouble."

Ordinarily I would have appreciated such man-to-man talk. This was no ordinary time. I absolutely did not want to have to think of him as too damn aged. So what if his middle was sagging, and his widow's peak was more pronounced than it used to be, and his forehead had a ladder of wrinkles now when he lifted his eyebrows? And that he hadn't been able to dodge a sheepherder's stupid elbow, something I continually told myself couldn't happen again in a hundred years? The sky color of his eyes hadn't dimmed any and his pouring hand was as steady as ever and his hearing was still keen as could be. Yes, he worked himself practically to the bone in the saloon and there were always so many bills to be paid and there had been those spooky Canada trips to help out on the money end, but none of that counted as much as my alarm at the thought of him as old, too old, to be the best bartender who ever lived, too old to possess the Medicine Lodge and its back room, too old to be the father who was half my life.

He leaned back against the breakfront, his arms firmly crossed, Franklin Delano Roosevelt at his shoulder as if backing him up about the vicissitudes of life. "Listen, Rusty, the hours, day and night in here"—he glanced almost apologetically to the gleaming bar as he spoke of this—"are starting to get to me. Been that way since the start of the year."

I argued with all my might that he could hire help behind the bar. Good help was devilishly hard to find, he argued back. Besides, he threw at me, what better time to sell than when the Medicine Lodge had been chosen the select joint in all of Montana? The Medicine Lodge, I came right back at him, was always that, anyway, whether or not there was a plaque on the wall, so why be in a rush to sell it? We went around and around like that, getting nowhere, until another awful disturbance caught up with me.

"The house, too?"

That brought him up short. The mate to the Medicine Lodge, the way we had lived these whole six years, back and forth across the alley with the spreading bower of Igdrasil sheltering our universe. "It's always gone with the joint," he said cautiously, "that was the deal when I bought the business." He must have seen me sag toward my shoe tops. "Don't get in a sweat. We'll see, we could maybe hang on to the house. For now, anyhow."

"For now?" I stared the question at him: What did that mean?

"Let's don't worry about the house for now, is all I meant." That seemed to me awfully thin reassurance. "We've got the joint to deal with, that's why I had to lay it on you like this."

The idea of life without the Medicine Lodge still stunned

me, but there was something even more daunting to imagine beyond that. Pop without the Medicine Lodge in his daily life. The human race's preeminent bartender without a bar to tend. Past the lump in my throat, I asked, "Wh-what will you do?"

"Oh, take life easy, I guess." Which did not sound convincing, even to him. He rubbed the sleek wood of the breakfront a few moments. "Who knows, whoever buys the joint might need somebody to fill in now and then."

This nightmare kept getting worse. My father's plan for the rest of his life was to turn into Howie?

"Pop, that's crazy," I all but bawled, "you say you're gonna sell the joint so you don't have to bartend anymore, and then you turn right around and—"

"Hey, excuse me all to hell for thinking out loud." He held up his hands to stop my torrent. "We'll come up with something." He attempted a smile that didn't quite take. "Maybe I'll quit smoking—that'd keep me occupied, right?" Seeing that didn't convince me of his sanity, he tried again. "Go fishing whenever we want. Maybe we'll take up fly-fishing."

By now I was looking at him totally slack-jawed.

"Okay, okay, I don't just know yet what we'll do. One headache at a time." He ran a hand through his hair, as if he could feel the streak of silver against the black. "Rusty, what I do know is time catches up with a person, and I'm trying to stay ahead of it a little." Gazing around one more time from the long, dark bar to the bright-eyed creatures on the wall to the dazzling bottles of the breakfront, he shook his head again. "Nothing lasts forever."

THE NEWS THAT Tom Harry was putting the Medicine Lodge up for sale brought on lamentations of practically biblical dimensions.

"Aw, hell, Tom, what do you want to do a terrible thing like that for?" ran the general howl of complaint, usually expressed much more profanely than that, as customers from one end of the Two Medicine country to the other dropped in to pay tribute to the saloon they had always known. Bill Reinking smiled sadly and called it the end of an era. Velma Simms asked Pop if he had lost his mind. The sheepherders were stricken, faced with a future in which they might have to hang out in a merciless dump like the Pastime. Even the flyboys were disturbed, grousing that the only good thing about their hole-in-the-ground duty was being up-ended.

And Cloyce Reinking, in one of our last script run-throughs before she went on to dress rehearsals with the Prairie Players, departed from Lady Bracknell enough to let me know: "This town will be a poorer place without your father there in his spot."

Listening at the vent after the news got around, I could tell the remarks were getting on Pop's nerves. The first few days, he would make some vague reply whenever someone asked what he was going to do with the rest of his life, but after that, his standard answer was, "Retire from the human race."

Zoe was as downcast as I was. She understood all too well what a change in the Medicine Lodge meant for us.

"It's funny," she said with a long lip, "your dad doesn't want you in his business and mine can't wait to put me to waitressing in the dumb cafe."

"Yeah. That's grown-ups for you. By the time we ever figure them out," I despaired, "we'll be them."

"Won't either," she said crossly. "We've got our heads screwed on different than that."

I had to hope so, did I ever. For there was one implication in Pop's decision that possibly was worst of all, that I couldn't bring myself to tell even Zoe about. That "for now" of his about at least keeping the house held a tremor I could feel in the distance, however near or far. It didn't take any too much imagination to conjure Pop one day saying, as people in our part of the country did when their bones started aching some particular way, "You know what, we maybe ought to consider someplace warm. These winters are getting to be too much." Someplace warm spelled only one thing to me, Arizona. Worse, Phoenix. The vicinity of Aunt Marge, our only known relative, in case something really bad happened to him in the onset of age and he could no longer bring me up by himself. Treacherous cousins and all else loomed in that, and if my mood could be depressed any further, that was guaranteed to do it.

We were on the landing, slumped at the desk, listless as puddles. Out front, at this early point of the afternoon, the barroom had no customers yet, but we could hear the small sounds of Pop puttering with things behind the bar, which he was doing a lot more of these days. The idle back room seemed to have caught a mood from the pair of us, rain slickers hanging slack, X-Acto knife looking dull and uninviting, model planes barely stirring in their suspended state. Attic of our imaginations, the big old expanse and its holdings had provided us with treasures beyond measure—costumery, an expanded vocabulary, a hundred bits we did, and of course, the listening post into the adult world. All of that, we knew disconsolately, was about to go. So were times together like this. My throat had been tight for days with that thought, and Zoe looked tragic most of the time now.

Dismally she whispered, "What's going to happen to all the stuff?"

"I wish I knew." Even Pop didn't seem to. "Maybe it ought to go with the joint," he wavered, "although it's worth something if we hang on to it somehow. We'll have to see how the cards fall."

The familiar swish of the saloon's front door roused us just enough to peek through the vent slats, more out of habit than interest, to see who had come in. Zoe and I made a face at each other. Mr. Snake Boots himself, Earl Zane, grinning from ear to ear.

"Hullo, tarbender." We watched him approach the bar, swaggering like a crow. As usual, he was full of himself, and there was a lot of him to be full of. "How's business at the old watering hole?"

"Drying up fast," said Pop, as if present company accounted for that.

"Don't worry your scalp, that'll change real soon." Earl straddled a bar stool, beaming into the breakfront mirror as usual. "I'll buy it."

"Buy what?" Pop glanced around the barroom for anything Earl could possibly afford.

"Your hearing going, Tom? The whole place. The Medicine Lodge."

Pop snorted an explosive laugh, the first gust in a storm of mirth that left him clutching the bar for support. I thought he was never going to stop with it. His laughing fit was so infectious, Zoe and I had to stifle our own with hands over our mouths.

"Damn, Earl"—he gasped and wiped his eyes with a towel as he made his way to the beer tap—"that's the best one you ever told."

"I'm not joking," Earl protested in a hurt tone. "You can't understand plain English all of a sudden? I guess I got to say it again. I'll buy you out, lock, stock, and barrel."

Shaking his head, Pop drew a glass of Shellac by feel. "Sure you will. There's only that one pesky little detail. What do you intend to use for money?"

"I'll sell the gas station, natch." He rolled his shoulders, as if luxuriating in newfound wealth. "Got it all penciled out. That and a mortgage will do the trick." He confided triumphantly: "I already been by the bank."

The three of us listening knew, in a single heartbeat, this was dire.

"I'll be an ess of a bee," Pop uttered in amazement. "You're serious." In the same tone of voice he used to tell me not to put beans up my nose, he told Earl: "You know, pouring drinks isn't like pumping gas."

The prospective buyer was offended. "I can pick that up along the way. You had to, sometime or other. C'mon, Tom, is the damn place for sale or isn't it?"

I did not imagine this, and Zoe would back me up in saying so: Pop looked up at the vent and the invisible two of us, with apology in his eyes. Then he moved slowly toward Earl, pushing the glass of beer along the bar.

"I said it's for sale, so it is. Set things up with the bank, and we'll get going on the deal."

HOW MANY WAYS could life turn inside out in the same year? Now the Medicine Lodge not only was going out of our existence, Pop's and mine and Zoe's, but was passing into the hands of the person who, if there were such an election, would be the strongest candidate for town fool. On top of that, although Pop hadn't agreed to it yet, Earl Zane wanted the trove of hocked items to be included in the deal—"It'd get me my belt buckles back"—which would mean our beloved back room and its treasures would fall prey to that weenie Duane, while I would be across the alley eating my heart out.

I was haunted by what-ifs. What if I hadn't had the bright idea of filling the swamper job myself, which somehow made my father envision me chained to the joint forever? What if the

Great Falls beer makers hadn't boosted our perfectly nice saloon into the select Shellac shrine of the whole damn state and prompted Bill Reinking's newspaper story? What if Zoe and I had been caught at that blind bit in the ballpark and spoiled Pop's big day—wouldn't that have been better, in the end? It wore me out, thinking about everything. Oh, sure, you can't undo what's done, but that doesn't necessarily get it off your mind. Past actions, guileless at the time, seemed to have a habit of ambushing later on, and that was greatly unnerving to a twelve-year-old sensibility. Suppers with Zoe turned into one long, glum wish list, each of us coming up with muttered hankerings for this or that to happen and miraculously set matters right again. Eyeing us mumbling into our meals that way, her parents plainly wondered what had gotten into us now.

Even Earl Zane had enough sense to agree with Pop that the sale of the saloon ought to be kept quiet until the absolute last minute. He admitted he had a few details yet to corral, such as working out final terms with the Californian who wanted to buy the gas station because he'd heard the Two Medicine country was such swell fishing, while Pop did not want to face the real howls of the imbibing community when they found out who would be taking over the Medicine Lodge. As soon as Earl strutted out the door that day, Pop was in the back room instructing Zoe and me to keep our lips zipped about what we'd just heard. "It's not a secret, exactly, we just don't want anybody to know about it until we say so, got that?" At least in that he was talking our language, and it was nothing for us to stay mum to the whole world, except for each other and our supper plates, for the ten days until the sale of the saloon was to be made final. Coincidentally, that was also opening night of *The Importance of Being Earnest*, and Pop made what amends he could by promising to drive us to Valier to see the play. "Gives you a little something to look forward to, hey?" he tried, without much success, to lift our spirits.

The majority of those waiting days went somewhere while I still was in my fog of what-ifs, and when Saturday morning came again, I had to be forcefully reminded of my swamping duties.

With reluctance I took up the broom and mop and pail for what might be the last time and followed Pop into the silent barroom. To my further astonishment lately—what change would he think of next, plastic surgery?—he'd meant it about quitting smoking, and was down to half a pack a day. Every so often he would have a cigarette between his lips and be thumbing the lighter before he remembered, as he did now. With a quick, guilty glance in my direction, he snapped the lighter shut and tapped the cigarette back into the pack, knowing I was vengefully keeping count of his daily total. Weaning himself off nicotine left him cranky, which made two of us. Even the animal heads seemed gloomy, their eyes not yet brightened in the soft morning light.

Neither of us said anything as we began our chores. As ever, he was behind the bar doing this and that in a rhythm all his own, although I noticed he went at things solemnly. With a lump in my throat, I was sweeping near the front door when the doorknob rattled.

"We're closed," I called out rather shrilly.

The doorknob rattled some more.

"Pop, somebody wants in. Real bad, it sounds like."

"That's their tough luck," he said, continuing to fuss behind the bar.

Now there was urgent knocking, so much so that I looked questioningly in Pop's direction.

"Can't they take a hint?" he grumbled. "Okay, if it'll stop the racket, see who it is."

I unlocked the door to someone no more than twice my age, but also twice my height and narrowly built, in sharply pressed tan slacks and a shirt with all kinds of pockets and flaps, as if he were on a safari. With reddest red hair topping that slender build, he looked like a man-size matchstick. He gave me and my broom an uncertain smile, then a lit-up one to Pop.

It took more than the latest odd variety of tourist to faze my father. "The joint's not open yet, chum," he called from behind the bar. "Come back in a couple of hours and I can take care of whatever ails you so bad."

"Actually, I'm not trying to buy a drink." The voice was as reedy as the rest of this apparition. He slipped past me and up to the bar in about four steps. "Are you Tom Harry? *The* Tom Harry?"

"The only one I know of. What makes you ask?"

The redheaded stranger smiled even more brightly. "Sir, it's such an honor simply to be in your presence. And what a break for me. If I hadn't found you, I hate to think—" He clucked at what a tragedy that would have been. Gazing around the barroom as if it were an uncovered temple, he began in a spellbound tone: "I'm Del Robertson of the Missing Voices Oral History Project at the Library of Congress, and—"

He broke off, peering past Pop's shoulder. "There it is!"

Pop whipped around as if some genie had escaped from one of the countless liquor bottles.

"The Roosevelt poster!" A long arm and finger extended past Pop, as if he couldn't see what was under his nose. "Right by the cash register, where I was told you always kept one. How perfect!"

"Glad you like the deecor"—Pop wearily started to come from behind the bar, not a good sign for the person on the other side—"and now that you've had a look, you might as well get on with your business somewhere else, okay? We don't have any missing voices around here."

The young man shook his head, chuckling. "You certainly haven't lost the gift of gab, Mr. Harry," he said, practically bouncing with enthusiasm. "No wonder you and your saloon are legendary."

If it was possible for my ears to perk up any more than they already had, they did so now. My own father and the Medicine Lodge, actual legends? Was that what a newspaper story could do?

"That's pretty flattering to me and the old joint here," Pop stopped short at the end of the bar, looking curiously at the interloper. "But that's about to be over with, so I don't think I'm worth your time, whatever it is you have in mind."

"Hmm?" Still gazing reverently at Pop, our caller had that head-cocked attitude of hearing only what he wanted. "No, no, not this saloon, although don't get me wrong, it looks like a perfectly nice place."

Pop started to say something, but my blurt beat him, startling all three of us. "What saloon, then?"

"The Blue Eagle, of course"—Del Robertson gave that out like a song known by heart—"when history was being made at Fort Peck."

❧ 4 ❧

H ISTORY IS ALWAYS being made, let's face it, but Fort
Peck did so on a scale all its own. The dam there was
the biggest in the world when it was built, and the huge work-
force brought in for what no less an authority than my fifth-grade
history book called "the engineering miracle on the Missouri
River" constituted a major New Deal effort to jack Montana up
out of the Depression. All that was common knowledge. What
was not, to the boggled twelve-year-old of the moment, was that
the old saloon sign tucked away in the back room wasn't merely a
collector's item from the mists of my father's early days of hiring
on as a bartender, it was a proclamation of proprietorship. Right
there at the famous site of the Franklin D. Roosevelt speech and
who knew what other exploits of the time.

"Pop, you didn't ever tell me the Blue Eagle was your own—"

"Yeah, yeah, never mind, that's another story." He studied
our visitor more closely, as did I. Crew-cut and lean, handsome
enough in a college-boy kind of way, Del Robertson had the
dashing look in vogue in the time of Kennedy, as if wishing for
a torpedo boat under him. He stood there restlessly, all pockets

and ambition. Even to me, newly hatched from childhood into adolescence, he seemed young in a way other than years—Pop would have said wet behind the ears—which made his appearance in the Medicine Lodge all the more odd.

"Look, fellow, you've caught me"—Pop glanced at me standing there with the broom forgotten in my hand—"us at kind of a busy time. And I don't really have anything colossal to tell you about bartending, it was all pretty much in there in the newspaper."

"It was? Which paper?" Out came a notebook and pen from one of the various pockets. "I'll have to look that up."

That stopped Pop. "If you didn't see the newspaper story, how the hell did you find me?"

"Hmm? Oh, I took some rolls of quarters into a phone booth and started calling every newspaper editor in the state to ask if they knew of a bartender by your name in their town." A modest shrug accompanied the telling of this. "Luckily, Gros Ventre isn't far down the alphabet."

Pop shut his eyes for a second, then opened them, blinking like an owl. "Bill Reinking is taking over from God." Sighing mightily, he turned back to the matter of the perplexing visitor. "Okay, so you know about the Blue Eagle," he granted, looking discomfited. He could see curiosity sticking out all over me. "Why'd you come hunting me up about something way back when?"

"Sir," Del Robertson's tongue practically tripped over itself in the rush to answer, "you're the Leadbelly of Fort Peck."

"I'm the *what*?"

"Don't take it wrong, let me explain," came stumbling out next. "You've heard of Alan Lomax, I hope?"

Pop squinted impatiently. "Didn't he use to pitch for the Yankees?"

"Ah, no. Lomax is a musicologist, the best there is." The

word was new to both Pop and me. Someone who cured people of music?

Evidently not, according to the copious explanation that ensued—I took a seat on a bar stool during it, and Pop leaned back against the cash register with his arms folded—to the effect that this Lomax person collected folk songs, in the old days lugging a recording machine like a big suitcase through the hollows and swamps of the South until, to cut the story short, he heard about a colored man in a Louisiana prison who played a guitar and wrote songs like nobody else's.

"Leadbelly," our young informant concluded, as if saying the name in church. "Huddie Ledbetter. Possibly the greatest blues performer ever. The songs poured out of him like, like down-and-out poetry. The essence of the blues." In illustration, he cleared his throat and tried to make his voice deep and growly. "*I's got to bobbasheely through life alone, 'cause I got no constant home.* Classics like that."

Boy oh boy, did I ever wish Zoe was here for this.

It intrigued me that something of the sort qualified as music, but Pop was unmoved. "Don't turn into a damn jukebox, okay? What's Leadbottom got to do with me?"

Another explanation poured out, the point being that after the songcatcher Lomax convinced Huddie Ledbetter to sing into the machine, other blues singers let him record them at it, too. "Muddy Waters, Jelly Roll Morton, the greats. It grew into one of the greatest collections ever done, all because Leadbelly led the way with that first session, if you see what I mean." Just in case, our overeager visitor spelled it out. "When potential interviewees are a trifle, ah, shy, an oral historian needs someone known and trusted to sort of"—he spun his hands as if churning up the proper words—"break the ice, let's say. With your reputation, Mr. Harry, along with the Blue Eagle's, you are the absolutely natural one for the Fort Peck project. You're the perfect"—at least he didn't say Leadbelly this time—"icebreaker."

"You want me to get Fort Peckers to spill their guts for you," Pop wasted no time cutting through that. "What kind of an ess of a bee do you think I am? Not a snowball's chance. Stick to blue music."

The collector of Missing Voices looked hurt.

"Sir, you misunderstand. Gathering people's own stories is crucial to preserving that chapter of history. It's a"—hands spun again—"a crime against civilization to let those voices be lost." I, at least, was impressed.

He paused to muster a new thought. "Let me put it this way. Fort Peck had so many workers—thousands, really—that I can't possibly know which ones would be the best to interview. But from what I've been told over and over, practically everyone there sooner or later was funneled through a certain institution"—he bunched his hands narrowly—"as historians call a social fixture in a community. No, please, don't try to be modest, Mr. Harry, it's true. By every reputation, the Blue Eagle saloon was a Fort Peck institution without equal." He had that spellbound look again as he gazed at Pop. "And naturally that makes you the institutional memory."

Pop groaned. "How the hell did I get to be the institutional anything all of a sudden?"

"The place in history finds the man," Del Robertson said sagely.

"Maybe you mean well"—Pop plucked up a fresh towel for bar polishing—"but I've got a business to tend to. Even if I wanted to, I can't go trotting off across the countryside with you trying to find yayhoos who worked at the dam."

"That's the lucky part," the response came as if it couldn't wait. "They'll be at Fort Peck, in droves. At the Mudjacks Reunion."

"That bunch? Getting together like high schoolers? When's this?"

Wouldn't you know. The eager-beaver historian named the exact day the papers were to be signed and the sale of the Medicine Lodge would be final. Not to mention the opening-night performance of Mrs. Reinking, carefully coached eyes and all, in *The Importance of Being Earnest*. There seemed to be only that single red-letter date on the otherwise numberless calendar.

Pop could not hide his relief. "Naw, I couldn't go with you then even if I wanted to. I've got something important to do, it's all set up. Besides," he concluded righteously, "I promised the kiddo and his friend I'd take them to the play over in Valier that night. Busy as a one-handed juggler, see?"

"But"—Del Robertson couldn't believe his day of days wasn't more sacred than ours—"it's a historic occasion, you have to be there! It's a monumental celebration! Twenty-five years almost to the minute," the earnest explanation of the Mudjacks Reunion was not about to let up, "since the dam fill was begun."

Something thrummed in me at hearing that. First the thirty-year winter. Now this. The way 1960 kept bringing historic numbers had to add up to something a person would remember into eternity, didn't it?

"That can't be ri—" Pop did the Fort Peck arithmetic in his head and frowned. "Okay, so Fort Peckers will be there thick as weeds. There's your setup. All you need to do is wade in with your recording machine and find the ones who'll gab to you, no sweat."

"That's just it." The lanky figure shifted uncomfortably. "I've been trying for weeks, out on the coast and other places." The strain in his voice showed the effort. "It's no use. Every time I track down someone who was at Fort Peck and they start in on their stories, inevitably it leads to something that happened in the

Blue Eagle, and when they realize I haven't talked to you first, they absolutely clam up. The last one told me, 'You better go see Tom Harry, he knows A to why about any of that.'" He paused, as if tasting such sweet words. "Isn't that such a great way to describe an institutional memory?" After that wistful moment, he went back to looking doleful but determined. "That's what I mean about needing you to break the ice, sir."

"No, you don't," Pop said, showing every sign of losing his patience. "Cripes, there were loads of other bartenders at Fort Peck."

"None like you, everyone says. Mr. Harry, I absolutely cannot get the interviews I need at the Mudjacks Reunion without you." Pop's shake of the head hastened the next plea. "Please, sir? It would only take a couple of days."

"Hey, are you hard of hearing or something? I told you no already."

"One day."

"Ever been thrown out of a joint before, Delbert? Because you're about to—"

"That's not my name."

"Then what the hell is?"

"Delano."

You could have heard a fishhook drop after he said that. Pop jerked a thumb at the poster picture of Roosevelt. "Same as him? How come?"

Delano Robertson, as we now knew him, blushed. "My father lived and breathed the New Deal and President Roosevelt. He was administrative assistant to one of the main members of FDR's 'Brain Trust,' Rexford Tugwell."

"Lucky you didn't get named after him," Pop observed. "Delano, huh? That's halfway interesting." He squinted in fresh appraisal of the visitor. "You're from back there?"

"Washington, D.C., you hit it on the nose." A boyish smile accompanied the admission. "Born and bred, strict in the District, as the saying is."

"How about that. You keep up with politics any?"

"Somewhat," came the cautious answer.

"What do you think of this guy Kennedy's chances?"

FDR's namesake was no dummy. With the Kennedy poster looming over Pop's shoulder, he said in that tone of voice a person uses in reciting the Pledge of Allegiance: "He's the better man. If sanity prevails, he'll win."

"Nixon's a rat," Pop growled in confirmation, "you can tell by looking at the ess of a bee." He was scrubbing back and forth over the same already gleaming spot on the bar wood with his towel, a sign he was thinking hard. "So you get paid for going around and listening to people, if you can manage to get them to talking in the first place? Not a bad racket." And not too unlike what went on in a certain barroom. "Where'd you learn this oral history stuff? Harvard?" he asked hopefully, knowing Roosevelt and Kennedy had gone there.

"Come again?" The red head tilted a little to one side, as if catching up with what had been said. "Oh. Actually, no. William and Mary."

"I guess you get a longer diploma that way." Pop tossed down his towel. "Hey, Delano," he seemed to enjoy trying out the name, "I can see why you'd like to have me glued to your side at the Fort Peck doings. But even if I wanted to, I've got a business deal that same day I positively have to be here for. Right, kiddo?" If he thought I was going to confirm the need to sell the Medicine Lodge, he was going to have a long, long wait; what he said may have been accurate, but that did not make it right. I sullenly kicked the leg of my bar stool until he took the hint and turned back to the other person whose hopes he was dashing. "Anyhow, before you go on your way, better have something to help you pack that name around. On the house. What do they drink at Willy and Mary?"

Delano Robertson smiled bashfully. "The same as any college, I suppose. Kegs of beer."

"'On the house' runs out after one glass," Pop made clear. While the beer brimmed to a perfect head, he included me in the proceedings by scooting an Orange Crush down the bar to where I was still perched. "This character with his ears hanging out is my son and swamper, Rusty."

Delano came at me on scissor legs for a handshake, as if we were long-lost brothers. "Twenty-five years," Pop was muttering to himself and perhaps the Roosevelt poster as he fussed the glass of beer to perfection, "where the hell does the time go?" This prompted me to give Delano a secret look of encouragement, not that he needed much of that. By now he was taking in the barroom, from the stuffed menagerie protruding from the forest-green walls to the pressed-tin ceiling that looked as old as heaven, to the ornately carved breakfront, with its cargo of bottles and glasses and mirrors, as though he couldn't get enough of it.

"This is priceless"—he plopped down on the bar stool next to mine and twirled as if on a merry-go-round—"the way you've kept this a classic saloon, Mr. Harry."

"Yeah, well, it takes some real hard running to stay in the same place these days," Pop agreed with that. I watched him think hard, his forehead furrowed the way that usually meant a wrestle with his conscience. "Here's the honest truth, Delano. Keep it under your hat, but I've about got a deal to sell the joint and—"

"No!" Delano cried out, whirling on his stool to face Pop. "I mean, that's totally surprising. The saloon and you, both the best of the kind, and for you to give it up now, at the height of—"

"Would it be too damn much trouble to let me finish what I'm saying, do you suppose?" Pop's glower sent Delano into retreat behind his beer glass. "That's one of the reasons I can't go galli-vanting off to Fort Peck with you. There's a last few things to be worked out on the deal that day, and then we're going to sign the papers, so I need to be here instead of there, see?"

"The time is out of joint," Delano brooded as if he were about to cry in his beer, "and the joint is out of time."

"Run that by me again?"

"Shakespeare, at least the first part." A tingle went through me, and I waited breathlessly for what Delano would cause next. "It's just too ironic," he went on in the same voice of gloom and doom, "that the very day you would be the center of celebration at Fort Peck will be your last as bartender here, Mr. Harry."

That gave Pop pause, but not for long. "I didn't bargain for everything piling up on the cockeyed calendar, did I? It's your tough luck it happens that way." All too plainly he was ready to drop the topic and the erstwhile young collector of Missing Voices, both. "Anyhow, drink up. You'll need the nourishment to tackle those mudjacks."

"Sir," Delano fashioned a fresh inspiration, helped by some fast gulps of beer, "I heard everything you said against coming along to the reunion, and I respect every word. But at least let me show you the Gab Lab. I have it all ready to go to Fort Peck, you'll see. It's parked right across the street. Please? It'll only take a minute."

Of course I was off my stool and halfway to the front door by the time he finished saying that, but Pop hesitated before taking his apron off and following him out.

I've always thought what awaited Delano Robertson in the main street of Gros Ventre was so unfair. Even yet, I can see it and hear it and almost catch a whiff of it. As he stepped from the sidewalk to eagerly lead us across to a green-and-white Volks-wagen van, bearing down on him no more than half a block away was a panicky mob of freshly shorn sheep, peeing and pooping and announcing in other ways how upset they were at being stripped of their fleeces, while in back of them, also supremely agitated, was Canada Dan, cussing the life out of the surprised pedestrian in the path of the flock. Pop and I looked on unsuspectingly at this inhospitable reception for the person who would change our life like night to day.

Our visitor froze in astonishment at the spectacle of a thousand undressed sheep madly advancing on him, which was a mistake on his part. Out front of the others, one ewe that must have lost her lamb as well as her wool and maybe her mind was frantically chasing back and forth, bleating blame at the world and stamping her hooves at anything in the way. She made a maddened run in Delano's direction. Can a person be buffaloed by a sheep? Whatever the fitting description, he bolted for safety as fast as his legs could carry him.

"They're just out of the shearing pen across the creek," Pop informed him as he scrambled ungracefully back to join us in the doorway of the Medicine Lodge. "Makes them a little excited." We watched the fleeceless animals, their bewildered lambs trailing them, jostle past by the hundreds. Sheep look so naked without their wool, like peeled eggs with legs. Besides that indignity, some of the ewes carried cuts where they had been nicked by the shearers' power clippers. You see pictures, all the way back to Bethlehem, of peaceful grazing flocks, but this scarred-up, loose-boweled parade would not make anyone envy a sheep's life. Delano Robertson remained wide-eyed and more than a little nervous about his van with the unsanitary swarm engulfing it. "Does this happen much?"

"Oh, hell yeah," Pop said, as if this was only ordinary traffic. "The Two Medicine country is deep in sheep. Wool and lambs are its bread and butter."

Eventually the last echelon of skittery ewes passed us by, along with Canada Dan, who spat a brown stream of tobacco juice toward us and groused, "It's getting so a man can't even herd sheep through town without a turster in the way, ain't it?"

Delano's face lit up. "The negative interrogative! It's a linguistic pattern that's dying out in most places." His hands flew to one of many shirt pockets again for the notebook and pen as he craned a look at the departing figure, still bristling like a porcupine and spitting in our general direction. "Where's he from?"

"All over," said Pop, alluding to the job history of the Two Medicine country's most hired and fired sheepherder.

"Canada," I said, giving Pop a look.

"I thought so," Delano nodded wisely, jotting in the notebook. "Linguistic patterns tend to mix along borders, likely French affecting English in him. The Gallic *n'est-ce pas* must have become *ain't it* in his cultural subgroup, don't you think?"

"Something must have affected the ess of a bee," Pop said, as if his eye still smarted. "That's Canada Dan for you."

Delano paused in his scribbling, puzzled now. "What's a 'turster'?"

"Tell you later," said Pop. "Show us this traveling contraption of yours. Watch where you step." The street was even more of a mess than usual after sheep had gone through, and Delano pretty much tiptoed as he escorted us to the van. Reaching it, he let out a relieved "Whew!" and flung open the double doors in the middle of the beetle-nosed vehicle. "Here it is, the Gab Lab!"

Pop and I stared into what looked like a camper combined with the guts of a recording studio. The camper part was straightforward enough: a gateleg table, seats and cushions that converted into a bunk, a white-gas stove cleverly hooked onto one of the double doors, and a small sink with a hand pump for water. Curtains on all the windows, a homey touch. But the rest of the interior held racks and racks of tape reels, as recorders used in those days, and two or three of the bulky machines were tucked away wherever they could fit, while headphones dangled from cabinet knobs. A typewriter was lashed to a little shelf all its own.

Pop could not help but observe, "Kind of tight quarters unless you're a sardine, isn't it?"

"Everything is within reach," Delano defended, sounding a trifle crestfallen.

"So how does this Missing Voices deal work?" Pop wondered. "You corner people and get them to gabbing about themselves and then—"

"—after the interview has been conducted, according to professional standards," Delano said patiently, "I review it and transcribe it onto paper, right here. It's fresh in my mind that way, and there aren't those questions later as to what this word or that was." He leaned toward us confidentially. "Alan Lomax's transcription typist thought Leadbelly had written an entire song about 'swimming' instead of 'wimmin' and it took the Library of Congress folklorists days and days to figure that out and fix it." That same shy smile. "That's why I came up with the idea for the Gab Lab and was able to convince the powers that be to let me outfit it like this." He beamed proudly at the chockful camper van. "It's the only one of its kind."

Shaking his head, Pop backed away from the van. "Okay, it's been seen. Good luck."

Immediately Delano had that pleading expression again, and began, "Mr. Harry, the Mudjacks Reunion is the chance of a lifetime to—"

It only brought him more head shaking from Pop. "Listen, I can tell you think you can't do this by yourself, but you'd better make up your mind to. I'm still not gonna be Leadbutt for you and lead you around by the hand to every Fort Pecker who's got some kind of a story. I gave you my reason and that settles it, right?"

Wrong, if I had anything to do with it. I was trying to come up with whatever would impel him to the reunion instead of signing the death warrant of the Medicine Lodge, when Delano slammed one of the van's double doors hard enough to show he did have a temper.

"If you're determined to turn your back on history"—he slammed the other one harder yet—"that's that."

Thrusting his hands into side pockets of his bush-jacket shirt and hunching up mournfully, he looked around at the town, mostly at the street with its sheep leavings, some of which he had stepped in. Without much hope, he inquired, "Is there a campground somewhere along the creek?" He was asking me because Pop, still shaking his head, was making a beeline back to the saloon. "Maybe I'd have better luck at fishing," Delano muttered, scraping his shoe on the curb.

Inspiration sometimes comes from the least likely source. "Fishing?" I repeated loudly. "Gee, I don't just know where you'd go, the creek has been too roily practically forever."

Pop stopped short in the middle of the street. He turned his head enough to ask, "You fished much back east?"

"Hmm? Oh, a tad."

Whatever a tad was, it did it. "Tomorrow's Sunday," Pop mused, as if it were his own sudden discovery. "We could show you the best fishing spot on the face of the earth, couldn't we, Rusty."

DELEGATING ME to escort Del to the house, where he could park his traveling home and office in the driveway overnight for a nice, early start on catching fish, Pop headed back to the Medicine Lodge in lifted spirits, calling over his shoulder: "You'll have rainbow trout running out your ears before we're done with you."

Delano had brightened measurably by the time he and I climbed into the van, probably at the prospect of a safe haven where marauding sheep could not get at him. Riding in the Gab Lab was an adventure in itself—wait till I told Zoe!—what with the recording gear and highway maps and other clutter its usual occupant had to scoop out of the passenger seat to make room for me. He apologized for his housekeeping and I told him not to worry, it matched ours. "There's only your father and you?" he asked, and I started in full bore about Pop and my mother splitting the blanket when I was real little, but before I could say more, he sympathized by telling me his parents, too, had divorced when he was a child and now were both dead, which effectively put him way beyond me in orphanhood, so I quit babbling.

As he drove, he evidently was still bothered by the events competing with the Mudjacks Reunion. "What is this play that's so vitally important?" he asked peevishly. "Something by someone local?"

"Oscar Wilde."

"Oh."

I figured it was my turn. "What's 'bobbasheely' mean?"

"Mmm, something like moseying along."

"Then why not just say 'moseying along'?"

"You wouldn't want vanilla to be the only flavor of ice cream, would you?" He had me there.

By then we were pulling in to the house, met by a stiff breeze along the creek, which was ruffling the front-yard trees. Igdrasil appeared to be doing a rain dance, its boughs swaying rhythmically and its leaves shimmering in countless motions. Fantastic

clouds, fat and billowy, hovered beyond the giant tree, as if waiting their turn with the wind. "I hope your father is a good judge
of the weather." Delano glanced up dubiously. "It looks stormy."

"That's nothing. We had a thirty-year winter, you know. It
never let up from Thanksgiving until—"

"A Packard straight-eight! What a piece of history!"

Unquestionably he had spotted the dark hulk at the end of
the driveway. The surprise was mine, next, when he enthused,
"Those old babies were absolute wonders—horsepower to burn.
Bootlegger specials." He imitated the rat-a-tat-tat of a tommy
gun so effectively, I gave a start. "Did your father pick it up in
a government seizure sale, do you know?" I didn't, but I was sure
going to ask now.

"Ah, well," he responded with a mysterious grin, "if only the
godly carriage could talk."

Grown-ups are like that, I had to accept one more time,
evidently even ones barely old enough to shave. Yet somehow
Delano was hard not to get attached to—maybe it was the
name—and I was prepared to keep him company for the afternoon, but he had work to do. "The Gab Lab is a trusty servant,
but a hard master," he said, if I heard him right. Before I could
traipse off and leave him to his undersize laboratory, though, he
made the mistake of asking, "Where's a place in town that serves
a good dinner?"

"YOU GET PAID money to listen in on people, Mr. Delano? Like
a spy?"

"Hmm? To listen to what they have to say, yes, but it's actually not like spying because—"

"Oh. You don't get to sneak up on them without their knowing it?"

"Not at all. Oral history is strictly face-to-face. Interviewer, interviewee, and the mike."

"But then if you can't listen to them without their knowing it, how can you tell they're not lying when they say things right to you? Isn't that what 'bare-faced liar' means?"

To say Delano had his hands full at the corner table in the Top Spot only begins to describe the situation, because along with attempting to eat a chicken-fried steak and contend with Zoe's barrage of questions, there was the surplus of conversation in the crowded cafe constantly at the edge of one's hearing. Pop's maxim that Saturday night buys the rest of the week held as true here as in the Medicine Lodge, as Zoe's mother bustled along the counter from customer to customer and to the other few tables, apologetically pouring coffee, while Pete Constantine, in his slipping cook's hat, manhandled matters in the kitchen. Trying to take it all in, our dining partner was having to stretch his attention in a number of directions at once.

"He's been to college for that, Zoe," I stuck up for his presumed ability to recognize truth or falsehood when it looked him in the face. "Isn't that so, Mr. Delano?"

"Just Del, all right? No need to be fancy among friends, hmm?" He took a couple of sips of the Spot's watery coffee to escape dealing with Zoe's philosophical inquiry into bare-faced liars, meanwhile trying to listen in on two oil field roughnecks at the counter mystifyingly talking about Christmas tree valves on a mud rig.

"Del"—Zoe dropped her voice to first-name confidentiality—"do they teach acting where you went to college?"

"Come again?" He tipped his head slightly in that habit of his, until she repeated, "Acting."

"Ah, a drama department, do you mean?" He grinned down at her. "Are you sure you need one?" He worked on his chicken-fried steak, the night's special, seeming puzzled to not find a recognizable steak under the gluey-looking brown gravy and breading, merely pulverized meat.

"Rusty, what do you know for sure?"

The voice so close behind my chair it made me jump was the nosiest in town, and quick as I was to be on my guard, Zoe's eyes already were flashing me a warning. Chick Jennings had been the postmaster before buying the Pastime saloon a few years back, and as Pop put it, he liked to know everybody's business but his own. "He runs that joint like he's still doing government work," the best bartender who ever lived scorned this most amateur one. "Doesn't put in the hours a real saloon needs. And he talks customers into the ground, which is why that joint is so dead."

Chick Jennings's jowly face now hung over me like the man in the moon as he lowered his voice confidentially. "Your daddy found a taker for the famous Medicine Lodge yet?"

"Not that he's told me about." Which was narrowly true; it had been overheard fair and square through the vent. Zoe radiated approval.

The Pastime owner looked deeply disappointed at the lack of gossip to take away. "Tell your daddy for me he beat me to the punch, putting the thing up for sale. The saloon business does wear a man down." He wagged his head in sympathy I didn't believe. "I never figured I'd outlast Tom Harry."

"I'll be sure to tell my father that."

Delano was following this, wisely silent. I knew Chick Jennings would not leave until his curiosity was satisfied, so I said: "This is, uh, Mr. Robertson. He's here to go fishing."

"That so? Where do you come from, Mr.—"

"Oh, look, your supper sack is ready," Zoe piped up as Pete Constantine's hand plopped the brown bag on the serving window.

Actually, it was understandable if Chick Jennings would rather talk than eat the Top Spot's version of food, but he wagged his head again about the call of duty at the Pastime and went off looking unsatisfied.

"I take it Gros Ventre is a two-saloon town," said Del, amused.

"His is a dump." Zoe dismissed the Medicine Lodge's competition so scornfully it did my heart good. "In Butte," she confided in the voice she used for secrets, "we call a saloon like that a deaf and dumb institute."

Professional listener or not, Del looked as if he had not heard that quite right. "Say again?"

Patiently she did, complete with explanation: "A bartender like him will talk you deaf, and you're dumb to drink there in the first place."

My turn to issue a warning as her mother sidled along the counter toward us, coffeepot in action. "Here she comes, Zoe, you better get busy eating."

With a world-class sigh, she fiddled a fork onto her otherwise untouched plate, then eyed Del's. "I bet you aren't getting enough supper," she expressed sudden concern. "Here, you can have some of mine." Before he could turn down the offer, she was dumping a major chicken-fried helping onto his. When he protested that he could not possibly eat all that, she assured him, "That's okay, you can just leave it."

Her mother arrived, clucking approval as she inspected the progress of Zoe's meal. "That's what I like to see, honeybunch, good appetite." Patting Zoe and giving me and my milk shake and cheeseburger her usual doubtful glance, she turned to Del with her most motherly smile. "I hope my little good-for-nothing isn't being too much of a nuisance."

"Not at all," he maintained with a straight face, "she's no trouble." That was an underestimation of Zoe if I ever heard one, but as soon as her mother left us, he took care of it. "I have sisters like you. Holy terrors."

Glowing at the compliment, she went back to peppering him with questions. I concentrated on my burger and shake until, in flirtatious movie style, she reached: "So, Del, are you married?"

"No," he reported, shy again. I could see something change in his eyes. "I came close right after college, but she chose a finance major from Richmond instead." He pulled his chin in, almost to his collar button, and intoned in that voice-of-doom style of old newsreels, "This is the way the world ends, not with a whim but a banker."

Zoe and I looked at each other in the same instant. There was no mistaking it. Shtick doesn't happen by accident. He had just done a bit.

After that, how could we resist showing him the keenest costume shop this side of Shakespeare's closet?

"HOW INCREDIBLE!"

Del turned in circles in the middle of the back room of the Medicine Lodge, gaping at it all, the hocked haberdashery filling the walls, and the tools and such piled in corners, and the lariat coils gracing the rafters. "There are museums that don't have this much!" He looked as excited as if he were the third kid in the room. "Where did this all come from?"

I explained Pop's policy of drinks for loot, as he called it. While I was doing so, Zoe skipped up to us with a set of Stetsons she'd swooped off the wall.

"Here, have a hat."

"No, really, I—" Del watched each of us clap one on like veteran riders of the plains and stand there looking at him expectantly. He gulped and glanced around, but the back room was an empty stage except for us, so he gingerly took the kangaroo-brown cowboy hat Zoe was thrusting at him—"This one goes nice with your shirt"—and put it on. It was not a bad fit, and feeling braver, he experimentally tugged it lower on one side of his forehead like every movie cowboy. "Git along, little doggies," he drawled, winning our instant approval.

Zoe and I trailed him as he toured the room. "That's a Texican saddle," he exclaimed, rushing over to the biggest and oldest of the horse gear. "It had to have come north on a cattle drive. That dates it to the eighteen seventies or early eighties, before the winter of '86." The first thirty-year winter! Just when you figured he was green as a pea, he would come up with something like that. "I like old things," he was saying, happy as pie. "You know they've lasted for a reason." Gazing around, he shook his head in awe. "Imagine, nearly the past century stored away in this room. It's like a King Tut's tomb of the prairie." Suddenly he lifted his Stetson as high in the air as his long arm would reach. "Hats off!"

Quick as a heartbeat, Zoe and I were lofting ours, too, even if we didn't yet know what the bit was that we were doing.

"To Tom Harry!" Del resoundingly completed the tribute, clapping his Stetson back on in emphasis. "Rusty, your father is a gatekeeper of history. A living legend in the Two Medicine country, that's obvious from all this." He shook his head in wonder. "The same as he was at Fort Peck."

Yes, but *is* now teetered on becoming *was* again. As Del sailed off around the room in search of further wonders and Zoe tagged after him, leaving me with a dark-eyed look of understanding, I stayed rooted in the spot where I had taken my hat off to my father. My mind kept spinning back and forth over the fact that these old, familiar surroundings would no longer be ours, very soon. The Select Pleasure Establishment of the Year, the oasis of the Two Medicine country, the back room that was my second home, this would all vanish from my life and his the minute he signed over the Medicine Lodge to a bee esser who could hardly even run a gas station. It didn't seem fair. Swallowing hard, I gazed up to the stairway landing and could just see that stupid weenie Duane Zane plastering himself to the vent. It pained me even more that this was the last Saturday night, the final time Zoe and I could have huddled there, gleefully listening in on the extravaganza of voices while Pop bartended to perfection, but instead we were stuck with being polite tour guides for this enthusiast of collections of all kinds.

I couldn't stand it.

In the infinitesimal time it took for the snap of my fingers to travel the length of the room to where he was perusing a wall practically curtained in reins and bridles and quirts and other leather accessories while she chattered at him, Zoe must have read my mind. Del paid no attention whatsoever to my finger snap, but she glided purposefully back to me, already radiating intrigue. We consulted in whispers.

"Should we let him in on it?"

"I dunno. We don't want him blabbing to people about it."

"Maybe he's smart enough not to."

"Maybe."

Together we contemplated the redheaded stick figure over there, engrossed in a workhorse harness. One of us shrugged, one of us nodded, and it somehow constituted agreement.

"Del? Can you keep a secret?"

"Hmm? I suppose." He turned around to us, blinking his way back to the land of the living. "I mean, absolutely."

Zoe specified: "Swear on the tailbone of a black cat killed in a graveyard at midnight?"

Interested now, he bobbed his head.

"You have to say it," she directed severely.

Concentrating hard, he recited it to Zoe's satisfaction. With that settled, we led him up the stairs to the landing and, fingers to our lips, sat him down next to the vent grille. Zoe allowed me to do the honors of silently levering it open and letting in the sounds of Saturday night getting under way in the barroom.

"Dode, I haven't seen you in hell's own while. How'd you winter?"

"Oh, I made it through to grass. Jesus H. Christ, though, did you ever see snow like that? I had to put stilts on my snowshoes to get to the barn."

The voices—mostly male, but with a wife's or a girlfriend's occasionally pealing in—came chorusing clearly as ever through the vent, joking and complaining—

"That honyocker was supposed to help out on this fencing deal, but he called up sick. Allergic to postholes, probably. So I guess I got to go at it bald-headed."

—arguing politics—

"I'm telling you, if the Democrats get back in, this country's done for."

"Are you kidding? What the Republicans already did to the country would gag a maggot off a gut wagon."

—gossiping tooth and nail—

"Didn't you hear? She left him, for some scissorbill at their high school reunion."

—toasting to faith in the future—

"Here's to eighty-pound lambs in the shipping pen and a new checkbook!"

—and ordering another drink just in case—

"Tom, when you get a chance, how about a couple more glasses of vitamin B for us down at this end?"

"You got it, two Shellacs coming right up."

—all of it as though the Two Medicine country possessed a communal throat that Leadbelly himself might have envied for its lifetimes of verses, all of it fairly singing into the ear Del Robertson was pressing to the vent slats.

"How amaz—" he started to say out loud, before two sets of small hands covered his mouth.

"Sorry," he whispered as Zoe and I withdrew our hands. "But it is amazing! Voices like these are usually so scattered, you can never collect this many in one place." He took on a tone of awe. "This is like discovering the Mississippi Delta of gab. Now I know how Alan Lomax felt." We smiled smugly. "I have to get some of this down," he muttered while urgently searching into the flap pockets of his shirt for the notebook and pen that held Canada Dan's contribution to the language. "It's pure *lingua america*."

"It's what?" Zoe or I or more likely both of us immediately whispered.

"I'll explain later. Let's listen."

As often as not, though, the lingo coming into his ear was also over his head. "I'm calling it a night," said someone, who indeed sounded as though he had spent a liquid evening, "I got to go out in the morning and do the round dance."

Hesitating in his scribbling, Del looked at us as if he wasn't sure he had heard right.

"Plow a field," my murmur enlightened him, "around and around."

"Mm hmm, how apt." He scrawled away madly until another in the chorus of lubricated voices proclaimed that if things didn't pick up in the sheep business pretty soon, his herder was going to have to live on sidehill pork.

Zoe took that one. "Poached deer." From Del's expression, you could tell he was thinking along the line of Top Spot specialties such as chicken-fried steak, until she rolled her eyes. "You know," she practically hissed in his ear, "shot out of season."

It went on that way, with him industriously listening and jotting until one of us asked, "Why don't you just set up your recorder?"

"I'd love to, but I can't. It's not ethical."

"Then why are you writing stuff down?"

"That's different," he maintained, not totally convincingly, "it's only random collecting."

"Like spying, you mean."

"No," he whispered insistently, "I don't mean that. All this is," he sounded like he was coming up with it from some rule book, "is a set of unstructured linguistic encounters."

Whatever it was, the three of us took in everything the vent had to offer until at last Zoe sighed fatalistically. "It's nine, I have to go. Bedtime," she pronounced, as if it were a jail sentence.

"Me, too." I looked at Del, but still wrapped up in the language of Saturday night in the Medicine Lodge, he had not taken the point. "You'd better, too, if you're going fishing with Pop."

RAINBOW RESERVOIR looked much murkier than I remembered—even though my memory of it was perpetually colored by being skunked in the derby every year and not catching much on these spontaneous outings of Pop's—and considerably deeper, given the runoff from the winter of big snows and then the spring blizzard and the unseasonal rains ever since. The water was lapping right up to the rocks we usually stood on to fish. Pop seemed unbothered by that fact. Lots of water meant lots of fish, he assured us, an equation Del lifted sleepy eyebrows at but didn't question.

"Pop?" Recent circumstances made me curious about the

reservoir dam, an earthen slope between the piney bluff where the parking lot was located and the similar shoulder of land across the way. "How does dirt hold back the water?"

He followed my gaze to the dam and the concrete spillway in its middle, with white water rushing down to where the South Fork of English Creek resumed, then shrugged. "Pile enough dirt together and it just does, that's all."

"I bet that took a lot of dirt at Fort Peck, huh?" I asked cagily.

"'The damnedest dirt dam in all of Creation,' as it used to be called?" He frowned at me and the topic. "Yeah, I'd say it took plenty."

"More earth than was moved in the digging of the Panama Canal," Del provided between yawns.

"There, see?" Pop told me. "All you have to do is ask something and a monkey comes out of a tree with the answer." He said it jokingly enough, however, finishing off the coffee in his thermos cup and taking last drags on a precious cigarette of his daily ration as he gazed up at the mountain skyline, which still held the pink of dawn. "Can't beat this if you want nature," he provided his customary tribute to the scenery practically in our faces, then got busy digging out fishing gear from the car trunk. Assembling his rod and reel with alacrity while the other two of us a lot more slowly did our own, it occurred to him to make sure Del was not incurably addicted to fancy fishing.

"Ever use bait instead of flies made out of feathers, did you, back east?"

"All the time."

"That's good, it ought to be in the Constitution that people have to fish with real bait. Here's how we do it, but don't tell nobody, got that?"

So saying, he shook out a prime chicken gut from the bait can and cut it into strips. Del cautiously watched us bait up before touching his share of the gooey stuff.

"Come on, you two." Pop lost no time picking his way down to the waterline, calling over his shoulder, "You can't catch fish if you don't have your hook in the water."

That may have been so, but a pesky breeze was riffling the lake as usual, and I was determined not to have my hook blown back in the direction of my ears. Using pliers, I put an extra sinker, like an enlarged lead BB, on my line, close to the hook and spinner. After watching me at it, Del took the pliers and, to my astonishment, crimped several sinkers onto his line. Busily casting, Pop was not paying attention to anything beyond persuading trout to take a bite of chicken guts.

I don't know that this is in the Bible, but there is a time to participate and a time to spectate. Something told me to hang back on the reservoir bank and see what Del was about to do.

First of all, he advanced to the lake by degrees, tinkering with his reel, plucking at his line, making twitchy little back-and-forth tries with his pole. Finally he reached the water, but as if sneaking up on it sideways. I had seen many, many peculiar stances in the fishing derbies, but never this. Gripping the pole in both hands like a baseball bat, he swung it all the way back until the tip nearly reached the ground behind him, then whipped it forward in a tremendous arc. Carried by the weight of the sinkers, the hook and line sailed and sailed, until dimpling into the lake three or four times farther out than Pop's cast.

"Where the hell did you learn that?" asked Pop, staring at the extent of fish line beyond his.

"Surf casting. In the Atlantic. Oops, got a bite."

It was the first of a good many. I was kept busy stringing Del's catch of rainbow trout onto a forked willow stick and cutting up bait for him, which I volunteered for to evade thrashing the water with my own pole, as usually happened. Pop was not ready to change a lifelong style of casting and take up catapulting, but I noticed his casts were more muscular than usual, and fish out toward the middle began finding his bait, too. The two men struck up the kind of conversation that catching fish on a scenic lake under a blue sky can lead to, Del asking this and that about the Two Medicine country and Pop inquiring in turn about life on the road in the Gab Lab.

"It still seems to me you're a glutton for punishment, Delano"—he shook his head but in a humorous way—"traveling around in a glorified tin can. It can't be any too much fun, either, when someone sees that microphone of yours and comes down with mental laryngitis. So what keeps you doing it?"

That question seemed to flip a switch in Del. "Sir," he began in a serious voice—

"Hey, I'm not your commanding officer, am I."

"Sorry, Mr. Harry. The interviews—"

"Cripes, are you allergic to first names?"

Somewhat bashfully, Del managed to come out with "Tom" and get back onto his train of thought.

"The interviews fill a historical need. If we don't capture people's own stories, history is told from the top down. Rome fell, and that's that, period. But the Roman Empire was so much more than the Caesars and gladiators and such," he went on like a classroom instructor, "it was a way of life and language that lasted on and on in ordinary people. That's where a hybrid language such as *lingua franca* spoken around the Mediterranean came from, people of all walks of life spreading the words, sorry about the pun." By now he was really getting wound up, a lot busier with this than with fishing. "And here in our own time, we have the technical means to actually document it when people put history into their own words and vice versa." He looked momentarily pleased with himself. "Actually, I put some of this in my grant proposal for the Missing Voices project. It seems to have worked." He sobered again. "But traveling around in the Gab Lab is going to produce oral history of a particularly valuable kind, I'm absolutely sure of it. Wherever I can manage to point that microphone, it's waiting to be found, *lingua america*."

He paused, suddenly embarrassed about sounding like he was reading all this off a card he carried in his wallet. "Alan Lomax has it easier in a way," he admitted with the shy grin that made him likable, "he only has to say he's crazy about the blues. *'Everythin' nailed down's comin' loose,'*" he growled illustratively. *"'Seems like livin' ain't no use.'* That kind of thing, you know."

Pop was listening as only he could, taking in every word while still tending to the business of baiting up and casting. "So why be crazy about history," he prodded, "when you can't even sing it?"

Del laughed slightly, then turned serious.

"I suppose this will sound idealistic, but why not? To try to understand human nature a little better, according to every history professor I ever had. They could all quote George Santayana in their sleep." His voice went so deep it seemed to come from his shoe tops: "'Those who do not remember the past are condemned to repeat it.'"

His fishpole swished as he made another two-fisted cast toward the middle of the reservoir. "Besides, I just somehow find it the most interesting thing in the world, listening to people tell about their lives. Maybe it started all the way back in nursery rhymes, but I can't get enough of stories."

Watching Pop, I could see that registered on him, but maybe not the way I hoped. "I don't know about you and Santa Ana," he said skeptically as he cast for more trout, "but I hear all kinds of bee ess when people start telling me their life stories. So, how do you know you're getting anything halfway true when they rattle off to you?" There: Zoe's question exactly.

"Tom, you might be surprised at the sobering effect of a microphone and a tape recorder," Del replied mildly. "When they know that their words will be preserved in an archive, most people stay quite honest. Careful in how much they say, maybe, but on the up and up with what memories they are willing to share." He was back to reciting, as if it was a creed. "Oral historians have to count on what's called the moral edifice embodied in remembrance."

"What's morals got to do with it?" Pop squinted across the boulders in Del's direction, twitting him a little or maybe not. "If you think you're gonna get anywhere at Fort Peck, you'd better not be picky about what some of those folks were up to back then." My ears pricked up, but he stopped at that.

"That's no problem." Del was grinning. "You know how it is, all sorts of things end up in a collection, mine as well as yours."

His pole swished in a fresh cast. Pop's did not.

"I'll go clean the fish," I said, grabbing up the whole catch and scrambling off along the bank toward the spillway to escape Pop's look. But I couldn't get away from what he was saying, loud and clear: "You know what, it sounds like somebody just might have let you snoop around the back room of the joint."

"Rusty was kind enough to let me poke my head in." Del's voice faltered a bit, then rallied. "It's a marvel, Tom, to see what you've gathered. How you've done it all—" He shook his head in tribute. "The Rockefellers spent millions on collecting for Williamsburg."

"It's a lot of years' worth of taking stuff in when cash isn't there, for sure," I could barely hear the gruff response over the rushing sound of the spillway. "That's over, a couple days from now."

THE REST OF that Sunday has blurred in me, the way a long stay in a hospital waiting room dulls away into a memory of dread at what was waiting ahead. I'm confident in saying fried rainbow trout was the special at the Top Spot that suppertime, but beyond that, all I am sure of is that Pop was busy at being busy going over the saloon's accounts one last time, Del was holed up in the Gab Lab doing whatever he could to get ready for the multitude at Fort Peck, and Zoe and I spent a pitiful afternoon in the deathly quiet Medicine Lodge, with not even the farewell whisper of a voice sifting from the barroom to the back room. It was like an all-day funeral.

Which changed like a thunderclap around bedtime that night.

Or rather, like the surprise barrage of thunder that could be felt in the floorboards of the house as lightning made the lights flicker, causing Pop to jump up from the kitchen table and his spread of paperwork while I scrambled to turn off the Selectrics game I was halfheartedly listening to, lest the radio tubes be blown out.

As the next terrific rumble arrived, we rushed to a side window, the same thing on both our minds. There, squarely beneath Igdrasil's biggest limbs, perfectly targeted if lightning struck the old tree, sat the VW van, just as Del had parked it.

Had it been either of us out there, the erstwhile Gab Lab already would be roaring to life and hightailing out from under that threat. The undisturbed faint light behind its drawn curtains indicated no such thing had occurred to its oblivious occupant.

By now the wind was picking up and rain had cut loose with

the other elements, drumming down so hard we couldn't be heard if we yelled out to him. "Damn," said Pop, and some more than that. The situation was as plain as the repeated lightning flashes and rolls of thunder. One of us would have to go out in the storm, and I hoped it didn't have to be me.

I underestimated. Pop was putting on his slicker, but handing me mine, too. "I'm gonna have to move the Packard some so he can pull in behind it at the end of the driveway. Quick, go tell him to hurry up about it."

As the two of us slogged into the dark backyard like sailors in rough weather, I barely heard his shout to me over the rain: "And tell the clueless ess of a bee to come sleep in the house out of this racket."

I splashed out to the van with the merciful message. Give Del some credit, he had that van going almost before I could scramble into the passenger seat out of the downpour. After parking out from under Igdrasil, he speedily threw pajamas and such in a bag and made a dash for the house with me.

Pop was there ahead of us, mopping his face and hair with a kitchen towel. I shucked off my dripping slicker in the hallway, while Del just dripped. "Whew. There's a lot of weather in this part of the country."

"You haven't seen any weather until you get to Fort Peck," Pop informed him. "Let's get you a bedroom. That one next to yours, Rusty."

However, Del seemed in no hurry to retire for the night now that he was under secure shelter, gazing around the house in that deer-eyed way of his and asking about this and that and the other. I kept hovering at the bottom of the stairway to show him to his bedroom, more than ready for my own after a day that had begun with fishing and gone downhill from there. I suppose I was out of sorts. All right, I was definitely out of sorts, yawning impatiently as Del toured the downstairs rooms as if this was Williamsburg West.

"Is this the original wainscoting?" he was asking as he trailed through the hallway a second time, running his fingers along the nicely carved panel wood. "How interesting. I haven't seen this kind since my grandfather's country place."

"I don't know whether it's original," Pop muttered carelessly, plainly thinking about bed himself, "but it's old as hell."

"Come again?" Del already was looking off to one side, maybe interested in the ceiling plaster now. That irritating haughty little habit of asking for something to be repeated got to me. Couldn't he for crying out loud pay attention to what was being said, the first time around? Couldn't he—

Suddenly I wondered. That slight stiff-necked turn of Del's head, as if to let in what he deigned to hear. Taking advantage of that to shuffle sideways a few feet, just past the corner of his eye, I experimentally snapped my fingers.

Del showed no response, although Pop showed plenty. Eyes narrowed and voice low, he directed me, "Do that again."

I instantaneously did, with the same result.

"Hmm? Do what?" Inquisitively Del looked around at Pop, then at me. There was no mistaking it, he had missed my finger snap both times.

"Delano," Pop was saying in the deadly tone he used on drunks who had to shape up or ship out, "am I right that you don't hear so good?"

Del drew himself up against that implication, or at least tried to. "What makes you think that?"

Hard stares from both of us were his answer.

I have to say, his confession was wrenching to watch as well as to listen to. You never saw a guy look so guilty of something not of his own doing.

"All right, now you know. I'm deaf in that left ear," he said miserably. He rubbed a hand tenderly across it, as if trying to feel the lost sense of hearing. "A lacrosse accident, when I was about Rusty's age. It broke the eardrum."

"Then why in all hell are you in a line of work where you have to catch every word people say?"

"Tom, this may sound paradoxical," he launched into desperate explanation, "but . . . what I *can* hear, I *really* hear. When a person is sitting on the other side of the microphone from me, I don't miss a thing, I absolutely don't." From the look of him, everything in Delano Robertson, ostensible oral historian, strained to make this understood. "It goes deeper in me than just catching some nice turn of phrase, I can *feel* the language making itself. It's, it's the words, yes, but the history they draw from takes me over in almost a kind of trance when people tell me their lives in their own way. An instinct kicks in, it seems like, and I know what to ask, how to keep them talking, what will draw them out." He spun his hands in front of him, as if trying to get traction on the notion. "It's hard to describe, but when I'm collecting people's stories, there's always that feeling I'm capturing more than what's being said. A kind of sixth sense of how much *else* there is, in back of the words." Stopping to read our faces, he weakly imitated Canada Dan: "I hope that's clear, ain't it?"

Give Pop full credit; he did not tell Del a bartender hardly needed a disquisition on the art of listening. Nor did he suggest the equally obvious, that a person with hearing loss might seek to compensate for it the same as someone with a voice like a bullfrog would take up blues singing. He stuck with the heart of the matter.

"Whatever you're hearing in your head doesn't change the fact you're half deaf and going around trying to make talk with people." He locked eyes with Del. "That's why you want me to be your bird dog at the reunion, isn't it."

"No, honestly, that's only the least part of it." Del's voice shook. "You and the Blue Eagle are absolutely up there at the front of people's memories of Fort Peck, I wasn't putting you on about what an institution you were. I mean, *are*. The reunion really needs you, Tom, it's not just me."

Pop squinted at him as if trying to believe what he saw. "Before you tie yourself in any more knots, let me ask you something. Why don't you just settle for a nice office job back there at oral history headquarters, instead of beating your one good ear against the situation this way?"

"I wouldn't last half an hour."

"Why's that?"

"The phone." Del pantomimed the problem. A right-handed person like him, to dial and be free to write and so on, naturally held the receiver in the other hand, to the left ear; he couldn't hear if he did it that way. "The powers that be would spot that in an office right away." He drew a finger across his throat in the slitting motion. "That's why I have to make it as a collector in the field."

"You're like one of those spy stories," Pop said grimly. "Every time anything clears up and halfway makes sense, some other damn thing comes along."

During this, Del sent him a silent look of appeal, and I admit I added an extra-strength one of my own. If rummy old sheepherders couldn't be left in that awful place of predicament, the lurch, how could he abandon poor one-eared Delano Robertson to it? He couldn't let that be on his conscience, could he? Could he?

He withstood us in silence as long as he could. "Lay off while I consolidate my thinking, okay?" he snapped. "Rule number one is, don't rush into things."

I wasn't letting him get away with that. "Are you sure, Pop? I thought it was, you got to play the hand you been dealt."

He gave me a darkly furrowed look. Followed by one at Del. "Cripes, why couldn't you have two good ears instead of getting yourself hit in the head by some goofy kind of stick?"

"Actually, I've asked myself that," Del said delicately.

"For starters," Pop now reeled off as if in an argument with himself, "Fort Peck isn't just a hop, skip, and jump from here, it's way to hell and gone across the state. And there's two half-pint actors with their hearts set on me taking them to a certain play in Valier at the same time, right, Rusty?"

I would like to say I instantaneously and bravely made my decision. In reality, for the longest few seconds I went back and forth like a swinging gate before deciding. Lady Bracknell would have to prevail without me. "Zoe can ride with Bill Reinking. I want to go with you and Del to the mud-thing reunion."

No sound followed that except for the rain drumming on the roof, accompaniment of the summer. Del tensely watched the two of us, his good ear slightly turned our way. Looking like he badly needed a cigarette, Pop lit one and proceeded to growl his way through any number of reasons not to go to Fort Peck—the howl Earl Zane would send up about postponing the sale of the saloon, the howl from Howie when he was tapped for bartending without any notice, the howl customers would put up when they came into the Medicine Lodge to lay eyes on its nationally famous bartender and he wasn't there, and so on.

Finally running out of growls, he took one last exasperated drag on his cigarette.

"The hell with it, let them howl. If it'll make the two of you quit looking like kicked puppies, we'll go gab with mudjacks."

As POP WOULD have put it, anyone with a brain in his cranium grasps what a lumberjack does. And it's no great mental feat to figure out a steeplejack, even if you've never seen one climbing the peak of a church. But a mudjack? If Fort Peck was the damnedest dirt dam in all of Creation, as he said, why weren't its builders called dirtjacks? Perched restlessly in back of the two very different heads in the front seat that mid-week morning while Del drove the Gab Lab at no more than the speed limit even on long, empty stretches of the highway—surely the only vehicle in Montana behaving so—I asked just that.

"Use your thinking part, kiddo." Still growly about the trip, Pop took the question as if he had been waiting for something to do besides watch grain fields go by too slowly. We'd had to pile ourselves and everything else into the van even earlier than for a fishing trip, and dawn found us heading east on the plains with the mountains of the Two Medicine country already slipping from sight behind us. The day came bright and washed after the latest deluge, but besides constant wheat and occasional farmhouses crouched behind scrubby trees planted as windbreaks—Igdrasil would have stood out like a redwood in this landscape—there was nothing much to look at. Boring as the geography was, I attached plenty of meaning to it. Somewhere not distant in the gray prairie to the north was the start of Canada, scene of those trips of his that had driven me wild. Were they really over, with the back-room accumulation to be dealt with somehow? I would have to worry about that some other time. Right now the lesson of the day was as basic as dirt, according to his tone of voice.

"Say you wanted to take one of those buttes"—he was squinting into the distance toward the only landmarks anywhere around, the Sweetgrass Hills, rising like three Treasure Islands on the horizon—"and use it to dam up the Missouri River. What's the slickest way to move that much fill?"

"Uhm, lots and lots of trucks?"

Wrong, his expression told me, not even close. "You'd be trucking for a hundred years. Naw, what you want to do is add water," he said, as though mixing the simplest drink. "Dredge up the soil, turn it into mud, a kind of slurry anyhow, and then pipe the stuff to wherever you want it. Dump enough of it and guess what, you've got a dam."

Okay, that explained mudjacks enough for me. But he wasn't through. Shifting around as though the passenger seat and for that matter the Volkswagen van was too small for him, he lit a cigarette, already his third of the day, and blew smoke as if letting off steam. "I bet you didn't know Fort Peck had the biggest dredges ever built." This tidbit of information was provided as if for my benefit, but doubtless for that of the straining listener in the driver's seat as well.

"Every piece of machinery on those mudboats was the biggest of its kind," we heard next. "Just the cutter heads alone stood higher than the feather on a tall Indian." He smoked and spoke very quietly, apparently drawn back in spite of himself to that time of making a mountain of mud and moving it. Del, hands tight on the steering wheel, looked agonized at not being able to write this down.

"Those things took a real bite out of the riverbank at a time," the dredge tale went on, "a whole hillside would be gone before you could give it a second look, and you'd wonder where the hell it went to. Then way down at the end of the pipeline"—he flourished his cigarette toward the horizon until the ash was about to drop—"you'd see this brown geyser shooting out, and mudjack crews all over the dam like an anthill that had been stirred up." He paused, with timing any actor would have envied. "It was quite the sight."

Was this great or what? Boats in the middle of Montana with teeth huge enough to eat hills. Geysers of muck adding up to the biggest dam on the planet. My very own father right there, witnessing the famous mudjacks at their muddiest. I was back on top of the world. The magnitude of Fort Peck in his telling of it gripped me the way the notion of a thirty-year winter had, and Zoe's magical presence in the back room, and the selection of the Medicine Lodge as the most pleasurable of all the saloons in the state, and family fame in newspapers far and wide, and Delano Robertson arriving in a cloud of sheep, the entire cascade of this one-of-a-kind year; the idea of outsize life, the feeling of being present as things happened way beyond ordinary in human experience. I suppose it was something like a mental fever, the headiest kind to have. Ever since Pop consolidated his thinking there in the hallway of the house, where my finger snap still echoed, my imagination and I knew no limits, and at twelve or at any other known age, there is no spell more dizzying.

Besides, as Zoe would have said, the Zanes didn't have their weenie hands on the Medicine Lodge yet. Temporary luck was better than none, right?

Now Del in his eager-beaver way began asking Pop about this, that, and the other at Fort Peck. Crouched there with the van's cargo stacked almost against my hip pockets, I listened for all I was worth. It was up to me to tell Zoe everything that happened, just as she had vowed to give me the full report on *The Importance of Being Earnest* and Mrs. Reinking's cross-eyed bit, so I nearly stretched my neck into the front seat when Del all of a sudden popped out with, "Is it true you built the Blue Eagle in one day?"

Pop snorted. "Where did you get that haywire idea?" He couldn't help looking rather pleased with himself, though. "I had the floor laid in one night, is all. There was a family of honyocker farmers by the name of Duff, they were working fools. Three of them hammered all night until their arms about dropped off, and I was serving drinks by breakfast time."

"How enterprising of you," Del enthused.

Pop shrugged. "You got to take the chance when it comes, that's rule number—" He caught my look and broke off. "Hey, is this as fast as this crate will go?"

"Hmm?" Del speeded up the van fractionally. He himself kept going full tilt at trying to find out about everything back there in the Depression years. Even his crew cut seemed to be standing at sharper attention now that he had Pop talking even the slightest bit about the Blue Eagle. I was burning up to ask the question that I for so long had wanted to, but did not get the chance before Del switched to, "Do you mind telling me, Tom, why you left Fort Peck before the dam was finished?"

Pop took so long to answer that I thought he wasn't going to. Finally his silence broke. "It was time." He was back to being rough as a rasp. "Every winter was colder than an Eskimo's butt, for one thing. And in the summer you'd fry." He shook his head. "Nature had it in for the place, bad."

"Yes, but you were right in the middle of so much that was happening," Del sounded wistful, "all that history being made."

"What the hell, aren't we always?"

And that was that, for anything worthwhile about my father's experience at the damnedest dirt dam of all time.

WE REACHED THE dam before I fully realized it. I was expecting something as grand as the Egyptian pyramids, rising against the sky, as mighty as eternity. But Fort Peck stretched across what must have been a gentle valley between high bluffs, and all that caught the eye at first was an immense sheet of water that met a very broad, grassy slope, like a glacier stopped by a rise of the land. As we drove down from the west bluff, though, I saw the fantastic gush of water way down at the foot of that rise, the entire Missouri River discharging out of a tunnel—I may have been imagining, but the air seemed to tremble from the force of that white torrent as we drew nearer—and there was no mistaking that the earthen bank of the dam simply was so huge, it seemed a natural feature of the landscape.

Del drove onto the dam and a considerable distance across to a wayside overlook where we could get out and stretch and have a look around. There on the tremendously tall and long dike, even Pop, I believe, climbed out like a pilgrim at a fateful shrine.

It still was quite the sight, all these years after a much younger Tom Harry marveled at the mud starting to fly. A mountain's worth of boulders lined the entire water side of the four-mile length of the dam, and the whole piece of engineering was staggering to think of, the heavy lid of rocks and gravel pressing down on what had started as mud fill, to compress everything in place and hold back the biggest river of the West. The sparkling lake, picture-perfect with circling white pelicans gravely looking down their long beaks at the water below, was like Rainbow Reservoir magnified countless times. I could see why the people who built one of the wonders of the modern world here would proudly hold a Mudjack Reunion, even if my reluctant father had to be taken by an ear—Del's deaf one—to join in.

As the three of us gazed around from the overlook, my curiosity finally burst. "Where was it, Pop?"

"Where was what?"

"You know! The Blue Eagle!"

He gave me a dodgy look, which was not at all the answer I wanted, until Del jumped in to my support. "I was going to ask if Rusty didn't."

"If it isn't one of you, it's the other," Pop grumbled. "I thought there was a law against double jeopardy." Nonetheless, he squared around toward the high bluff we had driven down and pointed halfway up the slope. "Okay, see that wide spot in the road? You're looking at the town of Wheeler. The highway was the main drag and there was a whole lineup of saloons, mine"—he stumbled slightly on the word—"right smack in the middle."

Where there was nothing but bunchgrass and tumbleweeds? I let Del ask the obvious. "What happened to the buildings?"

"Torn down or moved," came the curt response. "I bet we saw plenty of them on the way here—chicken coops and toolsheds."

I couldn't contain my dismay. "Even the Blue Eagle?"

"It was big enough to make a nice barn, kiddo."

Wheeler's fate of disappearance, Pop went on to tell us, was also that of the town of Idlewile. And of Parkdale, Park Grove, Midway, Valley, McCone City, Lakeview, Willow Bend, Delano Heights, New Deal, Square Deal, and Free Deal, all of the workers' shantytowns that sprang up at the dam site in the 1930s like Hoovervilles with paydays. Del and I hung on his every word as he described how twenty thousand people lived any crazy way they could while the wages lasted, in tar paper shacks and drafty government barracks and any other kind of shelter that could be slapped together and called housing. It made the life of Two Medicine sheepherders seem luxurious.

"Help me with something, please," Del asked as if stumped on his homework. "From everything I've been able to find out, the town of Wheeler had no shortage of saloons. The Buckhorn Club, the Wheeler Inn—"

"Yeah, and Ed's Place, and the Bar X," the recital seemed to improve Pop's mood. "The Dew Drop Inn, terrible name for a joint. The Mint and the Stockman, you can't have a genuine drinking town without those."

"—yet the one that sticks in people's minds is the Blue Eagle. How in the world did you win over so many customers against so much competition?"

Pop actually laughed a little. "Easy as pie. I took the front door off its hinges, first thing."

Del looked as if he hadn't heard that quite right, but I knew I had, and I still goggled.

"Word got around fast that the Blue Eagle never closed, day or night," Pop spelled out. "*Couldn't* close, no door, see? Three shifts were running on the dam, around the clock, so we had guys coming in from midnight to dawn as well as all day long." From the glint in his eye, this was one satisfying memory of Fort Peck. "Eventually I put the door back on and closed the joint late at night like a sane person, but that didn't matter by then." He shrugged. "You get the right kind of reputation, Delano, and you've got it made."

The other two of us could have heard more and more of his secrets of success, but he broke off the discourse all too soon.

"Enough of that. We better get to getting, or we won't be ready at the damn reunion."

Carried away by a sense of the occasion, however, Del insisted on taking a picture before we budged from the dam, and went scrambling into the Gab Lab to find his camera. He had to squirm in from the front seat through the space where I'd been sitting, because the back of the van was so loaded with our cargo, and we could hear him grunting as he shifted things around to reach the camera. "Do you think we brought too much?" I worried to Pop. "He doesn't have any room in there to get his recording stuff ready."

"Unless mudjacks have changed," he said without concern, "there's no such thing as too much. Delano will have to fend as best he can, it'll be good for him. This'd all be easier if he wasn't as green as goose crap." Edgily he walked to the railing of the wayside, peered over to the water, then grimaced toward the van. "I wish to hell he'd hurry up. This spot gives me the willies. It slid, you know."

I knew no such thing, which was becoming chronic where Fort Peck was concerned.

"This part of the dam gave way in '38," Pop impatiently enlightened me. "Killed eight mudjacks in the slide." He indicated the boulder-banked slope down to the lake. "It happened before they got the rocks onto it, this was all fresh fill, and a quarter of a mile of it along here slipped loose and slid into the rezavoy." He shook his head. "They were lucky the whole thing didn't go, or it'd have drowned out every place from here to Saint Louie."

My toes curling, I glanced down at the dam fill under us. "Wh-where were you when it happened?"

"Where would I be? Slinging drinks in the Blue Eagle."

"Found it!" Del sang out, brandishing the camera and motioning for us to stand together at the outer edge of the dam, which

I would have been happier to do if Pop hadn't mentioned the big slide. He held still for the photograph—it shows one of us big-eyed as a puppy for whatever the day would bring, and the other looking like he was about to have teeth pulled; you can guess which was which—but the instant the shutter was clicked, he had us into action. "Let's go to the government burg and see what's what," he directed Del, and we headed back to shore.

THE LITTLE TOWN carrying the Fort Peck name had outlasted all the others by housing the federal workers who tended the dam and its powerhouse, and it appeared determined to make up in neat identical streets of houses for the notorious messiness of the shantytowns. Lawns blazed green, like swatches of a golf course. Besides those spotless neighborhoods there was a tiny business section that Del cruised us into. Old hotel, post office, gas station, grocery store—the store had a big fresh sign saying ICE!

"Pull in here," Pop spoke up. "It's time to give your expense account some exercise."

Del parked and none too willingly pulled out his wallet.

"Give Rusty, oh, twenty bucks," Pop instructed, "that ought to do it." He turned to me and told me the plan. "Delano, better go in with him to help carry it."

Del balked. "The Library of Congress powers that be don't like odd expendi—"

"What they don't know back there won't hurt them. Call it emergency rations."

It was my turn to balk. "What if the store person doesn't want to sell that much?"

"No sweat," Pop waved that off and instructed me on how to handle matters inside.

Repeating over and over to myself what I was supposed to say, I advanced toward the store with trepidation. This was not like doing a bit when Zoe was the only audience. Beside me, Del looked as uncertain as I was.

The storekeeper glanced up as the pair of us shuffled in. "How do, fellows. What can I get for you?"

"Hi." Nervously I spread the money on the counter, my voice squeaking as I ordered up, "All the ice you've got, please."

Startled, the man behind the counter asked, "What are you going to do with it all?"

"I'm, we're from the Boy Scouts. This is our troop leader." Del did vaguely look like that, in his semi-safari shirt and tan pants. "We're selling pop to raise money for the big Scout Jamboree that's going to be at the dam, and our cooler tipped over on the way here and everything melted, and now we need all the ice you've got. Please."

"Funny I hadn't heard about any big jamboree." The store-keeper pondered that. "When's this?"

"Labor Day weekend?"

The thought of a horde of hungry, thirsty boys as customers across a three-day weekend made him sit up and take notice. Still, he questioned our purpose a bit further. "What'll this pop money you raise be spent on, exactly?"

"We need tents. Lots of tents."

"Dozens," Del unexpectedly put in.

"Hundreds," I adjusted his nice try.

The storekeeper rubbed his jaw. "Gee whiz, I sure hate to run out of ice this early in the day, so many people coming to the dam get-together and all. But if it's for a good cause—"

Del and I stacked bags of ice in every available nook and cranny of the van, with Pop supervising. "Drive down to the boat ramp," he directed next. There, he opened up the first of the cases of Great Falls Select stacked solid in the back of the van and dragged out the washtub brought along for this purpose. Professionally he iced the tub of beer with a number of bags of our monumental purchase and stowed some in reserve. The rest of the ice, he had us get rid of in the lake. Looking satisfied for the first time all day, he told Delano: "Get your apparatus ready. People are going to want a tall, cool one, and when they do, we nab them."

IN THE NEXT little while, mudjacks began arriving at Fort Peck as if they had come up the river to spawn. The reunion site was a riverbank park with picnic tables and scrubby wind-bent trees that provided mere spots of shade, and that, too, proved to be part of Pop's plan. He'd had Del unfurl the camper van's awning, supported by a couple of aluminum poles, and set up his table and tape recorder squarely beneath it, then supplemented that with a big tarp fastened onto the awning and stretched to the nearest couple of trees. The result was a nice, sizable patch of shade, and the three of us hung back there in the cool shadow, watching cars pour off the approach road and park in the bunch-grass in a mass of glittering windshields and hoods and fenders polished for the occasion, and people in their good clothes climbing out and greeting one another like long-lost relatives. We viewed the handshaking and backslapping and general camaraderie of the reunion until Del grew antsy.

"Ah, Tom, I do want to get as many interviews as I possibly can, so hadn't I better begin?"

"Not until the hats start to come off."

"The—?"

Very shortly it became evident what Pop meant. Those in the crowd who remembered what Fort Peck was like on a summer day wore straw cowboy hats or other ventilated headgear. (The three of us had on the best loose-weave Panamas from the back room.) Those who had been less mindful sweltered in Stetsons and fedoras, and they were the first to start lifting their lids and wiping their brows.

"Okay, let's get at it," Pop granted, and we sprang into action. He and Del lugged the loaded beer tub from the rear of the van to a prominent spot in the shade of the tarp while I started setting up some folding chairs borrowed from the Gros Ventre Chamber of Commerce's fishing derby resources. When those were in place, Pop briskly brushed his hands and turned to the waiting two of us.

"Remind me, Delano. Which one is your lame ear?"

"Hmm? The left, why?"

"Keep the good one closest to me so you can hear and try to act like a normal human being, is all. Rusty, just come on along and spectate nice and quiet, got that?" He squared his bow tie and set his jaw. "Come on, let's go hijack mudjacks."

I WISH I HAD adequate words for the performance that followed. Pop sifted into that Fort Peck crowd, meeting and greeting old customers he had not seen for more than twenty years, swapping remarks about how time flew, and in that gathering on that day my father was treated as if he was parting the waters of the Missouri River. "Tom, how you doing?" man after man greeted him joyously, and he would smile a little and respond with something like, "Still teetering and tottering." No question, the practically Shakespearean newspaper story accounted for some of the regard that enveloped him, fame finding its mark for all to see, but what Pop was experiencing went much deeper than that, I am still convinced. As we trailed in his wake like page boys behind royalty, Del kept slipping me a grin that said, *Didn't I tell you he's a living legend?* And that was openly true, for the people assembled here no longer were fledgling dam builders escaping the Depression for a night out in a boom-town saloon, but middle-aging husbands and fathers who saw in this familiar white-shirted bow-tied figure, with eyebrows knowledgeably cocked, a vision from when they were young and unmarred by what lay ahead of them in life. Memory does that, unerring as a spotlight. I noticed Pop didn't seem all that dis-pleased, either, with the attention that followed him through the crowd. But he dispensed with it as if he were on the job in back of the bar, staying on the move until, over at the edge of the throng, he spotted a lanky man in bib overalls and an old gray fedora.

"There's your first victim," he murmured as Del strained to hear. "Hey, Short-Handed," he called out, "how's the world been treating you?"

"Tom Harry, or I'm seeing things!" The bibbed man and Pop swatted each other on the shoulders until Pop managed to step back out of range and bring us in for introduction. "Delano, Rusty, meet Curly Martin."

"Used to be, anyhow," Curly told us with a forlorn grin, lift-ing his hat to display a bald head. Providing Del a handshake that seemed to startle him, our new acquaintance began talking a blue streak. "Son, you're packing around the best name this side of the Bible. If it wasn't for old Roosevelt, I'd still be living out in the tumbleweeds and eating gophers." Then it was my turn for a startling handshake, while Curly expanded the con-versation to Pop. "Tom, you old son of a gun, you sure bring back the memories. Remember the time that drunk Swede grabbed that milk-blond taxi dancer—what was her name, anyhow—and tried to drag her up onto the bandstand to sing with him? You threw him out halfway across the street, dang if you didn't.

Came back in with most of your shirt tore off and told us, 'Play "Roses of Picardy," get people to dancin' again.'"

I gaped at my father. Bouncing an objectionable customer halfway across the street was not news. But people danced in the Blue Eagle? Whose very same owner would not permit so much as a jukebox tune in the Medicine Lodge?

"That's another story, Curly," Pop coughed that away, "but what Delano here would rather hear about is something like when the dam slid. You were mudjacking that day, don't I remember?"

"Whoo, you know I was. Right there on the top of the dam when the goshdamn railroad tracks started to bow and the goshdamn ground turned to jelly right under my—"

"Hold it," Pop suspended the narrative. "See, Delano has come out here all the way from Washington, D.C., to collect stories like that from the old days"—Del was almost nodding his head off, ratifying that—"and so you'd be doing the world a favor by telling this into his tape recorder."

Instantly Curly dried up like a prune. "Aw, I'd be kind of bashful about doing something like that." He looked around as if for rescue. "Besides, the fellows and me are gonna see if we remember how to play music at all. I better be getting at that. Been nice visiting with you."

Looking stricken as Curly made his escape, Del started to call after him but Pop beat him to it.

"You know what, though, it's gonna be kind of hot playing music out in this sun. If it was me, Curly, I'd get myself ready with a nice, cold Shellac over there in the shade while Delano asks you a few things about the big slide."

Curly halted practically in midstep. "Now you're talking." He turned around to Del. "Where's this little piece of heaven?"

We watched Del eagerly usher him to the Gab Lab, with

Curly already talking a mile a minute again. I asked Pop, "Does he really play music?"

"Yeah, with the Melody Mechanics. He's guitar."

My hand still was feeling that handshake. "He's got a couple of fingers missing, doesn't he?"

"Sure, that's how he made his musical reputation—Short-Handed Curly."

Obviously there was a lot to learn about what went on in the Blue Eagle. But I didn't have time to pursue that because Pop kept on the move, picking out people to steer to Del, murmuring the names to me as faces fit his memory. "Cece Medwick from the boatyard, yeah, he'd be good. . . . Taine, he was the diving-barge boss, he'd have a lot to tell about the slide. . . . Chick Siderius, naw, he was always a management stooge. . . . Hey, there's Ron and Dola, they'd be just what Delano wants. They ran a cafe, more like a hash joint."

"What was it called?"

"What do you think, the Rondola."

All too soon, he sent me scooting off to keep the beer tub filled while he sorted through the crowd for other mudjacks to send over. Before long, quite a gang of them was bunched around that tub and the only ice anywhere to be found, and if these had been Missing Voices, they weren't by the time they had a couple of Shellacs and sat down under the Gab Lab awning to be interviewed by Del. I have to say, I was amazed at him. He was working at high speed yet somehow managing to draw the best out of each Fort Peck veteran. As he had tried to make us understand, his bad ear didn't matter when the person was seated across the microphone from him because he listened with all of himself, from his intent brow down his whole body, at times practically doubled up with anticipation and other times thrust back in his chair at the wonder of what was being said. Throughout, he made nearly silent clucks of encouragement between dealing out questions cannily attuned to whatever was being said, the five Ws and an H taken care of in the most natural kind of way. Maybe he was doing a bit each time or maybe it was just Del, but whatever the topic, he radiated such keen interest in the person in the interview chair that I almost wanted to jump in and start talking into his microphone myself. Besides that, he turned out to be a whiz with the tape reels; when the little counter on the recorder, like the odometer on a car, hit a certain number, he was there in a flash with a fresh reel, threading it on so quickly, I would have bet he had practiced it blindfolded. Even the safari shirt proved itself, its pockets producing batteries to keep the recorder rolling, old clippings about Fort Peck to help jog memories, labels to slap names onto the reels, and other supplies that kept things rolling smoothly. If only Zoe had been there to applaud his performance properly with "Swuft!"

I listened all I could between making runs of Select to the slushy tub; listened, entranced, to the mythic Thirties coming to life, little knowing that the Sixties would someday echo the same way. The interviews, as conducted by Del, were like jazz, or, yes, the blues; riffs of memory in a language all their own. So I learned that Fort Peck's populace had been such working fools that even the barbers wore bib overalls, and shantytown living conditions were so barny, you'd half expect to wake up in the morning next to a horse, but that never stopped married couples from pouring foundations in the dark—I figured out this meant making babies happen—and a job at the dam was as welcome as Christmas because when the eagle laid—payday—a person so broke he was dragging the ground would at last have some cartwheels—silver dollars—to rub together. And over and over, it was said that the day of the big slide, you'd have thought hell was afloat and the river rising.

What is it about human nature that dwells on close calls? As Del and I hung on their stories, the mudjacks, almost to a man, had stories of terror when the face of the dam slid, of riding the pipeline down the avalanche of mud as if on the back of a dragon, of being pulled from the island of mud and debris, of narrowly escaping drowning before the rescuers could get there. I listened with shivers, especially as they all said in one way or another that if the dam had broken, it would have been the damnedest flood ever.

But that was what this day was for, those memories, those tales. Del was supremely in his element, and the mudjacks gloriously in theirs, and the reels of tape ran and ran, the voices becoming permanent echoes of a certain time, a certain place, a rediscovered *lingua america*.

Eventually Pop showed up with another fresh supply of interview candidates, listened for a few minutes, then signaled me with a jerk of his head. "That ought to hold Delano for a while," he said with satisfaction. "Let's grab some grub."

Generally a reunion is an occasion with the worst of the past rinsed away by the passage of time, and this one now was determinedly lighthearted. On the flatbed of a truck the Melody Mechanics were playing vigorously—sure enough, Curly was strumming a guitar as if a few fingers were plenty—and between numbers an announcer with the patter of a livestock auctioneer worked the crowd to find out who had come the longest distance, who had produced the most children, and so on. The air had turned heavy—big prairie thunderheads were building up in the distance; I could tell what Pop meant about nature having it in for Fort Peck—but no one seemed to mind the weather this day. Skirting the throng, he and I stayed on course down to the riverbank, where the food tables were, then found a spot to sit under a scrawny shade tree with our paper plates of macaroni salad and hot dogs. We were barely settled before I could not contain the question one moment longer.

"What's a taxi dancer?"

"You would ask." He chewed on my question as well as his hot dog. "Let me put it this way. It's when you pay a dancer for how long you've danced with her, just like cab fare to go someplace."

"You mean, guys would, uh, hire these partners right there in the Blue Eagle?"

"Yeah, in the joint. It brought in herds of customers, savvy?"

I was starting to, putting two and two together, and it was adding up rapidly. "All those customers and taxi dancers ever did"—I could hear how dubious I sounded—"was just dance?"

He hesitated. "With some of the taxi dancers, that was kind of open for negotiation if the customer wanted to go farther than that, I guess you could say."

"So," I pressed on dangerously, "really it was like on First Avenue South in Great Falls?"

The sigh of ages, as the topic of prostitution no doubt has produced down through history. With his forehead scrunched, the famous owner of the Blue Eagle set to the task of explaining matters for me.

"Not every taxi dancer was a whore, if that's what you're thinking. Most weren't. Plenty of them ended up married to those dance partners, I could point out some of them here today."

He saw me trying to keep up with this and finding it hard.

"Rusty, here's the how of it. Things were different in the Thirties, and Fort Peck was even differenter, if that's a word. The Depression, when it hit"—he looked off across the still water of the man-made lake as though searching back into that time—"it did things to people it's hard to believe now. If you were on a farm out here, chances were your crops dried up and blew away year after year, until all you were left with was tumbleweeds and a foreclosure notice, and you lost everything. If you were a working stiff, you got laid off because some damn fool place called Wall Street crashed, and next thing you knew, the bank down the street went under and took your life's savings with it."

I had read all this in school, but hearing it from him sank in vastly deeper. He was grimacing painfully as he spoke.

"It changed people. They had to do whatever they could to get by. Curly wasn't only kidding about eating gophers—plenty of families in this part of the state were that desperate." He lowered his voice, as grave as I had ever heard him. "I still don't know why there wasn't a revolution. But people toughed it out until Roosevelt came into office and projects like this dam got under way. Then before long there's these thousands of mudjacks drawing wages, and others who showed up here because the mudjacks had money in their pockets." His voice gathered itself and he mustered a kind of smile. "Cripes, that was me, too, if you can imagine."

He drew a breath. "Okay, that's the long way around the barn to taxi dancing, but it's all connected, see. There were women who had to make a living, too, and getting out on the floor with a guy for two bits a dance was a way to do it. Any talk of business beyond that, let's say, was up to them, not me."

By this point I was practically memorizing his each word. Zoe was going to want every tiniest detail of this.

"The dance partner more than likely would buy the woman a drink or two and a few for himself," he went on doggedly, "so there's where it paid off for me. It was what you might call a sideline. Like letting the Medicine Lodge customers hock stuff. Same kind of thing."

Renting out women didn't sound to me like the same kind of thing. Was there even any way it sounded legal? The past casts a tricky shadow, I was discovering.

Pop read my face, then gazed off toward the truck bandstand, where the Melody Mechanics were producing another spirited tune and the crowd around them was clapping and whooping.

"Kiddo," he said softly, "you have to understand, every night in Wheeler was Saturday night." He listened to the raucous music for a few moments. "It was a different time back then. Everybody was young and hot to trot, excuse my Latin. Sure, people liked to drink in the Blue Eagle, the way I ran the joint, but what they really liked was to drink and dance and kind of get to know each other, the way men and women do. If I was going to be in business here, that's what had to happen." He tipped his hat back with a forefinger to look at me more openly. "Got all that?"

"I . . . I guess so."

"That takes care of that, then," he said, sounding like he was trying to convince himself as well as me.

"Can I ask you something else?"

"Nothing known to man has stopped you yet. What is it now?"

"Were you a bootlegger, too?"

He winced at *too*. "What makes you think I was?"

"The Packard. Somebody said it's a bootlegger special."

"Somebody did, did they?" He frowned in the general direction of Del. "That's bee ess, kiddo. I just liked the looks of the old buggy. Seemed like a lot of car for the money. Anyway, bootlegging . . ." He took a couple of hungry bites of hot dog before I could come up with any more pesky questions. "Naw, I never did any of that, not the kind you're thinking of anyway." This was not the definitive answer I was looking for, he could tell from my expression. "Here's how it was, see. Fort Peckers were a pretty thirsty bunch, so the joint would run low on booze sometimes ahead of a Saturday night. It's a hell of a ways to Great Falls or anywhere else out here, so the easiest thing was to run up to Medicine Hat and load up the car with Canadian booze."

"Why there?"

He shifted uneasily. "The Hat is kind of a crossroads, on the Canadian railroad and the highway to Calgary and like that. You can get a lot of business done there if you hold your mouth right. Anyway," he plowed on again, "that's all it was, some cases of rye and other Canuck hooch packed home in the Packard. This was after Prohibition, no law broken, *but*"—he underscored that last word with a careful look at me—"if the state liquor board didn't have somebody at the border to collect tax at two or three in the morning, that was their tough luck. Get the picture?"

It could not have been clearer if painted by Charlie Russell, so I nodded. My father, the living legend, maybe had not crossed the line of the law in the Blue Eagle years, but he had danced and driven right up to it, from all it sounded like. Yet, as he said, it was a different time back then. He couldn't change the past, I couldn't change it, we had to go on, and together; as he'd proclaimed more than once, we weren't doing too bad with what we had to work with, and we didn't give a flying fig for other ways of being father and son. I couldn't really argue with that.

Gazing off again into the gathering, he asked reflectively: "Now do you get why I wasn't red hot to come to this? Things happen sometimes that can be misunderstood."

"But everybody here seems to think you're"—I stumbled for the words—"something great."

"Yeah, well, that's what time can do to you, once in a while. Among other things." He turned my way, watching me anxiously. "That enough answers for you for one day? Rusty? Things still more or less okay between us after all that, I hope?"

Slowly I nodded again. "Still are, Pop."

"Right. Come on, eat up and let's go see how Delano is doing."

IT WAS SLOW going through the crowd, with Pop being greeted like strolling royalty by anyone who hadn't done so before, and as hard as I tried to envision these paunchy men and their broad-beamed wives as lean, young hot-to-trot drinkers and dancers, twenty-five years stood in the way. That was not the case for the majordomo of the Blue Eagle, who accepted slaps on the back and outpourings about the old days in an easy fashion, now that we could see Del industriously interviewing mudjacks, with beer still serving its purpose among those waiting under the shade of the tarp. "He's got it made," Pop said with satisfaction as we were closing the distance to the Gab Lab, "so all we need to do is keep everybody happy with plenty of Shellac and—"

He stopped in his tracks so suddenly I bumped into him.

"Damn," he let out under his breath. "Why doesn't he have anything better to do than prowl around here?"

"Who, Pop?"

"You'll see."

"I might have known who I'd find if I followed the trail of beer bottles," a voice with a scary amount of authority in it made itself known. A small man in a cowboy hat strutted over to us, looking annoyed. His meager face seemed set in that one expression, like a doll's head carved out of a dried apple. Everything about him was half pint in size, except for the star-shaped badge on his shirt pocket. "Tom Harry is still among the living, huh? Imagine that."

"If it isn't my favorite sheriff." I could tell from Pop's voice that the lack of warmth was mutual. "Been a while, hasn't it,

Carl, since you would drop by the Blue Eagle for some recreation of a certain kind."

"That's past history." The Fort Peck lawman, as much of him as there was, took me in at a glance. "Who's this? Got yourself a grandkid, you of all people?"

"My son," Pop said stiffly. "Rusty, meet Carl Kinnick. He's been sheriff in this county since the grass first grew."

"Hi."

Kinnick didn't answer me, merely nodded as if his neck hurt. "Tom Harry a family man? I'll be a son of a bitch." He smirked at Pop. "Will miracles never quit?"

Pop said levelly, "I hope not."

I started to worry, not even knowing why. At my age I didn't have Pop's long experience in reading people's character, but this person had *mean* written all over him.

Now the sheriff was back to giving Pop a gimlet gaze. "I wouldn't have thought you was the sentimental type, showing up at a shindig like this."

"Life's full of surprises," Pop offered with deceptive casualness. "Didn't I read somewhere that you've switched to Republican? After all those times of riding Roosevelt's coattails here?"

This evidently hit a touchy spot on Sheriff Kinnick. "The Democrats weren't worth it anymore," he huffed. "Adlai Stevenson was a loser if there ever was any invented."

"Kennedy maybe won't be," Pop laughed, "if the other choice is Dickybird Nixon."

"I'll take my chances," the sheriff said, as if it was costing him teeth. He went up on his toes to peek past us to the Gab Lab, where Del was poising the microphone just so while a lean gray veteran of dam work regaled him between swigs of beer. "Who's the jaybird over there people are yakking to?"

"Delmer Robertson," Pop improvised politically. "High-powered historian from back east. Talking to folks about working on the dam. Rusty and me are helping him with his on-the-ground research."

"They start them awful young in on-the-ground research, don't they," the sheriff said with a suspicious look at Del and then at me. "Present company excepted, huh, barkeep?" he shifted his beady attention to Pop. "Just to keep things on the legal up-and-up, let's see your event permit for selling beer."

I knew it. We were going to be thrown in the clink because this badge-wearing retreaded Republican son of a bitch—he used the word on himself—didn't like the looks of us.

"No need," Pop saved us, "I'm giving the hooch away."

Surprised, the sheriff laughed unpleasantly. "That isn't like you."

"Good works sneak up on a person, haven't you ever noticed?"

"Not hardly—I didn't get where I am by believing in fairy tales." Peering from under his cowboy hat, the little lawman watched one person after another fish out a bottle of beer from the icy tub and walk away without any show of money. He took another long look at Del and the recording apparatus, then sourly moved off, saying over his shoulder to my father: "Better be careful spreading those good works in my jurisdiction, hear? Every twenty-five years is about right."

I began to breathe again. My feeling of relief lasted only as long as it took Pop to get a gleam in his eye and call after the retreating figure, "Hey, Sheriff? Speaking of past history. Anything ever come of that case of the truck in the river?"

Kinnick halted and turned around, scowling. "Don't be funny. I'm still working on it. You'd have heard it all over the state if I got that solved."

"Just wondering. You know I always had an interest in law enforcement."

That unpleasant laugh again. "From a healthy distance, yeah."

Pop persisted: "Any of the Duffs here?"

"That tribe? Hah. They wouldn't show their faces after that."

"People surprise you sometimes, though, don't you find?"

Before turning to go, the sheriff preened up on his toes again, shaking his head. "You're getting soft, Tom. That's bad for your health."

I held in what I was dying to ask until the badge-wearing runt was out of earshot.

"What truck in the river?"

"Can't you take lessons from Delano in being hard of hearing?" Pop sounded on edge, although my question seemed to me perfectly natural. He still was watching the sheriff recede. Aware that I was not going to let the question rest, he lowered his voice and began: "If you really have to know, it was something that happened in '38, not long after the slide. A couple were parked in a truck on the dam one night. The thing somehow rolled into the water and drowned them both."

Put that way, it sounded like a pure accident. But if so . . .

"Why is the sheriff still working on it?"

"Kiddo"—Pop wrinkled his brow at me—"I don't know where you get it from, but sometimes you know more than the situation calls for."

He pulled out his day's half pack of cigarettes and found it was empty. "Damn," he said through his teeth, and opened a fresh pack. I didn't say anything. The commotion of the reunion picked up as the Melody Mechanics swung into "Pennies from Heaven" and much of the crowd sang along. Over at the van, Del could be seen, absorbed as ever in mudjack gab. The sun

shone, the famous dam stood strong as eternity, the Blue Eagle
was worshipped in memory, the sheriff was taken care of, everything was clicking just right for Pop on this day of days, except
for the bundle of inquisitiveness relentlessly tagging at his side.

"Okay, if it'll get it out of your system," he said, as if it had better, "I'll tell you." He lit the sinful cigarette, blew a wreath of
smoke, and began. "Like I said, the two of them were in the truck
in the middle of the night when it rolled. But that was only the
half of it. They were—"

I couldn't wait to tell Zoe about it.

"BARE NAKED? Both of them?"

"That's what Pop said."

"Watching the submarine races," Zoe whispered in her
knowledgeable way. Practically breathless, we were camped
beneath the vent, trying to sort through the happenings at Fort
Peck and those since, and at the same time follow along with
the voices rising and falling in the barroom, neither one a simple
task. For the moment, the tip of her tongue showed her concentration on the mystery couple. "But if they were married, why
weren't they home in their own bedroom instead of making out
in a truck?"

"That's just it, see. Married, but not to each other."

"Oooh. That's different."

So different that it kept me busy filling her in on the story as
I had it from Pop. The pair in the truck both belonged to a large
family working on the dam, which caused the scandal, but it
was the man's name that meant something. "Had a customer in
the old days," the echo of my father, in a summer snow of seed-
fall from a giant cottonwood the day of my arrival in Gros Ventre, "Darius Duff, how's that for a name? He was kind of a

political crackpot, but he knew things. He'd start feeling his oats after enough drinks, and one time he got going on Igdrasil, the tree of existence." I skipped the Igdrasil part to catch Zoe up on the mean little sheriff and how touchy he still was about the unsolved crime, if that's what the drownings amounted to. "Pop thinks it was an accident. The truck getting knocked out of gear when they were, um . . ."

"Screwing," Zoe helped out.

"Uh-huh, and it rolled down the dam into the lake, just like that."

"Wild!"

We paused to listen tensely to the voices out front, the familiar and the new. Nothing was changing there, although at the same time everything was, and I was impelled back to the rest of the story of the Mudjacks Reunion. How Del, exhausted but triumphant, finished the last interview as people were heading for their cars, calling out good-byes and vows to do this again in five years. Meanwhile Pop and I filled trash cans with empty beer bottles—"The Shellackers in Great Falls ought to put up a plaque here, too," he observed—and carefully stacked the empty beer cases so they wouldn't blow away. Now that the reunion was all but over, he acted more like his usual self, going about business as if nothing else on the face of the earth mattered, but a couple of times I caught him watching me tensely to gauge my reaction to the day and its revelations. I hardly knew how to measure it myself. This father of mine had proved to be everything Del credited him with, legend and institutional memory and icebreaker. Why not say it all the way? Leadbelly of the mudjacks. Yet he also was shown to have been something like a landlord of women who went with men for money—I may have been only twelve, but I could figure out that taxi dancing might have serious implications after the music stopped—and he and the sheriff poked at each other in a kind of scary way. What was I supposed to think?

When Pop wasn't busy glancing at me as we loaded up to leave, I eyed him, trying to decide. "Tom, you were fantastic! You too, Rusty." Del by now was practically floating against the ceiling of the Gab Lab as he stowed the precious reels of tape, recounting to us one mudjack's tale or another in giddy fashion. Gradually I made up my mind. When Del at last showed signs of running down, I butted in sharply.

"I have a question."

I looked right at Pop as I said it, and my tone sent Del silent. I could see Pop, his expression frozen, bracing himself against five Ws and an H and whatever else of the alphabet of inquiry possible about his doings in his Fort Peck years. I let that hang in the air just long enough before I asked, "Why was the eagle blue?"

I realize it was an imaginary whoosh of relief from him, and for that matter from Del, who sensed that this was one of those family matters where the stakes were dangerously high, but it cleared the air, nonetheless. With a look of replenished confidence, Pop enlightened me that the blue eagle was something from the New Deal, a symbol businesses showed off to say they were complying with wage standards and other codes of the National Recovery Administration, and he'd figured it made a good name to slap onto a saloon at the grandest New Deal construction project of all. "Anything to do with Roosevelt, Fort Peckers were hog wild about"—he got talkative now that my question had proved easy as a breeze—"so they thought it was patriotic to drink in the joint. Not bad, hey?"

Head cocked, Del had been crouched in the Gab Lab, happily listening. "Great story! History making itself felt in the thirst glands," he enthused, joking or not, I couldn't tell. "Tom, you absolutely must let me capture that on tape when we get back."

"We'll see" sounded more positive than it usually did from him. Hesitantly, Del put forth, "I, ah, hope you're glad you came?"

Pop paused. He gave that a rueful wrinkled smile, sharing some of it to me, before answering.

"'Glad' maybe isn't quite the real best word. But it's been interesting."

His gaze went distant as he cast a look at the dam and then at the vacant hillside, where the Blue Eagle once stood, and around at the reunion site, where he had walked like a king. I silently watched while he loosened his bow tie and folded it away, the same as I had seen him do so many times after his nights of bartending. Standing there as if catching his breath, he looked like he did after bouncing someone from the saloon, shirt crumpled and the gray in his pompadour mussed in with the black hair, brow furrowed but no wounds showing. I was the one hurting, with our life scheduled to change unimaginably as soon as we got home and the Medicine Lodge passed from our hands, and this father whom I loved, in spite of anything today's evidence said about him, would turn into an old man waiting for the marble farm. It didn't seem right.

After his breather, if that's what it was, Pop snapped to. "Delano, you don't have to kiss every tape," he called into the van, where Del could be heard still squirreling away things, "we need to get a move on or we'll be at the tail end of the traffic out of here." Already, departing cars were jammed at the approach to the road up the bluff, except for one coming off the dam and heading in our direction at a surprising speed, from the looks of it someone who couldn't wait to use the boat ramp now that the crowd was clearing away. Del hopped out, and while I made myself useful folding up chairs, he and Pop began taking down the van awning. Busy with that, they weren't paying any attention to the rapid arrival, but, naturally curious, I watched the car zoom right past the boat ramp and keep coming in a storm of dust.

Zoe had been following my whispered telling of this, as if she didn't dare miss a word. I stopped, seeing it all again.

"Then what?" she breathed.

"This big red Cadillac pulled up." The voices coming through the vent rose at this point, the woman's above the others. "And she got out."

❧ 6 ❧

B ACK IN BUSINESS in the old neighborhood, Tom?" The voice was husky, the smile a bit tilted, the appearance startling, to say the least. "Mudjacks haven't forgotten how to drink, I betcha. How was the take?"

Pop watched, wide-eyed—Del and I did, too—as this late-arriving surprise left the car to join us. The woman was, according to the saying I had never fully appreciated until then, an eyeful. In lavender slacks that had no slack between the fabric and her and a creamy blouse also snugly filled, the vision of womanhood providing us that slinky smile was not what is standardly thought of as beautiful, yet here were three males of various ages who could not stop staring at her.

As she came up to us, it became evident she was middle-aged, but unlike Pop's version, in the middle of resisting the years. Her complexion was that mother-of-pearl kind in ads in magazines, and whatever maintenance it took to discourage wrinkles had been done. Even more striking than any of the rest of her, though, was the mane of hair so blond it approached white; "milk blond" said it about right. She resembled someone well known, although in the surprise of the moment I couldn't quite think who, nor could Del, judging from his quizzical expression.

Pop seemed taken aback by her appearance, in both senses of the word. "It's nothing like the old days, Proxy," he said, not sounding like himself. "We were giving it away."

"For free?" she laughed. "You know what I think about that."

"Let's not go into it." He was awfully nervous all of a sudden, glancing back and forth from her to the two of us, his brow working. "So, what brings you to a reunion you've managed to miss entirely?"

More of that skewed smile. "You're here, I'm here. Nicer without all those curious types around, don't you think?"

Del and I standing there with our faces hanging out drew her attention, especially me. "Hey there, sunshine. Do I see a family resemblance?" she asked, as if looking for one.

Gruffly, Pop identified us to her, and her to us. "Meet Proxy Shannon. She used to"—he put it carefully—"work in the Blue Eagle."

She shook her head as if to say, *Men*. "The old marriage certificate reads 'Duff,' Tom."

"I know that. I just never liked it on you."

That exchange electrified me. Now I knew, absolutely knew, who this was. Wife, widow, survivor, whatever the unfortunate mate should be called, of the male half of that naked couple in that truck in the river. Talk about history, here was some a good deal juicier than Del's tape recordings. The sheriff had made it sound as if those with the cursed name of Duff would be too ashamed to show their faces around Fort Peck, yet she was certainly showing hers, bold as can be. Hungry as I always was for a story, I could hardly wait for more of this one.

Of course, Del knew none of that, and regarded the dazzling newcomer as a surprise pearl in the day's treasure chest of mudjacks. "Shall we get out of the sun?" He gallantly took the role of host, since the tarp tent still was stretched between the van and the nearest trees. "Here, I'll set up the chairs." I scrambled to help.

Pop seemed less than thrilled with Del's burst of good manners, but in no time the four of us were seated in the shade, with the water of the captured river lapping in the background, almost as if all this was intended.

"I could have sworn I heard you say you were giving away throat medicine around here," our unexpected guest kidded Pop, if it was kidding.

Del vaulted up to fish out a beer for her from the last remnants in the tub. "It's been such a phenomenal day, I believe I'll have one with you, Mrs. Duff."

"I could use one, too, Delano," said Pop, making me wonder what gets into grown men at a time like this.

"A phenomenal day at Fort Peck, huh?" the glamorous betrayed widow, as she now starred in my imagination, investigated Del as he returned with the clutch of Shellacs. "That's one for the books." She peered around him to the equipment cubbyholed in the van. "What are you, some kind of gypsy reporter?"

"Hmm? Not quite." He happily expounded to her about the Gab Lab and the mudjack interviews and how he couldn't have done them without Pop as the institutional memory and what a historic day this had been for the retrieval of Missing Voices, while Pop looked more and more as if he wished Del would lose his.

During this, she raised one eyebrow and then the other, which I noticed were not perfectly blond. Finally Del slowed down enough to ask, "Is your husband, ah, available for me to interview sometime?"

"He's out of reach," she said, without the slightest crack in

her expression. It was driven home to me how much Zoe and I
had to learn about facial control if we were going to be actors.
Next came a teasing little grin at Del, as if she'd caught him at
something. "Del-a-no. Is that your honest handle?"

He reddened, back to college boy. "As I've told Tom and
Rusty, my father worshipped Roosevelt." It was his turn now,
though. "If you don't mind my asking, Mrs. Duff—"

"'Proxy' will do, thanks. 'Mrs.' is for grandmas, and I'm not
there yet."

"—that's positively what I was curious about, the derivation
of 'Proxy,' I mean. A great historian once said names are the
signposts of the soul."

"The hair, honey." She tossed her head as if he might not
have noticed the bleach job that stood out like a full moon. "I
had to use peroxide in the old days. They've got better drugstore
stuff now. That's progress for you."

Until now Pop had not been saying anything, just sitting there,
nursing his beer and keeping watch on her. "If we're through
with hairdressing and the history of names, maybe you could
tell us why you're here. There's Nevada plates on that Caddie."
He couldn't help looking appreciatively at the big car with tail-
fins like a rocket ship's. "That's a hell of a long way to come, just
to wait until everybody packs up and leaves."

"Now, Tom, is that the best you can do for a welcome? Been
a little while since we saw each other, I thought absence is supposed to make the heart grow fonder."

"How'd you know I'd even be here?"

"Had a hunch. An old-timey Fort Peck get-together wouldn't
amount to anything without Tom Harry, would it." That came
from her with an admiring smile, genuine or not, I couldn't tell.
"Institutional memory, huh? Jeez, I wish I had one of those."

"I seem to have enough for everybody," he said with a pointed look at Del. "Okay, let's get to it, Proxy. You didn't come looking me up just to stroll down Memory Lane."

She studied her red fingernails. "I need to talk to you about a job."

"A *job*?" Pop couldn't help but laugh. "Excuse my saying so, but you're slipping. Don't you know I'm not running that kind of joint anymore, haven't been for more than twenty years? And, besides, I'm about to—"

"Don't get excited. Not that sort of job." That crooked smile. "I'm danced out anyway. Reno has plenty else to offer." My mind was practically flooded with all this. Nevada was where people went to get divorced quick, and Reno its center of that activity; Velma Simms had shed any number of spouses there. But this Cadillac-driving mystery woman from there, what possible job could she want from Pop in his respectable Gros Ventre life? Proxy Shannon in his telling, Proxy Duff in her own, this latest exchange told me she was no stranger to taxi dancing and the wilder doings in the Blue Eagle, besides being the victim of a husband who strayed to his death at the bottom of the Missouri River right out from where we were sitting. She'd had a lot busier existence than we were used to in the Medicine Lodge.

Naturally Del had his head cocked to hear every word she said—he had that look on him as if he wished his tape recorder was catching all this—and she glanced at him and then at me. "I didn't expect to have to do this in front of an audience." Again, I had the feeling that for some reason I was of particular concern to her. Del, though, gave a start, as if he'd been poked in the ribs. "Ah, maybe Rusty and I should go look at the scenery."

"Sit tight," Pop ordered. "You, too, Rusty. I'm not going to have two cases of itching curiosity to ride home with."

"Oh-kay," Proxy said in throaty singsong. "Then here goes."

A tiny indent of concentration—or was it calculation?—appeared in the place between her eyebrows as she peeled at the label of her Select bottle with her thumbnail before saying anything more. "I saw that newspaper piece about you and your famous joint, Tom. It set me to thinking."

"You can give your brain a rest," Pop duly headed her off. "I'm about to sell the Medicine Lodge. Gonna quit the business. Be a gentleman of leisure."

"I sort of wondered if that wasn't in the wind. 'Sure gonna miss you when I'm gone' is something I used to tell customers when their time was up, remember? Always good for a laugh, and they'd go away feeling better, the dumb joes." Her slanted smile seemed to excuse the three of us from that category, whether or not we deserved it. "But from the story in the paper, it sounded like you might mean it if you don't watch out."

"Didn't I just say in so many words I'm selling the—"

"It sounds like a real nice joint," she didn't miss a beat. "Right up there with the old Eagle, I bet. You always were the best at running a barroom. Jeez, Tom, you don't want to give up something like that. Sure, you maybe could use some time off, not work yourself half to death anymore—I feel that way myself sometimes. But you don't have to throw the whole business away to get to that." She paused. "I can about guess the fix you're in. Russell here"—either I was imagining it or she had said my given name as if trying to get used to it—"has some years to go before he can help out behind the bar, doesn't he."

"He isn't ever—"

"See, that's why I came all this way to make you a proposition." The other two of us were following this as if it were a volleyball match. Proxy gave us another sidelong look, then leaned sharply in on Pop. "What you need is a working partner. An A-1 bartender to take some of the load off."

"Now, there's a whale of an idea if there ever was one," he met that with something between a laugh and a scoff. "What's got into you? Have you forgot what a grind it is behind a bar? Slinging drinks to a full house isn't like cozying up to some guy who's feeling frisky, you ought to know that from those years of watching me at it." Amused now as much as anything, he shook his head definitively. "No slap at you, understand, but you wouldn't last one night tending bar."

"Not me, wise guy. Her."

Pop wrinkled his brow. "Who's 'her'?"

"Francine."

"Proxy, have you slipped a cog? I don't know any—"

"My daughter." The smile sloped more than ever this time. "Yours, too."

DUMBSTRUCK IS A word you use when you're out of others, but it fit then. Pop stared slackly at the tinsel-haired bearer of this news. Del rubbed his good ear as if to make sure it was working right. My head swam. What was it about Fort Peck that kept a person gasping to keep up?

More to the immediate point, how could this woman have a daughter by my father if she had been married to the man in the truck in the lake—I mean, it was conceivable, so to speak, but all kinds of questions followed that one. Starting with, why had he never known about this Francine person until this very day, as I only had to look at him to know this was total news to him. His brow bunched with so many furrows it looked like it was made of wicker. My own mind swirling, I tried to think straight, arithmetic first. Anyone dating back to the Blue Eagle in the 1930s would be a grown-up by now, would need to be if she was a candidate to tend bar. The revelation, if true, that I had some sort of adult sister boggled me as much as if I'd been told Igdra-sil the ancient tree was a relative.

Professional listener or not, Del was sitting there with his mouth pooched in a silent whistle of amazement. Pop was recovering enough to speak.

"This is wacky. If you've got a kid going back that far, sure as hell it came from Darius. He could barely keep his pants on, thinking about you, even after you were married. You and I only ever—"

"Nice try, Tom, but Francine doesn't take after him in any way whatsoever," Proxy brushed that aside. "Besides, him and me weren't that friendly there toward the end, if you take my meaning. I've always kept it a secret from the other Duffs about her being from some other pasture. But no question, Tom, she's yours." She locked eyes with him. "Women know these things." Then a different smile from her, that found time for me before returning to Pop. "Excuse me for saying she's a chip off the old bar, but you'll see. Wait till you meet her."

THE LONG, long drive back to Gros Ventre that night was like being in a darkened tunnel that stretched on and on. Instead of cruising home wrapped in the memory of our phenomenal day at Fort Peck, the three of us were under a far different spell, Del rabbit-eyed behind the wheel, me in a state of emotional commotion in back, Pop dourly smoking his way through one cigarette after another.

An uncertainty named Francine rode with us. When Pop demanded to see this supposed offspring with his own eyes, Proxy promised to produce her just as soon as she could catch a plane from Reno. "I figured we ought to do this sort of gradual," she'd generously left us with, "so everybody could get used to the idea of her." That did not show any sign of taking hold as the van monotonously traced the highway out of the deeper black with its headlights.

Ultimately Del cleared his throat a little. "Ah, Tom and Rusty, I feel like an intruder. This actually is none of my business. I mean, I can't help but think about it, but—"

"Delano, don't get started," Pop begged. "You wanted to hear about life at Fort Peck, you got one more earful than you bargained for, let's leave it at that." I watched him hesitate a couple of times before he half turned to where I was perched behind the seats. "How you doing, kiddo? Kind of a surprise, isn't it." The match lighting his next cigarette showed his face, so serious and seamed. Strange how a moment's glimpse like that can last a lifetime. "It sure as hell was to me." He shook his head, blowing a soft stream of smoke. "Shouldn't have happened."

I had no way of knowing if he meant Proxy materializing like a ghost risen from the reunion as she did, or whatever transpired on some unbridled night in the Blue Eagle twenty-some years ago, or what. The best I could muster was a shaky "Yeah?"

"You've got every right to be upset," he granted. "But this isn't what it's stacked up to be, as heaven is my witness." That was maybe not the best choice of words from a man never known to go near a church.

Trying to look like he was concentrating only on the road, Del was listening as strenuously as I was. "The odds are still sky high any kid of hers is not mine." Pop spoke as if it were flat fact. "Proxy and I didn't fool around in the Eagle. Strictly business, me in back of the bar and her on the dance-floor side. All those years we kept our paws off each other."

"Then why is she—"

"Except that one damn time."

The hum of the tires on the road surface was the only sound

for several seconds. Finally Pop hitched around in his seat toward Del. "How about you, Delano? You ever been in a squeeze like that? Where the brain shuts off and the other body part doesn't?" I sensed this man-to-man talk was for my benefit, somehow.

"Not quite to that extent," Del confessed.

"You're lucky, then." Pop shifted in his seat again, for once not lighting up a cigarette, simply gazing out at the night. "What happened between me and her came smack out of nowhere. Like I said, we'd behaved ourselves for, what, five years, working together since the dam work started up. And it wasn't many days before I was done with Fort Peck, I'd already put money down on the Medicine Lodge. But there was one last big Saturday night in the Eagle, and after we closed the joint, Proxy wanted me to have a drink with her to celebrate what the Eagle had been for us. One led to a couple or three." This still sounded like man talk directed at Del, but I had the very real impression of being the listener in the dark as the only parent I had ever known leaned against the bedroom doorway and told me what was most on his mind.

"We got sloppy," he was continuing that same way. "She was drunk, she was having trouble with that husband of hers, and I guess I didn't resist all that much. It was kind of a good-bye." He gave that the sigh it deserved. "Some good-bye."

Del judiciously left the question to me. "Then . . . then what?"

"We both came to our senses in a hurry, right after. Darius Duff wasn't someone to have mad at you, if he'd ever caught on. Proxy and I didn't go near each other again, and pretty quick the slide happened, and that was the only thing on anybody's mind. Then I pulled out for Gros Ventre, and the rest is another story, isn't it." Saying that, he turned his head toward me, our eyes meeting. "What can I say? Life throws you for a loop sometimes, Rusty. Try not to get all worked up about this, okay?"

Did he think I wasn't trying, ever since the fateful words "She's yours"?

He went on: "Hell, maybe Proxy just has a wild hair and nothing will come of this."

I didn't believe that the least little bit, and I doubted that he did, either. "What if"—my voice was so thin, Del was practically leaning out of his seat to hear—"it doesn't turn out that way?"

"Don't get ahead of the stampede," Pop warned crossly. His gaze moved off into the dark again. "We'll sort this out when they show up at the joint."

"But what about the deal with Earl?"

"Didn't I just tell you not to—" It took some doing, but he reined himself in. "First things first, right? Earl will just have to wait his turn in the complaint line a little longer. He's used to it."

So many conflicting thoughts contended in me that my brain felt knotted up. As much as ever, I did not want him to give up the Medicine Lodge, and if this Francine could turn out to be really a working partner and take the strain off the bartending, wouldn't that be the best possible thing? How much would she take over things, though? Everything? Would she live with us? Would she boss me around? What if she turned out to have a disposition like that other relative, Ronny the Phoenix menace? The doubts began to win in me. Come right down to it, I didn't really want to be related to anyone in the world except Pop, did I. Call me spoiled, if that's what being an only kid with free run of the back of a saloon amounted to, but I was utterly leery of my life changing that way. If I were to have a sudden sister, I would want her to be a duplicate of Zoe, smart and funny and ready to do bits and sharp of eye and keen of ear where the mystifying beings that were grown-ups were involved, and what were the chances of that?

In other words, I was irrevocably finding out for myself the drawback of the age of twelve, the awkward stage of not yet old enough to master such things but past the simple arithmetic of being just a child. The one certainty was that those two trains of thought, for and against a total newcomer in the family, put me in a real fix. Pop's familiar commandment not to get myself in an uproar or hydrophobic or some other upset state of mind was not helping at all. Opposite as were the outcomes I could imagine ahead, either one scared me to my eyeteeth to think about, and I never did know any way to shut off thinking.

The silence that had settled on the van lasted only as long as Del judged was respectful. "Ah, excuse my asking, but why is the husband missing in this?"

"He met with an accident," Pop replied reluctantly, "right before I left Fort Peck. Drowned in the river."

"MAYBE SHE DID it." Zoe had a ready theory when I told her about the bare-naked couple found in the truck. "Sneaked up on them and let them have it somehow."

"That's what I thought, too. But when I tried Pop on that, he said huh-uh there was no way she could have, she was in the Eagle with him and about a hundred other people when it happened."

"That lets her off the hook, then." Zoe couldn't help sounding disappointed.

"Yeah. That one, anyway."

GLANCING AT POP as much as at the road, Del waited for more, although I could tell it would have to come from me later on. Unfazed, he pursued in another direction. "That's an odd name, if I heard it right. Darius was a Persian king."

Pop laughed, the reflex kind when something is more bizarre than funny. "He was a strange bird in a lot of ways. Bony kind of guy who always looked like he could use a good meal—the Duffs were all built like hungry cats." That description cleared my mind a little. I would have been told I was jumping the gun again, but a family characteristic like that ought to settle the whose-daughter-is-she issue in a hurry, hadn't it? Look at the Zanes, senior and junior, you could tell at first glance they were the same make of fool. And while Pop and I didn't take after each other all that much except for build and our hair black as shoe polish, the likeness was unmistakable. Even Zoe had her mother's eyes. Resemblance didn't lie, right?

"Sometimes I thought Proxy married the ess of a bee"—Pop was still on Darius—"just to have somebody to fight with. He was a bright enough guy, knew his stuff about history and so on, but he'd argue politics until your ears would fall off."

Del was quick to pick up on the implication of that. "Against Roosevelt?"

"Can you imagine?" Pop sounded as indignant, as if this had all happened yesterday. "FDR was way too tame for him. 'Capitalism and soda water,' he called the New Deal. All the while he's drawing good wages on the dam like ten thousand other guys who would have been bums on the street without the government doing something. See what I mean? When it came to politics, he needed his bolts tightened." With a shake of his head, he delivered the final verdict: "Not the best customer there ever was."

Del absorbed all that for a few moments, then wondered, "Was Mrs. Duff—"

"Do me a real big favor and use her other name, okay?"

"Sorry. Was Proxy politically inclined then, too?"

Pop snorted. "Hardly. Her inclinations ran in other directions."

He dug for a cigarette, but halted before striking a match and turned to me. "How many is this today?"

"Four, on your second pack," I said crossly.

"I'm surprised it's not more." He lit up and took a lung-filling drag. "Damn, what a day," came the exhalation. "Anyway, that's Proxy for you. I have to admit, she's still a looker, isn't she." His tone of voice toyed with that. "Still a handful, too, when she puts her mind to something." He leaned back reflectively, his cigarette a glowing dot in the dark of the van. "Back there in the Blue Eagle she was a catamount, for sure."

"What's that?" I asked immediately, with Del looking glad I had.

"Pretty much the same as a wildcat, only multiplied by about ten." The bartender of the ages shook his head, as if still trying to believe her behavior. "There was the time she got into a big argument with another taxi dancer who'd tried to swipe a customer from her. I was busy behind the bar, I told them to knock it off and wasn't paying any more attention. The next thing I knew, Proxy is up on the bandstand, taking a running start. She sails off there and catches the other dancer around the waist with her legs and her arms locked around the head. They hit the floor like a ton of bricks, Proxy of course on top. She was just starting to bang the other dancer's head on the floor when I managed to pull her off."

I listened as openmouthed as I'd been about the making of mud until it piled up into the greatest dam in the world, and the all-night hammering that laid the floor of the Blue Eagle, and other wonders emanating from the front seat. The Gab Lab certainly was living up to its name on this round trip.

Still thinking back across the years, Pop sounded more than a little rueful now. "Proxy was quite an attraction for the joint, in more ways than one. And we got along together just fine when she wasn't trying to massacre somebody. The thing is, she was hellish good company when business got slow in the Eagle. Always had something to say, some tale to tell."

"She sounds almost, ah, institutional in her own right," Del ventured with a sideways glance at him.

"Yeah, well, that's a pretty good description." Pop in turn studied Del in the dim glow of the dashboard for a moment. "So, Delano. At least you got your Missing Voices. You'll be pulling out now, I expect?"

"Hmm? Oh, I was going to bring that up. Actually, I'd like to stay on while I transcribe the interviews, if that would be all right. Put the Gab Lab to further use."

"Help yourself," I was secretly glad to hear Pop say, "there's plenty of room to park in the driveway behind the Packard." He let out the same kind of big sigh as he'd done earlier. "Cripes, the Packard."

"What about the Packard?" I probably beat Del to it by a half a second.

Pop didn't say anything for about a minute. Then, "That's where it happened." His tone left no mistake what "it" was.

"In the *car*?"

"Kiddo," he said tiredly, "you have to realize, a sizable number of the population gets its start in a back seat, that's just life."

He turned around to me and I waited apprehensively for what else this endless day would bring. But he only said, "Better grab some shut-eye. We got a lot ahead of us when we get home."

7

WE THOUGHT SHE looked like a beatnik, when the Cadillac pulled up to the house that Sunday and, ready or not, here Proxy and her were. That's because we didn't know yet what a hippie was.

There in the driveway beside her mother—at least there did not seem to be any outstanding question about that—the young woman appeared frayed and tousled, maybe from the plane flight from Nevada, maybe habitually. She was in blue jeans on their last legs and a threadbare pinkish shirt, not a blouse, and beaded moccasins, and some other kind of decorated leather thing on one wrist.

Peer at her as hard as I could through the kitchen window, with Pop's description of Darius Duff to go by, the "hungry cat" part might have been more a matter of what she was wearing and how she wore it. This Francine person wasn't particularly bony anyplace I could see. On the other side of the resemblance question, certainly she was better-looking than either of us, in a sulky kind of way. Mainly, if this newcomer resembled anyone within a hundred miles, disregarding the way she was dressed, it had to be Proxy. Similar, very womanly figure, but not nearly so round, so firm, so fully packed, as the male clientele of the Medicine Lodge would have said. I still was unsure what to think. Because, plain as day, any other comparison—light complexion, facial features, characteristic tilt of the head—literally paled beside the matter of hair. Hers, in a kind of shaggy cut that did not come from any beauty shop, was the identical indelible hue as mine and Pop's where his had not silvered, as if the three of us had been dipped in black ink together.

Watching over my shoulder, Pop scrutinized the new arrival as intently as I did. "Cripes," he said mechanically about that family hair. With that and the pearly skin, if you closed one eye and concentrated, she did look like she was out of the same hatch as us, particularly him. He startled me by rubbing his hand on the crown of my head, as if for luck. "I don't know what we're in for, kiddo. But let's see how this pans out."

Out we went, to where Proxy was fixing her face in the side mirror of the Cadillac and Francine was eyeing the old Packard and Del's VW van curiously.

The usual breeze along English Creek rustled through Igdrasil's leafy branches overhead, sprinkling cottonwood fluff ahead of us as we approached. The four of us variously uttered "hey" and "hi" and "hello," and then it was up to Pop.

"I don't know any rule book for this kind of situation," he addressed Francine straight off, his voice tight. I had the impression he and I were being studied as fully by her as she was by us. "Proxy kept me in the dark about you."

"Same here," came the surprising reply. "She ought to start a mushroom farm." Francine swept her hair away from a hazel eye, the color of her mother's, further proof, if wanted, that these sudden arrivals into our life were two of a kind. Up close, she looked a lot like the movie actress Natalie Wood, but after a hard night. The line of her mouth was set in a pinchy way that seemed to say, the rebellious streak starts here. I began to wonder what I was in for with her for a sister, if that was going to be the case.

"Don't pour it on, you two," Proxy protested lightly. "I had my reasons. There wasn't any sense in upsetting things when there was nothing to be gained by it, and now there is, all around." She smiled sharply at Pop, as though he needed reminding why we were all standing across the alley from the Select Pleasure Establishment of the Year. "What could be better? You get a working partner, missy here learns the tricks of the trade from you, the joint gets a new lease on life—give me credit, Tom, I couldn't deliver more if I was Santa Claus."

Francine gave her the kind of look that came from long habit. "Mom, don't break your arm patting yourself on the back." Depending on how you wanted to hear it, that was either teasing or sarcastic.

"Kids these days," Proxy said imperturbably, with a glance that included me. "Right, Russ?"

Sticking close to Pop against the onset of these women, I was not actually tottering from one foot to the other, but the inside of me felt that way. Perhaps it came up through the shoe soles from the giant roots of Igdrasil, watered by the fates of past, present, and future. Which one would prevail was the decision Pop was struggling with mightily, as I could tell by the record number of wrinkles in his forehead. If he nixed this Francine—twenty-one or not, she did look a lot like a stray kid in those beat-up clothes and with that barely tamed hair—and turned her and Proxy down on the whole matter of paternity and responsibility, then that was that, the Medicine Lodge was a thing of the past for us. If he did the supposedly honorable thing and gave her a chance

behind the bar, he could look ahead to endless explaining to the
Two Medicine country who she was and why she was there.

"Let's sort this out a little more," he backed off the tightrope
of fates for the moment. "I'm not doubting you might have what
it takes, understand," he told Francine none too convincingly,
"but are you sure you savvy what jumping into something like
this would be like? You'd have a hell of a lot to learn. And bartending is long hours and short rest."

Francine's mouth twitched in a funny way. "Sounds a lot like
life, generally."

"Smile, chile," Proxy prompted with a terse laugh. "The man
needs a working partner, not a wet blanket."

Her daughter did not actually smile, but she stopped looking
like a rain cloud. "Sorry," she mustered, facing Pop. "Only trying
to be honest." She looked up at him, a head taller than she was,
and wiped the hair away from her eyes again. Up close, it was
apparent she'd had her dark eyebrows shaped the way women do,
perfect as a picture. At the moment she was not exactly a composed portrait, however. "Listen, I'm still getting used to not
having a dead Scotchman for a father. Makes me a little messy
upstairs." She fiddled with the leather bracelet on her wrist. "I
don't even know what to call you . . . 'Pop,' is it?"

"Tom," he said firmly, which for some reason I was glad to
hear.

"Oh-kay," she responded, sounding like an echo of her mother.
"So, anyhow, Tom, I'll bust my tail to learn the job." She spoke in
a rush now. "Mom says you're the greatest at tending bar. I'd
have to be a total wacko to pass up this chance, wouldn't I."

Well, at least that showed some spirit. Pop continued to look
Francine up and down. Having conscientiously told her the
drawbacks of bartending, now he had to tell her yes or no about

how she stacked up for the job. I still believe he had not made up his mind until that very moment. He glanced at Proxy, standing there a little akimbo in a milk-blond way that possibly suggested the old days in the Blue Eagle. I guessed what was coming when he rubbed the top of my head again as he spoke.

"All right, we'll give this a try." He cut off Proxy's flash of smile and Francine's relieved expression. "On my terms. There's not going to be any working partner, so don't get big ideas, Proxy. The Medicine Lodge stays in my hands, I'm the boss, period and end of punctuation." He looked squarely at Francine to make sure this was sinking in. "I'll hire you, which means I can fire you, got that?"

Her mouth twitched that funny way again, but she sounded fairly reasonable in saying: "That's jake with me." Automatically I filed that away to share with Zoe.

"See?" Proxy winked at me, or was it meant for Pop. "It all works out for the best, just like I—"

"One more thing." He held up his hands, as if stopping traffic. His gruff tone had Francine fooling nervously with the gizmo on her wrist again. "I'm not gonna spend my time explaining to everybody who comes in the joint that you're some daughter of mine who just happened to show up like Jesus in the manger." His eyes met Proxy's, although his words were still meant for Francine. "It's not fair to you, either. You shouldn't have to feed people's curiosity about something that goes back before you were born."

Drawing a deep breath, he acknowledged the hair problem and so on. "Okay, here's what we're gonna do when customers get nosy about any resemblance. We'll say Francine is my niece." He appeared uncomfortable with that white lie, if that's what color it was, but I could tell he was set in rock about this. "My sister's kid that I'm breaking in on the job out of the goodness of my heart. People can think what they want, but that's gonna be our story. Everybody got that?"

Wow, I couldn't help thinking, what a bit.

Mother and daughter glanced at each other. Whatever passed between them, it was Francine who turned to Pop with the hint of a sassy grin. "If that's the way you want to play it, Unc."

"Tom," he warned her.

By now Proxy was eyeing me, and I was instantly on my guard. There was something in the way she looked at me, as if I was a cause for concern. "Some little man will need to watch his mouth real careful, won't he."

"Rusty knows what's involved," Pop stoutly took up for me, squeezing my shoulder as he spoke. "He won't give the act away. Right, kiddo?"

I swallowed. "I'll, uh, watch my mouth."

That satisfied Proxy only so far. Now she was frowning in the direction of Del's van. "Then what about Carrot Top? Where is he, playing with his machinery?"

Pop indicated to English Creek, which was making that pretty sound of water dancing over rocks. "I told him to go fishing while we worked this out. Don't worry, I'll fill him in as soon as he gets back. Delano won't be a problem."

That seemed to take care of Proxy's concerns. "Then I can make myself scarce, can't I"—she patted the fender of the Cadillac—"and go tend to my business interests. How about if I just slip by here"—she nodded toward the house—"once in a while to kind of check on things?"

Pop chewed his lip a little before conceding that might not hurt. "But steer clear of the joint when you do. There are people around here who were at Fort Peck and would recognize you at the drop of a hat. We don't want the sight of you to give them funny ideas, do we."

Solo parent again for the second time in one lifetime, he turned to look speculatively at Francine, busy plucking cotton-wood fluffs out of her hair and dispatching them in the breeze. "I suppose we better get at this," he said as much to himself as to her. "Rusty can show you the house, how about. Give her the bedroom next to yours, okay?" It wasn't, but what else could I do but nod.

Pop turned to Proxy. "Hey, before you hit the road," he frowned, checking his watch, "come over to the joint with me. I need you to help me with the guy who thinks he's got a deal to buy it or I'll never hear the end of it from him. You're going to have to be Aunt Marge, whose darling daughter needs to learn bartending if she's ever going to amount to anything."

"That shouldn't strain me too much," Proxy said with a per-fectly straight face. The two of them started toward the Medi-cine Lodge, and the realization hit me.

"Pop, wait! I have to tell you something."

He swung around, Proxy halting as well. "What is it, kiddo?"

My big gulp did not constitute an answer, but it told him that what I wanted to say was for his ears only. Frowning, he came back and bent down so I could whisper it.

"Zoe has to be let in on it. She'll know something is fishy about Francine."

"Cripes. I didn't think about her." He pondered for several moments before whispering back: "She's gonna have to be your department. Hog-tie her into not telling anybody else about this, not anybody, right?"

"R-right."

Off he went with Proxy, leaving me with Francine as she dragged out of the Cadillac's trunk a hefty suitcase and a kit bag about the size of an extra-large purse, which from the sound of it must have had her toiletries in it. How do women find time for all the beautification involved, I wondered, although I was about to find out.

"I can take the ditty bag," I offered, but she said never mind, she was used to being a beast of burden. While I was trying to decide if that was a joke, she tossed her head to clear the hair out of her vision and said impatiently, "Lead on, Jungle Jim."

Ordinarily I did not have trouble making conversation, but I didn't know how to commence in this situation, and Francine was no help until I showed her to the bedroom next to mine. Looking it over, she said, "Seen worse." Noticing me stiffen more than I already had, she hoisted an eyebrow much in the manner of her mother. "Joke. Meant to be, anyhow." She gave the room a flourish of her hair. "It's nice enough. This takes some getting used to, is all."

I was with her on that, definitely. I watched as she stashed the kit bag in the corner by the dresser and flopped her suitcase onto the bed, flipping it open to establish residency, I supposed. Female undergarments brimmed into sight before I could hastily look away. Moving restlessly to the window after that, Francine looked down at the driveway, quite a parking lot now with the Packard, the Gab Lab van, our Buick, and the Cadillac. "So, who's Carrot Top that the old folks were talking about?"

I had to blink past that characterization of Pop and Proxy before delineating Del for her. I must have done a decent job, because she folded her arms on her chest and listened civilly enough. "Fine. Another one with Fort Peck on the brain," she said—not a bad summary, really—when I'd finished about Del. "Must be contagious."

Appraising me more openly than before, she tested the matter of the two of us with a little grin. "Russell, huh? Pretty distinguished. Where'd that come from?"

"I like Rusty better," I dodged.

"Oboy, I know what you mean. What were they thinking when they fastened fancy names on us, anyway? I always think Francine sounds like some dumb perfume." She bobbed agreement with herself. "The shorter the better, ain't it."

Sometimes you know when to take a shot in the dark. "Are you from Canada?"

That caught her by surprise. "All but. How'd you know? Grew up out in the sticks north of Havre—the boundary line was practically in the backyard."

"But she . . . your mom doesn't talk that way."

"Nahh. She wasn't around to pick up any lingo like that, was she. See, my father's"—she checked herself and flashed me a quick look—"my *previous* father's relatives raised me. Uncle Hugh and Aunt Meg. Square as cubes, but I didn't exactly get to choose, did I. They'd been at Fort Peck, along with all the other Duffs. So they did the honors on me, while Mumsie was busy in the divorce industry and so on. Wasn't there somebody named Reno Sweeney? Reno Proxy was more like it," Francine laughed, if something that short and sharp was a laugh, "all the time that mother of mine put in down there in Nevada." Boy, she could talk once she got going. "Anyhow, that's pretty much the story of Mommy and Francie. Probably won't make the nursery rhyme books."

I was about to ask more when she swung back to the window, craning to see what she could of town, which was mostly the alley and the backs of the buildings on Main Street. Off in the distance, past Igdrasil's snowing branches, though, the cemetery knoll showed up greener and prettier than anything else in sight because of the carefully watered grass. "This is one of those towns, huh?" She sounded as if she had been sentenced to Gros Ventre. "Dead people get the view."

"Maybe they need it more."

That drew me a keen look and then a sharp laugh. "Aren't you a kick. I'm glad some kind of sense of humor runs in the family. Something good should."

"Um, talking about family," I must have thought nonstop gab constituted hospitality, "I bet you were plenty surprised to find out Pop is your father."

"Better believe it, I was." She gave her hair a flip and said carelessly, "Kind of a nice change, though. It beats having a Communist one."

My jaw dropped. At the time, calling someone that was like saying the person was a mad-dog enemy of all things American. "You mean like in *Russia*?"

"Nahh, I guess not." Francine treated that as though it did not make much difference one way or another. "From what I picked up from Mom and the relatives, Daddy Darius was his own kind." For a moment, she looked more thoughtful than she had at any time yet. "As I get it, he figured the Russkies had it backward. His big idea was that people on the bottom ought to run things." Another flip of the hair, and that keen look at me. "Well, you know, not to stick up for the old devil or anything, but maybe they wouldn't do any worse job of it than the usual stupes." She regarded me for a moment, as if making sure, and of course she was. "Anyhow, he set out to remake the world and ended up in a truck in the river with the wrong woman. You heard all about that, I bet."

"Pop told me when you, um, came into the picture."

"Fine. Takes care of that." She stirred from where she'd been standing by the window. "Know what? I better get unpacked."

And I knew I had better depart before filmy undies and such came into further sight. But I was held by one matter yet. "Francine? Can I ask you something?"

"Try me."

"We're supposed to pretend to be . . . cousins, aren't we?"

"How about that." She glanced at me over the opened suitcase. "Nothing is ever simple, is it."

"But we're really . . . half brother and half sister?" I still was having trouble getting that relationship through my head. Maybe there was some other description of it that I was missing.

"Surprise, surprise, huh?" A sly little smile much like Proxy's caught me off guard. "So, buddy, which half is your girl part?"

The only response I had to that was a flaming blush. Backing out of the room, I rattled out: "I better let you get moved in. Pop will be here when he gets done at the saloon."

That's when I raced to the Spot to fetch Zoe.

THE DISCUSSION in the barroom, if voices raised to such a level can be called that, was reaching a climax when we slipped into the back and flung ourselves up the stairs to the landing. So much had been happening, I'd had time to tell Zoe only bits and pieces, particularly the juicy ones, like the undressed couple in the ill-fated truck, leading up to Proxy's arrival in the Cadillac at Fort Peck.

Ears and eyes plastered to the vent, the two of us eagerly caught up with what was happening on the other side of the wall. Right away we could tell that Earl Zane was not even touching the beer Pop had served up as a peace offering. Earl was having all he could handle in Proxy Duff.

"See, Tom got a little ahead of himself in putting the joint up for sale," she was explaining to him ever so nicely in a voice smooth as a purr. "This is what you might call a God clause, like in an insurance policy when an act of nature comes along and makes things go flooey. Tom just didn't know how much the matter was going to change when my daughter and me expressed our interest in keeping the saloon in family hands." It really was quite an appealing story in her telling, that if a young woman starting out on her own in life and who incidentally was Pop's niece merely required a bit of experience in the art of bartending under the tutelage of the master himself, was that so much to ask?

In conclusion, Proxy gave Earl a smile that I was learning to recognize as one with long practice behind it, probably all the way back to taxi dancing. "No reflection on you. These things happen."

Earl reacted as if the Medicine Lodge was being stolen right out of his pocket. His big red face looked like it would burst. "You can call it that claptrap if you want, lady"—his protest could have been heard all the way to the back room even had Zoe and I not been glued to the vent—"but I say it's backing out of a deal."

"Don't get yourself on fire, Earl," Pop was heard from, sounding strained.

Maybe on that dark drive home from Fort Peck, with more history attached to him than even he had known, he was pulled in paradoxical directions, the same as I was, and wound up teetering away from giving up the Medicine Lodge quite yet. Maybe the stage was set by the sorcery of drama that enveloped two theater-struck twelve-year-olds that certain summer. In any case, Zoe and I were the breathless audience as my father spoke his lines like a man taking his medicine.

"What's happened is, I need to hang on to the joint for a while and give the girl a chance. I'm sorry as hell you got your hopes up. My mistake, and I'll make it up to you if you're out any money on legal fees or whatever, all right?"

A cat will puff itself up when provoked. Earl did something like that now. "What did they serve at that Fort Peck get-together, loco weed? Goddamn it, Tom, you already put off selling the place to me once. It's getting to be a habit. A deal's a deal where I come from."

Zoe turned her head to whisper to me, "Del doesn't know what he's missing out on."

"Is there any ink on any sheet of paper"—this voice, calm and collected, level as a pistol, was Proxy's—"that spells out what you're calling a deal?"

"No," Earl admitted, "but—"

"Have you put down any earnest money?"

"Well, no, Tom understands it'll be along as soon as—"

"Then it hasn't reached the deal stage, has it, it's preliminary discussion, isn't it. And we've just discussed the change of circumstances."

"She's got you there, Earl."

"THAT'S ENOUGH OF THIS!" I might have considered that a cry from the heart if I wasn't sure Earl, like his mouthy son, had a heart the size of a prune. His eruption had Zoe and me bumping heads at the vent. The scene is indelible in me. Like always, Pop was behind the bar, but in the new order of things, had not put his apron on. Across from him, Proxy leaned against the bar with veteran ease as she faced the wrath of Earl perfectly poker-faced. As for Earl, though, the slats of the vent sectioned him, as if he might fly apart. His face had turned so furiously red, it was a wonder his hat didn't boil off. In the next slot down, his arms waved in the universal gesture of disgust. Below that, even his beer gut seemed agitated, barely contained by a rodeo belt buckle. "Tom"—he swelled up even more, turning aside from Proxy, as though that might make her vanish—"I'm gonna lay it to you, man to man. I don't like to have to do this, but you leave me absolutely no choice."

I tensed all through. I couldn't begin to imagine the extent of

the threat he was working himself up to—a fistfight? a lawsuit?—
and an inch from me Zoe was equally frozen in apprehension.

"Until you come to your senses," we heard him tell Pop in the
darkest of tones, "I am going to take my patronage right down
the street to the Pastime." Earl folded his arms magisterially.
"See how you like that."

For the first time since the Mudjacks Reunion, Pop smiled,
from ear to ear.

THAT WAS THAT, at least. With Earl Zane out of his hair as a
Medicine Lodge customer, let alone as its imminent proprietor,
Pop could turn to the Francine matter, and he and Proxy went
out the front door of the saloon so she could see the Medicine
Lodge in its full glory, with her doing all the talking as they
headed around back to the house. Zoe and I stayed put, so I
could catch her up, to the extent possible, on the situation that
began with that Cadillac making its appearance. The tip of her
tongue showed how hard she was concentrating to follow the
twists and turns of my report, but in the end she grasped what
counted.

"Rusty, you get to be an actor!" She meant, of course, main-
taining the pretense to all and sundry that Francine was merely
my cousin instead of my new sister. Not the hardest role ever,
surely, yet it felt more than a little tricky.

"You're in on it, too. So do you."

Plainly the prospect did not displease her. "I suppose. How
long will this Francine take to learn bartending?"

"That's just it, see." I voiced the uncertainty foremost on my
mind. "Maybe she's here to stay, if she's good at it."

A look came into Zoe's eyes I had not seen before. Careful to
make the query sound careless, she asked: "Do you like her?"

"I can't tell yet. She's kind of different."

We fell silent. Empty but for us, the Medicine Lodge for once was quiet in both its halves, the back room that had costumed our imaginations so many times that summer, and the barroom out front, where the grown-up world did its own performing. One and then the other, we gazed longingly at the vent that was our keyhole to that world, knowing our times of listening in secrecy depended on Pop's indulgence of us. Whatever else she proved to be, Francine did not seem to me the indulging type. What a rotten shame to lose our listening post just because she had arrived out of nowhere, I thought to myself, my mind stumbling this way and that until it hit on the obvious.

"Tell you what I'm gonna do, Muscles," I resorted to my best gangster growl.

"What would that be, Ace?"

"This." I reached over to where a spare rain slicker that Howie sometimes used was hanging and moved it to a peg where it concealed the vent.

"Real swuft thinking, Ace," Zoe ratified with a growl of her own.

BY THEN it was time for Zoe to dart off to her cafe chores, and I needed to catch up on developments at the house. Just as I got there, Proxy was making her farewells. Before getting into the big red car, she drilled Francine on the shoulder with a finger. "Don't do anything I wouldn't do, cookie."

"Some leeway there," Francine joked, or maybe not.

"I'll be back before you know it," Proxy was saying, as if anyone had asked, "to see how things are going. Have fun showing her the tricks of the trade, Tom."

Pop responded with a sort of grunt while tensely lighting a

cigarette. Opening the door of the Cadillac, Proxy paused to consider me, as if deciding on the right good-bye, and gave me a wicked wink that I would rather not have had. I didn't know why any attention from her got to me so much, but it made me feel like I was a target in her sights. Then, in a crush of gravel, she was gone.

There was an awkward gap now as Francine and Pop considered each other, as I supposed they were entitled to after twenty-one years of sheer ignorance of one another's existence.

As that started to stretch too long, he roused himself and her and me as well.

"Hey, no sense standing around like lawn ornaments, is there. Come on, I better show you the joint. Not you, kiddo." He'd evidently decided Francine was enough to deal with for the moment. "Hang on here and when Delano shows up, tell him I want to see him right away, savvy?"

Of course I did not like being left out of things, but I thoroughly savvied that Del had to be clued in quick on the make-believe niece. Pop, Francine, myself, Zoe, Del; this was becoming a bit with quite a cast. I drifted to the house in a mood new to me. The old place had not known a woman's touch, except for Nola's feathery occasional housekeeping, since the year of my birth. As if drawn to the source of difference as distinct as perfume in the air, I went upstairs again and gazed into the neighboring bedroom that was now Francine's. Her suitcase remained open on the bed, with female undies spilling out. An old blue denim jacket with a beaded yoke had been tossed over the back of a chair. From what I could see, the only thing that had been put away somewhere was the whopping kit bag, but I figured she had to start somewhere. Housekeeping did not seem to be her strong point any more than it was ours, so maybe that much of our habit pattern was safe. Yet disturbance of some sort was on its way, I couldn't help but feel it coming, almost like a change in the weather. Already it felt strange to have someone else in the gallery of bedrooms that Pop and I had shared, just ourselves, for the past half dozen years. There are some days in a person's life, definitely not many, that mark themselves into memory almost from first minute to last. The one thing I knew for sure was that this Sunday was not going to leave me any time soon.

"Anyone home?" Del's cheery hello downstairs snapped me to. "The angler returns in triumph!"

I was down there in a flash, bursting into the kitchen, where he was emptying his creel of fish into the sink. "She's here, over at the joint with Pop," I reported all in one breath, "he wants to see you. Right away, he said."

Still full of pride at his catch, Del grinned over his shoulder at me. "I don't suppose you'd care to tell me what the hurry is?"

"Huh-uh, it'd take too long. I'll start cleaning the fish."

As he went out, I began gutting the batch of trout, nice rainbows of a good eating size and a goodly number of them. Fifteen was the legal limit. I counted twice, and Del's catch was fourteen. That was odd, for someone fishing up a storm as he obviously had been, to be skunked on the last fish.

He was back before I was half through dealing with fish guts. His cheerful look was gone. "Quite a change of script by your father, isn't it. I guess he knows what he's doing." He scratched behind an ear. "Francine didn't seem exactly friendly."

"Maybe she just needs to get used to us," I tried to put the best face on things as he came over to the sink to pitch in on cleaning the rest of the fish, searching his maze of pockets for a jackknife. "How come you didn't limit?"

"Hmm? Oh, the angels' share."

"That's stranger than chicken guts, bub," I did a bit of a bit to prompt him.

He slit into a fish belly. "My father heard it from FDR"—you never knew what dose of history you were in for around Del—"when the Brain Trust and their top aides were called in to celebrate some part of the New Deal that had passed Congress. Eleanor happened to be on hand, and she ran the White House staff by her own lights, so the drinks were poured pretty weak." He slipped me a grin in acknowledgment of what Pop would have thought of that. "Anyway, Franklin Delano Roosevelt," he of course made the middle name resound, as if it was the main one, "takes a sip of his and holds the glass up to the light and says," here came a good imitation of that famous Fireside Chat voice, "'Gentlemen, we seem to be experiencing that phenomenon of evaporation called the angels' share.'"

I laughed but still didn't see what that had to do with fish. Rubbing the side of his head with a sleeve to satisfy an itch, mental or otherwise, Del went on. "It's silly, I suppose, but that saying caught on in our family." From being around Pop, I knew sayings were almost a second language, so I listened religiously to add this one to the collection. "Anytime a sock went missing or we ran short of milk at breakfast," Del elaborated, "we'd say it was the angels getting theirs. My father and I turned it into a joke when we fished together. We'd never catch the absolute last fish to fill out our limit. Leave that one for you know who. I won't say we were superstitious, but close enough." He spoke in that sober way the dead are recalled. "Families aren't easy to figure out, maybe you've noticed."

Was that ever the truth. Both lost in thought, we companionably thumbed guts out of split-open trout until Del rinsed a hand so he could scratch at a rib. "Phew. That is one brushy creek," he said in tribute to the hard-won trout. "There were places I had to get down on my hands and knees to crawl in to where I could cast."

"What's all the scratching about?"

"Oh, nothing. I just keep finding some kind of ladybugs on me. There must have been quite a hatch." He pulled up his trouser leg and rubbed his shin. He paused and peered at the back of his hand. "There's another one."

I looked with horror at the tiny dot crawling across his skin. "Don't go anywhere. Let me get Pop."

I raced across the alley and burst into the barroom. To my shock, there was Francine behind the bar by herself, already looking things over as if she owned the place, and Pop nowhere around. When I stammered out the question, she jerked her head toward the back of the barroom. "Said he needed to take a leak. What's up?"

This was no time for good manners. I went and pounded on the toilet door and hollered, "Del's got ticks!"

"Damn, what next?" came the muffled reply, along with the sound of flushing. Pop was out of there in record speed and headed out the back of the saloon for the house, with me chasing after and Francine belatedly following us.

We got there as Del was finishing with the fish, in between scratching. He looked up in surprise at all of us piling into the kitchen. "Are ladybugs this much of an attraction?"

"Ladybugs, nothing," Pop informed him grimly, "those are sage ticks. Quick, get upstairs to the bathroom. Stand in the bathtub and take all your clothes off."

"All my . . . ? Why?"

"You don't want them biting you, that's why. Hurry up, so we can look you over." Pop was already at the doorway and motioning urgently, standing flat against the wall so Del would not brush against him.

Francine hadn't said a thing during any of this, simply backing away to the safety of the living room, but from the crimp in her brow she must have wondered if this was what life in our household was going to be like.

"Come on." Pop surprised her as the others of us hustled up the stairs. "We need all the eyes we can get."

That may have been so, but with Francine crowded into the bathroom with us, Del hesitated at jumping in the tub and stripping, until Pop said impatiently: "She's not gonna see anything new in the human experience, get going." I was directed to cram his clothes in the wastebasket as he shed them, for soaking. "It's this tan getup of yours." Pop shook his head as Del peeled off the shirt of many pockets. "Makes you the color of a deer. Ticks see that and think you're their favorite food, venison."

I watched and certainly Francine did, while the naked Del, who had more to him than expected, stood shivering in the clammy tub as Pop started to examine him all over for unwelcome visitors.

"Francine, quit window shopping and go through his hair," Pop snapped her out of her attention to the other part of his anatomy.

I will say, she was equal to the task, telling Del, "Close your eyes, chum, here I come," as she straddled up to the bathtub.

Helplessly he ducked his head as she ran her fingers over his scalp. You would think a person with a crew cut did not offer much in the way of hiding places up there. Not so. "Ick, here's one," Francine exclaimed when she felt into the hair at the back of his neck. Pop told her to pick it off if it wasn't dug in, and she gamely did so, squeezing past me to drop it in the toilet bowl. That was the fate it deserved, as far as I was concerned. I hated ticks. That awful little goosey feeling on a section of skin as all those tiny legs kept the thing crawling slowly, as if exploring every pore. A tick wasn't like a mosquito, zeroing in and then gone. It kept on creeping for a prime spot to suck blood from. What was worse, the things were dangerous. Even if you didn't get Rocky Mountain spotted fever, which could kill you, a tick bite could hurt and itch for a long time. I silently cheered as Pop picked each one off Del's body and flicked it in the toilet bowl. By now there were three or four dark little bodies floating there. Then I saw the worst thing possible.

"There's one on his business end!"

Both men looked down as if afraid to, and Francine's eyes widened. The tick was at the start of things there, having crept from the red pubic hair as if coming out of the brush to find a picnic spot on a knoll.

Pop backed away a step, grimacing. "They head for the softest parts of the body, the damn things like to bite there. Is it moving any?"

"I . . . I can't tell," Del said shakily, staring at his threatened part.

"Real careful now," Pop advised in a delicate voice, "see if you can scooch it off with your fingernail. If it's bit into you, we'll have to try something a whole lot worse."

The other three of us held our breath as Del attempted to prod the insect just enough. Under his poking finger it seemed to move almost infinitesimally, and he took that as a sign to wildly bat it off, at some cost to himself. Wincing, he studied the area with all due care. "I don't see any bite."

"Good," Pop let out in an extended breath. "The rest of the family jewels okay?"

Cautiously Del felt around between his legs and reported, "Nothing there that doesn't belong there. Whew." We shared in his relief as he put his hands under his arms, hugging himself against the chill of standing naked in the bathtub this long. Abruptly the relief left him. "Oops."

"Let me see," Pop groaned.

When Del lifted an arm for him to look, an ugly dark dot was there, squarely in the middle of the armpit. I immediately felt queasy, and the tick wasn't even on me. "This one bit you, sure enough," Pop said, swearing suitably. "Full of blood." Rapidly he told Del to sit on the edge of the tub and me to go get a coat hanger. "Francine, there's some kitchen matches in the medicine cabinet, hand me some."

When I hustled back with the wire hanger, Pop mashed and twisted it, straightening the hook, until he had something hold-able, with a prong sticking out. He lit a match with his thumbnail, the sulfur smell curling Del's nostrils and mine and Francine's, and heated the end of the prong in the flame.

"Lift your arm," he told Del, and directed Francine to get a good grip on it and hold it steady in case he flinched. "This is gonna be a little warm. I have to make the tick back itself out, so the head doesn't break off in you."

It took exceedingly careful application of the hot wire onto the rump, if that's what insects have, and a bunch more matches, but at last the gorged tick gave up and dropped into the bathtub. I didn't have to be told to turn on both faucets full blast to swash the thing down the drain.

"How you feeling?" Pop checked with Del apprehensively.

"Not so good. It kind of burns."

"Right. We need to get you to the doc. Where can Rusty find you some clothes in the van?"

Duly instructed, I thundered down the stairs, while behind me Francine said she'd clear out, too, not to be in the way of medical progress.

Mere minutes later, as the two of us stood beneath the leafy sweep of Igdrasil, watching Pop and Del speed away in the Buick, she had to admit: "This burg isn't as dull as it looks."

———

AS POP TOLD it when they returned from the doctor's office and a very pale Del had excused himself to take refuge in the Gab Lab, the tick-bite victim had been given some pills and a strong talking-to about the idiocy of crawling around on the ground during tick season and the prognosis that Rocky Mountain spotted fever could take as much as a couple of weeks to develop, and there was nothing to do until then except to watch himself for strange rashes and fevers. "So he's not going anywhere for a while," Pop concluded, trying to settle himself down with a cigarette despite my frown at how many he'd already had since Francine stepped out of that Cadillac of Proxy's and into our existence.

"I hope that's the excitement for the day," he let out along with a blue zephyr of smoke. Squinting as if trying to make up his mind about something, he checked with Francine as she stood there with her hands parked in her ratty jeans and her bust testing the threadbare shirt. "Think you're ready to learn some bartending?"

"Ready as I'll ever be," she responded, probably truthfully enough.

When they made their entrance into the closed and deathly still Medicine Lodge—somehow there is an added dimension of silence in a saloon on a Sunday—I trailed them into the barroom. Pop glanced over his shoulder at me, and before he could ask what I was hanging around for, I alibied: "I thought I'd, you know, sweep and mop and like that."

Since I had done those swamping chores only the day before, after our return from Fort Peck, I could tell he was about to ask if I had left my mind out to dry. Luckily for me, he caught on in time that I was pining to be in on the session of educating Francine.

"Okay, maybe not too bad an idea," he granted. "Just stay out of our way where we're holding school." In pretty much one motion he donned his apron and plucked up a fresh towel and gestured for her to come on behind the bar, and she did so, pushing her hair away from her eyes as if readying for business.

"You know anything about this at all?" Pop began as he swished the towel tenderly on the bar wood.

"Sure, I've been in joints before."

"There's a world of difference being on the other side there with your fanny on a stool," he said evenly. "I should have asked before we started. Do you drink, yourself?"

"If you mean will I get tanked to the gills on the job," she laughed that off, "no, I won't. Give me credit for that many smarts"—that tiny pause—"Tom."

"That's only half the story. How about after work?"

She grinned saucily. "Maybe a little something before bedtime to settle down from this exciting town might be what the doctor ordered, huh?"

Uh-oh. I knew she was awfully close to putting beans up her nose with that answer.

Pop scowled. "Francine, you can't party and run a saloon. It's like any other business. You've got to be real serious about it or you might as well pick out your room at the poorhouse before you even start."

Sobered in more ways than one by this sermon, she bobbed her head. "All right, I won't drink the joint dry either before or after, honest."

"That's better." Pop led her down half the length of the bar to the beer spigot. "Here's where we start." He patted the draft handle. "The Shellac pump."

"The which? Wait, I bet I know. The Select whizzy that made this place famous."

"See, this isn't so hard if you have half a brain. First thing is"—he reached to the breakfront without looking and plucked a beer schooner—"you need to know how to fill a glass."

Francine pursed up without saying anything, unsure whether that was a joke. Pop drew perhaps the millionth beer of his career from the Shellac tap, and it sat there brimming to a head, pretty as a picture. He conjured another shiny empty glass from the breakfront and handed it to her. "Give it a try."

With a little lift of her shoulders, Francine stepped up to the beer spigot as casually as if it was a kitchen sink faucet.

I dawdled as close to this as I dared, slowly sweeping nonexistent dirt, because what she was about to try amounted to nothing less than the bartending skill of hand that had made the Medicine Lodge the cherished oasis it was. For without a basic good glass of beer, properly drawn and presented, a saloon was merely a booze trough. And while I knew it was an illusion, all the eyes in the place seemed to be watching her at this, every creature on the walls, for they were all of the male species, or at least had been. The horned ones, the deer and the antelope and the elk, with that antlered astonishment they carried into eternity. The wildcat with the blaze in its eyes. The buffalo with its one-sided gaze, like an old pirate's. Even the Buck Fever Case in the Charlie Russell painting appeared to be scratching his head at the sight of a female behind the bar.

Francine gushed the glass full. It was all foam.

Swearing silently, she tried with another glass. This one overflowed, a lot of good Shellac flooding into the sink under the tap.

"Fine, I give," she muttered to Pop. "What's the holy secret?"

"Draw it slow and easy, with the glass tilted a little. Then let it sit until the head forms just right."

Like a kid faced with a long-division problem, she nibbled her lip. "How much time is that supposed to take?"

"Hum 'Home on the Range' to yourself all the way through."

Skeptically she tried all that, and a presentable glass of beer resulted. Pop nodded. "Okay, that's half the battle. Go around to the other side," he directed, "and be the customer for a minute," flicking his towel to where he wanted her to sit up to the bar.

Francine came around past where I was sweeping for about the sixth time and snuggled onto the bar stool. "This seems more natural."

"Don't get ideas," Pop growled. From a dozen feet away he slid the glass of beer to a perfect stop in front of her.

"I get it. It's like shuffleboard."

"I wouldn't know. I call it a slick touch you only get by learning it. Now you come back here and try. Rusty?" Startled, I nearly dropped my idle broom. "Hop onto that stool like you're the customer," Pop directed, "so she can scoot the beer to you."

This was different, sitting up to the bar as though I was supposed to belong there. Feeling important with the perch, I patty-caked the bar like Earl Zane until Pop gave me a look.

Meanwhile Francine, puckered with determination, was drawing a bead on the spot where the foam-topped glass in her grasp was supposed to glide to a graceful halt.

"Whups," she said as I reared back out of the way of sloshing beer.

Pop made her try again and again. A lot of Great Falls Select ended up on the bar before she found the knack, more or less.

"Okay, that's that," Pop allowed, sopping up the beer spillage. "Now for the hard stuff."

Hearing this, Francine rolled her eyes, as if anything harder would send her right back to Reno, newly discovered father or no newly discovered father, but I knew Pop only meant the liquor, all the brands crowding the shelves of the breakfront. He reached under the bar. "I dug out a drink book for you. Study up from it when you get a chance and keep it handy here." He saw she was taken aback by the sizable volume. "Hey, don't let it throw you. We don't get much call for fancy concoctions in here."

"Glad of that." Saying so, she tilted her head the way he always did, as if reminding herself to be daughterly. "There's quite a bit to this job, ain't it."

"Bartending isn't tea and crumpets," Pop replied briskly. "While I think of it, let me show you a pouring secret." He flourished his favorite shot glass. It had the New Deal blue eagle embossed on the side, no doubt the notion of some federal Rooseyelter back in the time of Fort Peck. "Always use this as the house jigger. If anybody wants a shot and water on the side, give them one of those"—he indicated the stubby rank of shot glasses in the breakfront glassware—"but don't let this one get away. Here, feel why." He put the jigger in Francine's uncertain hand. "Feel the eagle on there, the top of its head?" She rubbed the shot glass between her fingers and thumb and nodded. "That helps when you pour, pretty quick you'll have a feel for when there's enough in the jigger and you won't hardly have to look."

He stopped to take stock, of both Francine and the territory he'd covered behind the bar. "Oh, yeah. Next, the concert piano."

"The huh?" She frowned around the barroom. "Maybe I'm blind in one eye and can't see out of the other, but where's there even a jukebox?"

"Don't need one, here's what makes music to our ears," said Pop as he stepped to the cash register, hit the jangly key that opened the till, and began instructing. "Rule number one is, when you make change from paper money, a five or ten or whatever it is, put it over here in this part of the drawer first, instead of in with the rest of the cash. That way if any argument comes up, you can make sure the mistake isn't yours. In other words, cover your behind."

Francine smirked at that but didn't say anything. Pop moved on to showing her the quirks of the ice machine. While there, though, she spotted his reading material tucked beneath the bar at the amen corner. "You dig Mickey Spillane?"

"Sure." Guardedly: "Why?"

"Me, too. *I, the Jury* is really something, huh?"

"Strong stuff." He regarded her afresh, as a hard-boiled master of fiction might have put it. "You read that kind of thing a lot?"

"Every chance I get. Done all the Mike Shayne books, waiting for more."

"Those're good, too," he enthused, the lesson session temporarily forgotten. At the time, tales of tough-guy private eyes and endangered damsels were over my head, or at least at a level I wasn't supposed to be perusing at my age, so I helped myself to an Orange Crush while the pair of them volleyed titles and characters. In his best humor for days, Pop commended her reading habit. "This'll help. You'll have a lot of time on your hands when business is slow."

"Don't worry," Francine said breezily, "I'm good at killing time."

Deciding she'd had enough behind-the-bar tutelage for now, Pop tossed down his towel. "Couple more things, and we'll call it good. The first one is what you might call the policy of the house." He looked at her in great seriousness. "No dating the customers. You get to going steady with some one guy, and the others aren't gonna like it." He paused for emphasis. "So no flirting, either direction across the bar, right?"

That seemed to make her bristle at the very idea, but she caught herself. "I get it, I guess. Playing favorites is bad for business, huh? Don't worry on that score, Tom. Ain't in this for romance, as my darling mother would say." Fidgety to have this over with, she asked, "Then what's the other thing that's bugging you?"

Running a hand through his hair, Pop looked consciously paternal as he surveyed her from head to toe and back again as she twiddled the leather bracelet. "Your getup."

Francine all at once looked scared, and it made me think she had a lot to learn about having a father.

He held up his large, capable hands to show her by example. "No fancy rings. Don't paint up with nail polish, either, now that I think of it. The customers shouldn't be looking at anything but that nice glass of whatever you're serving up, savvy?"

"Oboy." She was fingering the fancy leather bracelet nervously now. "I don't want to break any rules, but I'm really attached to this."

Pop studied it and her for a moment. "Yeah, well, okay, I don't know why you want to wear half a handcuff like that, but I suppose you can keep it on." He squinted critically. "Let's talk clothes. That outfit you've got on makes you look like something the cat dragged in." Before she could make so much as a peep of protest, he set her straight about proper apparel, Medicine Lodge–style. "First thing, we'll get you a bow tie. Rusty can teach you how to tie it. And if you're gonna wear pants—slacks, I mean—get some dark ones. The Toggery will have some. Nice white blouses to go with them." He looked at her moccasins. "Shoes, too. When you're bartending, you're on your feet all the time, squaw slippers won't do."

"Hey, wait," she protested, "didn't I see some bedroom slippers tucked away under the bar? What's the difference?"

"It's my old dogs that are tired"—he meant his feet—"that's

what. You want to keep yours from getting that way as long as you can. You need substantial shoes. Ask in the store for that grandma kind, I don't know what they're called."

Her dismayed expression said she knew what he meant. "Those black clodhoppers? Like nuns wear?"

"Those are the ones." He went to the cash register and counted out the wardrobe money for her. "Needless to say, this comes out of your first wages."

She tucked the money in her jeans, that hint of grin showing ever so slightly. "I haven't even started and I'm already in the hole? Only kidding."

Pop stuck to business. "So now you know what's involved with the joint. I'll work behind the bar with you the first week or so while you're breaking in. Get you through Saturday night. Then you're gonna have to be on your own."

With a swipe of her hand, Francine cleared the black mop of hair out of her vision. "It won't be the first time."

THE NEXT DAY came with Zoe and me hardly able to decide which subject to put our minds to first, Francine or Del. Since Pop was trooping Francine through the unglamorous side of bartending, such as slitting open whiskey cases, when we poked our heads in the back room, we opted for Del.

"Must of been quite the sight, that there tick on the business end." Zoe did her John Wayne/Marion Morrison drawl as we approached the driveway where the Gab Lab was parked.

"Cecily, old thing, it would astound the birds out of the trees," I replied in Wildean tones.

We sobered up and got our sympathy back in order as we reached the silent van, with its curtains drawn. In his tick-bitten condition Del perhaps was sleeping in, although that did not seem like him. In any case, the morning was far enough along that we figured he ought to be up, so we knocked on the big side door.

Only silence answered.

Zoe and I were not prepared for this. We looked at each other in sudden fright. She was the one who said it out loud, "What if he's dying in there and can't open the door?"

Why this overcame me so, I still can't explain, but it seemed a horrible fate to die in a VW van that Pop had likened to a sardine can. I panicked. If Del was breathing his last, there was no time to run for help. The side door was locked when I tried it, and so was the passenger one.

It was considerably belated, but one of us had the bright idea to go around and try the door on the driver's side. That came right open, and we scrambled in to look into the back of the Gab Lab, expecting the worst, but not what we saw.

In wrinkled fancy pajamas, gray-faced as a ghost, Del was sitting hunched over his tape recorder at the worktable. He had headphones on, big as soup bowls, and as we gaped, he would peer closely down at the recorder, where there was a tiny counting instrument like the odometer on a car, jotting down what the number was at that stage of the tape, then hit the recorder's PLAY and REVERSE and FORWARD buttons like a piano player playing one-handed. How someone with a crew cut managed to be tousled, I don't know, but he looked like he'd been worked over with an eggbeater. Thinking back, it strikes me as like something out of Beckett, *Krapp's Last Tape*, with the reel whirring methodically back and forth.

Zoe and I tumbled over the seat, startling Del out of his trance.

"Oh." Blinking at us, he lifted the headphones off. "Good morning, I guess it is."

"Does it hurt like crazy," Zoe asked straightaway, "where the tick got you?"

"Not quite that bad." He tried to seem sturdier than he looked.

I took a different medical tack. "Um, didn't the doctor tell you to take it easy?"

"I can't," he moaned, looking even more haggard. "I'll lose my grant! You have no idea how cutthroat the library world can be!" A wild look came into his eyes. "If I can't live up to what I promised in my proposal, the powers that be will take the Gab Lab away from me. There's a real push on to get Missing Voices into the library's holdings, and if I'm laid up . . ." He let that awful thought dangle. "I can at least transcribe. See?" He whipped the headphones back on, screwed up his face in listening concentration, then typed in blurts, a foot pedal stopping the tape recorder as he caught up with the last phrase. Off came the headphones, as if what we had just witnessed was proof of mental if not physical competence.

He must have caught our glances at each other, and around the interior of the van, mussed on almost every surface with uneven piles of typed transcriptions and scattered reels of tapes. "Things are a trifle out of order because of gaps in the transcriptions," he was forced to confess. "Talk about *lingua america*, the mudjacks practically speak a tongue of their own whenever they're describing something done at the dam." He shook his head as if to clear it. Gnawing the corner of his mouth, he lifted the nearest stack of typing as if weighing it, then let it drop. "Rusty? I hate to bother him, I know how busy he is, but could you ask your father to help me straighten out some of what I'm hearing on the tapes when he has time?"

I assured him I'd ask Pop right away, anything to make him feel better. "He said to tell you not to work yourself to death, there are more interesting ways to go," I passed along.

"Don't I wish he was in charge of the Library of Congress as well as the Medicine Lodge," he replied forlornly, grabbing for the next reel of tape.

FRANCINE'S DEBUT at the Medicine Lodge was as carefully supervised by Pop as if she was about to perform for royalty. "You aren't nervous or anything, are you?" he asked edgily before he opened the place for business that first day. "I'll be right here, just give me the high sign if anything stumps you, okay?"

"Ready as I'll ever be," she recited yet again, taking her post at the end of the bar nearest the street door as I watched every move through the vent. Zoe would have given skin to be here for this, but she could not talk her way out of chores at the cafe, and it was up to me to provide a full report at supper. Whatever was going to happen, the stage was surely set, with the barroom practically gleaming after all my sweeping and mopping and Pop's attention to everything Francine could conceivably need. Spiffed up according to Pop's dictates, in dark slacks and white blouse and a black bow tie that I had shown her how to master after half a dozen tries and with her hair even fixed better, she looked like a bartender. Some version of one, anyway.

As luck would have it, her first customers were a tourist couple on their way to Glacier National Park, and setting them up with a couple of beers was a cinch. They did appear puzzled as to why there was an equal number of bartenders to customers in this particular saloon on a quiet afternoon, but shortly they were on their way and Francine grinned down the bar to Pop. "I haven't disgraced the joint yet, huh?"

The first regular to come in was Bill Reinking, and I just knew he was going to be instinctively inquisitive at the sight of a young woman in back of the bar. So did Pop, even more so.

Before Bill could get a word out, he hurriedly produced the explanation he was going to have to make dozens if not hundreds of times: "New blood. My sister's kid, gonna learn the ropes about bartending."

"I see," said Bill, whether or not he actually did. Tipped off ahead of time by Pop, Francine had a bottle of good scotch waiting, and poured generously, and Bill, too, went off satisfied if still more than a little mystified.

It was Velma Simms who provided Francine's first real challenge. Things started not too badly, with Pop making introductions and Velma only raising an eyebrow a fraction. When Francine brought the ginger-ale highball over to the booth where Velma was going through her mail, though, she lingered and said, "That's a wild blouse." It was made of a soft material that seemed to have been poured onto Velma. "You buy it around here?"

"London."

"No crap! I bet it costs something over there, huh?" During this, Pop had come into the back room for something and wasn't aware of the one-sided conversation out front until I caught his eye and urgently pointed that direction. He emerged into the barroom as Velma, notoriously companionable only on her own terms, ran a look up and down the younger woman and said, "Like they say, if you have to ask, you can't afford it."

"Hey," Pop called to Francine too late to ward off the frost attack, "give me a hand with the beer glasses here, would you?" I noticed as she retreated behind the bar, looking back at the booth where alimony envelopes were coolly being slit open, that the little dent between her eyes when irritated was a lot like Proxy's.

After Velma, things went more smoothly, enough customers to keep Francine on her toes but not an overwhelming crowd, and with Pop close at hand as guardian angel, she kept things flowing reasonably well. My thoughts raced back and forth as I watched the activity in the barroom. This crazy year, which a person nearly needed to be an acrobat to follow, in its latest stunt had given me a sister, even if we didn't seem to be much alike in anything except hair follicles. I knew from my schoolmates that kids were not always happy when a new child came into the family, but did it have to work that same way at the other end of things, when a new grown-up showed up out of the total blue? I didn't think I actually resented Francine's arrival into my life and Pop's. I wasn't that much of a daddy's boy, was I? Yet how was a kid supposed to react to such an instantaneous change in the family, and for that matter, in the cherished routine of Medicine Lodge life? And Pop and Francine, this had to be real tricky for them to do, too. Down there at the bar, behind the big fib that they were uncle and niece, were they truly becoming like father and daughter? After all, she was a grown woman, and he admittedly was up there in years, and Pop by word and example had long told me habit dies hard. It bore watching, this dance of the generations.

Such thinking was interrupted as I saw him glance toward the door and stiffen at the sight of the next customers coming in. J. L. and Nan Hill were longtime friends of his and of the joint, but also old Fort Peck hands familiar with the Blue Eagle and its staff, if taxi dancers could be called that. The Hills steered their way to a booth as they always did because of J.L.'s shaking disease, while Pop in low tones instructed Francine in making a pink lady and drawing a beer into a mug with a handle large enough that J.L. could manage it without spilling.

Escorting Francine over with the drinks, Pop began a roundabout explanation of her presence. "I don't suppose you remember my having a sister, she wasn't really around Fort Peck so's you would notice." Boy, was he stretching the facts to fit the situation. He of course did have a sister, Aunt Marge, who had never been within a thousand miles of Fort Peck. Now, though, the so-called white lie had to be applied. "Anyhow, this is my niece Francine—"

"Pleased to meetcha." Francine all but curtsied, sensing something perilous from the way Pop was speaking.

"—she's here getting an education in bartending."

"This is the place for it," declared J.L., drawing the beer mug to himself with both trembling hands. "None better from here to China, unless it was the old Blue Eagle in Fort Peck days. I sure do wish we could have got to that reunion, seen all the faces again. I kind of miss the old days, Tom, how about you?"

"Sometimes," Pop equivocated, while Francine tried not to display the jitters at Fort Peck and Proxy's bailiwick surfacing in the conversation. And I knew what she did not, that the real threat of discovery was Nan Hill, who as washerwoman to establishments such as the Blue Eagle no doubt had knowledge of people's dirty laundry in more ways than one. Judiciously sipping her pink drink, she was searching Francine's face, as if trying to place it.

After enough such scrutiny, she turned to Pop with the verdict three of us were breathlessly waiting for.

"I can see the family resemblance—there's no mistaking that hair, surely."

With that, Francine passed all the examination any one person should have to undergo the first day on the job, and life in the Medicine Lodge settled to its true business, bartending. She did not do badly, as Pop graded it, on through the rest of the afternoon and evening. The true test to come, of course, would be whether she could handle the saloon by herself. And life with Pop and me.

✳ 8 ✳

THERE IS NOTHING like a new face behind the bar to either intrigue or alarm a saloon's patrons, and Francine's presence in the Medicine Lodge very quickly drew attention far and wide. Word spread like grass fire among the Air Force missile silo contingents and oil field roughnecks and the like, that there was someone young, female, and reasonably attractive now pouring drinks in the old joint, and they began to show up in droves. Saloons in the other towns must have dried up like puddles. And while her bartending skills were still very much in the development stage, right from the start she could hold her own with the flyboys, sassily kidding them as "junior birdmen," and laugh enough but not too much at the rough jokes of the oil rig hands, and meanwhile fend off flirting from just about every local male in her age range, including prominent bachelors like Turk Turco and Joe Quigg, by tossing off "Sorry, no free samples of the merchandise" along with a little mocking smile that seemed to let them in on the joke. As Pop admitted one night soon in a doorway conversation with me when she was finishing the bartending shift by herself, "She's got quite a mouth on her. But she maybe had to get one, to keep up with Proxy."

On the other hand, a number of the Medicine Lodge's long-time customers, such as Dode Withrow and other old-timers from the ranches, including the sheepherders, were less taken with her saucy manner and quick tongue, and missed having Pop stationed behind the bar in his bedroom slippers, faithfully listening to their stories and letting out "No bee ess?" as appropriate. No matter how attentive to them Francine tried to be, it was nowhere near the same.

I suppose Pop would have said it all balanced out on the teeter-totter. In any case, Francine now was there behind the bar of the Select Pleasure Establishment of the whole state, apparently as firmly installed as the beer spigot, and people were just going to have to get used to her. That included me.

"BILL TELLS ME you have an addition to the family."

Word surely was all over town if it tickled the ears of even Cloyce Reinking, I deduced when I met up with the former Lady Bracknell at the post office soon after Francine's bartending debut. You might not think going for the mail constituted hazardous duty, but was I ever finding it so. Occupied as Pop was with nurturing the newcomer behind the bar, he delegated me for the daily post office trip, which I ordinarily would not have minded. Nothing was ordinary since his change of mind about selling the Medicine Lodge, as I found out the first afternoon I had to pass the Zanes' gas station on my way and Duane popped out like the birdie in a cuckoo clock. "Your old man weaseled out of the deal," he sneered as I came into range, "he don't know how to keep his word." That got to me, but a broad daylight fistfight with a hereditary fool would not help matters in any way I could see, and so I only told him to stuff his remarks where the sun doesn't shine and from then on took to dodging around the block on my mail errand. Encountering Mrs. Reinking with the *Saturday Evening Post* and *Collier's* and a catalog or two cradled in her arms and lofty curiosity in her expression was no similarly possible mortal conflict, but something of a challenge nonetheless.

"Uh-huh," I tried offhandedly handling her inquiry about Francine having joined our living arrangement. "She's kind of a surprise." A little late, I remembered about watching my mouth. "I mean, we were never real close to that side of the family up until now."

"Is that so?" A persimmon smile in character for the ladyships of the world. "I hope not for anything as serious as leaving a baby in a handbag."

"Huh-uh. No. Nothing like that."

When she put her mind to it, Mrs. Reinking could be surprisingly astute about things. "It must make quite a change in the household for you and your father."

That was putting it mildly. "It takes some adjusting." I squeezed out enough truth without having to go into our domestic situation further, and hurriedly switched topics to her starring performance as Lady Bracknell, which I'd finally gotten to see when Bill Reinking kindly took me to the final night of the play. "You were outstanding! Zoe thinks so, too."

Her wintry features thawed into a genuine smile. "The two of you started something," she confided. "The Prairie Players are going to do *Blithe Spirit* this winter. I am cast—typecast, you might even say—as Madame Arcati."

"Neat! Do you get to—" I crossed my eyes to the best of my ability.

"I think not," she laughed lightly. "But I may resort to a turban. Madame Arcati, you see, is a medium and clairvoyant." Helpfully she explained that meant the character conducted séances with ghosts and could sense things that other people could not. A kind of fortune-teller of the past as well as the future, it sounded like.

We parted with her promise to enlist Zoe and me when she needed to learn her lines, and my silent wish for clairvoyance to rub off on me.

THE FACT OF THE MATTER was that Francine was not like any relative—sister, cousin, something in between as a half sister seemed to be—I could ever have dreamed up. For sure, the presence of a woman in a house that had not known one since I was an infant meant detours in routines Pop and I had followed as habitually as monks. Particularly, she hogged the bathroom for so long each morning that I regularly had to go out behind Igdrasil to take a leak. "They're that way," Pop counseled me about that propensity of womankind. But such quirks were the least of learning to live with Francine. Not only did she and I not start off on the same page of the book of siblings, we were not even in the same edition yet. Throughout life you meet people from the past, as natural as anything, but meeting someone from the future is far, far different. History only licenses us to drive in the past; the road ahead is always full of blind curves. Even I did not have nearly enough imagination to fantasize any of what the decade ahead would bring, with the flowering of a generation of Francines, restless and brainier than they knew what to do with and all too often as zany as they were brainy. The music coming that would leave Elvis Presley in the dust. The sprouting of communes and Haight-Ashbury and other such scenes. The whole youth revolt continually fueled by political assassinations, cities burning in racial rage, the despised Vietnam War, national traumas that seemed to come year by year after 1960. All I knew, those summer days and nights when history was forming up over the horizon, was that life had radically changed course with Francine's arrival, and I was scrambling to keep up.

THINGS MIGHT HAVE gone on that way, she in her hemisphere and me in my own, and mostly thin air between despite our best efforts, if the night hadn't come when she joined Zoe and me for supper. Until then she had been eating early with Pop so they could work the shift in the joint together on through the evening, and also to the point, he could keep on introducing her to all and sundry as his niece. This time he was busy with a beer delivery and sent her on ahead to the Top Spot by herself, and the next thing we knew, here she came giving us a knowing grin about all being in the same boat, eating-wise.

"Room for one more casualty?" she asked, as if Zoe wasn't openly dying of curiosity about her, and scooted in with us at the back table, already wearing her bartending bow tie and crisp white blouse. She dubiously scanned my usual shake and cheeseburger and Zoe's barely touched plate of the day's special. "Liver and onions, ain't it. That'll put hair on your chest." She flapped open a menu for any alternative. "What do they serve here that doesn't come with ptomaine?" We giggled a little nervously at this frank approach to Top Spot cuisine.

I have wondered since if Francine's tongue was simply looser than usual without Pop there with her. His wing, when he took you under it, covered a lot of territory. Out on her own, without him or Proxy to intervene, she must have felt—well, who knows what she was feeling, but she rambled on in a relaxed way as she went down the list of the cafe's none too appetizing offerings. Zoe and I could just sit there and listen to this mercurial visitor from the grown-up world, obviously not thought up by Shakespeare or Oscar Wilde but theatrical enough in her own head-tossing way. I have to stop and remind myself that Francine was only twenty-one at the time. To us she seemed as worldly as Scheherazade.

Zoe's eye was caught by the handiwork on Francine's wrist. Wider than a watchband, the wristpiece was an intricate weave of different-colored leather strips like fine basketry, only soft. "Ooh, that's some bracelet. Where did you get it?"

"Mmm? Made it myself," Francine still was absorbed in trying to find anything on the menu that appealed. "In leather class."

That roused my curiosity. "They have that in school where you were?"

"Nahh," she said offhandedly, still intent on the menu, "but they're big on it in juvie."

Zoe and I about fell into our food.

We looked at each other to make sure we had heard right, and we had. Juvie meant only one thing, any way it was said. A juvenile-offender correction facility. Alcatraz for teenagers.

"I give." Francine surrendered the menu, flopping it closed. "Liver and onions it is, you only die once." Our faces gave us away. "Whups. I see my mommy didn't spread the word about that little episode in my youth." Momentarily she frowned down at the wristband. "I sort of wondered how much my reputation had proceeded me. Not all that much, it looks like." With the rare realization that she might have said too much, she winked at us in the manner of Proxy. "Tell you what, let's keep it that way. What people don't know won't hurt them, huh?"

Depend on Zoe, she came right out with it. "How bad a crime was it?"

"I took a car, is all. People got excited. Jeez," a note of annoyance crept into her voice, "I was going to bring it back later that night. I just got a little delayed."

"How old were—" Zoe and I blurted together.

"Old enough not to know better," Francine breezed past that. "Fourteen." In other words, no great amount of age beyond that of two thunderstruck twelve-year-olds.

If she was going to keep talking, we were going to keep asking. It was my turn. "So how long were you in juvie?"

Frowning, she toyed with a tendril of her hair. "Year and a half. That judge was really touchy about cars."

"Have you decided, dear?" Mrs. Constantine hovered in briefly to take her order, alternating a warm smile at Francine as a new customer and a stern expression at her non-eating daughter. Zoe and I could hardly wait until she was out of earshot to resume our question barrage.

"What did Proxy say when you got caught?"

"She wasn't around to say anything. Hardly ever was." This was given out carelessly, as if a missing mother was of no concern. "My aunt and uncle weren't any too happy with me"—she gave the offhand shrug that was becoming familiar—"but what did they expect? If there'd been anything to do besides watch wheat grow, maybe I wouldn't have swiped that car."

Zoe was torn, I could tell, between devouring every word of this and dying to fire off more questions, and for that matter, so was I. With extreme mutual willpower, we waited for Francine to go on.

"Anyhow," she picked up her story as if she had nothing better to do, "me being in juvie got Proxy's attention for sure. Came and got me when I was sprung. Decided to turn into a real mother and hauled me off to Nevada." She shrugged again. "It's been a roller coaster ride ever since."

For someone who had been locked away for not inconsiderable theft, this new addition to the family sounded blindingly honest when she wanted to. But not, it was dawning on me, to the extent of having volunteered her automotive indiscretion to Pop. Nor had Proxy seen fit to mention the matter, had she. If I was sure of anything, it was that Tom Harry would not put a car thief in charge of the saloon that was his lifeblood. So he didn't know, but now I did. Talk about the weight of knowledge; it all of a sudden felt like a ton.

Zoe, bless her up, down, and sideways, took up the questioning while I was sitting there, stunned with the burden of truth. "What did you do before coming here? I mean, what kind of work?"

Francine glanced around with an expression as if the hard-used cafe was all too familiar. When not showing a sidelong smile similar to her mother's, her mouth had a tendency to look like she was tasting something fishy. That dubious approach to life came out in her voice now. "Pearl-dived." Which meant she washed dishes. "Slung hash." Waited on tables. "Took rental cars down to Vegas when they ran short, go bring them back when Reno started to run out. Little of this, little of that, not a hell of a lot of anything." She picked up her spoon and drew idle circles on the tablecloth. "Just between you and me and Pat and Mike and Mustard, I think that's why that mother of mine came up with this brainstorm of getting me into a line of work that's got something going for it, like bartending. Don't you guess, Rusty?"

"Huh? Oh, sure." How the question popped out of me right then, I don't know, but when better? "What does your . . . what does Proxy do for a living?"

"Her?" Some more tracing with the spoon in concentrated fashion. "She's a promoter." Zoe and I glanced at each other, trying to figure that out—the only promoting we knew anything about was advancing from one grade to the next in school—until Francine took mercy.

"Mom," she gave the word a sly little twist, as if all three of us knew the strange ways of parents, "is more or less in the divorce business, see. Nevada dude ranches have always been big on divorcees in for the quickie piece of paper. New crops of grass widows. So they send her around up here"—from the vague swing of her head that seemed to include everywhere north of Nevada—"to travel agencies and private investigators and so on, anybody with a stake in marriages going on the rocks. Casinos use her, too, same kind of thing—spreading the word where people might be interested in coming on down to Reno." She kept looking fixedly at the whorls the spoon was making on the tablecloth. "Those, and some other ways of earning a buck." The slight lift of the shoulders that was casual, but also not. "She's usually got something going."

Her supper arrived, along with Mrs. Constantine's beaming wish for good appetite, and she dug in, while mine now sat as untouched as Zoe's.

"Hey, don't let anything I said put you off your feed," Francine favored us with as she chewed a piece of liver. "You can't let other people's behavior drive you crazy. Learned that in juvie."

MY STOMACH KEPT turning inside out during the rest of that meal. Francine's offhand gossiping about herself had left me in what Pop would have called a "picklish dilemma." Was it up to me to tell him his long-lost daughter had a criminal past, at least of the juvenile sort? Would that make me a squealer against my own flesh and blood? What if I did tell him and he took it wrong, thinking I was doing it because I resented her arrival into the family? Would I only be making trouble, and be blamed for bringing up something bothersome from the past? When you go through a gate, close it behind you, remember.

For once, even Zoe was less than certain when we put our heads together at the table after Francine finally went off to tend bar.

"You want him to keep her on so he doesn't sell the joint—"

"Yeah."

"—but you don't want him out of it about what she did to land herself in juvie."

"No."

We deliberated silently on the matter.

"Maybe"—inspiration surfaced in Zoe as it so often did—"she'll take care of it."

"Who, Proxy? Fat chance. She hasn't said boo about it so far, so why would she—"

"No, no, not her. Francine, I mean. She about talks her face off, doesn't she? So she might blab it herself to your dad, like she did with us, sooner or later."

I seized on that, particularly the "later" part.

"Good thinking, Muscles. Maybe I'll wait and see what happens."

❧ 9 ❧

"Guess what Bill Reinking had on his mind today."
Looking deeply thoughtful, Pop was at his desk on the landing, a typical rainy afternoon, when I came back from the post office.

"Don't keep me in suspenders, Pop," I joked as I trotted up the stairs, still clutching the mail under my slicker to keep it dry until I handed it to him—bills, mostly—and went to hang up the dripping coat. At least I hoped I was joking, for the most average thing seemed suspenseful since Francine came onto the scene. I was pretty sure she hadn't told him about her juvenile detention past yet, if she was ever going to, and the Gros Ventre *Weekly Gleaner* generally had more serious matters on its mind than who had stolen a car way back then, so there was a pretty good chance this wasn't that.

What was it, though, that had him sitting there, as if waiting to explore the human condition with me? I could tell simply by listening that the vent was safely closed. He had not said anything about keeping it a secret from the new presence in the barroom, but I had the impression he didn't at all mind it happening that way for the time being. Right now he looked more than ever like the master of all he surveyed, having a cigarette in a relaxed manner that suggested this one didn't count toward quitting smoking, gazing around the back room, as if collecting his thoughts from the loot assortment. Now that Francine was catching on as bartender enough not to disgrace the joint, he even had the leisure to help Del with mudjacks lingo, the Fort Peck reunion evidently a rosier experience to look back on than when he'd had to face it. So I was not able to pick out any imminent disturbance of the peace in my father's universe at the moment, and had to let him take his sweet time in telling me what was on the mind of the *Gleaner* editor.

"Okay, picture this," he said at last when I was more than ready to. "Bill comes in a little while ago and is sitting there having his scotch and I'm just hanging around, visiting with him. Francine minds her manners, goes off to the amen corner to leave us alone, and we're shooting the bull like always, when guess what he brought up?"

He seemed to be enjoying the story so much I almost hated to parrot back, "Gee, what?"

"He's president of the Chamber of Commerce, you know." News to me. Pop paused for effect, but couldn't hold it in for long. "He asked me to honcho the derby this year."

This was quite something, all right. While other towns marked the close of summer with harvest festivals and homesteader days and rodeos and such, Gros Ventre had decided the proper way to celebrate was to catch every fish humanly possible. The derby had grown much larger and more popular across the half dozen years since my ill-fated introduction to it. Which was why the best I could come up with at the idea of Pop, chickengut fisherman that he was, in charge of the annual rod-and-reel extravaganza at Rainbow Reservoir was "No bee ess?"

He started to correct my language, but then laughed a little sheepishly. "I must be getting a reputation for having time on my hands, you suppose? I don't know, though." He looked almost embarrassed. "Being in charge of something like that is awfully damn civic. I'm not sure I have it in me."

Now, it would have been perfectly fine with me if he decided not to have anything to do with the exalted fishing derby in any way, shape, or form, which would mean I didn't have to, either. However, if it would give him something to do after Francine could handle the Medicine Lodge by herself and Del departed to wherever Missing Voices led him to next, what could be wrong with that?

Quickly I worked up enthusiasm. "Sure you have. He's just asking you to boss a bunch of people for their own good, isn't that what 'civic' means?"

"I told Bill I'd think it over." He glanced at me, as if making sure. "You really figure I could do okay at it?"

"Hunnerd percent cinch, Pop," I vouched.

"Okay, we'll see," he said, and for once it did not sound as if it meant maybe.

NEXT CAME THE morning, not long after, when Francine startled me by showing up in the kitchen as I was heating my breakfast. Ordinarily she slept late and I would only eventually know she was out of bed by those constant bathroom sounds of faucets being turned on and off and lids clattering on the sink counter and other toiletry noises that always left males in the dark. In this new order of things, Pop was sleeping in as well, claiming to be catching up on years of late nights, and usually he and she would grab a bite at the Top Spot before setting up the saloon for the day. So I wasn't prepared when she wandered in this early, her hair not even fixed, more like the black mop back to the day she had arrived, and she had on the same pinkish shirt and over-the-hill blue jeans from then. "What's buzzin', cousin?" Her usual greeting was delivered with a yawn.

Thrown as I was by her appearance, I mechanically did the polite thing. "Morning. Want some tomato soup?"

"Not hardly." Instead, she prowled around, opening cabinets, making a face at what she didn't find. "Don't you have anything edible in the place, like cornflakes? Oatmeal? Raisins, even?"

"Huh-uh. There's some old bread we haven't thrown to the magpies yet. You could maybe make toast."

"I'll settle for some joe, thanks just the same." She prepared the coffeepot and stuck it on the stove while I poured my breakfast into a soup bowl and sat down to it. Joining me at the table while waiting for the coffee to perk, she seemed to have something on her mind. Whatever that was, it didn't seem right to me for the only sound in the room to be my slurping up soup.

I asked, "Sleep well?"

"Fine." This was said, though, with another yawn stifled with her sleeve, the leather bracelet sliding a little on her wrist. By now Pop was letting her close up the saloon by herself most nights—"She needs the practice, shutting up of any kind," he said humorously enough about Francine's shotgun style of conversation; little did he know—so she was keeping late hours. Rare sunshine was flooding in through the kitchen window on us, not a cloud anywhere beyond Igdrasil's leafy outline, the old Packard, and Del's van, sparkling with dewdrops in the morning light. Squinting against the brightness, she asked, as if just reminded, "How's College Boy doing?"

"No tick fever yet," I reported. "He's still awful busy typing up the mudjacks so he doesn't get canned from his job."

She smiled with one side of her mouth. "He better not work

himself too hard. He gets any skinnier, ticks wouldn't have anything to climb on, huh?"

I didn't care to join in on this reminiscence of Del in the flesh,
and, coffee now ready, she went and poured a cup and took quick
sips before rejoining me at the table.

Francine sat there for a little while, not saying anything, which
was unlike her. After enough gabby suppers in the cafe, Zoe and
I had become used to her going on at length to the effect that it
didn't matter whether Kennedy or Nixon won the forthcoming
presidential election because we were all going to get blown up
anyway when Russia and the flyboys cut loose with the missiles
out in those silos, and other extended observations that did not
help one's appetite. Yet you couldn't really write her off, we kept
finding to our fascination, even when she was telling us we'd all
end up in incinerated fallout shelters with nothing to eat but
tubes of toothpaste. Even at her worst she made you think, and
that's worth something in a person.

As now, when she sat there tracing a roundabout pattern on
the oilcloth with her thumbnail before giving me a sudden, keen
look. "Want to know something?" I kept at my soup. In my experience, when someone said that, they were going to provide the
something, whether or not that's what you wanted.

"You're the first to find out, bud." She leaned across the table
in confidential fashion. "Decided I'm gonna change my name."

Just like that? Was she kidding? Could a person do that?

"Oh?" I stammered in surprise, wondering if I ought to get
Pop up to hear this. "You mean, from Duff to—ours?"

"Nahh, it's too late on that," she tossed the Harry family
name exclusively back to Pop and me, to my considerable relief.
"I mean the other one. I'm sick of being Francine. It sounds like
some constipated saint."

Now I was fascinated. "What are you going to change to?"

"France."

The kitchen went so silent, my eye blinks probably could have been heard, until I managed, "Like the country?"

"Mm hmm. Got kind of a romantic touch to it, ain't it. How's it grab you?"

"It's, um, real different."

"That's what I thought. Sounds kind of hip, don't it. 'France,'" she said in cool-customer fashion, "yeah." She grinned at me over her coffee cup. "The boys in the joint are gonna have something to get used to, huh?"

So were the rest of us, starting with Pop. When he arrived on the scene somewhat later for a wake-up jolt of coffee, his initial reaction was predictable—"Like the country? Not even 'Frances,' like the saint sounds like?"—but shortly he threw up his hands and said she was a grown-up and her name was her own damn business.

As it proved out, France, as she was now, guessed right about the flyboys and roughnecks having a good time adjusting to the new her when they came in the joint, with the playful ones teasing her as "Frenchy" at first. But that wore off soon enough, and her adopted name or nickname or whatever it was ceased to be anything I paid particular attention to on life's list of surprises.

PROXY WAS ANOTHER matter. Put it simply, she spooked the daylights out of me whenever she showed up.

Not far into the evolution of Francine into France and the reaction in the saloon, Zoe and I were on our way back from supper, chattering a mile a minute as usual, when we saw the red Cadillac parked in the alley behind the saloon. Leaning against a fender, taking long, thoughtful drags on a cigarette was the unmistakable blond, shapely figure, and we needed to do some fast thinking.

"Just remember," I whispered urgently, "you've seen her—"

"—through the vent, right," Zoe tallied in a similar rushed whisper.

"—but she's never seen you—"

"—but she knows I'm in on it about Francine, I mean France—"

"—so you better look surprised or something at meeting her so she doesn't get suspicious about how you recognize her. Ready?"

"Piece of cake. I'll just say, 'I've heard your name mentioned, Mrs. Duffy.'"

"No, no, *Duff*, get that straight or she'll bite your head off. Come on, she's looking at us."

You really knew you had been looked at when Proxy gave you the once-over, with that suggestive gaze and tuck of a smile at a corner of her mouth. She studied Zoe to the maximum as we came up, Zoe giving back as good as she got.

"Remind me here," Proxy saw in a hurry that Zoe was thoroughly attached to me, "you're exactly who?"

Dramatically Zoe began regaling her with Butte and the Top Spot and suppers together, until I finished off the introduction with what really counted. "She's in on it."

"Right," Proxy said, as if sucking a tooth. Me, she gave a little shake of her head. "You're starting early, Russ," whatever that was supposed to mean. Her attention shifted from us, thank goodness, as she restlessly looked up and down the alley. "Is Tom around? He's not at the house, and I didn't want to barge into the joint and upset things."

"He's gassing up the car"—with Earl Zane still spitting mad over losing out on the saloon, this now had to be done at the truck stop at the other end of town—"he should be back pretty quick."

"Oh-kay," Proxy said, grinding out her cigarette with a practiced foot, "we can inspect the scenery until he gets here. So, sonny. How's that daughter of mine doing at slinging drinks, does he say?"

I was not going to be drawn into any discussion of that. "Pop will want to tell you himself, I don't want to spoil it."

She studied me the intent way that made me uncomfortable. "You getting along okay with Francine, I hope?" She included Zoe with a half wink that said any of this was just between us.

"Sure," we chorused. Then, though, some urge sneaked up on me and I turned this conversation on its head. "She's changed her name, that's a little hard to keep up with, but we're getting pretty much used to it."

"She's what?"

"Didn't you know?" I couldn't resist, and Zoe beside me was trying to keep an equally straight face. "She goes by 'France' now."

"Like the—?"

"Sure thing."

"Is that all." Proxy nonetheless looked a bit bothered by the news, resorting to another cigarette. She smoked the same unregenerate brand of coffin nails my father did, no Kools or Salems for her. "'France,' huh? Isn't that something. Shows she has a mind of her own," she said as though that was a novelty.

Zoe's attention was caught by the strange license plate on the Cadillac and used it as an excuse to ask with a wonderful air of innocence, "Do you have a job in Nevada?"

Proxy seemed amused by the question. "More than one, angel eyes. Force of habit." Well, that tallied with her daughter's version that she always had something going. Now she slanted a look at Zoe, although I again had the feeling she was speaking mostly to me. "I don't suppose you know what a stand-in is."

But we did! We had learned all manner of things theatrical from Cloyce Reinking. Bursting with curiosity, we demanded to know what classic of drama Proxy was attached to.

"Naw, not a play." She brushed aside a mere stage role. "A movie they're shooting in Reno and the desert there."

Suspiciously I asked, "So who are you the stand-in for?"

"Marilyn Monroe, natch."

Zoe and I fell silent. This couldn't possibly be true. Could it?

Meanwhile she was telling us she didn't know why anybody would think it would make a good movie because all it was about was catching wild horses, but Clark Gable was in it, too, "and a bunch of others." It sounded very much like what a person might pick up from reading a Reno newspaper.

"Then what's Marilyn—" I began trying to pin her down.

"—really like?" Zoe finished.

"Don't get me wrong," Proxy's voice dipped to a more modest tone, "we're not buddy-buddy, her and me. I'm part of the furniture, as far as she's concerned. See, I stand in for her when they're setting up the shots, is all. The hair and skin and so forth, we register about the same with the cameras."

Zoe barely beat me to the next question. "How'd you get a neat job like that?"

Proxy shrugged as if there was nothing to it. "I'm in Harrah's one night, just seeing what's going on, and I reach out and give one of the slot machines a yank as I go by. 'Why'd you do that, doll?' a guy behind me asks. 'This machine loves me,' I tell him. He laughs and says, 'Wait a minute, stand over here in the light, would you?' He turns out to be the movie director on his way to the blackjack table." She shrugged again. "Long and short of it is, he tells me they need somebody awfully blond for a stand-in, and how about me, so I said why not?" She laughed in a dry way. "You watch, I bet they swipe my line about the slot machine. Those movie people."

Whether or not there was a lick of truth in any of that, she could weave a story, for sure. Skeptical as we were, Zoe and I had listened as if hypnotized. "But if they need you to be the stand-in," I finally challenged insofar as I could, "how come you aren't there instead of here?"

"Oh, that. The shooting's shut down awhile. See, they have to dry Marilyn out. Booze and pills together." She twirled a finger at her temple. "Real bad idea."

That still was the kind of gossip that probably could be picked up at any Reno slot machine. Like me, Zoe didn't know how much to believe, but it sounded so good in the telling, it seemed a shame to write it off entirely. "Maybe she'll go on the wagon and you'll have to turn right around and go back to Nevada," she tested out, knowing I would feel a lot better about matters if that happened.

"I'm not holding my breath. Things happen when they happen, buttercup." Proxy was growing restless about waiting around in the open and glanced at me. "What do you suppose is keeping that father of yours?"

I shrugged and should have quit with that, but instead did something I could have kicked myself for afterward.

"We could wait for him in the back room, I guess," I more or less invited before Zoe's expression told me that was not the best idea.

In a blink Proxy dispatched her latest cigarette. "Lead on, I'm housebroken."

THE BACK-ROOM ASSORTMENT caught her interest the
moment we stepped in. "Well, looky here. Tom didn't tell me he
was running a pawnshop as well as the joint." Damn, she was
swift at sizing things up. I had to hope she wasn't swuft as well.

"This is some bunch of stuff," she marveled, looking every
which way. "Kind of like money in the bank, huh?"

I mumbled an explanation about drinkers sometimes running
short of money, avoiding any mention of Pop selling off the loot,
as I wished he hadn't called it, on those trips of his.

A reminiscent gleam came into her eye. "Yeah, that had a habit
of happening at the Blue Eagle, too." She gave a throaty laugh.
"You wouldn't believe what some of those characters wanted to
trade."

Zoe had been darting fearful glances at the slicker covering
the vent, but when Proxy's back was turned I silently mouthed,
"It's okay, it's closed," and she relaxed into the natural role of
tour guide. With Zoe showing off the variety of items from
cowboy hats to crowbars, Proxy was unexpectedly interested in
it all, like a shopper turned loose in a shut department store. I
hung back a little, staying out of the way, brooding over the way
this milk-blond force of nature kept showing up out of nowhere
and disrupting things.

"What the devil is this, a gospel meeting?"

So taken up with Proxy's visitation, I hadn't heard Pop's car,
and I came to with a start as he stepped in from the alley. He did
not sound all that pleased at finding the three of us in the back
room, and I edged in behind Proxy to let her handle it. Zoe
wisely had shut up, too.

"How's every little thing, Tom? I figured I'd stop by and find out how our girl is doing, besides lopping her name in half," Proxy said casually. "I see you're letting her run the joint by herself."

"Some of the time," Pop allowed, coming over to where we were clustered by the saddles and spurs. "She's got to learn to be on her own."

"So?" Proxy's eyebrows alone pretty much asked the question. "How's she shaping up behind the bar?"

"Not bad." He paused, glancing at Zoe and me and then giving up on keeping us away from grown-up talk. "The flyboys and roughnecks are like bees to honey around her, but she knows I mean it about no dating the inmates, and she hasn't been."

"I'll lay down the law to her about strictly sticking to the job, too," Proxy said, looking relieved. "Men, they are such a nuisance. Present company excepted, natch." She generously included me in the grinning glance she gave Pop.

"Let's don't get into that can of worms." I noticed he was giving her the same funny look he had when she pulled in after the Fort Peck reunion, guarded yet attracted. Shaking that off, he turned away to where his apron was hanging on its usual hook by the landing. "I know you'll want to visit with Francine—I mean, France. Cripes, why couldn't you give her a name that can't be fiddled with?" Zoe's eyes sparkled at that. "I'll take over out front"—he tied the apron on—"and send her—"

"Before you do that," Proxy interjected. Zoe and I took note of the actressy way she looked around the room, as if only then discovering its treasures. "Quite the collection you have here."

Pop paused, looking unsure whether he wanted to hear this. "It adds up, if you stay in business long enough."

"If I know my history from the old days in the Eagle, customers don't always make good on paying up later." She patted the weathered stirrup of a saddle that obviously dated back to roundups long ago. "I bet a bunch of this is never gonna be got out of hock and it's yours to do with, am I right?"

"That happens some. Why, you in the market for a saddle for the Caddie?"

Proxy didn't crack a smile. "I was just thinking of someplace where they buy all sorts of stuff, and there must be a junior fortune here if it was handled right." Clearly she thought she was talking over the heads of Zoe and myself, which showed she didn't know our heads. We put on bored faces, idly spinning the rowels of the rank of spurs while listening with all our might.

"You were, were you," Pop was saying gingerly. "And where is it you think something like that takes place?"

"Canada, slowpoke."

My insides lurched.

"The railyard district in Medicine Hat," she specified. "Come on, Tom, you know what I'm talking about. No place like it when we used to know it, was there." The kind of slick, knowing smile I didn't want to see accompanied that. "Still that kind of place, if I know anything about it," she sailed right on. "I've been back to the district now and then since, doing business, and you'd be surprised at what they can come up with when they like what they see." I suppose she did not actually bat her eyes, but she might as well have. Proxy's general type of business already had involved Pop with a surprise daughter. Now it was threatening to set him off again on those trips I hated so much. As far as I could see, she was a specimen of catamount that made the wildcat mounted on the wall seem like a kitten. Catching my distress, Zoe nibbled her lip anxiously.

Pop squinted as if trying to draw a bead on what to say next. I couldn't tell if he really was tempted or simply thrown by Proxy's latest big notion. In any case, hesitation was not a good sign in him around her.

"I'm kind of busy with something else," he put her off. Who knew I would ever be thankful for the fishing derby? "For now," he went back to safer ground, "let's just concentrate on the bartending daughter."

Agreeably enough, Proxy said that was fine and dandy with her, and as he went in to mind the barroom, she left Zoe and me with a grinning *adios* and went out to the Cadillac to wait for France. It is strange what you have to pin your hopes on in this life. I now had to wish for Marilyn Monroe to be dried out enough to need a stand-in, if she really did, because when Proxy was here instead of there, I could feel my father being lured away from me a little at a time.

BY NOW DEL was showing signs of emerging from his camper cocoon. Much to his relief, Pop's sessions of helping with the mudjack lingo had enabled him to send off a first batch of Fort Peck tapes and transcriptions to the powers that be at the Library of Congress, and with every new day bringing no sign of Rocky Mountain spotted fever, Zoe and I no longer had to dole out sympathy when we dropped by the van to see how he was doing. Our report of Proxy's visit elicited his old bushy-tailed interest, right down to that deathless detail, that she claimed she was a stand-in for Marilyn Monroe.

"If that's so, Marilyn Monroe had better watch out she doesn't end up as a stand-in for Proxy," he said with a chuckle. Actually taking a break for a minute from the tape recorder and typewriter, he yawned and stretched in the Gab Lab chair. "By the way, how's 'Uncle Tom's Niece' playing to the audience at large?" This was different. He hadn't brought up Francine to us before, still embarrassed over the tick on his business end, we figured.

Zoe looked at me meaningfully, and I had to nod in surrender. After all, I'd had the privilege of dropping the news on Proxy.

"Not bad," she took over with that arch hint of more to come that we had picked up from *The Importance of Being Earnest*. "People are going to have to get used to the fact she's changed her name, though."

"Say again?" Del tilted his head to employ his good ear.

No further prompting needed, Zoe delved into Francine becoming France, with me furnishing the crucial detail she'd always thought Proxy had burdened her with a name that sounded like a constipated saint.

"She thinks she got a bum deal on her birth certificate"—Del did a wickedly effective Groucho Marx bit with his eyebrows—"she should try being named after a president."

"Yeah, but," Zoe was struck with a thought that nobody else saw coming, "that was his middle name, sitting there waiting. President Roosevelt's, I mean. So you got off pretty easy, people usually have dumb middle names. What's yours?"

"Oh, nothing worth mentioning. Now, if you don't mind—"

"That's not fair. We'll tell you ours, won't we, Rusty."

"Sure. You first."

"Theodosia. It's Greek."

"Thomas," I owned up to. "Like Pop."

Still nothing from Del. "Listen, I have work to do and—"

"I bet it's something like Sylvester, isn't it," Zoe persisted as devilishly as only she could. "Or Algernon. Or—"

"All right, all right." He picked up a pencil and threw it down. We kept waiting.

"It's Delano."

As soon as the word was out of his mouth, Zoe knew something was up. I was already staring bullets at him.

"For your edification," he none too willingly was admitting to, "my full name is Philip Delano Robertson. My father thought if you speak it fast, it sounds kind of like . . . well, you know."

I did not even have to say anything, merely kept staring at him. Was any grown-up trustworthy at all?

"I know what you're thinking, Rusty"—and he was all too right—"but it wasn't like that, honestly. I didn't turn Phil into Del to win over your father, I decided to make the change when I left Washington to come out here."

"Cross your heart and swear to go to heaven in a flash of—"

"Absolutely. Look, I'm using it on the Missing Voices tapes"—he grabbed the nearest one to show us the grease-penciled label on the reel—"and the transcriptions and all else. Professionally and"—he spun his hands as if making the one catch up with the other—"personally as well, I go by Delano now. It's a better name, it has more to it," he said with conviction. "I don't know why it's taken me this long to do it. Slow learner."

He must have seen we needed more convincing. "Honestly, it's an old, old tradition of new arrivals to this part of the country," he resorted to, "and I can absolutely see why Francine, I mean France, would do it."

"What, call herself after someplace in Europe?"

"No, change her name to the extent she has. Amending it, let's say, the way I'm doing with Delano. History is full of examples," he said, as if that was justification enough, "people did it all the time when they came west." He hit on an inspiration. "Alan Lomax even discovered a song about it." Clearing his throat, necessarily or not, he proceeded to twang out:

Oh, what wuz yer name in the States?
Wuz it Jackson or Johnson or Bates?

Mebbe Gaitskill or Gaither or Gates?
Oh, what wuz yer name in the States?

We clamored for more, but he declined. "I really shouldn't have got going on this matter of France, as she now is," he reproved himself. "Terrible manners. I don't know what's getting into me. I've never even thanked her for pitching in at picking deadly insects off me." Serious to the roots of his crew cut now, he looked out the van window toward the Medicine Lodge, as if setting his sights on it. "I suppose I really ought to take care of that when I get a chance."

Right then we should have seen what was coming, shouldn't we.

THE VERY NEXT day, another wet one keeping us inside at the back-room desk, Zoe and I were settling in over the Flying Fortress that still lacked a tail, what with all else that had been taking up our time. Out front, the saloon had just opened and was still empty, with only the distant clink of glassware as France—we were calling her that with hardly a second thought now—fussed with chores behind the bar. Zoe was ritually checking the vent, which we were about to shut so we could jabber all we wanted while we worked on the bomber tail.

"Ooh," she whispered as I was starting to cut out the balsa wood tailfin with the X-Acto knife. "Rusty, guess who."

Looking much as he did when he appeared in the Medicine Lodge that first day, all legs and pockets and red head, Del was stepping up to the bar, shaking off the worst of the rain as he came.

"Top of the afternoon," he said lightly. "Good weather for amphibians."

"Yeah, ain't it." France came partway down the bar, wiping her hands on a fresh towel. "Two Medicine country liquid sunshine, everyone tells me this is." She glanced up at the clock. "Looking for Tom? He's at the Spot having lunch with his fish derby committee, so he'll maybe be a while."

"No, no, I only came by to say thanks for helping out there when I had to be, ah, searched." He twitched his shoulders self-consciously. "I hope it wasn't too embarrassing."

France responded with that cunning little turn of mouth she had inherited from Proxy; it could serve as a smile or not, depending. "Angel of mercy, that's me." Turning more serious, she asked: "You over your bug bite?"

"Pretty much. Still an itchy spot." Del tried for the bright side: "At least it didn't result in sudden death."

"Mm hmm. Well, that's always good."

Bomber tailfin abandoned one more time, the two of us at the vent watched in suspense while she rubbed the bar with her towel and he stood there, gangling like a hollyhock.

"Actually," he came around to as if it was a big decision, "while I'm here, I think I'll have a drink."

"Fine. What'll it be?"

"Hmm? Beer, please. Sorry, let me do it right." Slapping the bar, Del pulled in his chin to make his voice deeper. "Herd me up a Shellac, *s'il vous plaît*." Not a bad bit, Zoe and I silently agreed.

France snickered and stepped to the Select spigot. When the glass was brimming to a nice head, she slid it to him. "Here you go, straight from the horse."

Matters now had reached a pivotal point of bartending ethic, whether to withdraw to a respectful distance and let the drink be imbibed in solitary pleasure, or to stay in the immediate vicinity, doing some little thing and provide small talk and a listening ear if wanted. Pop always knew in a flash which to do. Looking less than certain, France glanced to the amen corner, where one of those mystery novels with the perpetually endangered blonde on the cover waited as usual, but then began drying the same beer glasses she'd dried five minutes before. "You've really been holed up working, huh? How's it going?"

"Phenomenal," Del responded, dabbing away a little beer mustache. "Another week or so and I'll have all the interview tapes transcribed and sent off. I couldn't have done it without Tom. Fort Peck was a world all its own."

"I bet. I've heard a ton of that from Proxy." Another dry glass received a thorough wiping. "Then what? You moving on, I guess?"

"I'm afraid so." He did the bit with his chin jacked down on his voice box again. "Back on the trail of the Missing Voices." Zoe and I heard this with a pang we could feel in each other.

"Oboy, this place could use some noise around this time of day," France skipped past his imminent departure. "Tried to talk Tom into putting in a jukebox, but he says if people want music, they can go sing in church." She wrinkled her nose at the Buck Fever Case painting across the room. "If I owned the joint, I'd put in a jukie right smack over there."

Del ventured, "And have to listen to fifty versions of 'she done me wrong' songs?"

"Nahh, not just yokel vocals. I'd make sure to sneak in some Mose Allison. 'One Room Country Shack' and so on. You dig that kind of thing?"

"Do I! Absolutely!" Del nearly ascended off his bar stool. "Mose Allison is a Mississippi Delta bluesman of the first order. A direct descendant of Leadbelly and Muddy Waters and Blind Lemon Jefferson and—" He rattled off names until building up to an encore of the growly blues he had performed at the reservoir that fishing day with Pop and me. *"Everythin' nailed down's comin' loose. Seems like livin' ain't no use.* Sensational stuff, isn't it? Pure *lingua america."* Finally he caught himself. "Sorry. I tend to get carried away about musicology."

"That's okay," she said, giving him a strange look. "Passes the time anyway."

That caused him to check the clock over by the Select Pleasure Establishment plaque and conscientiously down some more of his beer. "I really should get out of your ha—your way so you can go about your business."

"Aw, feel free to stick around and flirt with me"—she gave him a grin so fresh it was comical—"I need the flattery and you need the practice." Her face sobered as she saw him redden all the way to his ears. "That's what's called a joke, you know."

"Right, right. Good one."

France fiddled with something under the bar while Del kept rolling the beer glass back and forth between his palms. "Actually, I need to drink up and go back to transcribing." As if it had just occurred to him—which may well have been the case—he dug deep to pay. She came, took the money, delivered the change, and began to move off down the bar. Del wrenched around on his stool in that direction.

"Ah, France . . . I was wondering, I mean I wanted to ask. Have you had a chance to see any of the countryside around here? Glacier Park, for instance?"

"Not hardly," she laughed unhumorously. "Been too busy with—" She rolled her eyes to indicate the totality of the barroom.

He managed to sound bashful and eager at the same time. "What would you think about driving up with me on Sunday? The park is only a couple of hours from here."

I instantly knew what was going through her mind: the house

policy, no dating a customer. Yet, and I was entirely with her on this, too, Del didn't really qualify as a customer, did he? He was . . . well, Del; practically an attachment to the household; friend of the family, inadvertently; soon to head down the road in pursuit of other Missing Voices. Obviously an exception to any rule, and in my pulling for her to say yes to him, I was not at all alone. I speak for both of us, Zoe was as eager as me to see Rosalind and Orlando, Algernon and Cecily and Jack and Gwendolen, duplicated in front of our eyes.

France did it her own way, grinning a little slantwise as she answered: "Promise we won't end up picking ticks off each other?"

Even from the length of the barroom away, we could see Del's ears redden again. "No buggy stuff, scout's honor."

"Okay. Sunday's it."

ALL THAT COULD be gotten out of them afterward about the Glacier Park trip was "It went fine" from her, and "It was quite the day" from him, not exactly the dramatic dialogue Zoe and I were hungry for. Pop added a few furrows to his brow when he learned of their date, but he only said, "Opposites attract, but usually not for long."

And in fact, Del did not show his face in the saloon in subsequent days but hunkered in to the Gab Lab again, and France seemed the same as ever, matching wisecracks with customers when she had to and minding her own business in the form of bar chores and hard-boiled novels otherwise. Still waters run deep, though, notoriously so. It was only a few nights into that week when I stirred from sleep with the sense that something was wrong.

Groggily I sat up and sniffed hard; one more time the house was not on fire from Pop smoking in bed, so that wasn't it. No, what woke me, I realized, was that France had not come in yet, even though the radium green of the alarm clock showed it was considerably past closing time at the saloon. I strained to hear if she might be in the bathroom, but faucets weren't running, the toilet wasn't flushing, none of that.

Now I started to be really alarmed. Had something happened to her? Just as I was about to jump out of bed and wake up Pop, I heard small noises outside. For the next minute or so I listened almost hard enough to get ear strain, but it did not really take that much. No matter how careful a person is, the side doors of a VW van opening and closing make some sound. So do creeping up the creaky back steps and easing open the kitchen door and trying to tiptoe through the house in the dark, as she more or less successfully was.

Wait till I tell Zoe about this development, I thought excitedly as I rolled over and pretended to be asleep.

HOW MUCH DID YOU say them jellied eggs is, girlie? Price gone up again, ain't it."

There was only one voice like that in the Two Medicine country, rough as barbwire and about as welcome, and I had heard its grumbles so many times, it simply made me groan to myself as I checked on the barroom out of habit, not many afternoons after Del's excursion into the joint. Like many another of the sheepherders, Canada Dan drank for a week or so when he got started, and plainly he was launching the kind of drunken spree that Pop dealt with all the time but France had not encountered until now.

She had been in a chipper mood since taking up with Del, but any midnight rendezvous in the van was hours and hours away yet, and in the meantime, here sat this ornery customer taking up residence in the otherwise empty saloon. It would be some while yet before any of the regulars were due in, so I entirely sympathized that she had his less than welcome company to fend with by herself. Even through the vent, I could tell that when she wasn't having to get up and draw him another beer, she just wanted to be left alone in the amen corner to keep on reading the latest from her and Pop's shared stash of tough-guy books, *Say It with Bullets*.

"Just like I already told you, twenty-five cents, cheap at half the price," she joked, although she sounded a little strained and sulky. "Girlie" surely was nowhere on her list of preferred names, but then Canada Dan was never going to be a candidate for the diplomatic corps.

"Two bits a cackleberry, Jesus H. Christ, what's this world coming to?" The grizzled herder pawed around in the wages he'd spilled out onto the bar, another of his less than endearing habits when he was on a bender like this, evidently trying to decide whether he could afford to eat as well as drink.

"What the hell," he made up his mind, "bring on the hen fruit, one for the gullet 'n' one for luck." I had my back-room chores yet to do—Zoe was at hers at the cafe, before she could join me for another session on the perpetually unfinished B-17—but for whatever reason, I couldn't tear myself away from the duo in the barroom.

What a contrast they made, the unshaven and unsteady gray-headed customer in shabby herding clothes and the feminine young bartender in a sharp white blouse and her raven hair by some bathroom miracle attractively done in ringlets. Appearances aside, France seemed capable of holding her own with the hunched, muttering figure at the end of the bar, gamely bringing the glass crock and serving up a couple of its distasteful contents to him with plate and fork.

With a shaky finger he pushed a bill to her out of his mess of money and ate an egg in about two bites, chasing it with beer, while she went and made change. "There you go. Have a good time," she left him with, and moved off to the other end of the bar to dive into her reading again.

Canada Dan wiped his mouth with his sleeve, staring down at the bar, his second egg untouched. He called out, "When's Tom coming in?"

"He's not. I'm the regular bartender now," France informed him coolly. "Lucky you."

"Huh, yeah." He was staring down at the bar again. "Girlie? Didn't I give you a ten-spot?"

France never even glanced up from the page. "Not unless it had Abe Lincoln on it."

I was dumbfounded. She stubbornly wasn't making a move toward the cash register, where in accordance with Pop's rule the greenback in question should have been set aside as proof against any doubt.

Canada Dan swayed on the bar stool but was firm on the money matter. "I'm sure as anything I had a ten, right here"—he jabbed a finger on the cash on the bar—"and now look, I got this chicken feed back from a five. That ain't right."

Irritably she called to him, "It was a five. If you'd keep your dough in your pocket, where it belongs, you wouldn't get so confused."

The herder argued on, his voice growing louder. "It ain't fair. Treating a man like a turster. Swipe his money right out from under his nose. What's this place coming to?"

"Have another beer and forget it," came her flat reply from down the bar.

"Uh-uh, nothing doing." With that flair a drunk can sometimes have, all at once he was on his feet, staggering but determined. "Going down to the Pastime," he declared with injured dignity. "See if they can treat a man honest there."

"Fine," France said sweetly. "I'll miss you with all my heart."

As he made his unsteady way out without so much as looking at her, alarm grew in me at the prospect this presented. Canada

Dan on a weeklong bender, telling his troubles at the rival saloon, run by that gossip Chick Jennings and now frequented by Earl Zane to boot. As surely as night follows day, they'd spread word around town that Tom Harry's barmaid would swipe money from you right under your nose. And while I wildly hoped not, there was the awful thought that they might be right. But Canada Dan might have been mistaken about a ten-dollar bill, too; I couldn't let the reputation of Pop and the Medicine Lodge depend on that.

Closing the vent decisively, I slipped down the stairs and out the back door and dashed for the house. Pop was in another session with Del in the Gab Lab, straightening out Fort Peck lingo, and I didn't dare burst in on them anyway with something like, "France is being called a thief and maybe she is, if she didn't learn her lesson in juvie." No, instead I rushed up to my bedroom and the dresser-drawer stash of money from my swamping chores. Pop always paid me off in silver dollars and I let them accumulate until there was a model-plane kit or something else I wanted to buy. To my dismay, I didn't have as many as I'd thought, and had to scratch together quarters and dimes and nickels to make the final dollar, panicked that I was losing too much time. Jamming the handful of coins large and small in my pocket, I raced down the alley to head off Canada Dan.

I rounded the corner of the block where the Pastime was situated just as he approached the entrance, muttering angrily to himself.

"Dan! Wait!"

"Uh?" He jerked around as I panted up to him.

"Francine"—I wasn't going to confuse him with her latest name—"sent me. She looked in the cash register again. Said you were right, she shortchanged you, she's real sorry. Here."

"Well, ain't that something." Drunk as a skunk or not, he

closely counted the loose change and four silver dollars I handed him. His sour old face leered down at mine as if we shared some dirty secret.

"Tell her I knowed she was wrong and I'm just glad she caught up with herself," Canada Dan rasped. "It wouldn't do to be cheating good customers."

THIS WASN'T LIKE me, but I didn't even tell Zoe about the incident, let alone Pop. It was just too murky or too open to question, too something. Canada Dan's word against France's? I didn't want to be responsible for bringing that kind of thing to anyone's attention. After all, maybe she had made an honest mistake, or not made one at all. I kept telling myself I'd settled the matter—with my own money, even—and that ought to be that.

The next few days passed without disturbance, and the welcome lull brought the end of the week and a new movie at the Odeon for Zoe and me to capitalize on as usual. By now Charlie Hooper at the ticket window must have thought she was tubercular, but in any case, with a few of her tragic coughs, the crying room was once again ours.

As soon as we were settled in the dark, waiting for the show to start, we prattled about assignations in the Gab Lab and wondered what Del and Francine would do without each other when he left, and otherwise plumbed the mysteries of adult behavior, to call it that. Ourselves, we were joyously splurging, Almond Joy candy bars added to the usual Neccos—thanks to a found dollar I must have missed, back under my socks, in that frantic scramble to ante up to Canada Dan; everything nailed down did seem to have a habit of coming loose lately—and if luxurious entertainment of this sort wouldn't get my mind off life with a startling sister, what would?

The movie was not likely to wear anyone out with thinking, for sure: *G.I. Blues*, starring Elvis Presley, with the rest of a cast that no one had ever heard of, deservedly. Shakespeare and Oscar Wilde had nothing to fear from the plot. Tanks roared across the screen, crushing small trees and blowing things up in the opening scene, but this merely served to establish that Elvis was one of a happy-go-lucky bunch of peacetime American soldiers stationed someplace in sunny West Germany, where there didn't seem to have been a lick of damage done by World War II.

Zoe and I watched in silence except for the sound of Neccos in our mouths as the soldiers made a bet that their leading seducer could not maneuver the town's standoffish nightclub dancer into a one-night stand. Presto, and the seducer was transferred to Alaska and Elvis had to fill in for him, as well as sing every five minutes, and it took no great guessing where this was headed. Elvis, slender in those days and with a flattop haircut so unmilitarily high that from a distance it looked like the eraser on a pencil, had just wiggled through the title song when a rattle of candy wrapper told me Zoe was putting her attention to an Almond Joy. Even through a mouthful of chocolate and almond she could sound more dramatic than anything happening on the screen: "You're real worried, aren't you."

"About what?"

"Francine. France. Whoever she is right now."

"Wouldn't you be if some car snatcher who's been in juvie showed up out of nowhere and said, 'Guess what, I'm your sister'?"

Her imagination refused to give in. "What about this: her and Del fall in love and get married, and they run the saloon, and your dad can quit bartending and go fishing all he wants and take you to ball games and everything. What would be the matter with that?"

"Proxy would have her nose in everything even deeper, that's what."

"Right. I forgot her."

I wished I could. Why did she call me Russ and sonny all the time, with that disturbing smile of hers, as if only the two of us were in on some kind of secret?

By this time Elvis was singing on a stage in a rathskeller, when someone punched a selection on the jukebox and it blared "Blue Suede Shoes" loud enough to drown him out. This somehow led to soldiers starting to slug one another. Seasoned critics of this sort of thing by now, we agreed the fight scene did not stack up well against the one in *The Alamo* cantina; not enough bodies were flying through the air and breaking up furniture. Peace was quickly restored and the story line went back to the bet about a one-night stand.

"How could they ever get married, anyway?" I thought out loud during this break in the action, unwrapping an Almond Joy; it was such great candy, two goodly pieces when you opened it, so that you always felt there was reward ahead. "France and Del, I mean. She calls him College Boy behind his back all the time."

"She'd have to get over that," Zoe deliberated. "Learn to call him honeypie or something instead."

"Oh, sure, can't you just hear her?" I said, munching. "'My little chicken dumpling, please pass the salt.'"

"You never know what they're going to do. Sometimes my mom calls my dad Peterkin."

"Whoa. What does he call her?"

"Nothing."

By now Juliet Prowse was fully in the story, as the nightclub dancer whose routine was mostly twirling in circles when she wasn't doing the splits. She was leggy and toothy, and to our discerning ears didn't sound German or even French.

"What kind of accent do you call that?" one of us wondered.

"Goulash," the other readily volunteered.

Things worked out, as they do in movies. Elvis was pressed into babysitting for a G.I. buddy, the baby began squalling—"Just think, if they had crying rooms in Germany, the movie would have to end right there," I pointed out—and in a panic he called Juliet, who, being a woman, knew to coo over the baby and give it a bottle, and these ministrations somehow took all night, so Elvis won the bet. Sure, after that there was a misunderstanding and a spat, but reconciliation in time for Elvis to sing the last song with Juliet practically turning to butter as she listened. "Uff courze I marry you," she said before he even asked.

Elvis sang a final song to the assembled troops and fräuleins, and then we were back in the dark for real, the Odeon's marquee shutting off behind us as headlights of pickups and cars dwindled and vanished while the two of us headed home, quiet the way we sometimes were when one of us had grown-ups on the mind.

"Don't get all shook up," Zoe said sympathetically in parting.

"Uff courze not," I said, as if I believed it.

FRANCE AND POP were both behind the bar the next morning, Saturday, when I showed up for my swamping duties.

He was breaking in France on this aspect of bartending, too, so she was washing and shining up an army of glasses while he checked the beverage supply, going over things with her as he did so. "Just remember, if a guy says, 'Gimme a ditch,' that's plain bourbon and water, and you use the cheap stuff down here in the well," he stipulated, replenishing the supply of run-of-the-mill bottles beneath the bar. "If he wants to drink fancy, he has to ask for a Lord ditch," he turned and put a hand to the higher-quality Lord Calvert whiskey kept for show in the breakfront. France dabbed in "Fine" and "Got it" at intervals as instruction of that sort went on. They seemed to be becoming more comfortable with each other, despite the generational equator dividing their worlds that made Francine's lips start to twitch whenever he got going on something from the old days of the Depression and the Blue Eagle era that he and her mother had shared, and that drew a gruff "Don't get big ideas" from him if she suggested something like the Medicine Lodge serving edible snack food instead of pickled eggs and pig knuckles. At least in that respect, then, they were father and daughter as if handed scripts in pink covers, with me doing my best to ad-lib between the pair of them. It was a role much on my mind again that quiet morning while they went about their chores behind the bar and I did mine in the rest of the barroom, spittoon and toilet duty first, to get the worst out of the way. I had just grabbed my broom and come back in to start sweeping when I heard Pop exclaim, "When did this show up? Been missing since last Saturday night, hasn't it? I thought you said somebody must have walked off with it."

I snapped my head around, to see him holding up the eagle shot glass.

"Oh, yeah, meant to tell you," France said as if the jigger's reappearance didn't amount to much. "I came across it behind some stuff under the bar." She shrugged. "Don't know how it got away from me."

"That'll happen," Pop said good-naturedly. "Sometimes I'd lose my head if it wasn't tied on, hey, Rusty?"

"Uh, you said it."

"But you need to keep track of something like this," he ser-

moned for France's benefit, twirling the shot glass so that the
blue eagle caught the light. "Don't let it be wandering off and get
lost for good."

"Oh-kay," she said with a slanty smile, "I'll remember that."

I was in a trance as I slowly pushed the broom. Was I jumping
to the conclusion? Or was the conclusion jumping out at me? My
top-drawer dollar had mysteriously disappeared and reappeared
exactly the same way, hadn't it. Put that together with juvie and
Canada Dan's ten-spot, and now I knew I had to tell Zoe.

"YOU GOT SOMETHING on your mind besides your hat, Ace,"
she sensed right away.

"Funny you bring that up, Muscles. I'm in a sort of a fix."

"Bad one?"

"Not yet, but it could get there." If I was learning anything
this adolescent year, it was that pretense can be one hundred
percent serious underneath. "So here's the setup." I stayed in
character in more hardy fashion than I felt. "There's this person,
see, who maybe keeps doing something not too legal but doesn't
get caught at it, and then turns around and undoes it on account
of guilty conscience or something, if you get what I mean. Pretty
risky way to behave, you think?"

Zoe gasped. "Doesn't France have any more smarts than
that? She's not back to taking cars, is she?"

"No, that's the weird part, it's dumb little things." I ticked off
my missing dollar that came back and the shot glass story, getting around to what had happened with Canada Dan. Zoe listened as only she could, her dark eyes never leaving mine, her
generous mouth pursed in contemplation.

The instant I was done, she said, "And you're in a fix about
whether to tell your dad or not."

"You got it."

The tip of her tongue indicated deep thinking about my dilemma while I waited in agony. "Maybe," she said at last, "maybe she's a kleptomaniac."

"Wh-what kind of maniac is that?"

"It means somebody who steals, they can't help it. It's in their blood or something," she said knowledgeably. "There was a rich lady in Butte, when she went in Hennessy's department store, a clerk would follow her around and write down what she tucked in her dress. At the end of the month they'd send her a bill."

"That wouldn't work on France," I despaired. "Zoe, what am I gonna do? What if she gets to be more and more of a stealing maniac? Takes a car"—the Buick; the Packard, even; once I started imagining, there seemed no limit to where her acquisitive habit might lead, this was no mere matter of the angels' share—"or all the money she can lay her hands on, or something?" I concluded helplessly, "But if I squeal on her to Pop, that's that for her bartending."

"Del."

Zoe left it at that until I gasped, "You think he's one, too?"

"That's not what I meant," she said impatiently. "Del must know her pretty well by now, don't you think?"

"Sure. Right down to the skin."

"So maybe he could"—she spun her hands that way he did when trying to come up with the right phrase—"sort of give her the word. Tell her somehow that she's got to quit taking things that don't belong to her. Some nice roundabout way, he's good at that. He's about to leave anyway, isn't he?"

"Any day now, he says, as soon as he hears from the powers that be."

"There you go, then. Piece of cake, Ace."

"Yeah, well, maybe." I drew a deep, deep breath of resolve. "Let's go ask him."

"AH. THE FEARSOME twosome."

Del was not doing a bit, though, when he admitted us into the van and sank back into his Gab Lab seat, only acknowledging us in a distracted way. He had a peculiar glazed expression while he kept gazing around the Gab Lab as if enumerating every item in it. I fidgeted, waiting for him to show attention in our direction, but there was no sign of it. Zoe urged me on with a little snap of her fingers that he didn't hear.

I mustered, "Del, I was sort of wondering if you could help me out—us out, I mean—by . . . what's wrong?"

He sat up so abruptly it made me step back. "Where's your father?"

"In the back room. Paying bills. Why?"

"I just found out something he had better know." He shot to his feet, still wearing that queer look as he ducked out the van door. "Come on. You may as well hear this."

Zoe and I looked at each other, agape with the sense of deliverance. From the way Del was behaving, France must have walked off with something of his, and now he knew the situation without my having to spell it out to the end of the alphabet. Hurriedly, we trailed him as he marched down the driveway and across the alley to the Medicine Lodge. He stepped into the back room like a man on a mission. Pop looked down from the landing, cocking an eyebrow at the sight of our contingent.

"Hey, Delano." His greeting carried a note of surprise. "Stuck on something a mudjack said?"

"Can you have France come in here? It's important."

"What for?"

"It's important."

"I grasp that it is," said Pop, studying him from A to why. "Hold on, if there's nobody at the bar, I'll have her lock up for a few minutes."

While he went and attended to that, Del walked in a tight circle, hands thrust in his pockets and shoulders hunched so high he looked like a scarecrow, still wearing that strange expression he'd had in the confines of the van. Watching him, Zoe picked at her elbow nervously and I kept swallowing with a dry throat. Was he going to charge France with something so awful, it would get her thrown into the adult version of juvie? That was more than I bargained for, but it was out of my hands now.

Pop arrived back, took one look at the circling figure, and simply folded his arms and waited.

France came buzzing through the door from the front, towel still in hand like a true bartender. "What was it you wanted, T—"

She jammed to a halt at the sight of us all. Natalie Wood stopped by a cop for something. Apprehensively she asked, "Somebody call a prayer meeting?"

Pop inclined his head to the determined keeper of the Gab Lab. "So, Delano, what's eating you?"

As though an electrical current was running between us, Zoe and I shared that held-breath feeling of drama, the theatrical high point when Rosalind reveals her identity to Orlando, when Lady Bracknell bestows her lofty blessing on Algernon and Cecily and Jack and Gwendolen, when the confusions of love are solved and all's well that ends well. Only in this case, one lover was about to lower the boom on the other.

Del shifted restlessly, looked around at us all, and blurted it out.

"I'm not leaving."

The big room was silent as this registered on us in individual ways. I nearly swallowed my Adam's apple for good.

"Isn't that phenomenal?" Del was grinning as much as his face could hold. "The powers that be were so impressed with the mudjacks tapes and transcripts, they want me to stay and keep right on with the Missing Voices, here. Do another series of interviews before a subgroup vanishes from history." He beamed at each of us in turn, last and longest at France. "They, ah, gave me another grant." He looked almost bashful. "Alan Lomax usually gets them all."

There went that, I savvied before he was even finished speaking. Not a chance in the world that a diagnosis of kleptomania would be forthcoming from him if the midnight meetings in the van were going to go merrily on. According to the way he was gazing at her, France could be stealing the fillings out of his teeth and he wouldn't notice. Beside me, Zoe was thinking the same, I could tell. We had to be happy for Del, fellow bit player that he was, and glad he wasn't going away yet, but we knew there was no approaching him about France and her problematic habit, now. We weren't up to the role of heartbreakers yet.

"Well, swell, Dellie." France sounded relieved and enthusiastic all in the same breath. She gave him the nicest kind of smile. "We'd miss you around here."

"Yeah, we wouldn't want things to get dull," Pop seconded that. He squinted companionably at his partner in mudjack lingo. "So, Delano, who's got their voices missing now?"

"Sheepherders."

Roomful of silence again.

No one wanted to be the first to say it. Finally, twisting her towel as if wringing out the words, France ventured, "You dead sure about that, Dellie?"

Pop was looking nearly as stunned as if he had been hit by a flying elbow. "She's right, where the hell do you get the idea sheepherders are vanishing? Cripes, most of the time you can hardly turn around in the Two Medicine country without bumping into one. Delano, are you sure you don't have any tick fever?"

"Trust me on this." Del held up his hands as if heading all of us off. "I did some research, before I came out here from the Library. You have to understand, the sheep business is in what economists call a gravitational decline, which means steep. Sheepmen are simply up against too much." He fingered his elaborate shirt, not a stitch of wool in it, as evidence. "Synthetics, cheaper imported lamb, new grazing regulations, higher costs of everything—the usual kinds of horsemen of the apocalypse that do in old family businesses." He paused somberly. "It's sad, of course, but it can't be helped. And when sheep ranchers go, it's perfectly plain what that will mean for herders."

"The marble farm," Zoe said in a ghostly voice.

"Well, no, they're not exactly going to die off like dinosaurs," Del belatedly sought to temper that. "But their numbers are bound to decline, and now's the best chance to record their lives for the archive." He paused again, as if a thought had only now struck him, or at least gave a good imitation of it. "Ah, Tom, I wonder if I might ask you for a favor."

"While that's going on," France saw her chance, "hadn't I better get back to tending bar?"

"What? Yeah. Do that." Pop and the other two of us tried not to be too obvious about looking on while she and Del did not quite blow kisses to one another, but the hint was there. As soon as she was gone, Del turned to Pop, bright as a button. "What I was wondering . . ."

"Delano, I know all about your wondering and the answer is no. I cannot trot around hunting up sheepherders with you, I have a fishing derby to get everything ready for and a joint with a green bartender to oversee and every other damn thing that takes up time in life. Got that?"

Even if his words had not registered on Del, Pop's danger-ously wrinkled brow would have. "I just thought I'd ask," he murmured, burying his hands in his pockets again.

"Besides"—Pop started to reach for his cigarettes until he saw me looking—"herders aren't anywhere you can get to them right now, anyway."

Del went stone still. He turned his head to one side as if to make sure he'd heard what he'd heard. "They're not? Where did they go?"

"Where they always do this time of year," Pop said impatiently, "when they're not in here drinking their wages away. Way to hell and gone up in the mountains, herding on the national forest."

Zoe was nodding, even she knew that. Evidently the self-trained expert on the subgroup called sheepherders did not.

"But . . . but," Del spluttered, "when do they come back down?"

"Shipping time," said Pop. "That's, oh, three or four weeks yet. You can take life easy for a while."

"No, I can't! My grant calls for an immediate start," the ins and outs of oral history practically poured forth in a babble, "the powers that be think I already have interviews lined up and waiting. I had to, ah, stretch matters a trifle in the proposal."

"You got to be kind of careful in proposing," Pop advised. But he didn't like to see Del in distress any more than we did. Squint-ing in thought, one eye in particular toward half closed, he mut-tered: "Of course, there's always that ess of a bee Canada Dan."

Del brightened as if a switch had been thrown. "Perfect! I never did get to ask him what a *turster* is!"

"Dode has him herding some kind of bunch up the South Fork," Pop was saying to me. "Seen the wagon on the way to fishing, remember?" Before I could even bob my head, Del was asking eagerly, "Do you think he'd consent to be interviewed?"

"I wouldn't predict what he'll do from one breath to the next"—Pop seemed bemused at the thought of Canada Dan fending with Del and vice versa—"but you can try him." Then his conscience must have kicked in. "Better take Rusty along, he knows Dan. That might help."

Del was back to buoyant just that fast. Gravely he bowed in our direction. "I don't suppose you'd be interested in coming along, Miss Zoe, parental authorities permitting?"

"Pleeeaase?"

"Don't worry, Tom. I'll keep an eye on them."

"I was more thinking about them keeping an eye on you."

I WAS NOT any too enthused about being assigned to this. To me, Canada Dan represented several kinds of a headache, from that wayward elbow that floored Pop, up to and including the dispute with France that had cost me five dollars. As far as I was concerned, he could fester in obscurity forever and it would serve him right.

Pop did have a point, though. It would be just like the old cuss to give Del a hard time or even run him off, simply because he could. With me on hand representing Pop and the Medicine Lodge, sort of, his manners might—*might*—improve. Riding in the passenger seat to be navigator, I was silent with such thoughts—at least it was a brief respite from having a kleptomaniac half sister on my mind—as Del drove us toward the sheep camp that afternoon, a rare sunny one. Dode Withrow's pasture was nice green bottomland where the South Fork of English Creek ran down a long coulee. With the mountain cliffs stretching up and away everywhere ahead of us and the Rainbow Reservoir dam at the far end of the creek, like the front step to their succession of heights, our journey from town was actually quite a scenic excursion. Zoe occupied the back of the van, perched behind the seat as I had been on the Fort Peck trip, she and Del talking away.

Gandering through the windshield at the wall rocks and crags of the national forest that rose and rose all the way to the Continental Divide, he exclaimed, "What luck that he's not herding somewhere up there. I wonder why not?"

"Maybe he gets nosebleeds in high places," Zoe theorized.

Del chuckled that away as he turned off the county road onto the rutted set of tracks where I was pointing. A not very large flock of sheep grazed picturesquely at the bottom of the steep coulee. "Likely he's been given this spot down here because it's less rugged terrain for a man of his age, wouldn't you think, Rusty?"

"He's afraid of the timber."

"Hmm? Run that by again?"

"Canada Dan is scared to death of herding in the timber, where he can't see all his sheep every minute and he's no good at it. The ranchers know it and they don't put him any closer to the mountains than this." I did not add that Canada Dan only got herding jobs at all because he was living and breathing and handily available when he wasn't drunk.

By now the van was jolting down the track to the creek, where the white-canvased sheep wagon sat next to the willows. "I see," Del said in a less sure voice as a stumpy figure came peering out the Dutch door of the wagon at our approach.

When the van bumped to a stop in the small creek-side clearing, Zoe and I scrambled out while Del composed himself in more professional fashion, smoothing his various pocket flaps and so on. We were met by a mottled white-and-gray sheepdog, growling as it came.

"Quit, Moses," Canada Dan called off the dog but not his distrustful eyeing of us. "What's this, a Sunday-school picnic?"

"Whoo," murmured Zoe, getting her first good look at the herder. People still had goiters then, and Canada Dan had a dandy, as if he had swallowed a lemon. Long underwear yellowed with age showed at the neck of his shirt. The cud of tobacco that had given me so much spittoon work showed in his cheek. The hard effects of time and weather and drink showed on the rest of his face and personage. Not exactly a picture of hospitality standing planted there in the wagon doorway, but Del forged ahead.

"Mr. . . . ah, Dan? I wonder if I could have a little of your time."

"There's plenty of it out here in the sticks, that's for sure." He gave me a grudging nod out of respect for Pop and included Zoe because she seemed to be with me, but Del received something between a frown and a scowl. "What's on your mind, when you're not in the way of my sheep?"

Del forced a chuckle about that incident and explained about his interviewing mission.

"That a fact?" Canada Dan stepped down out of the wagon as though he had to inspect him for common sense. "You come all the way out from town to talk to a mutton conductor?" Spitting an amount of tobacco juice that did not seem to diminish the cud in his cheek, he shuffled over to us and gestured to the nearby grazing ewes and lambs, as if we were welcome to them. "Got the goddamn mutton on the hoof for you, that's for sure."

"Rusty," Zoe was whispering, "what's wrong with those sheep?"

Before I could tell her, Del had caught up with the bedraggled nature of the creatures in Canada Dan's care. "What kind of a, mmm, flock do you call this?"

The herder laughed harshly. "What's it look like? It's the hospital bunch, next thing to pelters. Some has got maggots. Others got blue bag, can't nurse their lambs. Some is just old and broken down, like me."

"I see. Well, that doesn't really matter, I suppose." A false supposition, if Zoe and I had ever heard one. Plain as anything, these sheep were down on their luck, and anyone assigned to herd them was even deeper in misfortune. Dode Withrow may have been ready to wring Canada Dan's neck for that loss of lambs in the spring blizzard, but he had since given him what amounted to a charity job. Tending these cripples and invalids barely qualified as sheepherding. Nonetheless, Del held out an inviting hand toward the open van and its recording equipment waiting at the ready. "Let's just step in and I'll get the tape going and—"

"Nothing doing." The one-man subgroup of Missing Voices backed away from the van. "Come on in the wagon, where we can gab comfortable-like."

Momentarily thrown, Del was quick to improvise. "I'll be right there, just let me grab a portable recorder." It hardly rated that description, Del digging out a hefty machine with a handle on it like a suitcase. While he was hurriedly threading tape reels, Zoe scrambled to find him a spare microphone, and I commiserated in a low voice, "Pop always says if there are any more ways Canada Dan can be a pain in the wazoo, they have yet to be invented."

"No, no, it's all right. I'll get this done," he said with determination. "I need to send in something in a hurry so my grant doesn't get pulled. Alan Lomax is always around to scoop up loose funding."

Anticipatory audience of two, Zoe and I followed as he swung the recorder and then himself into the sheep wagon. The design of a sheep wagon is on a narrower wagon bed than, say, the prairie schooner we all know from history books, and the canvas roof is more snug and igloo-like, compressing the inside into something remarkably on the order of a grown-up dollhouse: small stove, miniature cabinets, a bunk where one person will just fit. A really dirty dollhouse, in the case of Canada Dan's abode. The grimy cooking utensils on the blackened stove showed he had the cooking philosophy that a washed pot never boils. I recoiled at how tight the quarters were, and sensed Zoe doing the same, but Del seemed right at home. Setting up the tape recorder and microphone on the little gateleg table where Canada Dan had slid in on one side, he took the other, and practically knee to knee, he beamed across at his interview subject. "Ready for some conversation, are you?"

"I guess I got nothing better to do," the herder muttered unpromisingly. Since Zoe and I would practically be on top of the pair of them no matter where we tried to sit, I took the initiative in saying we'd wait outside, if that was all right. "Suit yourself," our host grunted. "Moses is shaded up under the wagon. He might growl at you now and again, but he don't mean it."

Shading up sounded right to us, and we scooted under the wagon box, where we could lounge against some sacks of sheep salt and cottonseed cake in something like comfort. The dog kept watch on us with those pale border collie eyes, but made no sound. Zoe reached to pet him. "Huh-uh," I warned in a whisper. "Sheepherders don't like to have their dogs spoiled by petting."

"Poor pooch," she whispered solemnly.

"Shall we get started?" Del's voice reached us. We grinned at each other. We could hear everything, right overhead. This was as good as the vent at the saloon. "Your full name is . . . ?"

"Daniel Korzenowski."

"Age, please, Mr. Korzenowski?"

"Too goddamn much of it, that's for sure."

Del chuckled a little, waiting, but that seemed to be the full answer. "I'm only asking for archival purposes, you understand. So, the year of your birth?"

"Back there a ways, let's just say."

"Mr. Korzenowski—Dan. Surely you don't want me to have to guess the year you were born."

"Don't matter to me."

"Very well, then. Eighteen hundred and ninety-"

"Eighteen hundred nothing! Nineteen hundred even, damn it."

"That makes you sixty, am I right? As old as the century."

"Both of us are showing it, too."

"And born where in Canada?"

"Who said I was hatched up there? I'm pure hunnerd percent American. Born right up here this side of the border, on the Milk River. My folks was homesteading, or thought they was. I don't know where you got that Canada notion."

"Hear that?" Zoe was whispering in wonderment. "He doesn't know he's called Canada Dan?"

"He knows. He just doesn't want to."

"Sorry about that, I must have misheard something," Del scrambled to recover. "What can you tell me about life on the homestead? It must have been rugged in those days."

"Rugged! That don't begin to say it." This set the raspy voice going without stop. The family was skunk broke most of the time, to hear him tell it. If grasshoppers didn't get the crops, hail did. The nearest neighbors were a mile away and the nearest town was thirty, so if a person was sick or hurt in an accident, you might as well say your prayers. Zoe and I listened hard as he came to the part about riding horseback to a one-room school. "My schooling stopped in the third grade. Had to help out at home, it didn't matter none that I was just a kid." That gave me a twinge of sympathy for him, although a person can be deprived and still be naturally ornery. Del let him talk on, occasionally nudging or coaxing with a quick question, until steering him toward the sheepherding life.

"It ain't for everybody," the coarse voice started in slowly. "You see this sheep wagon—not exactly the Waldorf, is it. Out like this, you have to live with muskeeters and mice and skunks and pack rats and all those. Hell, I been in places where I couldn't leave my bridgework out at night."

Beyond that, though, the interview turned rocky. Del would try to keep things on a historical track, and his veteran of sheepherding would wander off to some topic like the weather. I had listened in at Fort Peck enough to know that, thanks to Del's lines of questioning, the mudjacks' stories had a beginning, middle, and an end. Canada Dan's started anywhere and went no particular direction. Del's patient tries at getting him to describe the herding life down through the years produced mainly prolonged gripes about gut-robbing ranchers and tardy camp tenders. "You wouldn't believe what a man has to put up with."

At last Del managed to slip in: "The Two Medicine country is known for its fine summer grazing in the mountains. What can you tell me about that kind of herding?"

This may sound strange, but Canada Dan could be heard not saying anything for some moments.

Zoe and I looked at each other. Was this it? Was he going to kill off the interview and throw Del out of the wagon?

Then we heard him say tightly, "Them mountains. It's rough up there. Coyotes. Bear. Poison lupine. If it ain't one thing to raise hell with your sheep, it's a goddamn 'nother. I'm more of a flatlander myself, in my herding. Makes better sense. Now, if them ranchers had any brains worth mentioning—"

"You were right," Zoe mouthed silently to me. "Afraid of the timber."

Del gamely kept on with questions for a while, but there is a limit to how many sheepherder gripes you can listen to in one stretch, and we were growing bored by the time we heard him wrapping up the interview. We were out from under the wagon as he exited it, the herder right behind him, and I was more than ready to depart the company of Daniel Korzenowski and go back to town. To my surprise, Zoe piped up, "Can I ask Mr. Dan something?"

Del was looking worn but, trouper that he was, he said of course she could, "But let's get it for posterity." He knelt and had the recorder going almost instantly. "This next voice is Zoe Constantine," he intoned into the mike, "at the advanced age of twelve, trying out a career as a seeker of Missing Voices. Go ahead, Zoe."

He passed her the mike and she took it in both hands and asked Canada Dan, innocent as anything: "Have you been around pack rats much?"

I could have kissed her. Why hadn't I thought to ask this myself?

"Only about as many as there is Chinamen in China," Canada Dan said gruffly into the microphone she was aiming practically down his gullet. "Why're you asking, girlie?"

"I was only wondering. When a pack rat takes a thing . . . does it ever bring it back?"

"Funny question, ain't it." The herder rubbed his whiskery jaw. "But I've known it to happen. Something shinier catches its eye and maybe it'll leave the first thing out where you can find it."

Now we knew, did we? Francine was maybe a pack rat kind of kleptomaniac. Surely a less serious sort, right? Not the kind that I should get up my nerve and tell Pop about?

Zoe thanked Canada Dan sweetly, and Del shut off the tape recorder, and that should have been that. Except Canada Dan turned to me with a crude grin.

"How's the piano girl doing in the bar? Learning any new tunes?"

I didn't have time to think, only react. "She's doing fine," I answered nervously. "Pop is awful glad to have her helping out, you know how hard it is to find good help."

"Yeah, it's a bugger"—he gave me more of that nasty grin—"getting somebody who knows what they're doing behind a bar."

Del had only half caught our exchange, broodily heading toward the van. All at once he stopped and turned back.

"Ah, Dan, before we leave, I'd like to try something, if I may. Could you walk through the sheep with me? I'd like to pick up some ambient sound to add to the interview, if you wouldn't mind."

"You want to take a constitutional through a hospital bunch of sheep?" Canada Dan cackled. "I thought I'd heard of everything." Capitalizing on what would plainly be a good tale to tell during the next drinking spree, he swept an arm toward the grazing ewes and lambs, those healthy enough to be on their feet. "Sashay on in, the mutton population is ready and waiting."

"I need something from the van, I'll be right back."

Giving each other the look that says, Now what, Zoe and I tagged close after Del as he vaulted into the Gab Lab and grabbed his headphones from the desk equipment. "What do you want those for? What's 'ambient' mean?" we demanded in whispers.

"That interview needs all the help it can get," he said grimly. "I'm going to try for a sound portrait. I'll explain later." He plugged the headphones into the portable recorder and clapped them over his ears. "Wish me luck, *amigos*."

Drawing on whatever limited wisdom he possessed, Canada Dan had been doing some thinking. "Sheep don't take real good to being disturbed. You kind of got to pussyfoot through 'em, and even so, they spook easy." You just never know when things will mysteriously chime. Del was being instructed in how to bobbasheely, sheepherder-style. The squinched-up keeper of sheep next took charge of Zoe and me before we knew what was happening. "You shavetails stand there and there; don't let the buggers get in the brush. Stay, Moses." He pointed the disappointed dog to the wagon. In the same rough tone, he told Del, "C'mon, if you're still of a mind to do this."

The hospital herder set off into the flock at the slowest of gaits, Del right behind him, hefty recorder in one hand and the microphone deployed in the other. Stationed where we were, motionless as sentinels, the coulee began to speak to us, Zoe and I listening for all we were worth. Grasshoppers whirring in flight over the meadow. Creek water rattling musically past. A magpie yattering in the willow thicket. With the headphones alerting him to every slightest sound and using the microphone like a baton, Del was gathering it all out of the air. A few of the sheep blatted restlessly at the moving men, and now a bell tinkled as a dark-fleeced wether hobbled toward them.

"There's Coalie," Canada Dan said, as if introducing the animal. "He's a lead sheep, or anyway was, until he ruptured hisself. I told Dode any number of times we ought to turn him into coyote bait. Here, you old bum." He dug in his pocket and fed the sheep some pellets of cottonseed cake. "Old good for nothing," the herder said gruffly, "about like me," and moved on.

Del kept quiet except for an occasional brief question as Canada Dan eased through his band of casualties. "This ewe, now, she got snagged on a down tree. See that rip in her side? I turpentined it up good, keeps the flies out. She'll come around." He pointed to another with blue stains at the bottom of her legs where dip had been applied. "Hoof rot. Awful, ain't it. There's just no end of things can go wrong with sheep. Keeps a man hopping to tend to 'em, the poor critters." Like a doctor on his rounds, the herder led Del through the woolly forms, the mike all the while picking up the ambience of the sheep camp around the rough old voice like no other. You can tell when something remarkable is happening. Zoe had the same spellbound expression I did. This wasn't the Forest of Arden, Canada Dan definitely was not the smitten shepherd Silvius, but there was a recognizable touch of dramatic magic in the portrait in sound Del was orchestrating.

UPON OUR TRIUMPHANT departure, the van was not even out of the coulee before Zoe was leaning in from the back seat, bursting with the question, "So why is he called Canada Dan? How come he's not Milk River Dan or Polack Dan or something?"

Del had been grinning his head off ever since he shucked the tape out of the portable recorder and hopped in behind the steering wheel. Now he sobered up enough to lift a hand toward me and invite: "Any theory, Sherlock?"

"Uh-huh," I had been working on this, "I bet it still has to do with him being spooked about the mountains. I can about hear Dode Withrow say something like, 'He'll push the sheep out in the open all the way to sonofabitching Canada instead of putting them in the timber.' You can ask Pop to be sure."

"Ooh." Zoe wrinkled her nose at the thought of being tagged that way all through life.

"That would make sense." Del thought it out as if a grant depended on it. "A behavioral nickname rather than an associative one. I'll have to note that in the interview transcription."

"Why, what's the difference?"

"Well, one is the sort of nickname that comes from some physical characteristic people associate with a person, such as—"

"Short-Handed Curly," I furnished.

"*Exactamente*," he trilled in whatever language that was. "Behavioral ones, though"—he went back to seriously thinking out loud as the van reached the county road and trundled toward town—"come more from something a person picks up a reputation for doing. Wrong Way Corrigan getting himself turned around on his transatlantic flight. Mittens Mitchell, the shortstop who couldn't field grounders. That sort of thing." Del winced a little. "Canada Dan. Poor old bugger," he did a decent imitation of that barbwire voice. As if reminded, he sent me a puzzled look. "Did I hear right, back there? He called France 'the piano girl'?"

"Oh, yeah, sure, you know how she is, with those long fingers. We heard him tell her she ought to be playing the piano on stage somewhere, didn't we, Zoe."

"You bet," she made up as fast as I had, "a concert pianoist."

"Pianist," said Del, still in a puzzled tone.

"That's it. Just what he said."

"Hmm. Imagine him coming up with that. He's full of surprises." Del checked over his shoulder with another questioning look. "So, Miss Zoe? Is there a pack rat in the storeroom of the Spot?"

"Oh, no, no, no. Farther away than that. In Butte."

———

ALONG WITH MY SOUP and crackers, I was digesting Canada Dan's knowledge of takers of things when Pop showed up in the kitchen the next morning, uncommonly early for him these days.

"Recuperated from the excitement of sheep camp yet?" he asked as he poured some evaporated milk into the pan to stretch the breakfast soup for himself.

"Getting there, I guess."

"Glad that worked out. I kind of wondered, looking at you and Zoe when you got back, but Delano seemed as happy as if he had good sense." The Romeo of the VW van doubtless had spent an even happier night, according to how late France had come in, but I kept my mouth shut about that.

Pop himself was looking pleased about something. Before even firing up the coffeepot, he announced, "The weather's better," which meant it was not raining pitchforks that very minute. "What do you say we go up to the rezavoy? I ought to look things over before the derby." He was in such a good mood, I could tell what was coming next. "We'll grab our fishpoles, just in case we feel the urge to catch rainbows while we're there, hey?"

If fishing would gladden his heart, even temporarily, it was up to me to try to muster the urge, and I took over fixing the thermos of coffee while he rustled up a bait can of choice chicken guts out of the freezing compartment of the refrigerator. Taking care to be quiet while leaving the house and crossing the yard— France and Del still were in bed, innocently separate beds at this time of day—we skirted around to where the cars were parked under Igdrasil's leafy care. To my surprise, Pop opened the trunk of the Packard instead of the Buick to deposit our fishing gear.

"We'll give the old buggy some exercise," he answered my questioning look, "get it ready for the big day. Climb in." A little leery of the vehicle, I did so, as happened usually only once a year, Derby Day itself. Big and boxy as the Packard was, you might expect it to be as gloomy inside as a hearse, but it wasn't, really, with the luxurious seats almost like sofas and the instruments on the dashboard set in fancy chrome and a good, hardy smell to it all, like that of the Medicine Lodge's back room, of old leather and hat sweatbands and other traces of men at work, no doubt lingering from Pop's last loot trip to Canada. Installed behind the fine-grained wooden steering wheel as the straight-eight cylinders purred us out of town, he looked so contented that I was determined not to get carried away with the car's history, especially that event in the back seat involving him and Proxy and subsequently Francine, as she came to be. However, I may have been noticeably untalkative on the way up the creek valley to the reservoir, as he glanced over across the spacious front seat every so often and remarked on the hay crop or Canada Dan's sheep camp as we passed it or other this and that. I responded as best I could, although it is hard to get something off your mind—the consequential back seat was right there behind me like a historical exhibit—when it doesn't want to leave.

The reservoir was discharging water plentifully when we arrived, the spillway frothing in a way Pop remarked he hadn't seen it do in years. Even so, there seemed to be a lot more lake than usual, the blue surface reflecting the sky like a closely held mirror.

"It's kind of high for fishing," I invoked the only angler lore I possessed as Pop busied himself with our gear, "isn't it?" For starters, the boulders where we usually stood to cast our lines were underwater.

"Bill Reinking has been hearing that from folks, too," he acknowledged, with a mild frown at the level of the lake. "We've decided to say a hell of a lot of water means a hell of a lot of fish. It stands to reason, right?"

This dictated fishing from the bank, a challenge to my already questionable casting ability, and I immediately began to worry about making a fool of myself on Derby Day if I couldn't get my hook and line out farther than, say, those rocks we ordinarily stood on. That weenie Duane Zane would be right there, sneering and making mocking remarks, I could count on that. Determinedly I postponed this particular fret, not wanting to spoil Pop's outing today. "That's nature for you," he was shrugging off the extra feet of water for trout to hide under, "you got to play the hand it deals you."

For once we were not out in the first blinks of dawn, but otherwise this fishing trip was almost like a memory coming to life, the morning brilliantly blue over us, the mountain cliffs so near and high, the timbered canyon bending away out of sight behind Roman Reef at the far end of the lake, and in the other direction, the olive-green stands of willow and greener cottonwoods marking the course of the South Fork and eventually English Creek, all the way to town, distantly visible beyond the dirt face of the dam. Much else seemed so close to the same as it was our first time here, six years before. Pop appreciatively taking in the scenery while he had a cigarette and drank coffee from the thermos and fitted together our fishing poles—it was a ritual I'd known by heart ever since. Yet while it was the same two of us here, the picture had changed with us, from then to now. The difference was that I had grown taller while he had only grown older, time's unfair trick on a father and for that matter, a mother.

"Got the chicken guts ready, kiddo?" His question snapped me out of such thoughts, and I began cutting up gooey strips of the guaranteed surefire bait, a nasty task that had not changed at all over the years. Meanwhile, committee chairman to the hilt, he was surveying the setting for the derby, figuring out loud where portable picnic tables and extra trash cans ought to go— the Mudjacks Reunion was turning out to be a valuable rehearsal— and shrewdly settling on a strategy against the Rotarians and their despised beer booth. "Gonna let the esses of bees do it, same like always," he confided to me, "I don't want any ruckus over that. But I'm having Zoe's folks set up a food booth, and nobody can kick if they just happen to sell soft drinks along with the grub, right?" He chuckled in satisfaction. "Lots of wives will steer hubbies right past that Rotary beer, you can bet your bottom dollar."

"Swuft, Pop," I had to hand it to him. Now, were it not for the fishing part of the fishing derby, I could look forward to the occasion with something approaching anticipation. Slim hope of that, though. In all the years I still had not caught anything that rated more than honorable mention in the posted results, and anyone with a pole got that. Sighing to myself over the stubbornness of fate, I picked up the bait can and my rod and reel and trailed Pop along the causeway of the dam, to where he declared the rainbow trout were surely awaiting us hungrily.

The footing was not any too good without the boulders to stand on and with the soil of the dam soaked from all the rain, causing him to crease his brow and think out loud that the derby crowd had better be confined to the shore bank, so that he and the committee wouldn't spend the whole damn day pulling people out of the lake. I agreed that sounded like further shrewd chairmanship. Satisfied, he tested his reel and his wrist, addressing the hidden population of the reservoir. "Watch out, rainbows, here we come."

I stood back and let him cast first, so I could watch the knack, as he called it. It had something to do with the flip of the wrist, which whenever I tried it merely sent my baited hook whirring out in a feeble arc instead of sailing a good distance into the water. Practice was supposed to make perfect? It hadn't even made me passable in casting, as yet.

Be that as it may, I was about to give it the usual try when I recalled Del's introduction to Rainbow Reservoir those weeks ago. Surf casting, he'd called his strenuous let-it-fly overhand style. I thought about that for a minute. Where was it in any rules of fishing that you needed to have an ocean of surf instead of a lapping lake in order to cast like that? Sneaking a quick look at Pop, obliviously busy with his own fishing, I decided to hell with flip of the wrist. I planted my feet, gripped my pole with both hands like a baseball bat, and with a mighty grunt gave a two-fisted heave that sent my hook and line sailing way, way out into the reservoir.

"Hey, not bad," Pop called over when he saw the ring on the water where my line had gone in. "You're getting the knack."

I would have settled for that cast for the whole day, content to let the morsel of chicken gut sit on the bottom of the lake or wherever it had ended up. But something that felt like it wanted to start a tug-of-war had other ideas.

"I've got a bite!" I hollered, although I had much more than that, my pole curving as the fish nearly pulled me in the water. I dug my feet in as best I could on the slippery dam bank and gripped the pole for dear life while trying not to lose my head. Supposedly the greatest allure of fishing is the thrill of the fish putting up a fight. I say it's tricky work, attempting to levitate an extremely reluctant living object out of the water on the end of a thin line and a long stick.

"Hang on to him!" Pop grew excited now, putting aside his pole to scramble over and coach me. "Don't horse him, just keep your line tight and reel in slow and walk him out, that's the way."

It took what seemed an unearthly amount of time, with the stubborn fish thrashing and twisting and turning but gradually drawing closer to shore. We were of the drag-'em-out school, not bothering with fanciness like a net, so in the end I tottered backward up the bank, towing the glistening trout out onto solid ground, and Pop pounced on it before it could flop back in the water.

It was a beauty, royally speckled with the colors of the rainbow that gave the species its name. And it was king-size, a foot and a half long if it was an inch. Pop looked even more proud of it, and me, than I was myself. The two of us stood gazing down at my whopper of a catch, thinking the exact same thing. He was the one who spoke it.

"Too bad you couldn't have saved that for the derby."

This was my chance. Now if ever.

"I was going to bring that up. The derby coming and all."

"Yeah? So?"

"I think I better not fish this year, don't you? I mean, it wouldn't look good if I won and I'm your son, see what I mean? What if there's another rainbow like this one, its mate or something, and I caught it, too, now that I know how?"

The unlikelihood of another leviathan trout yielding itself up to me aside, the rest was pretty much unarguable. He started to say something, but I sneaked in ahead, "Then everybody would want to know what my bait was, and they'd find out about chicken guts."

The hint of amusement in his eyes telling me he knew what I was up to, he finally gave a resigned shrug. "Okay, you win. This year you can be assistant to the Derby Day committee chairman, how's that grab you?"

Right where I most wanted to be grabbed, heart and soul.

"That's that, then," he said, giving me and my prize catch

another glinting look. "I better get to catching fish if I'm not going to be disgraced by my own kid."

While he went back to baiting up and casting, I was excused to clean my champion trout, conscientiously tossing its guts into the gushing spillway so as not to litter the bank, and covering it with moss out of the lake to keep it cool in our creel. Rather than stretch my luck and fish some more, I found a relatively dry spot to sit and watch Pop at it.

How peaceful everything seemed, and how fleeting. Fishing is supposed to clear the head and put a person at one with nature and all that. I can't really say I felt any divine inspiration, but this excursion did give me a pocket of time alone with my father, without other people complicating the scene. It came to me more as a whisper of suggestion than the fundamental adage that it is—if this is not biblical, I shall always believe it should be— that all of us need someone who loves us enough to forgive us despite the history. Watching the figure who fathered me, now with gray at his temples and a certain stiffness in his casting arm, I no longer cared about his quirks and questionable habits, about whatever happened in the Packard and the Blue Eagle and any other of his circumstances out of range of my knowing. I had to hope that he could forgive in turn my tardiness in what I was about to do.

"Pop?" I raised my voice just above the lapping of the water. "Can I tell you something, just between you and me and Pat and Mike and Mustard?"

"I guess so, if it won't cause blisters and blindness." Still smiling over my catch, he glanced around at me. "What's on your mind now, kiddo?"

I drew the biggest breath I could, and let out the words along with it.

"You maybe ought to watch her a little closer. France, I mean."

"What for?" He remained mainly interested in casting his line out far enough to impress the fish. "Seems to me she's doing okay on her own behind the bar. But if you've heard her messing up on drinks, I suppose I better give her a refresher on—"

"It's not that."

"So? What is it then?"

"She's maybe a pack rat."

"Say that again?"

"See, she has a, uh, kind of a jail record from taking something that didn't belong to her," I rushed on, "she told Zoe and me so, but we figured it would be better if she told you herself, so you wouldn't think we, that is me, was squealing on her, but she hasn't, has she, so—"

"A kind of a jail record?" he exploded, although it wasn't clear if it was at her or at me as the bearer of the news. "Rusty, are you sure she wasn't pulling your leg?" he demanded, his brow drawn down in the severest way as he studied me.

"I don't think so, Pop. Why would she kid about a year and a half in juvie?"

By now he was reeling in furiously, the chicken gut bait skipping across the surface of the water. "Cripes, they must have thrown the book at her if that's true. What'd she 'take'?"

"A car. When she was fourteen."

I saw him wince hard. Pole in hand, fishing abandoned, he stalked over by me and sat down heavily.

"Okay, let's think about this." He started trying to parse through the matter. He was welcome to it, after all the brain-bending I'd done on it. "Let's say that's the straight scoop and she served her time. It ought to have taught her a lesson, right? Scared her straight, if nothing else." Making every effort to be fair to her, he countered the juvie record. "I've been keeping a real close eye on the cash register, just to be on the safe side, and

I'm pretty sure she's not taking from the till." He tapped his forehead. "I'd know."

"Maybe not there, but—"

"Not there? Then where? Come on, spill it."

I reminded him of the eagle jigger he couldn't find no matter where he looked behind the bar, and then days later, there it magically was, and related the similar tale of my silver dollar that went missing and showed up again.

He could hardly believe it about France's personal version of shoplifting, on us. "What the hell would she bother with little things like that for?" he said in bewilderment. "And why bring them back?" Then something like a sudden headache seemed to come to him.

"This maybe explains something," he began slowly. Reaching in his shirt pocket, he pulled out a cigarette lighter, a shiny ACE IN THE HOLE one. "Couple of days ago, I was certain as anything I had left this on my nightstand. Just, you know, in case," he tossed off, as if that had nothing to do with smoking in bed. "But when I remembered while we were opening up the joint and went back for it, damned if I could find the thing. Then the other night when I turned in, I reached over to the nightstand for a book off the pile and the lighter was right there, sort of tucked behind the stack. It really threw me, how I could have over-looked it the first time. Made me wonder if I was ready for the funny farm."

I doubted that a mental institution was in prospect for him or me, either, although I would not have bet against incarceration of some sort for my ersatz cousin, if recent behavior was any indication. I felt a whoosh of relief that I hadn't been accusing her of behavior imperceptible to anyone else. Now I stayed quiet to let him try to sort matters out. "What's she doing, playing some crazy game with us? Damn it, she's a grown-up, she better act like one." Firm as a father could be, he drew a conclusion: "I'll tell her to cut out the nonsense and—"

I couldn't let it end there. "Pop, there's something else she's doing."

He looked at me with extreme reluctance. "What's the something else?"

Haltingly, I told him the story of Canada Dan's ten-spot. "And I saw Velma Simms count her change two or three times that last time she was in."

By the time I was done, he was squinting so hard, it looked like it hurt. "That puts a whole different light on it." His voice sounded hollow, barely hearable over the gushing spillway. "Shortchanging any customers is a death warrant for a joint, that's rule number one." Taking out the lighter again and fumbling a little, he lit a cigarette as for once I watched sympathetically. As the first puff of smoke settled, he wondered aloud, "Why do you suppose somebody—I'm not naming names, understand—didn't tell me any of this before now?"

"Maybe they," I guiltily took the little cover that was offered, "wanted to give her a chance. See if her conscience might start kicking her in the wazoo."

"I suppose that's it. Can't blame them too much for good intentions, I guess."

He smoked in silence for a while.

"That still leaves us with what to do about her," he finally broached. "I hate to have to can her, the way things have been going. We're right back in a fix about the joint, if I do. And there's no getting round it, she's my—our own flesh and blood." He looked sick about the situation. "Then there's Delano, he couldn't fall any harder for her if you hit him with a club."

He ground out his cigarette in the damp soil. I could tell he was casting around for some other answer than firing France, and slowly he brought out: "Tell you what, we're gonna have to put up with her until I get done with the derby. Howie's too old to cut the mustard anymore, full time, so I don't see any damn choice but leave her behind the bar for now." Frowning again as if it hurt, he concluded, "But then she's gonna have to turn honest or hit the trail."

"I TOLD."

"Whoo. Was your dad mad?"

"More like sad." Rapidly I filled Zoe in on what had transpired at the reservoir. Our conversation was hushed, even though the saloon was not yet open, and so neither was the vent. Looking like a man trying to juggle hot potatoes, Pop had gone on to derby business at the community hall as soon as we got back from fishing, and France was out front, setting up the bar as usual, if she hadn't lapsed into stealing ashtrays or some such.

"Poor Del," Zoe mourned. "He's in for a real snotty surprise when he finds out about her, isn't he."

No doubt I was touchy about the matter, but Del seemed to be drawing more sympathy over the disclosure about France than was I, directly related to the juvie veteran and presumed pack rat. The elements were not helping my peevish mood, the day having deteriorated practically by the minute ever since Pop and I left the reservoir, with dark clouds rolling in over the mountains behind the Packard, as if racing us to town. Now rain was pouring down yet again and thunder was rumbling like beer kegs rolling off the delivery truck. More thirty-year weather.

"Yeah, but," I started, "isn't it a whole lot better for him to find out now than—"

Unexpectedly the door from the barroom flew open, making us both jump.

It was the piano girl herself, France barreling into the back room and, from the look of it, not simply to replenish something behind the bar.

"Hi, you two, think the rain will hurt the rhubarb?" she wise-cracked, and to our surprise, started racing directly up the stairs to us. "Not if it comes in cans, huh? Guess what, forgot my bow tie. Tom will bug me about it if he catches me not wearing it. Gonna borrow that slicker to run back to the house for it." She meant, Zoe and I realized in a single convulsive gulp, the one hanging over the vent.

Panicked, I leaped up, nearly bumping France backward at the head of the stairs. "Huh-uh, that's Pop's. He gets really, really upset if anybody uses it but him. Come on, I'll get you a better one down here." I pattered past her to the hanging haberdashery below.

She gave me an odd look, and then one to Zoe, sitting there by the raincoat with a theatrical expression that implied if it were up to her, she would waft the forbidden garment onto France's shoulders like a royal cape. "Some people have funny habits," sighed Zoe in universal regret.

"Yeah, the dumb bow tie is in that category, too," France said, reluctantly turning to trot down the stairs to where I was flour-ishing some sheepherder's yellow slicker. "Don't let the joint float away before I get back," she left us with, and dashed out into the downpour.

"That was close," Zoe said.

"What isn't, with her," I said.

AS IF PROXY had some sixth sense about showing up when no one was looking for her, the very morning of the fishing derby she came wheeling into the driveway, casual as you please. Our soup spoons poised to dig into breakfast, Pop and I heard the definitive crunch of the red Cadillac on the gravel. France wasn't even out of the bathroom yet.

"What is this," he burst out, already beset with assignment sheets and voluminous other derby busywork spread around him, "some crazy phase of the moon?"

Swearing under his breath—considerably beyond mentioning the Nazarene—as he scooped together the paperwork and reared up from the table, he got hold of himself enough to instruct me to pour breakfast back in the pan and then fetch France for the awaited confrontation.

"We're gonna get her straightened out right here and now, or know why not," he vowed as he marched out to conscript Proxy for that duty.

All too aware of my part in bringing this about, I mounted the stairs with my heart thumping at every step and knocked on the bathroom door.

"Hold on to your irrigation hose, can't you," the occupant responded laconically, "I'll be a couple more minutes."

"It's not that. Pop told me to tell you your mom is here."

Something clattered in the bathroom. "Proxy?" came the muffled question, as though she might have some other mother. "Now? She sure knows how to spoil a good time."

Back downstairs, where Pop was waiting stiffly—I could tell he was bottling up everything until France arrived on the scene—and Proxy was lounging around the living room as if she owned the place, I met once more with that unsettling gaze, as if she were sizing me up. After a moment, she cracked a smile. "Hey there, Russ. The big day, huh?" Turning back to Pop, she kidded: "Jeez, chairman of the whole fishing shebang. You've come up in the world, Tom. If you don't watch out, you'll be mayor next."

"I have enough headaches already," he said shortly. Anything further was cut off by rapid steps on the stairs and France making her appearance.

"Hi, Ma," she came in talking fast, "come to see if all fishermen are liars or only liars fish?" When I say making her appearance, this day she really had worked on how she looked. She must have cleaned out the Toggery of its most exotic items, a vividly striped red, white, and blue blouse and a fringed buckskin vest that went with her leather bracelet, plus crisp new blue jeans. Topping it all off, her black hair, with a fresh sheen to it, had been teased nicely into a kind of crown effect. In a word, she was an eyeful, and the three of us stared as if making sure it was her, the old Francine.

"Look at you," Proxy eventually said, guardedly. "Bartender clothes have changed since my day."

France glanced in nervous appeal at Pop, and he came through with, "She's not behind the bar today. The joint's always closed for the derby."

"Civic, huh?" Proxy adjusted to the situation. "So much the better." She gave France a sort of maternal wink, if those two things do not cancel each other out. "It'll give us a chance to catch up with each other. I don't know about you, but I'm not much for hook, line, and sinker. What do you say we go into Great Falls, ladies' day out?"

Now France really showed the jitters. "Sorry, no can do. I didn't know you'd blaze in here like this. See, I'm going to the derby with"—she managed a twisty shrug and toss of her head that ended up pointing out the window, toward the Gab Lab parked beneath the bower of Igdrasil—"well, Del."

I swear Proxy took in the van and the Packard beyond it, shined up for the day's event, in a single lightning glance.

"It's like that, is it?" Her tone said she remembered all too well how such things were. "I thought Carrot Top is supposed to be chasing down voices out on the coast by now."

"He got a grant," I helpfully provided.

"He's after sheepherders," Pop supplied simultaneously.

"He'll be here for a while yet," France imparted at the same time.

Proxy scrutinized the trio of us, the crimp between her eyes saying more than she did for a few seconds. "Oh-kay, the young folks will have their fun," she conceded. If there is such a thing as a warning smile, she gave France one now. "Just don't let having a good time get in the way of what counts, all right?" With that, she briskly gathered herself. "Well, I guess I might as well hit the road, busy as everybody is around here."

"Don't rush off." Pop's tone erased the look of relief on France. He looked regretfully at Proxy. "We have something to talk over." Here it came. I was divided between anticipation and apprehension.

Pop wasted no words: "Things have been going missing."

Mother and daughter went rigid in the same instant. You could have heard a false eyelash drop in the silence before Proxy at last sighed, "What things?"

"Little things that disappear and then, surprise, surprise, show up again," Pop said pointedly. "Wouldn't you say that's what happens, Francine?"

It is never good news when a parent resorts to your full name. The blood seemed to have drained out of her. "Oboy. That again." She defensively looked back and forth from Proxy to Pop. "People are always thinking I steal."

"How come they think that?" he pressed.

The leather bracelet was getting a nervous workout. "See, I did kind of take something, back when I was wet behind the ears"—I did not appreciate that she indicated in my direction as illustration of that condition—"and didn't know any better. Learned my lesson, honest."

"In juvie, right?" Pop did not relent. "For auto theft?"

Resigned to that reputation, she dipped her head. "I figured you'd heard about it from one source or another." With a hurt expression, she gestured around to Proxy and me as if we were the suspects. I couldn't tell if I was watching a master class in acting or if she was as sincere as the day was long, but she rallied to look Pop in the eye. "It's not something I wanted to tell you myself, is it. 'Hi, I'm your daughter and, guess what, I was a teenage convict.'"

"Past history," Proxy rushed into the full silence following that. "No sense getting excited about something that happened way back there. Tom, anyone deserves a second chance."

"I don't want to have to be the one to keep count all the time," he flung back, as frustrated as I had ever seen him. "Damn it, Proxy," he exploded, "the two of you don't get off that easy, especially you." He looked pained to have to do this to her, but driven to it. "Does it run in the family or what, one Jones after another acting up, until a man can't count on any kind of behavior but bad?" His old companion from the Blue Eagle days flinched almost to the roots of her milk-blond hair, but sat and took it. "Let's try a little past history," his temper kept going, "such as why did I ever give in to you when I knew better? Both times, no less. Second chance," he ground out woefully, "I could use one myself, every time you show up."

There may have been more to his outburst, but if so, it did not register on me in my stunned condition, trying to catch up with the thunderclap of what I had just heard.

"If I'd raised you," he finally switched back to the daughter situation, "you would've had that stealing habit taken out of you in the first five minutes." Dazed as I was, I realized he had the look in his eye that told a customer to settle down or clear out, and Francine knew it, too. "You better get serious about life," he concluded bluntly, as the object of his ire stood there rigid as a cadet, "or you'll end up somewhere a hell of a lot worse than juvie."

Probably it was piling on, but Proxy couldn't stop herself from saying crossly, "Francine, you told me you'd kicked that kind of fooling around. No more sticking this, that, and the other in your pocket, you promised."

The younger woman blinked, as if coming to. "Fine, I shouldn't have done any of that, but why does everybody have to flip about it? I put the stuff back, didn't I? That's something in my favor, isn't it?"

It was an impressive try, but not even her bravado could withstand two deadly parental stares. I could see her lip quiver as she confessed, "It's a tough habit to kick. I have to fight it like crazy every time. That's . . . that's why I put things back, see."

"There now." Proxy saw an opening. "No real harm done, huh? Just a little confusion, and now that everybody savvies the situation, she can straighten herself out like you said, Tom."

"That isn't all," he said ominously.

"Then what is?" She cast a questioning glance at Francine, who was looking genuinely surprised.

"The way she makes change."

Absorbing that for a moment, Proxy tried to laugh it off. "Tom, you always was one to pinch pennies until Lincoln needed a hernia belt. Come on, you know how it is, all the way back to the Eagle, and I bet it's no different in this joint—guys get to drinking and they spill chicken feed all over the bar, and you have to make change from it all night long, it won't come out exactly right a million percent of the time, how can it? A few dimes' difference here and there—"

"No, he's right, Mom," Francine blurted. "I shortchanged a sheepherder because he got my goat." She faced Pop as if pleading before a judge. "I know what you told me, the old poots come in from six months in sheep camp and don't always know how to act around people, and we have to just leave them alone to soak up drinks and talk to themselves, and I've been doing that, really I have. But this one made me so mad, I took it out on him, five bucks' worth, in his change." To Pop's credit, he listened as if I had not already given him my eyewitness report on Canada Dan and her. "He caught me at it, but I bluffed him down, so nothing came of it," she finished her side of the story.

Proxy was giving her a look that could be felt ten feet away.

"But see, I made up for that," Francine protested.

"Made up for it? How?" Pop demanded.

She tugged at the fringe of her vest like a little girl. "I felt kind of bad about doing it to the old coot. So the next customer in, I overchanged."

"Over . . . ?" He couldn't believe what he had just heard. "Gave back too *much* change?"

"Sure thing. It was what's-her-name, the stuck-up one."

"Velma?" Pop ventured cautiously.

"You got it, her. I slipped the same five into the money back for her drink. Watched her count it a couple of times like she couldn't believe it. But she didn't give back the fiver, did she."

We sat there like the three monkeys, fixed on her. Nothing stirred in the room except Francine's nervous fingers. Pop came to life first, mustering himself as if facing the most difficult of barroom behavior cases.

"Look, bartending doesn't work that way. I don't know what kind of cockeyed conscience you have, but you can't cheat one customer and pass it along like gravy to another one and have it come out even. All that'll get you is both of them thinking you're playing fast and loose with the cash register. And word like that gets around, don't think it doesn't. The joint's reputation would be down the drain in no time." Plainly this was his limit. "I hate like everything to do it"—he threw up his hands— "but I'm gonna have to can you."

Francine looked dismally resigned to the verdict, but Proxy did not.

"Cut her a break, Tom," she pleaded. "She's just a kid."

"Twenty-one?"

"Some people grow up slower than others," Proxy hedged. She turned to her daughter. "Honey," she said sorrowfully, "you couldn't have messed up this chance any worse if you'd tried." She paused for effect. Marilyn Monroe could not have done a better job of creating breathy expectation. "But that's in the past," she reasoned, although it barely was. "You're going to quit doing it, aren't you, dear. Stop taking dumb-ass things that aren't worth taking in the first place?"

"I guess I have to get with it or split the scene, don't I," came the sulky answer, along with more demure tugging at the vest fringe.

"You're damn right you do," Pop weighed in. He looked exasperated but uncertain. If I knew anything about it, his own conscience was giving him too much trouble. I saw him start to say something, stop, squint as if squeezing out a decision, and then deliver it in the slowest of voices: "I'm probably going to kick myself for this, but if I give you another try, will you behave different?"

Francine tossed her head, as if deciding to change her life then and there. "I'll do better," she vowed, "but you've got to do something for me, Tom. You and Rusty."

Me? Why? How did I get into the bargaining? Alarm must

have been written all over me because Pop said, "Don't come unglued, kiddo. Let's hear what she means."

"Don't tell Del about what I got myself into?" she practically whispered it. "I mean, let me clue him in, after today." She gave us an intensely pleading look. "Honest, I'll tell him everything. Just not right now, okay?"

Pop seemed to consider this from up, down, and sideways before finally replying. "As far as I can tell, you haven't been shortchanging Delano," he said drily. "If he's happy to be in the dark, we'll keep our traps shut for now. Right, Rusty?"

"Uh, okay."

Proxy had the last word. "See how things work out when you don't get excited?"

BUSY FUSSING the Gab Lab into readiness, Del looked on curiously as we poured out of the house, Pop rushing off to deal with last-minute derby details, Proxy gunning the Cadillac down the alley, Francine giving a quick yoo-hoo wave and calling out that she'd be ready after one more little thing in the bathroom, and me scooting across the yard to stay safely out of her vicinity.

"The family gathering go all right?" Del asked, a smile on him as big as the day, when I reached the van. He was busy stuffing extra tape reels and other odds and ends of recording gear into his safari shirt.

"Right as rain," one of Pop's sayings that I never understood in the first place came to my rescue. I still was trying to cope with the mental lightning strike back there in the middle of his tirade to Proxy. I had to try to find out in a hurry, France would be there any minute. "Say, mister," I piped up in a stagey voice, "how are you fixed for answers?"

"They're running out my ears, my good fellow," Del generously joined in the bit while still putting things here and there in his shirt. "In what manner may I enlighten you?"

"Is Jones ever one those nicknames, like Canada Dan?"

He stopped loading his pockets to think that over. "A behavioral one? I can't imagine how, a plain standard family name like that. What makes you ask?"

"Oh, there were a couple of tourists in the bar," I made up as fast as I could think, which was none too fast, "and so, one of them did something the other one didn't like, and the other one seemed to be calling him a name like that, something about how with him it was one Jones after another acting up until you couldn't count on any kind of behavior from him but bad, so I wondered."

He clucked his tongue in sudden understanding. "Ah, of course, *that* kind of jones. Small *j*. It means a compulsion, something you keep doing, against better judgment. Monkey on the back," he did a sudden scary bit, twitching jerkily, as if trying to shake off a clinging simian. "Got a jones about that, man." I stood petrified, needing to hear no more but at the mercy of Del's encyclopedic tendency as he parsed the matter further. The expression, he guessed, might have come from the jazz world, where various kinds of unwise behavior were not unknown. "That tourist must be a real problem case," he finished.

"Huh? Yeah. Awful."

"Who's a problem case?" The whippy voice caught us by surprise. "Nobody I know, I hope." Coming up on the van from the yard side, the piano girl, as I couldn't help thinking of her ever since hearing it from Canada Dan, looked tense as a tightwire walker, but then she often did. Her fixed grin of greeting, if that's what it was, flashed at me before settling onto Del. I shook my head so swiftly my eyeballs rattled, to show her I hadn't told him about her pack rat episodes and the rest.

"*La belle France*," he greeted her in a goofy boyfriend way. "You look sensational," he admired, taking a good, long look. "Ready for all the fishing?"

"Can't hardly wait." Her fingers played in the buckskin vest fringe as she worked up to saying, "You know what? I've gone back to Francine. By popular demand, sort of."

"Hmm?" Del puzzled over her name switcheroo a moment, then smiled unconcernedly. "'By any other name,' as the poet said," he proclaimed, a gallantry that evidently was as far over her head as mine. Nonetheless, Francine gave him a gaze full of reward.

The lovey atmosphere was growing too thick for me. Besides, I badly needed a chance to sort things out in my head. "I have to put the banner on the Packard," I started to make my escape, "I better get at that."

"I'll give you a hand," said Francine.

"No, no, I can do it myself, honest."

"Uh-uh, I insist."

Knowing I was in for it from her—Pop obviously had not learned about the shortchanging episode from the angel Gabriel—I fetched the banner out of storage and trudged down the driveway to the hulking old car, my problematic half sister shadowing me as if I might get away. Behind us, Del was happily trying his portable tape recorder, "Testing, one, two, three . . ."

I wondered if she knew the Packard was where it happened—*she* happened—because of its spacious damn back seat. If so, she didn't let on, and simply surveyed the banner as I flopped one part of it—CATCH 'EM—onto the trunk and then the other—TO THE LIMIT! She still didn't say anything until we were nearly done tying the thing to the taillights and trunk handle and so on.

"Been thinking, buddy." She kept her voice low so it wouldn't carry to the van. "You did me a real favor by tipping off your— our, dad about me messing up the way I did. So big kissy thanks."

I was wary. "How was that any favor?"

She tossed her head, as if clearing that black mane of hers out of the way. "It makes me get myself squared away. Don't have any choice now, do I."

Skittishly watching her, I wondered if a person could make a jones go away just like that. The one that was giving me a waking nightmare didn't show any sign of going anywhere.

ZOE COULD TELL right away I was a mental mess.

"What happened?" she asked in a stage whisper, speeding out of the cafe after I feverishly tapped on the window. "A knock-down drag-out?"

"Just about." There wasn't time, as we headed like homing pigeons to the Medicine Lodge and the sanctum of the back room, to tell her all that had happened at the house. I rushed through the parts about Proxy showing up unexpectedly and Francine owning up to pack rat behavior and Del being kept in the dark until the right time, whenever that was, while she listened hard. I was wrapping it up, none too tidily, by the time we mounted the landing and claimed our spot under the mute vent, the saloon silent around us, front and back.

She waited until I reached my stopping point to say in some puzzlement, "So didn't everything work out peachy keen? France-*cine*"—she caught up with the renaming—"has to go straight or hit the road, right?"

"That isn't all," I echoed Pop.

Sounding worried, Zoe examined me more closely. "Rusty, you look peaked. You aren't going to throw up or something, are you?"

"Huh-uh, it's not that."

"What, then?"

"I think I found out—"

The words wouldn't come, until I forced them to.

"I think I found out Proxy is my mother."

❧ 11 ❧

I T MADE A crazy kind of sense, gaps filled in, veils lifted, the full story revealed after all this time. Pop's pained version of my mother, whenever I ventured to find out anything whatsoever about her, must have been that she was a jones, a bad habit, not a phone-book Jones as I'd thought. By his own saying so, Proxy fit that; the jonesiest kind of compulsion, according to his outburst in the house, overcoming him twice. It was the *twice* that hit home with me.

The first time, that "one damn time" in the Packard, with Francine as living proof of unrestrained behavior. But the other: it did not take much imagination to conjure it happening in Canada, he on one of those trips to sell off back-room loot and she in the business of taxi dancing or worse, and they cross paths again, by every indication in Medicine Hat. "The railyard district, Tom," in that silky voice. "No place like it when we used to know it, was there." And out of that intersection comes me, nine months later. An awful lot was explained that way. Proxy's fishy manner of looking at me. Pop's hazy description of my nativity, the housekeeper story much more convenient than one beginning, "See, there's this taxi dancer I used to know who keeps turning up like a bad penny and we got a few drinks into us one more damn time, and—" As for Francine, she could be in on the secret, or this all could have transpired without her ever knowing, given Proxy's motherhood record of being absent for years at a time. Either way, it would make me the last to know that the girlishly named missing mother I had tried so hard to imagine was actually a milk-blond hustler full of schemes, wouldn't it.

As this spilled out of me, Zoe had the logical question. "So why didn't your dad and Proxy get married when they knew they were having you?"

"I bet she wouldn't do it," I hazarded not much of a guess. She was a different breed of cat, Pop had outright said so. And not the marrying kind at the time, particularly with a scandalous first husband to live down. No, it made sense to me that Proxy, as she was then, would have dealt herself out of any matrimony, and probably me into the nearest orphanage, except for Pop saying something like—I could almost hear him—"Then I'll raise the kid myself," and depositing me in Phoenix, and the rest was history.

"Whew." Zoe's eyes were big with awe at this family saga of mine and, given her dramatic instinct, maybe a touch of envy. "Are you going to let on to your dad that you know?"

"I . . . I can't make up my mind." Neither choice held real appeal. I'd been gritting and bearing it ever since two dangerously smiling women came along out of nowhere to upset our perfectly sound bachelor life, and forbearance was getting profoundly wearing. Yet there are some questions you don't like to ask because of the answers they might bring. What if I mustered myself to question Pop as to whether Proxy was in truth my mother, and he let his conscience run away with itself and replied, "You know what, she is, and now that it's out in the open, she and I ought to fix this family situation and do it right for a change and get hitched and we all live together. How's that grab you?"

Right where I did not want to be grabbed, that's where. If it was selfish not to want to share my father's life and mine with a catamount, then I was hopelessly selfish.

Shocked, Zoe asked, "Your dad wouldn't really do something like that, would he?"

"Who knows?" Hellish good company, he'd characterized Proxy in their Blue Eagle time together. The first part of that, I could agree with. "He complains about her and how she's always up to something, but he ends up doing what she wants. That's what scares me. You saw her in the back room—she's not making eyes at him just for practice."

Biting her lip in sympathy, Zoe watched me without knowing what to say, for once. In the stillness of the back room, not even the model planes stirred overhead, and the menagerie of items down on the floor and along the walls was like a museum everyone had passed through but the two of us. I could see her working on my predicament as mightily as I was, but the answer wasn't revealing itself.

The bang of the door from the barroom side flying open jarred us both.

"There you are." Pop peered up at us, sounding like a man in all kinds of a hurry. "Time to shake a leg, kiddo, we've got to get out to the rezavoy. Your folks will be looking for you, princess." On whatever checklist a fishing derby chairman has to carry in his head, however, he paused for a regretful second to scratch one off. "Tell your dad we won't need any chicken guts this time around."

THE DERBY DAY crowd, even as early as Pop and I and the Packard pulled in to the parking lot on the bluff, already was starting to put the Mudjacks Reunion to shame for size and high spirits, and while the dam was modest compared to Fort Peck, it held an even more impressive amount of water than when I had caught my trophy trout. By now Rainbow Reservoir was practically brimming, as if all the weather of the year had collected within its banks in liquid form. If a hell of a lot of water did mean a hell of a lot of fish, then Pop and Bill Reinking were in luck. As we were getting out the loudspeaker equipment and other derby paraphernalia he was in charge of, being greeted all the while by people bristling with rods and reels, Pop surveyed the scene of the crowd, staking out spots along the gravelly shoreline. "How about that, maybe I knew what I was doing," he said with satisfaction, looking toward where someone from his committee had roped off the muddy top of the dam, as he'd directed. "Not that it wouldn't be fun to see a Zane or two slip into the water, hey?"

Just then we heard a familiar twang, Turk Turco calling out from where he had parked a highway department flatbed truck, donated or at least borrowed for the day, on the shoulder of ground just above the dam to serve as the speaker's stand. "Over here, Tom, we'll get the glory horn set up for you if Jojo doesn't electrocute himself doing it."

"Montana Power to the rescue," Joe Quigg grunted as he swung heavy batteries onto the truck bed to operate the loudspeaker and amplifier.

Pop gladly yielded the equipment so he could move on to overseeing the refreshments area, more his department, and in my unsettled mood I trailed close behind him as he plunged into all that needed doing, questions to be answered, directions given, decisions made. Booths had to be set up, the Rotarians with their inferior beer, the Constantines at their Top Spot hot dog stand, the Ladies' Aid with their tables of baked goods, and the Goodwill ones beyond those. Across the years the Gros Ventre Fishing Derby had grown to such importance that the state Fish and Game agency, known as the Frog and Goose guys, now dispatched a couple of game wardens to sell hunting licenses and provide free fish gutting for the contestants; Pop wisely put them and their gut buckets farthest away from the food booths. Even the Air Force flyboys had a booth this year, under the banner THE MINUTEMAN MISSILE—AMERICA'S ACE IN THE HOLE, where they gave away blue ballpoint pens. Then there was the sign-up table and the judges' setup for measuring and weighing fish, that whole side of the parking lot a community encampment where my fathomless father was something like the temporary mayor.

To me now, that culminating day of the summer—of the year, really—seems like one long, twisty dream, everything that began with Proxy's Cadillac nosing into the driveway and the thunderous disclosures that followed, and then the tremendous gathering at the derby, as if the audience had come to see what Tom Harry would bring about next. There are some days in a person's life, only ever a few, that are marked to be remembered forever, even while they are happening. As if in a trance, I watched Pop master his chairmanship tasks—"I wouldn't make too much of that 'ace in the hole' business if I were you, Sarge, there are some jokers in this crowd...." "I'm sorry, Louise, but like I told Howie, the ladies will just have to get by with one table for pies...." "You didn't think to bring a tub of ice, Fred? That's sure too bad, I guess people will have to get used to warm beer"— the most important person in the Two Medicine country, at least for the day. I should have been busting my buttons with pride for him, and mostly I was, but the repeated history of him and Proxy, creeping closer all the while, incessantly kept haunting me. Her for a mother. What does it take to empty a head of something you do not want there?

Trailing after him with this churning inside me as he strode from one derby duty to the next, I was sticking so close, I was nearly riding his shirttail. It wasn't until he ducked around to the side of the Frog and Goose booth to catch his breath and have a cigarette that he had a chance to read my face.

"Hey, you doing all right, kiddo?"

"Trying to."

"Don't let this morning's commotion get you down." He lowered his voice just enough. "We got Francine onto the straight and narrow or else, didn't we? That's something." Busy even when he wasn't, he was keeping an eye on the derby doings while talking to me. "You know what, I still kind of wish you were fishing today, it'd take your mind off other things." I must have shown alarm, because he gave me a wry look. "Relax, you're right, I can't have the chairman's son catching the prize rainbow. Go have some fun while I tend to things, can't you? See what Zoe is up to, how about."

SHE SAW ME coming as I wended through the crowd to her folks' hot dog stand, and as quick as she pantomimed blindly eating a ballpark wiener, my spirits climbed, although it still was heavy lifting.

"I'm sprung, Muscles"—at least I wasn't so far gone I couldn't feebly do a bit—"what do you say we vacate the space?"

"That's an idea if I ever heard one, Ace. Let me have a chinnie with the warden." With business at the Top Spot stand keeping her mother hopping and her father laboring over the grill of curling frankfurters, her parents were as glad to shoo her out of the way as Pop had been with me.

Off we went, life finally feeling right to me with Zoe at my side. She fell quiet as we roved the scene of the event. You could have walked away with the town, so many people from Gros Ventre had come out for the big day. Even Cloyce Reinking was on hand, in spousal loyalty to Bill's Chamber of Commerce position, we figured. Spying us, she provided a comically elevated eyebrow, very much as Lady Bracknell might have done at the news that people pursued fish when foxes were so much more visible to the eye, and we couldn't help but giggle.

On the other hand, it was a middle finger lifted in our direction when Duane Zane came tagging after his father, Earl passing Pop's vicinity with his nose in the air.

As if the Zanes were a bad omen, Zoe grew more somber when we wandered past family bunches visiting gaily with one another along the reservoir shore while waiting for the derby to start. At the section where ten- to thirteen-year-olds were grouped, my horse buddies Jimmy and Hal and some others spotted us and waved and hollered. "Come on," I tried to put some enthusiasm into my social role, "better say hello to the guys, they're in our grade."

"Huh-uh," she surprised me, squirming her shoulders. "Later."

I gestured to our curious classmates that we were urgently wanted by waiting parents and we kept going. Zoe was looking vacant eyed in a way that I knew was no bit.

"Something the matter?"

"Ooh, nothing, really."

"Zo-oe, tell me."

"It's hunnerd percent dumb."

"Come on." I snapped my fingers all the way back to Shakespeare. "How now, unhappy youth?"

A teeny smile trembled on her at that, but then she looked away and around at the crowd. "You know everybody here. And all the kids. For me, they're"—she struggled to put it into words—"it's all going to be new, Rusty."

As fumbling as her emotion was, I felt in a flash exactly what she meant. The calendar was closing in on us, bringing on the jaundiced feeling that kids get when summer is leaving in a hurry. Without ever having to say so, we shared the haunting sense that our education together would end when school started. And if Zoe was on the verge of crying, that made two of us. It was right there in our faces; there might be other summers, other years, but never again like this.

I tried to make the best of it. "School doesn't get us for a couple days yet."

"Saved until the bell, I guess," she said with the bravado I loved in her.

"Don't worry ahead," I said as if I wasn't a prime example. "We'll employ our brains and think of something, Muscles."

That twitched a grin out of her, and at the same time I saw her eyes widen as dramatically as ever. "Here they are," she whispered, ready for the next act, "the piano girl and her main squeeze."

WHATEVER THEY had been up to, Del and Francine were conspicuously tardy in arriving. I could tell by the giddy expression on him as he hopped out of the van that she had not yet told him anything, except maybe any cooing between kisses. Francine met us with her best poker face, and I supposed it counted in her favor if she was dead set on bluffing her way through the day without upsetting Del in his work. But then?

That was when and this was now, Del all business as he flung open the side doors of the Gab Lab. "And now, for a sound portrait of the Gros Ventre Fishing Derby, stay tuned," he intoned like the most baritone of radio announcers, and began scooping up recording gear.

Zoe and I had watched him at this before, but it was new to Francine, as were the glistening reservoir and the natural setting tucked against the mountains and the mob of people at the booths and the throng down along the shoreline. "Jeez, Dellie, everybody and his twin brother are at this bash. How do you go about this?"

"An estimable question, mademoiselle." He paused in checking the connections on the portable tape recorder and scanned the busy scene. The answer seemed to come to him from the dam, where so much overflow was gushing out the floodgate and cascading down into the South Fork that it sounded like a natural waterfall. "Aha!" He cocked his good ear. "The sound of white water, as some poet must have said."

"Ambience," Zoe confidently defined for Francine's benefit, who looked like she needed it.

"Let's go, derby fans." Del set off with headphones slung around his neck and the recorder swinging at his side like a suitcase, the three of us in his wake. Swiftly he headed for the speaker-stand truck, where Pop was going over last things with various committee members about to take up their assignments, everyone jaunty as free spenders at a carnival.

Memory heightens these things, but I have my own sound portrait as clear to the inner ear as if it all was happening again now: Francine saying sweetly to Turk Turco and Joe Quigg as we passed their side of the truck, "If it isn't my favorite customers";

and as quickly as she had gone by, Turk moaning wistfully, "It must be nice to be a ladies' man"; and Joe telling him, "Eat your heart out, Turco, you're never gonna have red hair and a crew cut"; and Del glancing back at them with a distracted "Hmm?"; and Zoe silently delighting in it all with me, as we had done so many, many times by the sift of the vent. If only the rest of life were as clear as the voices of that time.

The next was Pop's, as he greeted Del and Francine with a mock frown, or maybe not, glancing up from dispatching the last of his committee volunteers. "Get lost getting here, did you?"

Right away Francine looked guilty, but one thing about Del, you couldn't deter him when he had something in mind. "I'm glad we haven't missed anything," he went right past Pop's remark. And immediately inclined his head toward the rushing spillway. "Tom, Mr. Chairman I should say, I need to go out there for a few minutes. It sounds like Niagara. It'll be phenomenal on tape."

No doubt remembering the tick episode, Pop gave him a warning look. "Promise not to slip and fall in?"

"Absolutely."

"Okay, then, I guess, go to it." He shook his head at Del's determination to catch noise while several hundred people waited to catch trout. "Make it snappy, we're about to start the fishing."

Wasting no time, Del ducked under the rope, holding it up in hopeful fashion for Francine. "Coming?"

"Not this kid." She and her clean new britches shied back from the muddy dam. "I'll cheer from here, thanks." I didn't blame her, knowing how single-minded Del could be when he had the microphone on and the tape reel hypnotically turning; not exactly lively company. Resigned to going solo, he was already concentrating on his recording gear, checking his multitudinous pockets for things and automatically clamping the headphones onto his ears as he set off across the causeway to the floodgate, careful of his footing while lugging the hefty recorder.

Watching his progress, Pop suggested in a way that did not want any argument that Zoe and I hop up on the truck bed to sit during the derby, so he wouldn't have any more wanderers to keep track of. The morning confrontation still clouding his brow, he turned and considered Francine standing by herself, looking more than a little lost. "You, too, I guess, toots." His expression lifted as he jerked his head toward the truck bed. "All the problem children in one bunch, okay?"

Relief flooded her. "Fine," she said hastily, and started to scooch up onto the truck beside Zoe and me before conscience seemed to catch up with her.

She worked her mouth, as if tasting the words carefully first. "Tom? I'm sorry about . . . you know, everything."

"That puts you back in the human race," he accepted gravely. "Come on, rest your bones until Delano gets back." She hopped up as Zoe and I squirmed over to make room for her.

With the three of us under control, Pop looked all around the reservoir scene and drew a sighing breath, the kind that told me he really wished he had time for a cigarette. His eye caught mine. "I got a fishing derby to run instead, don't I." Setting his face the way he did when he was about to open the Medicine Lodge for business, he signaled to Bill Reinking over at the sign-up table that all was in readiness. Seeing this, Turk or Joe did something to the sound system that caused the customary feedback screech, startling everyone but Del, earmuffed as he was by his headphones out on the concrete apron of the spillway, setting down his recorder to punch buttons and read dials. "Cripes, it sounds like we're murdering a cat," Pop muttered as he climbed onto the truck in back of where Zoe and I and Francine were perched. Gingerly taking the microphone Joe handed up to him, he cleared his throat a couple of times and began the proceedings.

"WELCOME, EVERYBODY, TO THE GROS VEN-TRE FISHING DERBY AGAIN THIS YEAR," his voice resounded out over the reservoir and the clapping gathering. "HAVE YOU NOTICED THAT BLUE SKY? NO WATER FOR A CHASER TODAY, BY ORDER OF THE MAN-AGEMENT."

The crowd applauded louder now, perfectly willing to let the maestro of the Medicine Lodge take credit for the day's dry weather. Zoe of course watched Pop in his master of ceremonies role as if he were Shakespeare come to life, and Francine gave his opening effort a twitchy grin, but a grin. Myself, I prayed he wouldn't get carried away and be reminded of a story, as he'd done at the beer banquet; success does not necessarily strike twice when it comes to bartender jokes.

Squinting hard at a sheet of paper the sun was catching, he rolled on: "BEFORE WE GET STARTED THROWING FOOD TO THE FISH, THERE ARE SOME FOLKS I HAVE TO THANK FOR—" and I relaxed about at least one peril.

While he was conscientiously droning through that list, more than ever I felt like a spectator to a colossal dream, memory min-gling with all I was witnessing. In the nearest area of contestants strung thick along the reservoir, the little kids pointed their fishing poles in as many directions as quills on a porcupine. Remembering when I was like them, how mature I felt. At the same time, an inch away from me on one side sat wondrous Zoe, the summer's gift, whom I would have given almost anything to have for a real sister, and all but touching on my other side, the actual one, Francine, the newcomer whose middle name seemed to be Trouble. Trying to fit the contradictory two of them into my own small world, how childish I felt, hopelessly twelve years old in circumstances that would have taxed much older brains. Meanwhile my singular father, author of disappointments and triumphs and regular surprises in between, stood there, bigger than life, on his stage for the day, his voice rolling out over the water and shore, as central a figure in this panorama as he had been on the occasion of the Fort Peck reunion. Tom Harry as historic as Leadbelly. How clear and simple that had seemed before Proxy pulled up in a Cadillac typhoon of dust. Before the story of my life started coming unraveled in me.

Zoe, thank heavens, had been restlessly dandling her legs over the edge of the truck bed and taking everything in while I was so absorbed with myself. I snapped to at her sudden words under Pop's amplified ones, "Whoa, is that supposed to be like that?"

Francine and I saw in the same instant what she was pointing to on the downstream face of the dam, a portion of the earthen slope that did not look mud-brown like the rest but was glistening, the way the sun reflects off something wet.

"Pop!"

"Tom!"

Our simultaneous yells surprised him to a stop in midsentence, and he must have sensed the situation from the alarm in our shouts. Quicker than I would have thought humanly possible, he was madly motioning everyone to stay back from the causeway and roaring into the mike, "DELANO! GET OFF THE DAM! DELANO!"

It was no use, nothing at this distance was. The headphoned figure out there, blissfully tuning in the roar of the spillway, was deaf even to amplified shouts, and Francine's anguished "Dellie! Look up, damn it!" never stood a chance.

I suppose you never know what you will do in such a situation, until you do it. I launched off the truck bed, running as hard as I could toward the dam, Zoe right behind me.

"HEY, NO!" Pop's shouts now were followed by the death shriek of the mike as he scrambled off the truck in pursuit of us. No one else was near enough to be of any help, except Francine, who with presence of mind caught up with Zoe and wrested her, struggling and howling bloody murder, back toward shore as I raced onto the causeway.

There's a saying that you run from danger with your heart in your mouth, and that was even more true as I ran headlong into it: not brave, not even close, just blindly determined to reach Del before a reservoir full of water did. As best I can re-create the experience, adrenaline replaced the blood in my system and instinct took over from sanity. I simply ran and ran, the causeway seeming cruelly long, the kneeling figure ahead ever at an awful distance. How I kept to my feet on the muddy top of the dam, I do not know, except maybe through the gripping fear of falling. By now Del, taking his sweet time with his cherished equipment, was just yards away, but I felt the dam do something under me. Stories of the slide at Fort Peck had it all too right; there is an odd sensation of time suspended when the ground begins to move.

Out of breath, or so scared that my breathing wasn't working right—it pretty much came to the same—I floundered onto the concrete apron of the spillway and practically bowled Del over as I snatched his headphones off.

"Ow!" He grabbed a smarting ear, a look of surprise on him at my bad manners. "Rusty, what—?"

"The dam's leaking, come on!"

You most definitely did, Del, but not before scooping up your recording equipment. Not waiting around to argue the point, I already was flinging myself back along the causeway toward where Pop and Turk and Joe and some others had rushed down to the dam and out as far as they could risk on the shifting soil, and were hollering every kind of encouragement, although I have always wondered if any of it ever registered on you, if you were deaf even to Francine's screams of *"Drop it! Dellie, leave the damn thing!"* and Zoe's wailing urgings to us both. In any case, when I reached firm enough ground to whirl and look back for a second, you were lugging your precious tape recorder in a struggling crab-legged run, like a man in some ridiculous picnic race.

Which is why I made it to the safety of the shore, and you didn't.

"Watch out, it's gonna go!" Pop cried, grabbing me around the waist and practically carrying me with him as the bunch of us stumbled our way up the shoulder of higher ground, Zoe still in Francine's clutch as pandemonium spread among the crowd. People would be saying for the rest of their lives they were there that day, when the Rainbow dam broke. Actually it was a series of collapses, avalanches almost in slow motion, as pockets of soil big as sidehills slid off the core of the dam, one after another.

The wet patch Zoe had spied proved to be Del's undoing. He was nearly to the end of the causeway—"Come on, you've got it made!" Pop shouted, as I would have if I'd had breath left—when that section simply slipped sideways off the dam, carrying him like a surfboarder riding a wave of dirt.

Surely it happened in a matter of seconds, but in memory it took much more than that, the long-limbed figure swept into the cascade of soil, the tape recorder tumbling to its own fate. Pop clutched me so hard it hurt as we watched Del disappear from sight.

Whatever is worse than a sob burst out of me as I buried my

face in my father's chest, and he ducked his head to mine, still gripping me tight.

"Don't," he said brokenly, and choked up in a spasm of his own.

It was Zoe, farther up the slope, who cried out, "There he is!"

Not much of him, actually, the red head the only thing that wasn't mud-colored there against the side of the bluff, where he had been flung, and was clinging to a rock outcropping like a swimmer to a reef. If she had not spotted him in time, who knows?

He was barely holding on by the time Turk and Joe could scramble down to him, risking themselves so close to the cascade of earth and water. Between them, they managed to drag him up the slope and get him to the truck, where he collapsed on the running board. His head back against the door, Francine hugging him, muddy mess that he was, and Pop and Zoe and me asking him a dozen ways whether he was all right, Del ultimately gasped out, "Now I know what the mudjacks were talking about."

All of this was happening in the thunder of water as Rainbow Reservoir disgorged a coulee-wide torrent before hundreds of disbelieving eyes. The story of that day was far from over. For the floodwater had no place to go but down the course of the South Fork and on into the English Creek valley, where Gros Ventre lay in its way.

❋ 12 ❋

"THIS WAITING IS driving me up the wall, kiddo."

Up and over and out into some neighborhood of frustration constructed specially for a proprietor of a historic saloon downstream from a dam disaster, was more accurate. You might think the aftermath of a flood is destined to be an anticlimax. Even biblical stories lose ground after Noah and the Ark, don't they. Yet I remember fully the suspense of those next days, when Pop and I were reduced to living in the Packard at the swollen Red Cross camp on the cemetery knoll above town, while waiting for the authorities to allow the stranded population of Gros Ventre back to their homes and businesses, if any still fit that description.

During the nerve-wracking wait for the water to go down, he looked more worried than I had ever seen him, his face fixed in a cigarette squint and his hat down on his brow as if it was raining, even though it finally wasn't. When he and I weren't pitching in on unloading emergency supplies from trucks or standing in endless toilet lines or eating ladled-out tent meals, I would catch him staring down at the watery ghost town somewhere under its shroud of trees for long spells at a time.

Not that I was very well pulled together myself. Pop hadn't really said much about my mad dash onto the dam before it broke except to ruffle my hair with a rough hand and mutter, "That was close. Cripes, that was close." Something of a celebrity around the camp, I kept being greeted and hailed by those who witnessed my feat at the reservoir—even Duane Zane mumbled, "Nice going, guy," when I bumped into him in the chow line—but it was a good thing heroism is not transparent, because only now did I feel scared through and through. Not so much from that narrow escape, but of whatever lay ahead when the slowly receding water showed what we had been left with.

Until that could happen, Del of all people was our saving grace. Maybe lacrosse had taught him to shake off life's body blows in a hurry, but in any case, no sooner was the disaster camp being set up and reporters flocking in than he found a radio station van and wangled the loan of a portable recorder. Pop and I were pounding in tent pegs as the latest delivery of emergency shelters was being unrolled when we heard Zoe let out an "Ooh." We had practically inherited her while her parents volunteered at the meal tent, and depend on it, she first spotted Del striding our way, Francine keeping up with him, as inseparable as his shadow.

Pop straightened up with a grunt at the sight of the two of them, or rather all three, counting the recorder swinging at Del's side. Suspicious, he asked, "What are you gonna do with that thing?"

Del could hardly contain himself. "Tom, it's the chance of a lifetime! A sound portrait of this camp," he gestured around, as if scooping in the atmosphere of the flood aftermath by the armful. "Just think, if we had something like that from right after the Fort Peck slide. It would be historic!"

Certainly there was plenty of sound, diesel generators sputtering to life and the anxious tones of neighbors asking after one another and the bellow of Red Cross bullhorns making announcements and countless other noises of people laboring to get their lives together on a makeshift basis. Pop listened a few moments as if the commotion hurt his ears. "Yeah, well, you're welcome to it, Delano."

"Ah, I was hoping," Del stood on one foot and then the other, "you could go around the camp with me a little and point out people I might talk to. Break the ice, so to speak."

Pop just looked at him. "You know what, I could do without any more chances of a lifetime for a while." He cut off Del's immediate further plea with a tired shake of his head. "Have Francine lead you around, she knows enough of these folks by now."

She shook her head so fast her hair flew. "Not like you, Tom. Please? Pretty please? Dellie needs you in on this." She gestured awkwardly. "You . . . you're trusted."

That drew another sizable look from Pop. "Dellie needs his head examined," he growled, "and he's not the only one." Puffing out his cheeks, he turned resignedly to Del. "Okay, let's get at it. You stick close with us, kiddos."

The two of them set off into the confusion of the camp, Francine and Zoe and I tagging after. You really had to hand it to Philip Delano Robertson, gawky fledgling westerner from points east; not all that many hours before, the worst flood in Two Medicine history had done its best to inundate him, and here he was his bushy-tailed self again, somehow managing to listen to Pop and deploy the microphone toward anything that caught his interest and adjust settings on the recorder slung at his side, all at the same time. For his part, Pop singled out personalities who would stand out in a portrait, sound or otherwise, starting with Cloyce Reinking, sitting outside a tent like a queen in exile. She sent Zoe and me the kind of look that passes among old theatrical confederates, then turned to Del's mike with aplomb.

"So what do you think, gang?" Francine muttered as we hung back out of range of the interview. "Am I washed up?"

"Wh-why?" I responded, really asking *What now?*

"Are you in some kind of trouble like got you thrown in juvie?" Zoe breathlessly went the full route.

"Nahh, that's not what I meant." Francine toyed with the leather on her wrist. "My bartender gig. What if the joint is a total wreck?"

Leave it to her to blat it right out. At least her tongue was honest. Zoe wisely left the matter to me. Where I found it in me, I don't know, but I sounded more like Pop than he himself sometimes did: "You got to play the hand you been dealt. That's rule number one."

Francine gave me quite a look for a few seconds, then one of those grins that didn't leave the corner of her mouth. "Thanks, champ. I'll remember that."

On through the course of that day and the next couple, anytime anyone looked up, the tall intent red-topped figure and the tall silver-streaked familiar one were on the prowl through the camp, the one wielding the microphone like a magic wand, the other introducing him around as if he was the sound portraitist of the ages. Through it all, Francine stuck right there at Del's side, helping out any way she could. Appearances can deceive, but she gave every sign of being genuinely attached to him, rather than, as might have been suspected, snuggling up because the Gab Lab happened to be the coziest accommodation in the camp. He, of course, continued to look at her like she was the perfection of a rose. Zoe had a better sense of these things than I did, and she pointed out that Francine had a lot to offer a man if he did not know about her habit of taking things. Still, I couldn't help wishing Del savvied what he was getting with her.

THE LAST DAY came, with Pop summoned along with some other of the town's leading lights to a meeting with the camp administrators. Zoe and I were again killing time by trailing after Del and Francine, so we were right there when he slipped the microphone into the circle of law-enforcement officials briefing Bill Reinking and the other reporters on the final tally of lives lost in the flood. Nearly all the victims were tourists who had been camping or fishing or picnicking at creek side, names that meant nothing to us, the kind you read in newspaper stories of distant terrible happenings. Until the Polish-sounding final one.

Swallowing hard, she and I retreated into the maze of tents and makeshift avenues of people either sitting around with nothing to do or rushing this way and that. Hearing Canada Dan's name read off crushed the best efforts of our imaginations, the possibility that he and Moses had herded the hospital bunch up onto the coulee slope that day and the flood rushed by below, man and dog and ailing sheep safely high and dry. Twelve years old was awfully early to meet up with what inevitability does to possibility. Never had I expected to be choked up over the fate of one ornery old sheepherder, not even a very good one. But that was Canada Dan for you.

In the general hubbub I almost didn't hear when Zoe said in a tight voice, "What if the dam had gone out that day we were at his sheep camp?"

That was one I hadn't thought of.

"Curtains, Muscles," I tried to make light of it but it came out as a kind of croak.

Without saying anything more for a time, we wandered the encampment. Never had I known Zoe to be so downcast. Her eyes glistened, next thing to crying, although I could tell she was fiercely determined not to.

"Don't get all shook up," I managed, "we lucked out like crazy at the sheep camp and the dam. That's something, isn't it?"

She nodded miserably. "I know. But—"

"But what?"

It took her a couple of tries to say it.

"I heard my dad telling my mom, if the cafe is in real bad shape, we'll have to go back to Butte."

I felt as if all the air had been sucked out of me. I was trying to stammer something when Pop's voice caught up with us.

"Been looking all over for you," he beckoned impatiently, "let's get to getting." He had the news that people who ran essential services, such as the bank and the mercantile and gas stations, were about to be allowed into town ahead of everyone else. The first trace of his old self in many hours flashed across his drawn face. "Guess what, they couldn't leave the Medicine Lodge off the list. Princess, better go tell your folks what's up, okay? We'll see you in town."

Zoe sped away. Casting around for Francine and Del, Pop spotted them at the edge of the graveyard next to the camp, crouched over the recording equipment, catching the sound of wind in the long grass bordering the cemetery. "Hey, you two!" he hollered. "They're letting us back in town, if you can tear yourself away from the marble farm. Make it snappy, Proxy's waiting at the Packard."

That was the next jolt down to the bottom of my shoes. Now her, all of a sudden, along with everything else?

BY NOW THE camp was buzzing, with everyone anxious to find out what shape the town was in, and we wended our way to the cars through a chorus of encouragement to Pop to get the Lodge open for business the first possible minute, and he steadfastly said he would have to see what was what. My mind was taken up with what lay directly ahead, the red Cadillac poking out beyond the black bulk of the Packard, and there she waited, in the lavender slacks and creamy blouse and the hair still the shade of tinsel on a Christmas tree, leaning against a fender as composed as you please. My mother the Jones. Abandoner of children until they suited her purpose. Seducer of my father anytime she really put her mind to it. The wild card in the deck.

I asked darkly, "Where's she been, anyway?"

"They weren't letting anybody but emergency vehicles through until now," Pop excused her, naturally. But that was the kind of parent she'd be, all right, I could feel it in my bones. Absent until you least expected her, and then everything had to revolve around her.

Proxy met us with a more off-kilter smile than usual, as if she had been caught up in something that took a tricky amount of thinking. Immediately, though, she fastened onto me with one of her disturbing gazes. "Aren't you something, Russ. I hear you go around saving people's lives."

The only answer I was willing to make to that was something inconclusive, kind of a shrug and nod at the same time, for history was unmistakably in the air, that midnight episode at Fort Peck when a truck went in the river. The story practically cried out in my very being. If something like my action had occurred then, Darius Duff might still be her husband and Francine's apparent father, and I'd be, what? Nonexistent? The offspring of Pop and someone more fitted to be a mother? It is the kind of thinking that does not get a person anywhere, but it ruthlessly leads you on even so.

"Twice in one lifetime, Tom. What are the cockeyed odds on that?" I caught up with what Proxy was saying as she bummed a cigarette and he lit hers and then his while we waited for the procession into town to get under way.

"We don't have much luck around dams, do we," he interpreted that. "I hope it's not as big a mess as the time at Fort Peck." He glanced keenly at her. "I still have bad dreams about that, how about you?"

"It can't be," she said, ignoring the dreams part. "The slide took a whole frigging year to fix. Don't be so down in the mouth. Francine will be good help getting the joint back in shape in no time, you'll see." The little crimp appeared between her eyes, as if this had just occurred to her. "Fact of the matter is, I can spare some time myself to hang around and try to be useful."

My heart flip-flopped. Here she came, right into our lives.

"Yeah, well, we'll see how it all sorts out," he responded, a far cry from turning her down flat, as I wildly wished would happen. "We need to get ourselves in there first and take a look at things." Pacing and smoking, he kept an eye on the law-enforcement types in charge of dispatching cars into town, meanwhile frowning around in search of Francine and Del. At the last minute they showed up, dodging their way toward us, still lugging recording equipment and looking like a couple you couldn't separate without surgery.

Watching Proxy, I had the feeling Del was a complication she gladly would have done without. However, she did the polite thing, remarking to him that he was quite the survivor.

"It's quite an experience," he replied, not in his usual bouncy way, but looking straight back at her with Fort Peck knowledge in his eyes.

Evidently his close call was on Francine's mind, too. While the others went on making talk, she drifted around to the other side of the Packard, where Pop had dispatched me to roll down the windows to let stuffy air out.

Half covering her mouth with her hand so only I could hear, she began, "You want to know something, buddy boy?" Not much choice when it's put that way, is there. I glanced sideways at her, her expression that same flat-honest one as when she told of being in juvie.

"You were crazy to run out there to Del," she said so low it was practically a whisper.

Neither admitting nor denying, I cranked down the rear window as if it took all my attention.

"Lucky thing, too," she murmured, "but that's not what I mean. Me, I couldn't have. Didn't, did I."

Modesty, if that's what it was, found my tongue. "One of us crazy is probably enough."

"Fine," she laughed sharply. Then gave me a strange, warm grin. "I can dig that—somebody else's turn for a change."

"Let's go, everybody!" Pop ended that with a shout, finally getting the high sign from someone wearing a badge. Del sprang off toward the Gab Lab with headphones dangling and recorder swinging, although not before one last promissory look at Francine. In the rush to go, the next thing was Proxy proposing that she and Francine ride with us, inasmuch as she didn't want to take the low-slung Caddie down there into the flood mess, and Pop drily telling her the Packard always had room to spare. One more thing to unnerve me. It was happening already, the slapped-together family, with Proxy's bossy style that hit like lightning when it happened.

But as we went to jump in, Francine all of a sudden backed away. "Know what," she said, as if it had just occurred to her, "my things are in Dellie's van, I'll ride with him." Her expression was hard to read, except it was one hundred percent resolved. "Always up for an automotive adventure, you know me."

About to climb in the notorious rear seat, Proxy whipped around and started to say something. But then thought better of it, simply smiled a few moments longer than that kind of smile should be held, and left things at, "Oh-kay, it's like that, is it. See you and the lady killer in town."

"Parting is such you-know-what," Francine bestowed, and bolted off. Proxy came up to the front seat with us, lodging me uncomfortably in the middle between Pop and her. "She's got it bad." Solemnly she watched her daughter trot away down the line of cars. "When you get to that age, keep your head on your shoulders, Russ."

"She could do worse." I was grateful to Pop for sticking up for Del, and then he nosed the Packard into our spot in the line of cars, and we all went silent as the caravan slowly wound its way past the marble farm toward town.

THE RIDE IN, while short, seemed as momentous as my arrival to Gros Ventre half of my lifetime ago, the sign at the city limits still standing on its higher ground before the highway curved decorously down to branch into streets, the same green roof of trees over everything ahead. The difference rapidly made itself known at ground level, a foot or so of dark water still standing wherever the soaked soil could not absorb any more. As we reached the first houses Pop said, *"Damn,"* once and definitively, at the ravages of the flood: driftwood snagged on porches and household goods sluiced into yards, and a smelly scum of mud and mildew everywhere, as if the town had been dropped into a swamp.

Bulldozers and graders had cleared a rough lane through the muck and debris of Main Street and were working on the back streets now. As the Packard crept past silent mud-coated storefront after storefront, I saw the Top Spot, sitting grimy and abandoned, and the Odeon, darkened and ghostly, and had to fight back a choking feeling. Emotion piled on emotion in me. You are only young once, the saying goes, but that is a terrible miscount. On that slow journey through the stricken town, I was young any number of times over, and each time different, young and lost without Zoe if her family moved away, young and spooked out of my wits at the unsettling tinsel-haired woman next to me emerging as my second parent, and most of all, young and stricken myself for my beleaguered father and what lay ahead of him at the Medicine Lodge.

At last the car eased to a stop at the familiar end of the street, and we sat saying nothing—even Proxy—for a short while. Still standing, the poor old saloon looked its age and then some, like a ghost town derelict abandoned to history. Flood debris had buckled the front door so that it stood drunkenly blocking the entranceway. A water stain so ugly it made me want to puke dirtied the building up to the plate-glass windows, and we could tell the flood had to have left the same rind of filth inside.

Taking in the scene, Pop looked as sick as I felt, but at last only said, "That door's had it, we'll have to try the back."

WHEN HE WRESTLED the rear door of the saloon open, what awaited us was beyond the meaning of mess. The water had swept through savagely, mingling spittoons and boots, bedrolls and saddles, empty Shellac bottles and anything within reach on the walls, and mud, mud, mud. The back room that had been the realm of exploration and costumes and every wild bit of imagination Zoe and I were capable of was a sodden dump now. It took everything in me not to break out bawling and cause Pop more woe. Grief does not always come out in tears.

Things were no better when we checked on the barroom: bar stools collected in a tangle like a beaver dam and booths still bleeding maroon where the flood had sat. Even the painting of the Buck Fever Case was curling away from the bottom of the frame. Pop took a look behind the bar and swore to himself.

Proxy had been silently biding her time. Now she gazed around, appraising everything as if it was hers. "How's the insurance?"

Pop wobbled a hand. "So-so, like it always is."

"Then the thing to do is get the place going even before it's cleaned up," she said, the soul of reason. "You can't do business if the joint isn't open, isn't that the truth? You remember how it was, everybody at Fort Peck needed a stiff drink and some company right after the big slide, they practically stampeded in on us."

"That was different," he answered hollowly, both hands braced on the bar as if he needed the support. "The Missouri River didn't touch the Blue Eagle. This place was underwater for days and days." The age lines in his face appeared painfully deep as he gazed around at what was left of the Select Pleasure Establishment of the Year, the plaque still on the wall and the animal heads shiny-eyed above it all and the posters of Roosevelt and Kennedy intact but peeling at the corners, while everything below showed where English Creek had lately been. Besides the wrecked stools and booths and the rest, the floor was a mud bank to a depth that made a swamper's heart sink.

"Come on, don't let this get you down," Proxy did not let up. "The beer and whiskey didn't float away—"

"It might as well have, everything else did."

"—and we get Francine in action behind the bar, things will improve lickety-split. Now that she's straightened herself out, she can take on more of the running of the joint, spare you some of the headaches. You'll see." This was said as if it was a done deal, making my head spin. "The house didn't look bad," she was saying next, "so that's a load off the mind, isn't it." True enough; on our way into the back, we could see across the alley that the house seemed to be simply waiting patiently for its missing porches, front and back, and other than those it did not appear to have suffered much water, thanks to its high foundation. The Buick, too, had survived in gunboat fashion, two-toned with muck halfway up its sides but still squatting in place on the driveway. Survivors under the leafy protection of Igdrasil, whatever its powers were.

"I never was any great shakes at housekeeping," Proxy dealt herself in further, "but I bet I could hold things together over there while Francine and you get the joint back on its feet." She glanced impatiently toward the one functioning doorway of the barroom. "What's keeping her and Lover Boy, anyway?"

"Delano probably stopped to record a frog crossing the road," Pop sighed, wearily drawing himself up behind the bar. "Then we're supposed to count on Francine being here to save our skins, just like you've been doping it out, hey?" he mulled, looking no less haggard. He held up his hands before Proxy could say anything. "I'm not contesting that. If it wasn't for her, I think I'd sell off the joint for whatever it would bring. Earl Zane might still be fool enough to buy it for practically nothing." He studied me as if I held some kind of answer. "I don't know, that might still be the best way to go. Get us all out from under."

I was torn. Was I ever. If the Medicine Lodge went, so might the problematic sister and the mother from nowhere. Women with slanted smiles out of our life. But without the saloon, what would Pop's life and my own amount to?

"Tom," Proxy negotiated with the patience of a taxi dancer and more, "you're not seeing the chance here." She swept a slow hand around the mess that was the barroom. "The joint is an attraction after what's happened. People are gonna be curious, word will get around and they'll come in for a look and buy a few rounds. I'd bet my bottom dollar on it." I am almost sure she didn't wink as she said the next, but the effect was the same. "And plenty of them are going to be hard up for ready money, aren't they. You can stock up the back room again in nothing flat."

"I hear what you're saying," Pop said tensely, "but—" And I had, too, even before Proxy came right out with it.

"Speaking of ready money, there'll be every kind of construction crew passing through here after what's happened, won't there." Either she forgot about me in her effort of working on Pop or figured I didn't have anything to say about the matter. "Judging by Fort Peck," she gave a knowing grin, "some interesting stuff might turn up to be traded in, huh? And I bet we could—"

By now it was all lining up like the script of a nightmare. Canada. Medicine Hat. Those trips.

Without thinking—no, with all too much thinking left over from solitary parentless nights while blizzards blew and worries piled up, I let out in a burst, "Pop? Remember what you promised."

Startled, Proxy shot a look at me and then at him. "That didn't sound much like a Christmas list."

"It's something between Rusty and me," Pop said, as if coming to. He started to say more, but broke off on seeing Del outlined alone in the doorway at the rear of the barroom, however long he had been standing there. The other two of us followed his gaze to the unspeaking figure. Accompanied only by what he lugged at his side, Del appeared strangely unmoored without Francine inches away.

"The lost are found," Proxy greeted him but peered past. "Where's that daughter of mine? We need to put her to work."

"Gone."

The word hanging in the air, he stepped on into the barroom, pale as he'd been during the tick bite episode. "Oh, and she said to tell you she's borrowing the Cadillac."

For a second or two, the trio of us at the bar took that in as dumbly as the stuffed animal heads. Recovering first, Proxy started, "She didn't ask—gone where?"

"The coast. The Pacific one," Del added punctiliously, his face blank. "She said it was time for her to leak into the landscape." He plowed through the mud on the floor as if not noticing it, to where the three of us were congregated at the bar. "And she told me to go to her room and get this." He swung what he was carrying onto the dully gleaming surface.

I recognized the ditty bag right away, although not ahead of Proxy. "Her toiletry stuff, is all. I'll take it and—"

"I'm afraid not," Del overrode that, pushing the kit bag away from her. "She made me promise to give it to Tom and Rusty. You'll see why, she said."

Pop's brow narrowed. I hovered as he dug into the contents the distasteful way men do in women's purses and such, until his hand found something that made his face change. Ever so slowly he lifted out a bottle of hair dye and set it on the bar top. Midnight Black, the label read.

"Why'd you try to pull this?" he said in a deathly tone, squinting at Proxy as if she was hard to see.

She sagged against the bar. The other three of us in the picture composed from that bottle—father, brother, lover—stood
waiting for whatever truth she had in her. If Del was right and
there was a moral edifice embodied in remembrance, we were
owed a masterpiece of confession.

"I had to do something with Francine," Proxy began in a
defeated voice. "She was getting to be more than I could handle.
Didn't have any direction in life and about to turn into man bait.
What's a mother to do, that stupid old saying." With an effort,
she met Pop's steely gaze. "Then I stumbled across that newspaper piece. You seemed to have everything going for you, just the
right material for a father. Having a kid sounded like it suited
you, Tom, like it never did me." Still looking stricken, she glanced
at me, and our eyes held for a long moment. "And Rusty for a
brother, who'd maybe take her mind off herself for a change,
that fit right in, too. I figured the two of you would be good
for her."

"Besides a famous saloon she just might inherit," Pop spoke
in his same unrelenting tone, "if the two of you played your
cards right."

Her expression turned strangely wistful. "That didn't hurt,
either."

"I bet it didn't. It might even have been the main point."

Proxy had nothing to say to that, her silence the deepest confession of all. All these years later, she still was under the spell of
the Blue Eagle. A storied saloon, an institution of its kind that
bestowed reputation and a good living on its possessor—no wonder it was such a tempting memory. I almost could sympathize.

Pop simply looked at her for what seemed an eternity, as Del
and I stood silently by. Finally he flicked a finger against the bottle of hair dye. "Just for the record. Francine isn't mine, is she."

"Don't I wish." Proxy stirred from her slump against the bar.

"She's Darius's, tooth and nail. Her hair's even like the Duffs had, trying to be red." The rest was spoken even more dolefully. "She takes after him in how damned spiky she is, too. That's one reason I let his side of the family raise her. It turns out not to be the best decision I could've made, huh?"

The admission seemed to take a lot out of her. Blinking hard, she smiled, with the effort showing. I honestly felt her gaze coming before it returned to me. This was what I had most feared, the moment when she would openly say something like, "That leaves Rusty. Our real kid. We better call it a draw about Francine and the joint and so on, and get ourselves together about raising this one right, now that we both know how, don't you think? A family's a family, even with a few interruptions." My imagination could hear it all before she actually said, "So, anyway, Tom. The back-room business we could do, up north? If Russ could see his way clear to let you out of whatever you promised?"

Pop shook his head.

She sighed the way he sometimes did. "Then I guess there's nothing for me to hang around for."

I waited breathlessly.

"No," he said, "there isn't. I couldn't trust you as far as I could throw you, after this."

Proxy showed a flash of pain, remorse, regret, who knows what at those words, but shrugged like the veteran of life that she was. "That's the problem with being inventive. It's not always appreciated." Trying for her tough smile, she turned to Del, who had been listening as comprehensively as I had. "So, Prince Charming. Can I bum a lift back to the camp, see if I can catch a ride to the Falls from there?"

Before he could respond, Pop slid a key along the bar to her. "Never mind. Take the Packard. For good. I have a hunch you're not gonna see that Cadillac again."

Hesitantly she reached for the car key and turned it over a time or two before pocketing it. She angled her head a certain way as she looked back along the bar to him. "Who knows, I may bring the old jitney back sometime."

"Don't hurry," he said with emphasis.

She shook her head regretfully. "You're one of a kind, Tom. Too bad we didn't take a little time for ourselves in those years at the Eagle and explore that some."

"Lots of things in life are too bad, Proxy," he said quietly. "Time to move on."

My mind a muddle of emotions, I watched her go, the small, sad smile as she gave the barroom one last sideways glance, and then just the back of her, the hair and figure that defied mere motherhood, as she picked her way through the flood's leavings and out to the old car.

Finding his voice, Del broke the spell she left behind. "Francine told me all of it. She said we'd never be able to stick together, with her habits and me as I am." Wincing, he went on: "She's either too honest or too much the opposite. It's beyond me. Whatever, that's that, as I've heard someone say before." Looking bleak but trying to get over it, he asked, "Can I use the phone if it's working? The powers that be are going to be wondering if I still exist."

"Help yourself. It'd be nice if somebody got something done around here that didn't draw blood." Pop signaled me with a motion of his head, and we excused ourselves to the back room.

Light-headed with the mercy of Proxy exiting from our life, I followed him into the strew of waterlogged items, still trying to catch up with all that had happened. Francine gone, leaving everyone a little scorched, more than a little amazed, definitely a standout memory. Even now I half expected her to materialize at the base of the stairs to the landing, black bow tie tied as nicely as the ribbon on a gift box, flashing a sassy grin and saying "Oboy, some mess in here, ain't it." Whether or not it was her and her checkered conscience and a Cadillac heading west that was on his mind, too, Pop wore a pensive expression as he gazed around at the watery remains of the Medicine Lodge.

"Pop," I broke in on his mood, there was no help for it, "can I ask you something?"

"You know I've been pretty short of good answers lately," he said ruefully. "But fire away, I guess."

"Do you wish she'd been really your daughter?"

He hesitated, studying me as if making sure I could stand the honest answer. "Fifty-fifty," he teetered a hand. "She wasn't too bad a bartender, you know." Stooping, he rescued the Blue Eagle sign from a seaweed-like tangle of horse harness. "How about you? You gonna miss having a sister?"

I started to say no, then veered toward yes, and in the end I simply shook my head in a way that said I didn't know how to answer that.

"Francine had that effect," he grunted, standing the hard-used sign in its place against the wall and stepping back as if he had done a day's work.

This was taking an awful chance, but I had to know. "Are . . . are you going to miss *her*? Our mother, I mean?"

"Who?" He looked over his shoulder at me with a puzzled squint.

"Proxy. She's my mother, too, isn't she."

He went still as death. "How'd you come up with that?"

"From that funny way she was always looking at me like she owned me," it poured out of me. "And you were in Medicine Hat together back when, from what she said. And you called her a jones, and that's what you always said my mother was, and you gave in to her both times, you said, and so the second time must have been me, like the first time was supposed to have been Francine, and—"

His expression worsened as I kept on and on. I hoped he wasn't having a heart attack. Finally he got me stopped. "Rusty, we need to talk this out. Come on up."

We climbed to the desk on the landing and sat facing each other, the vent soundless, as if listening to us.

He worked his jaw a time or two, the wretched look still on his face. "Cripes, where do I start?" He drew a ragged breath and the words came haltingly.

"I can see where you thought Proxy and me had it bad for each other. Particularly me for her—she's the kind that gets under a guy's skin, in more ways than one." Tense as I had ever been, I watched him give a little shake of his head, as if clearing it. "But she and I missed our chance way back there when she fell for Darius. That's what that fling in the Packard was about, as much as anything. Kind of a consolation prize for both of us, if you see what I mean."

Maybe I was beginning to. Yet I wasn't at all prepared for his next words.

"Your mother, your *real* mother, passed away. Earlier this summer. I didn't have the heart to tell you. She'd been taken care of, the funeral and all, by the time the landlady figured out how to let me know. The phone call came, and you were flying high about how you're gonna be an actor and so on, and I just couldn't do it to you then. And things kept coming up, where the time never seemed right to tell you." Hunched forward with his arms on his knees and his hands clasped, he looked at me as if from far away, although our knees were practically touching. "Kiddo, it was real hard to know what to do, as you can see."

I could barely hear myself ask, "What did she die of?"

He didn't answer that for the longest time. Then said with

resignation, "That's the rest of the story. She drank herself to death, finally."

"Where . . . where was she?"

"Canada." He nodded. "Medicine Hat. I can see how it threw you when Proxy brought that up, but she was only ever there with me a time or two on those booze runs from the Eagle. Nothing ever happened between us, she was just along for the ride." His eyes changed. "Different situation with your mother. See, she was a chambermaid in the railroad hotel up there after we . . ." His voice faltered.

"Split the blanket," I helped.

"Right. Jonelle, that was her name, Jonelle Jones, her folks' idea of something cute, I guess," he recited this with care, "Jonesie, she liked to be called—" I could tell he had to drag the next out of himself. "She wasn't cut out to have a kid. I was scared to death she'd drop you on your head or something. One day when you were only about a month old I came back to the house from the joint for something, and there was a hell of a smell in the place. I could hear you upstairs whimpering—you were good, you didn't squall much, but when you were hungry, you would kind of whimper like a puppy. I went in the kitchen, and the pan where she'd been heating milk for your bottle had burned through the bottom. I found her in the living room, passed out drunk. That did it. I could see what was going to happen. Somebody who drank like a fish and me with the saloon. You could get a divorce in Nevada about as easy as changing your underwear. I drove her there, and you to Phoenix."

The unspoken fact of ever since, twelve years' worth, must have stood out all over me.

"You might as well know the whole thing," he read my face. "I was paying her to stay away from you all this time."

"Pay—? Why'd you have to do that?"

"She had custody of you," he said huskily. "Came with the divorce. That's the way it works—the woman always gets the kid."

This news hit me like an anvil. Stunned, I tried to make sense of it. "But you've always had me."

"Yeah, well," he looked uncomfortable but told it all, "kidnapping is kind of a strong way of putting it, but that's what the law could have charged me with all along." I listened as if hypnotized. "And she always held that over me. That she had legal right to you and I didn't have a leg to stand on if she pressed the case. I had to buy her off, right to the end."

"Buy her off with—"

"You got it. Those trips. She would call, always late at night in the joint. The same story every time, she'd run out of money, drank it up, I could tell by her voice, and threatened to come down here and get you and call the law on me." He gazed into the remnants of the hocked items, the glorious loot that held more meaning than even Zoe and I imagined into it. "So, yeah, I'd have to load and go up there to Medicine Hat and sell off whatever I could for fast cash and deal with her, same old way. She could go through money like it was water, so I'd only give her enough to get by on, and parcel out the rest to whoever she owed"—I at last understood the plague of bills down through the years at this desk—"until it happened again."

It was dizzying, the back room now as deep in drama as when this one-of-a-kind father held me over the rim of the Grand Canyon to spit a mile. He saw me staring toward the tarp that had drifted into the corner, beneath the surviving saddles.

"Rusty, listen. I've never stole. Got that?"

A moment of hesitation that was its own explanation.

"It's kind of a fine line, maybe," he started in slowly, "handling things that don't come with a bill of sale, but every pawnshop in the world has to deal like that. If a foreman on a big road job or an oil rig showed up late at night and said he had some surplus stuff he'd like to trade in, I didn't figure it was up to me to ask any too many questions. Maybe the stuff had walked off the job, maybe it hadn't."

This seemed the hardest part yet for him. He started to say something more, halted, then turned up his hands as if letting the words free.

"Kiddo, I'm no saint on the wall. That's been my history, I guess you'd have to say. What I did at Fort Peck, throwing the Eagle open for the taxi dancing and what Proxy got up to, it meant I could afford to come to this town and buy this joint. Anything I did here, it let me afford you." He looked squarely at me, anxiety etched deep in his face. "Okay?"

You got to play the hand you been dealt. He always had, and if I was going be the son he deserved, I could do nothing less. To this day I have not regretted saying, "Okay, Pop, if that's the how of it," which seemed to be all that needed to be said.

His relief was brief, as was mine. "Can I come in?" Zoe called from the back doorway, coming in. "Whoo, this is some mess."

"That's for sure, princess," Pop greeted her, tiredly passing a hand over his face. "How is it at the cafe?" I tensed for the next turn of fortune in this epic day.

Dodging her way through the clutter on the floor, she shrugged elaborately but couldn't hold in the news. "My mom says she's seen worse in Butte. She has my dad already trying to cook hamburgers."

Her big grin faded as she trotted up the stairs and got a close look at us. "What happened? Where is everybody?"

"Mother and daughter are no longer with us," Pop said levelly. "Rusty can tell you the whole tale."

Zoe edged along the railing of the landing, sensing trouble. "When will you get the saloon open?"

Pop did not say anything for a moment, then sighed. "Princess, I won't. I can't hack it." He flung out a hand toward the barroom. "The joint would need new booths, stools, ice machine," he went on down the list. "New bartender, for that matter." He was speaking as if to Zoe; I knew this was his way of softening the blow for me, but I still felt the words hit my heart. "I'm gonna have to sell the joint for salvage," he finished. He looked over at me apologetically, which hurt worse yet. "I don't see any choice, kiddo."

"Ah, Tom?"

All three of us jumped at the sound of Del's voice calling through the vent. We were not used to being listened to from the barroom. "If you're through, can I duck around for a minute and discuss something with you?"

"Sure, come on back," Pop spoke up. "We'll compare war wounds. You and me, Delano. We sure know how to pick women, don't we."

"Maybe it's not an exact science, Tom."

In no time Del joined us in the back room, halting at the bottom of the stairs, as if too bashful to come up. The bleak expression was gone, replaced by something mixed. He shuffled a little, as if looking for where to start, then began with it.

"That was quite some phone call. The powers that be loved the sheep camp sound portrait." He looked embarrassed, happily so. "They played it for Alan Lomax and he called it a phenomenal piece of Americana. He said Canada Dan's voice was the most original he'd heard since Leadbelly's."

Putting his hands in his pockets and lifting his shoulders, Del swayed a little as he spoke the next words.

"They want me to stay on and do as many Two Medicine sound portraits as I can for as long as it takes. Ranchers, rough-necks, hay hands, game wardens, forest rangers, any field of work I can think of—maybe even a bartender," he said hopefully. "That's besides the Missing Voices, of course. With everything involved, I figure it might take me all fall and maybe the winter, and that set me to thinking." He gazed up with that bright-eyed expression from the first time he had set foot into the Medicine Lodge. "Since I'm going to be here anyway, Tom, if you could stand some help—in the saloon, I mean—behind the bar, I mean—well, here I am."

Zoe and I were as still as statues, a moment that stays with me a half century later. We watched my father's face change. Slowly he asked, "You mean, if I could pound enough bartend-ing into Francine's head to get by, I might be able to do the same on you?"

"That's more or less what I was thinking."

"Bartending isn't tea and crumpets, Delano."

"Probably not."

"It's long hours and short rest."

"So is oral history, actually."

"The pay's not much, you know."

Del grinned. "Then I'll have to count on the rewards being great, won't I."

Furrowed with thought, Pop reached in his shirt pocket for a cigarette and pulled out an empty pack. "Cripes"—he crumpled it and tossed it into the rest of the trash in the back room—"the joint needed cleaning out anyhow." Squinting at the redheaded figure standing on one foot and then the other down there at the bottom of the steps, he came to life, and Zoe and I with him. "Okay, it's a deal," he said gruffly, rising to his full height and smoothing his pompadour to blend the white with the black.

"Let's take that front door off its hinges and get our aprons on, Delano. Rule number one, you can't do business if the joint isn't open."

IT IS ALL these years later, long after my father in great old age joined generations of the Medicine Lodge's customers in the marble farm on the knoll overlooking Gros Ventre—"That's another story," as he would have said—that the chance of a lifetime has come to me. What a set of chapters our lives have been, imbued with Pop's historic one, since we have all gone on from that phenomenal year of 1960. Delano Robertson to become the latter-day Alan Lomax, the now gray crew-cut eminence of sound portraits and *lingua america*, presiding at the Library of Congress Archive of Oral History. Francine to knock around San Francisco in ways that probably should not bear inspection, until she found her niche as stage manager at the Fillmore West and grew to be a mother figure to bands of tie-dyed musicians and their raucous successors ever since. Proxy to disappear into her own style of business one more time, leaving us with those unbelievable tales of hers and the remarkable coincidence that when the filming of *The Misfits* was finally done, early in it Thelma Ritter yanks the lever of a slot machine she and Marilyn Monroe happen to be passing in a Reno casino with the explanation, "This machine loves me."

And Zoe and I? I suppose ours has been a combination of the stories of lovers since time immemorial, of unrequited longing— the Gros Ventre school years—and of separation—college plus my military service—and of reuniting, falling for each other all over again when Cloyce Reinking saw fit to invite us both home, unbeknownst to each other, to her New Year's party after I came back in one piece from Vietnam. No sooner were we married than our luck held and our acting careers found their arc, in repertory theaters across much of the country ever since.

We have gone from being those young snips Algernon and Cecily in summer stock, to performing our goodly share of Shakespeare together, to gray-headed roles such as George and Martha butchering each other's nerves in *Who's Afraid of Virginia Woolf?* Now, though, there is one play that is going to be mine alone. Zoe simply tickled me in the ribs and said, "Go for it, kiddo." I successfully auditioned for the much-anticipated Chicago revival of *The Iceman Cometh*. And in the time it has taken me to tell this, it is now opening night. Famously, Eugene O'Neill gave the lead actor, Hickey, one of the most sought-after roles ever written: bravura speeches, mocking the pipe dreams of the other customers in a saloon. I have the credits to play Hickey, a cinch and a stretch, both. But when tryouts came, I chose something else. The actor woven into everything that happens onstage, the bartender, Rocky. He pours the drinks for the lost dreamers, eternally swabbing the bar while listening to their stories, ever listening, and, yes, in the end has his own tale. It is my chance to give the performance of a lifetime. After all, I know the character by heart.

A third-generation Montanan, **Ivan Doig** is the author of thirteen previous books, including the bestselling *The Whistling Season* and the classic memoir *This House of Sky*. He has been a National Book Award finalist and has received the Wallace Stegner Award, among many other honors. He lives in Seattle.